## WHAT WAS WRONG WITH HER?

Jacie hoped he could not feel her tension, the strange emotions coursing through her body. She was supposed to be feeling revulsion, fear, for this savage who stared up at her with dark, piercing eyes in a way that set her heart to pounding. She could feel her own fever rising. This man, this strange and feral man, was making her wonder what it would be like if *he* were her husband and showed her what it would be like to be *his* woman, *his* wife.

But perhaps what disturbed her most, Jacie realized, was the reality that never, even when he had held and kissed her, had she felt this way about Michael.

**Books by Patricia Hagan**

*Midnight Rose*
*Heaven in a Wildflower*
*A Forever Kind of Love*
*Orchids in Moonlight*
*Starlight*
*Love and War*
*Say You Love Me*
*Passion's Fury**

Available from HarperPaperbacks

*coming soon

Harper Monogram

# Say You Love Me

Patricia Hagan

HarperPaperbacks
*A Division of* HarperCollins*Publishers*

This is a work of fiction. The characters, incidents, and dialogues are products of the author's imagination and are not to be construed as real. Any resemblance to actual events or persons, living or dead, is entirely coincidental.

HarperPaperbacks *A Division of* HarperCollins*Publishers*
10 East 53rd Street, New York, N.Y. 10022



Cover illustration by Doreen Minuto

Printed in the United States of America

HarperPaperbacks, HarperMonogram, and colophon are trademarks of HarperCollins*Publisher-*

ISBN 0-06-108222-8

# Say You Love Me

# Prologue

**Texas, 1840**

*Violet held the infant* to her breast, though it seemed a sacrilege, somehow, to offer milk intended for another baby.

*But that baby is dead,* a voice inside reminded her cruelly. *Born dead. She never got to draw the first sweet breath of life.*

Violet looked down at the baby through a mist of tears. She was a week old, and precious as only one of God's earth angels can be. A downy fuzz covered her tiny head, promising a crown of sable black hair, and already her blue eyes had a lavender cast, which meant they would eventually be the same color as her mother's.

Violet felt the empty burning in her heart at the thought of how her own baby was buried before she even had a chance to hold it in her arms. Then just three days afterward, Violet's twin sister Iris had given birth. "Momma named us after flowers," Iris had declared, "and I'm going to do the same with my little girl. I'll name her Jacinth, which is what hyacinths are called in England." But Iris's husband Luke had immediately shortened the baby's name to Jacie, and Jacie her name would be.

Violet lifted her tear-streaked face to the sky as she knelt among the clumps of sagebrush with the infant in her arms. "Why, God?" she asked. "Why is it that Iris is always blessed with the bread of life, while I'm left with only the crumbs?"

There was no sound save for the infant feeding. Violet knew that God was not going to answer her. Not this time. Probably not ever. It was just something she was going to have to work out for herself, within her own tormented soul.

Even though it was early morning, the summer heat was smothering, and perspiration trickled from her every pore. But there was no shade to be had, and the sun's rays were searing. Violet could have stayed with the other members of the small caravan traveling from Georgia to Texas; they were camped in a grove of cottonwood trees beside a cool stream. But after the terrible things she had said to Iris, Violet had wanted to be alone with her misery and guilt, away from everyone.

It all started one morning when Iris remarked that Violet looked ill. "It's because you have so much milk in your breasts," she had said worriedly. "I'll let you nurse Jacie too, and—"

"Oh, you know everything, don't you?" Violet had lashed out at her. She lay huddled on a pallet in the back of their wagon, still weak and sore from the birth, in body and in spirit.

Iris knelt beside her holding the baby, though she was feeling weak herself. They had both delivered early, no doubt due to the ordeal of travel. "I know how you must feel, Violet. I can't imagine anything more heartbreaking than losing a child, but you have to let me help you. If you don't, you'll come down with milk fever, and you could die."

"You think I care?" Violet glared up at her. "Well I don't. I wish I was back there on the trail beneath that pile of rocks with my baby, because I don't have anything to live for now."

"You have Judd."

Violet lowered her voice to a whisper, for despite her despair, she did not want the others in the caravan to hear the embarrassing truth about her marriage. "Judd won't want me anymore when he finds out our baby died. You know as well as I do he wasn't planning on me coming to Texas. He was walking out on me and our marriage, till I found out I was in the family way."

"That's not true," Iris said, though she knew it was.

Violet got to her feet, her legs wobbly, all the resentment smoldering within igniting to give her strength. "It is true. Judd never loved me, and everybody knows it. It was you he wanted to marry. The only reason he proposed to me was because you were marrying Luke. Oh, yes, I knew about the gossip, how everybody said Judd married me because it was as close to you as he could get. I knew it that day twelve years ago when we had our double wedding on the porch. His hand holding mine was cold, and so were his lips when he kissed me, because it was you he wanted and always had been. It was always you. And he knew later that you could have given him the children he wanted, because you and Luke had four fine sons, while I couldn't conceive. And now you've got a healthy baby girl, and I've got nothing."

Violet paused to draw a ragged breath, not caring that Iris's face had turned ashen. In the past, in all those hurting years of growing up, Violet had swallowed her frustrations and kept the pain inside, but now, when her life had crumbled about her, she could hold back no longer. "We were twins," Violet reminded Iris coldly, "but not identical—oh, no, far from it. You were the pretty one. Dainty and pretty, just like Momma. But I took after Poppa. I was big and gangly—I even got his ugly hooked nose." She tapped her nose with a shaking finger. "You and I were never alike in any way. It was you the boys flocked after, while I was the one people said was destined to be a spinster."

Iris shook her head in protest, her silky black hair flying about her face. "You're wrong, Violet. You're not ugly. And in his way, Judd loves you. He's been good to you—"

"He never beat me," Violet conceded. "But he never really loved me, and when the years passed with no babies, I knew I'd just about lost him."

When the Panic of '37 finally hit Georgia, everybody started heading for Texas and the two square miles of land offered to any family brave enough to make the journey. Judd was the first to take off—without his wife. When he did come back he was wearing a shiny badge and bragging about how he'd joined the Texas Rangers. After trying to eke out a living on a fifty-acre dirt farm, Luke, too, decided the promise of over twelve hundred acres of land was too good to pass up. He and Iris made plans to follow Judd back. Violet was better off staying in Georgia, Judd had said. Being a Ranger would keep him away from home most of the time.

"If it hadn't been for me getting pregnant, like a blessing out of the blue, I'd never have seen him again. But that doesn't matter now, because that blessing turned out to be a curse, and it's all over. All of it. I don't have anything left to live for, but you've got everything. Even the daughter you always wanted. Your baby lived and mine didn't. Now I wish I'd died with her."

Iris had heard enough. "Stop it. Talking this way is blasphemy. You had a terrible delivery, Violet. You could have died, but God spared you, and it's a sin for you to say you wish He hadn't."

Violet began to cry, her whole body quaking. She felt so awful, with her breasts swollen and aching. "I don't care. You said I'd never be able to have another baby—"

"I can't be sure. No one can."

Violet made a face. "Well, you should know. After all, you were the doctor's little helper, weren't you? Always traipsing around with Poppa when he made his calls. After he died you just took over, like you always do. Folks had something else to talk about besides how pretty you are and how your handsome husband adores you and what wonderful sons you have. They started calling you a 'medicine woman' and treated you like some kind of God."

Iris's eyes filled with tears. "Violet, don't say these things. You don't mean them. You're sick, and I understand. Now please take Jacie and nurse her. We won't be leaving today as early as we usually do. Luke insisted you and I should get some rest, since we're only a day away from Nacogdoches now."

Iris did not tell her about the other men's protests that they should keep moving because of the fear of Indians. An old prospector had happened by late the night before and warned them that they should get to the fort at Nacogdoches as soon as possible. Apparently, twelve Comanche chiefs had met with Texas commissioners a few months ago in hopes of a peace treaty—only there had been bad trouble instead. The Comanches had balked at giving up the white prisoners they were holding, and troops had then charged into the council room and started shooting. When the smoke cleared, all of the chiefs had been slaughtered, and the incident had set the Comanche nations on the warpath.

The other men had not told their wives of the danger, knowing how terrified they would be, but Luke and Iris kept no secrets from each other. He regretted that a delay of a few hours was all he could get the others to agree to after telling them Violet was sick.

Jacie began to mew hungrily, and Iris held her out to Violet. "Take her and rid yourself of some milk. We'll talk later, and I'll make you see you're wrong about Judd. He loves you, and everything will be fine once we get to Texas. You'll see. I love you too, Violet. I always have. And so did Momma and Poppa."

Violet started to move away, but then her eyes fastened on the locket Iris always wore on a ribbon around her neck. It contained a daguerreotype of Iris, given to her by their mother, because they looked so much alike. Violet had been hurt, feeling it was a cruel reminder that she was not pretty like her mother and her sister.

Violet's hand shot out, and she gave the locket a vicious yank, breaking the ribbon. Squeezing it in her fist, as Iris stared in wide-eyed wonder, Violet said through clenched teeth, "I am sick of staring at this symbol of the difference between us day after day, year after year. I think I hate you, Iris."

Even as she had spoken the words, Violet felt awful and knew she did not really mean what she was saying. At the same instant, her breasts suddenly began to ache even more. Finally, she yielded to the agony and roughly jerked Jacie from Iris's arms. "Give her to me. I'll nurse her. Maybe then I'll feel like I'm useful for something in this life," she said miserably.

She retreated to the distant scrub, but now she felt worse than before. Her breasts were no longer swollen and gorged; Jacie had drunk her fill and slept contentedly, tiny fists curled against her cherubic cheeks, droplets of milk drying at the corners of her little pink mouth. But guilt over the way she had treated her sister was making Violet sick to the depths of her soul. Iris had never been cruel or mean to her. It was not her fault the way life had turned out for Violet.

Violet thought of Judd and prayed Iris had been right in saying he would still want her after finding out their baby had died. Violet loved him with all her heart and could not remember a time in her whole life when she hadn't. She had sworn to be a good wife and was certain that when the babies came, Judd would love her for being their mother if for no other reason. But could she hold him now, she wondered in anguish, when there would never be any children for them?

She opened her hand and looked down at the locket, murmuring, "I've got to give it back, and I've got to apologize. God forgive me, how could I have said such terrible things to my own sister?"

She got stiffly to her knees, careful not to wake the baby, and was about to stand when she heard a strange noise, like thunder on the plains, piercing the stillness of the day. Glancing up, she noted the sky was clear. At the next moment she realized that what she heard was pounding hooves against the dry, parched land. Then came the screams of the women and the alarmed shouts of the men as they tried to gather their wits and attempt to defend their families against the rapidly approaching Indians.

The whoops and cries of the Comanche drowned out all other sounds as they swarmed down on the helpless caravan, arrows singing through the air. Some were aflame, and they pierced the canvas of the wagons, setting them afire.

Violet watched, paralyzed with horror, clutching Jacie tightly against her. A silent scream constricted her throat at the sight of Iris's oldest boy, Lukie, being taken down by an arrow to his neck.

She fell forward, bracing herself with one arm against the ground as she continued to hold the baby while peering over the top of the camouflaging sage and scrub. She could see it all—the people she had come to know so well in the past weeks and consider friends, family even, all being slaughtered. Shuddering, she felt bile rise in her throat as she helplessly watched Luke trying to shield Iris, who crouched on the ground clutching one of her dead sons in her arms.

The last thing Violet saw before mercifully fainting was Luke falling dead, a tomahawk buried in his skull.

Iris was denied the relief of fainting. Instead, she was frozen in a kind of shock, unable to speak or move as the wild-faced savages leapt from their ponies to surround her.

She was the only one spared.

The Indians talked excitedly among themselves. She was beautiful, their leader declared, bragging how he had seen her from afar and decided she would bring them much pleasure before following her white brothers and sisters in death. Another argued he should have her first, since it was his tomahawk that had felled her defender.

But one warrior's gaze fastened on Iris's bosom. He shouted to his comrades to leave her alone and, dismounting, walked over and yanked her to her feet for closer scrutiny. Her legs would not support her; he held her up only long enough to make sure the stain on her dress was not blood, and then he let her slump to the ground in a sobbing heap as he announced triumphantly to the others, "She has milk. Our chief will be pleased to have her for his son."

The Indians nodded and muttered approval, thinking how Moonstar, the wife of their chief, had died only a few days before. Her son was being fed by other nursing mothers but now that he was four years old, his demand was great and the supply limited. The chief would be pleased to have a woman with milk for his son alone.

The warrior signaled for her to be taken away. "She will live," he said. "At least until she is of no more use to Great Bear. It will be up to him to decide. Then he will let us take our pleasure as a reward for bringing her to him."

Iris did not understand what they were saying and did not know she had been spared. If she had, it would not have mattered, because she had no reason to live any longer.

Her only solace amidst the carnage was having been spared the horror of witnessing her infant and her sister being slaughtered like the rest of her family—like the rest of her world.

Violet struggled to pull away from the peaceful oblivion that shielded her mind from the nightmare of reality. But a baby was crying. *Her baby?* No. Her baby had died. Yet she heard the hungry wail and fought to respond, an aching in her arms and in her heart.

Her eyes flashed open, and she looked about in panic as the horror came rushing back. Lying beside her on the ground, Jacie flailed at the air with her little fists, kicking against the warm blanket that constricted her.

Violet ignored the baby as she got to her knees with heart pounding and dared to peek out through the brush that had mercifully kept the Indians from spotting her.

What she saw made her blood run cold. The carnage was sickening, and she couldn't bring herself to walk through it to look for her dead family. She wanted to remember Iris, beautiful Iris, as she was in life.

The baby began to cry louder, furious to be neglected. Pausing only to catch her breath and make impatient smacking noises with her lips, she jerked her head from side to side, instinctively seeking to be fed.

Dizzy, stomach rolling, Violet managed to collect herself. She turned away from the silent, grisly scene but knew the image would forever more be burned into her mind and soul. Buzzards circled overhead. The Indians would have made sure there were no survivors.

How long had she been unconscious? The baby was hungry again, so it had to have been several hours. Then she noticed the sun was melting toward the west; It was late afternoon, which meant she had been asleep most of the day, probably due to her weakness, as well as to her having fainted in terror. It was no wonder the baby was screaming.

Picking up Jacie, Violet fed her, and the baby settled down contentedly. Violet tried to think what she should do, for despite the grief and anguish she felt, she wished to survive. The baby seemed to be sweating, so Violet pulled the blanket away from her, feeling a strange lump in one part of the hem as she did so. Curious and grateful to have anything to take her mind off her woes, she investigated and was startled to realize that Iris had sewn some money inside the blanket. "I will see that she gets it one day, Iris," Violet said aloud in a choky voice. "I'll never be able to tell you I'm sorry for the awful things I said to you, but I'll take care of your baby. I'll treat her like she was my own—"

Violet stiffened.

. . . *Like she was my own.*

Slowly, she absorbed the words and wondered if she actually dared make them so. Who would know? she rationalized, pulse racing. There was no one left who knew about her baby being born dead, or that the one she would call her own was actually her niece. No one would ever find out. Certainly not Judd, who would mercifully be spared such grief and heartache. There would be no harm in such a deception, only good. Jacie would have parents to take care of her, and Violet would not have to worry about losing the only man she had ever loved.

Her eyes fell on the locket where it had fallen to the ground when she had fainted. Loosening a few threads in the blanket's hem, she hid the locket inside with the money. One day perhaps she would give everything to Jacie and tell her the truth, but not while Judd was alive. Till then, it would be Violet's deep dark secret.

She fell asleep then and was not aware when the soldiers finally arrived after seeing the smoke. They immediately set about the grisly task of burying what was left of the bodies as quickly as possible. It was not until they had finished and were preparing to leave that they heard the sound of an infant crying in the gathering shadows of dusk.

Two of the soldiers went to investigate, daring to hope a mother might somehow have managed to hide her baby before the Indians were fully upon them. They moved cautiously in the dusk, making their way toward the sound. Seeing the squalling infant, arms and legs kicking mightily as it lay beside a woman's still body, the men exchanged fearful glances.

Violet stirred and moaned softly as she tried once

more to answer the needs of the baby—her baby, she reminded herself groggily.

"She's alive," said one of the soldiers. He dropped to one knee. "Are you hurt, ma'am?"

Wild-eyed with fear, Violet grabbed Jacie and held her tight against her.

"It's all right, ma'am. No need to be scared. We're soldiers, and we're going to take care of you. But I need to know if you're hurt."

Violet shook her head. Jacie was howling lustily, but she could do nothing for her at the moment and commenced to describe how she, along with her baby, had escaped death.

The soldiers wanted to know how many men, women, and children had been in the caravan so they could tell whether any captives had been taken. Days later, when she was told that there was one woman not accounted for, Violet would not let herself think it might be Iris, that the Indians might have taken her with them. She had seen her die, hadn't she? But the massacre had happened so fast; she could not be sure what she really saw. Still, the missing woman's body had probably been dragged away by wild animals before the soldiers got there. She forced herself to dismiss any doubts from her mind.

Violet was taken to the post infirmary after an all-night ride and put to bed with Jacie in her arms. Toward noon, Judd came into the room, eyes red-rimmed and swollen, shoulders slumped. His deep despair over Iris's death had ravaged him, making him age overnight.

"I don't feel like talking right now," he said in a barely audible voice. "Don't reckon you do, either. We'll have time later." He turned and walked out.

Violet smiled. Yes, there would be time, lots of time, because he would never leave her now, not when they had a child.

Violet knew that Judd was truly hers, at long last, for he would no longer torment himself with wanting Iris.

Then and there, Violet promised herself that if it took till her dying breath to make it happen, one day she would hear him say that he loved her.

Those precious words were all Violet was living for.

# 1

## North Georgia, 1858

*Zach Newton, hands on* his hips, looked down at the dark-haired girl with the shining lavender eyes and shook his head. "Miss Jacie, you're goin' to get me in a whole heap of trouble." In more ways than one, he thought, wondering if Jacie Calhoun knew how excited he got just being near her. "Mr. Blake will have my hide if he knows I'm teachin' you how to jump. You know how he feels about that."

Jacie dismissed his protest with a wrinkle of her nose as she stuck one booted foot in the stirrup and swung herself up into the saddle. She didn't think anything about Zach cupping her bottom as he gave her a boost, confident he regarded her in the same way the rest of the plantation workers did. She was a tomboy; she had grown up around most of them.

They knew she would much rather wear trousers and spend her days galloping on her horse than wear dresses and do boring things like learning to tat and sew.

Comfortable in the saddle, she took the reins and said, "Set the bar on the top."

He swung his head from side to side again. "Miss Jacie, I ain't gonna do it. That's too high for you."

She leaned down and tweaked his cheek playfully between thumb and forefinger. "Do be a dear for me, Zach, please. Michael will be coming home from Richmond today. I won't have another chance for a while, because it's next to impossible for us to slip off this way if he's at home. Besides, his mother is giving me a big party for my birthday next week, and I'll be busy with that."

Like everyone at Red Oakes, Zach knew about the party. People would be coming from all over because it would be the first social since old man Halsey Blake had died. The mourning period was over and it was expected that Michael was going to want to marry Jacie soon. Zach didn't like that one bit. When Mr. Halsey had hired him as an overseer, Zach had taken a shine to Jacie right off.

He had been all set to court her, till one of the other overseers tipped him off that Michael Blake, the future master of Red Oakes, had designs on her himself. Zach couldn't see that. After all, money married money, and the Calhouns sure didn't have any; in fact, Jacie's father was nothing more than a blacksmith on the plantation. But she was a fine piece of woman-flesh, and Zach couldn't blame Michael for thumbing his nose at anybody who thought he was courting someone beneath his class.

"Are you going to set the bar?" Jacie asked impatiently. "Please, Zach. I can make it. I know I can."

"I just don't see why you're riskin' your pretty little neck," he grumbled.

"Because it's something I haven't done before."

He felt like telling her he could think of something else she probably hadn't done yet, and how he'd sure like to teach her about that too, but held his tongue. "Well, it's your neck." He went to the hurdle and set it the way she wanted.

Jacie set the horse into a gentle trot toward the far end of the clearing. She would need a good distance to get up the speed necessary to clear the bar.

She felt herself sweating, but it was not from fear. Jacie could not remember ever being afraid of anything in her whole life. It was the scorching August day that made her perspire. The old shirt she wore, one that belonged to her father, was plastered to her, and her hair was damp against her neck.

Halsey Blake had cleared this strip of land, intending to plant more scuppernong vines between the river and the cornfields, but he had died before seeing it done. Michael had been too busy learning to run the entire plantation; therefore the section remained barren and made a wonderful place for Jacie to sneak off to so Zach could give her riding lessons. The tall stalks of corn kept them from being seen by anyone at the big house.

She reined the horse about and saw that Zach had placed the wooden crossbar in the highest slot. He waved at her and yelled, "Dig in like I told you, and let the horse decide when to jump."

The horse pawed the ground impatiently and tried to toss his head, but Jacie held the reins, pulling down on the harness. The horse might be ready, but she wasn't, because she wanted to savor the moment of anticipation. To Jacie, life was a series of hurdles that could be conquered only by courage and determination. Each time she felt she was about to make a fateful leap, it was exhilarating, and she tried to make the feeling last as long as possible.

She thought of Michael; Zach had been right when he said Michael wouldn't approve. Michael's brother Edward had died of a broken neck in a riding accident when he was only fourteen. Even though Red Oakes was known for its fine stock, hurdle jumping had not been allowed since the tragedy.

But Jacie loved riding, including the hurdles, which she was determined to conquer despite the ban.

She pressed her thighs against the horse and leaned forward to whisper into his ear, "Do it, boy." At the same time, she dug her heels into his flanks and gave the reins a flip. The horse took off at a full gallop, his mane slapping Jacie's cheek as she raised herself slightly in the saddle. She was braced, she was ready. She had done it before and knew what to expect, knew that when the horse started to leap up and over, she would instinctively stretch herself to almost lie along his great neck as he cleared. She would go limber for just an instant, then brace herself for the jolt sure to come when his hooves hit the ground on the other side.

The hurdle loomed closer. Jacie could actually feel the anticipation rippling through the horse. Zach stood back, watching intently, nervously.

The horse was about to lunge. Jacie commanded herself to yield to the movement. It was going to happen. She was going to make the highest jump ever and she laughed out loud at the sheer thrill of the moment.

The sound of a voice, sharp and loud, angry and frightened, rang out in the stillness.

"Jacie, no!"

She tensed, did not relax her body as the mighty horse lunged. Losing her balance, she fell backward and to the side. Her shoulders struck the ground first, then her head. She felt a sharp pain just before a dizzying blackness consumed her.

"Jacie, can you hear me?"

The frantic urging came out of the thick fog that enshrouded her. Her head felt heavy and was throbbing. She heard a groan and realized it came from her.

"Jacie—"

"Here. Let me put this under her nose," another voice interrupted.

Something sharp, acrid, and quite annoying filled her nostrils. She fought against it, slinging her head from side to side, which made the aching worse. Her eyes flashed open as she protested against the foul odor of the ammonia. "No. Take it away."

She saw two faces staring down at her anxiously, and one of them belonged to Michael. Groggily, she reached to brush back the unruly curl that forever seemed to topple onto his forehead. It was a gesture he adored, and he caught her fingertips and pressed them to his lips. "Thank God, you're going to be all right," he said, then darted a nervous glance at the man beside him. "She is, isn't she?"

Dr. Foley said, "I think so. She's had a bad bump on the head, but there are no broken bones. She's a very lucky girl."

"And a very foolish one," Michael said, frowning. He could wait no longer to scold her. "What were you thinking of? You could have been killed."

It was all coming back to her, and Jacie felt the anger rise up in her. "I was doing fine till you came along and ruined everything, Michael. If you hadn't yelled when you did, I'd have made that jump."

"But you had no business trying. I'm going to have Zach Newton's head for this. He ran to get Doc Foley and I haven't had a chance to speak to him since. But I will, you can be sure of that."

Jacie saw the pinpoints of anger flashing in his blue eyes. She had seen his temper erupt in the past. He was a man to be reckoned with when angry, and she was not about to allow him to vent his rage on Zach for something that was her idea in the first place. "It's not his fault. Promise me you won't punish him."

"He knows better than to go behind my back like that," he said through clenched teeth.

"I had a right to do what I wanted. How did you find me, anyway?"

"I went looking for you as soon as I got home from Richmond. Your mother said you'd gone riding. Then Sudie told me she saw you and Newton going through the cornfield, so that's where I headed."

"Sudie . . ." Jacie nodded to herself. "I might have known. She's always watching me."

"Because she adores you."

Jacie knew that was so, and it was also the reason she was not really angry with the little Negro girl. She was only eight years old, and since it was a rule at Red Oakes that children under ten did not work in the fields, Sudie tagged after Jacie whenever possible, offering to help with whatever she might be doing.

Michael ran his hands through his hair in frustration. "You try my patience, Jacie. God knows, you're the most headstrong woman I've ever met. You never listen to anything I say. What am I going to do with you?"

Dr. Foley closed his worn leather bag. "I'll stop back by in the morning and see how you're feeling. Will you be here or at home?" Everyone knew Michael Blake had plans to marry Jacie Calhoun, so it was easy to assume he would make her comfortable in his house while she was recuperating from her fall.

"Here, of course," Michael confirmed.

But Jacie protested. "No, I won't. I'll be home, because I'm fine. I knew how to fall, just like I knew how to make that jump, if I'd had the chance," she added tartly.

"I'd rather have you here where I can see that you're looked after," Michael argued.

"I'll be fine. Mother is going to be worried if I don't get there soon, anyway, so I'd better leave now." Glancing about, she found she was lying on a sofa in the parlor. "Where is your mother, Michael?" she asked, wondering why Miss Olivia wasn't fluttering about in her usual nervous way.

"She's taken to her bed," Michael explained after Dr. Foley had let himself out. "The accident reminded her of Edward's death, so Dr. Foley gave her some laudanum to calm her."

"I'm sorry," Jacie said.

"As for your parents, your father was here, but Dr. Foley told him you'd be all right, so he went back to work. Your mother is sitting with mine till she falls asleep.

"You were unconscious for a while," he added, frowning. "You gave us quite a scare."

"I'm sorry," she repeated, and started to get up. She was certainly not going to keep lying there apologizing for something he had caused, albeit not intentionally.

He held her down gently. "Please stay."

"I don't want to."

"Jacie, you're angry." His expression softened. "But I'm the one who has a right to be. Zach had no business—"

"I told you not to be cross with him. He did what I asked him to do because he's my friend."

"He isn't the sort of person you should be around. In the first place, he's a hired hand and—"

"So is my father," she blazed.

He knew he had erred, but he pressed on nevertheless. "Zach Newton is also a rowdy when he drinks too much, but at least that's on his own time. My father liked his work, so I've kept him on, but that doesn't mean I want you having anything to do with him, or with any other man around here."

Jacie was tired of arguing. "I'd really like to go now," she said firmly.

He gave a sigh of resignation. "All right. I'll have a carriage brought around."

"That's not necessary, and you'd best stay with your mother yourself. She's going to be so angry with me when she wakes up that she'll probably cancel my party." Jacie suspected Olivia hadn't wanted to hold the celebration in the first place and that it was all Michael's idea.

"Nothing is going to spoil that party. It's going to be very special, I promise. It's time to let everyone know that mourning has ended, and Red Oakes is ready to start living again. But most of all, it's your birthday." He smiled, eager to end the tension between them.

Jacie really was looking forward to the day. Michael had even insisted on sending her and her mother to Atlanta to have elegant ballgowns made at his expense. It was thus understood he would be officially proposing soon. Otherwise, such generosity might have been considered improper. Still, Jacie felt uncomfortable about Michael's mother. "Be sure and tell her when she wakes up that I regret what happened. Sometimes I get the feeling she really doesn't like me."

"That's not true, though you do worry her with some of your antics, and you know it. Like that old Indian—"

"His name is Mehlonga," Jacie said impatiently. "He's my friend, and he's teaching me all about herbs and Indian medicine."

"And he's also a renegade Cherokee who's been hiding in the mountains nearly twenty years because he refused to go to a reservation. He sneaks in here to teach the slaves that they should be afraid of white men's medicine. He's been a real thorn in Dr. Foley's side, and mine, too, and I wish you would stay away from him."

Jacie's ire was rising again. "I don't blame him or any other Indian who refused to give up their land and go on that horrible march. They call it the 'Trail of Tears' and—" She threw up her hands. "Oh, what's the use? You have no sympathy for them."

"I admit that," he said without apology, "but this

isn't a good subject for us to be discussing, so let's not continue."

She was glad to end the conversation, well aware it would always be a delicate matter between them. Neither Michael nor his mother would ever change their feelings toward the Indians, although Jacie had heard conflicting stories as to why. According to the family tale, Michael's grandfather, Jasper Blake, had been murdered by the Cherokee for no reason. Mehlonga, however, had told Jacie it had to do with the discovery of gold on Cherokee land and how Jasper tried to steal it from them. She had been tempted to ask Michael about it but was afraid it would only make him resent Mehlonga even more.

Jacie insisted on leaving, and she hurried over to the blacksmith shop to find her father hard at work, as always. His face blackened with soot, he held an iron horseshoe to the fire. "I see you're all right," he said, glancing up only briefly. "I told Michael you would be. He was all upset. Guess he doesn't know what hearty stock you come from. Still and all, you had no business jumpin' that horse when you know how he feels about it, and you ought to know he don't approve of you hangin' around with Zach Newton. Better watch yourself, girl. He ain't proposed yet."

"Daddy, you fret too much." Jacie was used to her father's endless grumbling. He made no secret of the fact that he was anxious for her to marry Michael so she'd be well taken care of for the rest of her life.

He looked up from the fire long enough to scowl at her and then returned to his chore and his badgering. "It'll be you who's frettin' if he decides he don't want a wildcat like you for a wife, Jacie Calhoun. You better hear me and mind your ways. Michael Blake can have his pick of any unmarried woman in the state of Georgia, and you know it. There ain't a one among 'em who wouldn't give anythin' to marry up with the owner of one of the richest plantations around."

"I don't care about his money. I won't marry Michael unless I'm sure I love him."

"And you're sure you do." He said it as a fact, not a question.

Jacie did not respond. That was something she had been thinking about lately, a lot, because she was not sure exactly what being in love meant. Michael was the only man who had ever kissed her, and she felt all warm and wonderful inside when he did, but was that love? She wondered. And the only person she had ever been able to talk to about it was Mehlonga. She could discuss anything with him, and when the subject was love, he always said she'd know when it came, because a spirit inside would speak to her heart, and then she would have no doubt. But Jacie had not heard a spirit, and she had felt nothing but the tingling feelings Michael so easily evoked with his touch, feelings that were nowhere near her heart.

"You ain't sayin' nothin'."

"There's nothing to say." She turned toward the door. "I'm going home now."

"You do that," he called after her. "And you mind what I say and quit upsettin' the folks at the big house, or you'll find yourself livin' in a shack the rest of your life. Hear me now, girl."

Jacie heard him, all right, but longed instead to

# 2

*Jacie took a sip of the* concoction Mehlonga gave her and made a face.

"Drink more," he urged. "It will stop the pain in your head."

"What *is* this?" She shivered with revulsion.

"Boiled turnip roots."

They were sitting in their secret meeting place, a grotto formed in the rocks by a stream running down through the mountains. Jacie thought it was uncanny the way Mehlonga always seemed to know when she'd come there looking for him, like today. She had wanted the company of a good friend, and before long he had come out of the woods.

She forced herself to finish drinking, then said, "I want you to show me how to make it, because I want to learn all I can."

He reached into the deerskin pouch tied about his

waist and brought out a pinch of something green. Patting it on her forehead, he told her, "These are the crushed leaves of the tulip tree. They also soothe a headache."

He was a stern-looking man, his face etched with wrinkles from many years in the sun. He had a hawkish nose, a short, spiky gray beard, and eyes that seemed to bore right into a person. He had a turned-down mouth that never formed any hint of a smile. He took life quite seriously, and life had been hard. "The remedies are closely guarded secrets," he said, "passed down from one family and healer to another."

He described taboos surrounding the ritualistic gathering of herbs and plants. "If a poisonous snake crosses your path, it is a bad omen. You should return home and not work with your medicine for the rest of the day. Remember not to pick the first plant when you start out. It has to be left as a symbol to all plants that you know what their blessings are.

"But enough teaching for today," he said sternly. "I feel something bothers you besides the soreness from your fall. Is it because the spirit has still not spoken to your heart, and the time is near for you to marry Michael?"

She sent him a wry and mirthless smile. "It's your fault, you know. If you hadn't told me to listen, I wouldn't be worried about it." She leaned back against the rocks, and taking the crushed leaves from where he had stuck them on her forehead, she tossed them into the water below, staring as the current carried them away and out of sight.

Mehlonga watched her intently but did not speak. He knew when to keep silent.

After a few moments, she said, "Daddy says I should marry Michael, that he's a good man and he'll take care of me."

"Is that what you want?"

"I don't know. I only know that he is good to me, and he adores me."

"As your mother has adored your father?"

Jacie glanced up sharply.

"Remember how we met?" he prodded. "You were only a child, and you were lost. I found you crying, and I took you back within sight of your home, but while we were together, you told me you wanted to run away because you were so unhappy there."

Jacie remembered. It was the only time she had actually left, but there had been many days since when she wished she lived anywhere but with her parents. For they were without a doubt the two most miserable people she had ever encountered. Her mother seemed to cry all the time, and her face was a cross patch of wrinkles; her father practically lived at the blacksmith shop, working when he didn't have to, to keep from going home.

They had fights, especially when Jacie's mother drank too much cider. She would whimper that Jacie's father didn't love her, and when he got mad, so would she, and they would curse each other. Jacie had confided everything through the years to Mehlonga but assured him she had no fears her marriage to Michael would be like that.

"It might be if you do not love him as he loves you," Mehlonga countered. "He might turn to drink, as your mother did, which would make you angry, and then the trouble would come."

"That won't happen. I won't let it."

"Listen for the spirit to talk to your heart," he warned again, "as it spoke to mine to tell me I loved my Little Crow."

Jacie made no comment, knowing he was slipping into painful memories of how he had lost his wife. He had told her about it, how when the soldiers came to take the first Cherokees forcefully to a reservation west of the Mississippi, he had been away, gathering herbs high in the mountains. When he returned, Little Crow was gone. He tried to follow after her, only to learn she had been among the first to die on the arduous journey when hunger, cold, and disease took the lives of one of every four Indians. Mehlonga had gone home and avoided the soldiers ever since, not wanting to leave the place where he and Little Crow had been so happy together.

Finally he spoke. "Sometimes I think I would like to go there, to the west to join my people. I am getting old, and I would like to live my last years among them."

"Would you really travel so far, not knowing whether you would be happy after you got there?"

"I have not been happy since I lost Little Crow, so it makes no difference. It's just something I want to do."

Jacie knew Mehlonga had loved Little Crow with a love too deep for her to comprehend and wondered if her parents had ever loved each other at all. Once, during one of her mother's drunken tirades at her father, she had screamed at him that he probably wished she had also died in the Comanche massacre that had killed her sister, Iris. He had stormed out of the cabin without answering. Her mother had become hysterical then, and Jacie remembered being horrified by it all.

"Mehlonga," Jacie said quietly, "I've listened to all you've told me about love and spirits talking to the heart, but the fact is, Michael is going to ask me to marry him at my birthday party, and I'm still not sure I love him. He expects me to say yes. So do my parents. I don't know what to do."

"And I cannot tell you what to do. Just keep listening, child. Just keep listening."

Jacie was more confused than ever but told herself she had to forget about whether or not she loved Michael and just accept his proposal and endeavor to make him a good wife.

After all, what else was there for her?

Michael took the white velvet box from the wall safe and went to sit down at his desk before opening it. Lifting the necklace from its satin cradle, he held it up to the light streaming through the window. It was exquisite, the diamonds glittering to compete with the stunning purple of the amethysts. The jeweler in Atlanta had followed his design but had to rush to complete the piece in time for the party. The amethysts had to be ordered all the way from South America and were a long time arriving.

Michael was proud and pleased over the creation. He had wanted to give Jacie not only a special gift for her eighteenth birthday, but also something as a memento of the night he asked her to be his wife.

It was hard to remember a time when he had not loved Jacie. They had grown up together, and by the time he was twelve and she was ten, Michael knew he'd never meet anyone prettier. She had hair the color of a crow's wing, but it was her strange and beautiful lavender eyes that took his breath away. That was why he had chosen amethysts for the necklace, knowing the splendor of Jacie's eyes would surpass even the beauty of those precious stones.

Michael never had any doubts that he would make Jacie Calhoun his wife, but his parents were not pleased when they began to notice that he was thinking of her romantically. She was not of his class, they said, and he was expected to marry well, but he was stubborn and swore that when the time came, he would not court anyone else.

The year he turned sixteen they sent him to England to study at Oxford. He argued that a planter did not need such an education, but they insisted he follow family tradition; all the Blake men studied at Oxford. And so off he went.

Through his father's acquaintances, Michael was introduced to young ladies from London's finest families. Groomed to marry among their own class, they all had charm and grace, but Michael knew there could be no one for him but Jacie. And not merely because he found her so pretty. He loved her for her zest, her spirit, and when others raised eyebrows over her daring and sometimes unorthodox antics, Michael was merely amused.

He made friends among his classmates, who took him to the streets of London to learn another side of life—the pleasures of the flesh. But those women were merely a harmless diversion that meant nothing beyond the moment, because he never stopped thinking of Jacie. As a child she had learned to read and write along with him, sharing his tutor at his insistence, against his parents' wishes, so they were able to keep in touch through their letters.

His time abroad seemed to pass slowly, and Michael began to count months, weeks, finally days, until at last he was on his way home with but one thing on his mind—to make Jacie his wife as soon as possible, his parents' objections be damned.

But fate had cruelly stepped in to decree otherwise, for Michael arrived home to learn that his father had died suddenly while he was in transit. The responsibility of running the vast plantation had fallen upon his young shoulders, and along with it, the obligation of the ritual of mourning, which could last from six months to two years. His mother declared the longest period. Marriage during that time was out of the question.

Jacie was around, of course, and Michael treasured what time he could be with her. She loved horses and could usually be found at the stables, but she avoided the blacksmith shop. Michael knew she was not close to her father, who was a cantankerous sort. Actually, no one liked to be around Judd Calhoun, but he did his work well, which was all that mattered to Michael.

As for Jacie's mother, Violet, Michael yearned for the day he could get Jacie away from her. She was cold and distant to everyone except Judd, doting on him to the point of obsession, though Michael heard she drank too much sometimes and there were terrible fights. But Jacie never divulged family secrets.

She also never complained that her mother mistreated her, but Michael had his suspicions about that, too, and felt her constant cheerfulness was actually a facade to hide the misery she endured at home.

It had always seemed to him that Violet only tolerated her daughter, that she felt that Jacie was actually in the way of her adoration for her husband.

But Michael could not dwell on his love for Jacie or his concern over her unhappy parents, because he was determined to show everyone he was capable of running the plantation at least as well as his father had done. By working tirelessly, he had succeeded in doubling cotton and corn production and at the end of two years was richer than his father had ever been.

He was proud of his accomplishment but happier still that the time had finally come when he could remove the crepe band from his arm and officially come out of mourning. His mother would probably, as some widows chose to do, wear black for the rest of her life.

He was still gazing at the necklace and dreaming of the happiness ahead when his mother tapped on the study door as she opened it. "Michael, I want you to—" she began, then stopped short. Too late, Michael put the necklace back in the box.

"What do you have there?" she asked, hurrying to the desk. "Let me see. Is it Jacie's present? You told me you were having something made in Atlanta."

Michael braced himself. He had hesitated to show it to her, dreading her reaction. Reluctantly, he opened the box.

Olivia gasped and sank into the nearest chair. The piece was decidedly finer and more expensive than any of her own jewelry.

"I designed it myself," Michael told her.

"I think this is far too extravagant for a birthday gift," she commented archly.

"It's more than that," he said evenly.

Their gazes locked, each challenging. Finally Olivia said, "I think it's too soon, Michael."

"Father has been dead two years, Mother." He got up and went to put the necklace back in the safe. "I've waited long enough. I'm going to ask Jacie to marry me at the party. She can set the wedding date any time she wants. The sooner the better, as far as I'm concerned.

"I know you don't approve of her," he added coolly, "but I love her. I always have and always will."

"I just worry about what people will say, Michael. I'm afraid she won't settle down after you're married. The Blake name is highly respected, and—"

"And *what?*" he flared. "What are you trying to say, Mother? There has never been a breath of scandal about Jacie. True, she's mischievous now and then, but always she is a lady."

"She was not behaving like a lady when she rode that horse, using a man's saddle no less, and tried to jump that hurdle. Not only did she nearly get herself killed, but she brought back terrible memories." Olivia blinked and dabbed at her eyes with the lace handkerchief she plucked from her sleeve.

"She meant no harm."

"I expect you to honor your father's decree that jumping is forbidden at Red Oakes. And another thing, people are already talking about her and that old fool Indian. That's why I came in here to see you. I want you to forbid her to see him. Why doesn't the law do something about him, anyway?

"I mean it," she said waspishly as she stood to leave. "You put a stop to it. You tell her if she is going to be a Blake, she can start behaving like one by not associating with savages."

Michael could only stare after her as she headed for

the door. He was not about to reveal that Jacie was quite stubborn about her friendship with Mehlonga.

Olivia turned. "One more thing. You will need to send a carriage to Atlanta to meet the morning train from Charleston."

"And who is coming from Charleston, Mother?" As if he didn't know.

"Why, Cousin Verena and Cousin Elyse, of course. You didn't think they would miss a party at Red Oakes, did you?"

"I didn't want them here. I intentionally left their names off the list."

"And I intentionally included them. They always look forward to visiting."

"They don't know when to leave. We have a wedding to plan, and I don't need Verena interfering. She always puts her nose in family business."

"Verena adores you. She'll want to share all the excitement."

Michael was about to protest but his mother breezed out the door, effectively ending the conversation. He slumped in his chair, miserable.

He did not mind being around Elyse. She was nearly his age and sweet and charming. If not for his losing his heart to Jacie all those years ago, maybe he would have given serious consideration to marrying Elyse. They got on well together, and he hoped she and Jacie would be good friends.

It was Elyse's mother, Verena, first cousin to his father, that Michael did not particularly enjoy being around. She always sided with his mother in any dispute, especially one concerning him, and he knew once she heard about Jacie's friendship with an Indian, she would be openly critical.

But there was no more time to brood over unwelcome house guests. Glancing at the wall clock at the sound of a knock on the door, he saw that Zach Newton was right on time. Michael had postponed talking to the overseer about the jumping incident until his temper had cooled. "Come in," he called.

Zach entered and drew a deep breath, savoring the delicious smell of the fine leather furniture. He liked this room but didn't get to see it often. He could just imagine sitting himself down in the big sofa in front of a roaring fire on a cold winter day, a snifter of good brandy in his hand. But he was never called in for social reasons, and by the way Michael was glaring at him through steepled fingers from behind his big mahogany desk, Zach knew he was in trouble.

"You wanted to see me?"

"I think you know why," Michael said tightly.

"Miss Jacie asked me to teach her to jump. I didn't see no harm."

Michael suddenly slammed both his fists on the desk. "She could have been killed, and you know jumping horses is forbidden here!" he shouted at the overseer.

Zach did not wither before Michael's angry glare and fired back in defiance, "Miss Jacie is a good rider. She wouldn't have fallen if you hadn't scared her the way you did. As for not allowin' jumpin', that's a ridiculous rule and—"

"That is not for you to decide!" Michael bolted to his feet. "Get something straight, Newton. I make the rules, and you either follow them or get your gear and get off my land. The only reason I'm not kicking your butt over this is that Jacie made me promise not to. Now get out of here before I do it anyway, damn you."

Zach turned on his heel and hurried out, silently cursing all the while. Damn wet-behind-the-ears upstart. Who did he think he was, threatening to beat up on him? Zach just wished he would try, because he would find out just how little a fancy education in Europe meant in a fight.

As for Jacie, Zach knew now she had to feel something for him, otherwise she wouldn't have bothered to take up for him like she had, telling Blake to go easy. Maybe one day he would have his chance with her, after all. Married women took lovers sometimes, and once she got a taste of a sissy like Blake, Zach would be only too glad to show her what it was like to tumble in bed with a real man.

# 3

*Halsey Blake had known* from the first pair of horseshoes Judd Calhoun struck that he had found a treasure of a blacksmith. He knew just how to hone the heel calk and how to round the nail crease for a perfect fit. Big and brawny, Judd could make the anvil sing.

Judd had been desperate for work, having just returned from Texas with a wife and baby. Halsey wanted to keep him around, so he had a better cabin built for him than the one he usually provided, which was a mere square pen of logs roofed over with boards supported by rough posts at the door. Halsey even let Judd pick the site, a picturesque knoll overlooking the winding Oconee River. The cabin was elevated three feet above the ground on four corner posts, so air could circulate beneath. The fireplace was at one end, made of sticks and clay, the chimney carried up outside. The roof was extended to hang over the porch.

But it was not the porch Judd preferred. He liked to sit out on the lawn beneath a spreading mimosa tree, where he now aimlessly whittled at a stick while waiting for the Blake carriage to arrive. He wished he didn't have to go to the party. Brushing wood shavings from his new trousers, he thought again how silly he felt to be wearing a frock coat. But Michael had insisted, ordering him to be fitted by his own tailor and footing the bill himself. Judd figured he would get three wearings out of his outfit—today's party, Jacie's wedding, and one day down the road, his own funeral.

One down, two to go, he thought mirthlessly. Not that he had any fear of dying. No, he reckoned he'd had a real good life, considering other folks. But there were times when he wondered how things would have been if he'd stayed in Texas. He had liked being a Ranger. But when the Indians had slaughtered poor Iris and her family, Judd couldn't wait to take his baby daughter and get the hell out of that wild land.

"Well, Daddy, how do I look?"

He looked toward the house. A lump came into his throat as he saw Jacie and was struck as always by how she was the spitting image of her aunt Iris. And he had never seen her look prettier. Her ebony-colored hair was pulled back and held by a tiny cluster of fragrant gardenia blossoms, soft ringlets tumbling to her golden-tanned shoulders. Her gown was fashioned of deep purple silk and satin and overlaid with delicate pink lace flounces on the bodice and the skirt, and she wore elbow-length gloves of white kid and a sheer stole that matched the lacework of the gown.

She held her skirt daintily to keep from dusting the hem as she came toward him. "You aren't saying anything. Do I look awful? Should I go back inside and put on one of my old dresses?" She was forever attempting to get a smile out of her father by teasing him but rarely succeeded. He was such a somber man, and she had always wondered what had happened in his past to make him so unhappy.

Suddenly, Judd could keep his thoughts to himself no longer. "You look just like your aunt Iris did on her wedding day," he blurted.

Jacie knew her mother and her sister had had a double wedding, just as she knew her aunt's death had been something neither of her parents had ever gotten over. Rarely was Iris mentioned, and it made Jacie feel awkward to hear her father speak of her now. She changed the subject. "I never dreamed I'd wear such a fine dress. It was sweet of Michael to buy new things for all of us."

Judd snorted and returned to his whittling. "He knew if he didn't, there wouldn't be no party, because you sure couldn't go dressed in the rags I've been able to provide for you. Just wait, girl. This is only the beginnin'. Once you and him are married you won't want for anythin' the rest of your life."

"Maybe you and Momma will come and live with us. The house is certainly big enough." Jacie knew with certainty that that would never happen.

Judd began to rock gently to and fro. "I'll live here till the day I die and then I want to be buried right here under this tree. All I want is to know you're looked after when I'm gone."

"I will be, but don't you worry. You're going to be around a long, long time, Daddy. You'll be rocking your grandbabies in that very chair. You'll see." She rushed to kiss the top of his balding head.

Judd tensed. It always made him feel funny when Jacie touched him, because thoughts of Iris and how much he had loved her came to mind.

Jacie moved away, sensing his usual rejection. She could not remember a time in her life when he had hugged her or kissed her, and if she tried to hold his hand when they walked together, he drew back. Sometimes she dared wonder if maybe he blamed her for how unhappy he was, married to her mother. Perhaps she had been born at a time when he was thinking about leaving but felt duty-bound to stay after becoming a father. And she had often wondered why she had no brothers and sisters.

"That boy is gonna propose to you tonight," Judd said. "He spoke to me about it awhile back. Asked my permission, proper like. You're a lucky girl."

Impetuously, Jacie dared ask, "What if I told him no? What if I told him I'm not ready to get married yet, that I'd like to experience more of life before settling down?" She was not about to confide how much she had been thinking lately about Mehlonga's dream of going out west, and if he did go, how she wished she could go with him. Only for a visit, of course, but even to think of actually seeing the other side of those mountains filled her with excitement.

"Don't you even joke about such a thing." He shook the knife at her. "You tell Michael yes, or so help me, I'll take my shavin' strop to you."

Jacie dismissed his threat. He might seem to resent her at times, but he'd never whipped her.

"Somethin' else," he said gruffly. "Miz Blake told me to see to it that you quit hangin' around that old Indian. She don't think it looks nice, and neither do I. It was different when you were little, but you're grown up now."

"I enjoy being around Mehlonga. He teaches me about healing ways. I want to learn everything I can."

His tone softened as he was again reminded of his beloved. "You're just like your aunt Iris. Her pa was a doctor and she was his shadow, learnin' everythin' she could from him. After he died, she started tendin' folks. They called her a medicine woman. Maybe you took after her that way too. But if Miz Blake don't like you seein' that Indian, you give it up, you hear me? And I don't imagine Michael likes it, either. It's time you started actin' like a woman about to be married."

"Just because I get married doesn't mean I have to forget all my dreams."

"What dreams? The only dream you ought to be havin' is about bein' Michael's wife, havin' his babies. What kind of nonsense are you talkin' about now?"

"Do you see that mountain in the distance?"

Judd followed her gaze.

"Sometimes I can't help thinking how there's more to this world than what I've known here. Roads I've never walked. Rivers I've never seen. Flowers I've never smelled. I guess what I'm trying to say is that I'm always going to wonder—"

Judd slapped his forehead and looked at her as though she had gone daft. "That's the craziest thing I ever heard of. One of the richest men in the state of

Georgia wants to marry you and you're wonderin' about rivers and flowers."

Jacie was unmoved by his censure. "Haven't you ever thought about it, Poppa? How life might have been if you hadn't settled down here?"

A shadow crossed his face. "Listen, girl. I crossed them mountains once. Some of me is still on the other side, and the empty parts filled up with pain and made me wish I'd never gone. I'd be better off. A lot of folks would." His voice cracked. "So don't go talkin' to me about how you want to do the same damn thing."

Violet heard everything from where she stood listening inside the cabin at her bedroom window. Judd's words cut deeply, because although they had never discussed it, she knew he blamed himself for what happened to Iris and her family. He probably reasoned that if he had not gone west to return with glowing tales of the life awaiting, Luke would not have wanted to go. The trip would not have taken place and the horror would not have happened. But she also knew that Judd would have left her for good, and that was where her own nightmares began—with the reality that her lie, her deception, was what had kept him tied to her all these years. But she had loved him so much, had prayed he would learn to love her too. Only it hadn't happened, and she had come to believe they would all have been better off if she'd told the truth back then.

She wanted to love Jacie, but every time she looked at her she saw Iris, which needled her conscience. She had tried to be a good mother all the same. Now Jacie would be moving into the mansion and Violet was happy for her, but also glad to have Judd to herself at last. Without Jacie around to remind him of Iris, Violet dared hope it was not too late to make him love her after all.

The sound of a horse approaching took Violet's attention, along with Jacie's and Judd's, to the road beside the river. It was not quite time for the carriage to arrive.

It was Zach. He reined to a stop near Judd and was about to state his business when he saw Jacie and froze. "Lord," he whispered under his breath. He had never seen her look so beautiful.

Dismounting, he could not tear his eyes from Jacie, and for the moment he forgot why he was there.

Judd had to prod him and was a bit irritable, because he had never liked Zach's interest in his daughter and didn't like how he was looking at her now. "Well, what is it? Don't stand there oglin'. We're waitin' to go to a party and have no time for you."

Zach continued to stare at Jacie as he told Judd, "I reckon you got time for Mr. Blake. He sent me to tell you them horses he bought up in Richmond last month just got here. He wasn't expectin' them till next week. Some of them got hooves in bad shape, and they're limpin'. He wants you to carry some work clothes with you so as soon as you've put in an appearance at the party you can high-tail it over to the stables and take a look at them. He said to apologize to you, Miss Jacie"—he flashed her a big grin—"and says he knows you understand about things like that."

"She understands like I do that lame horses are more important than a party I didn't want to go to in the first place," Judd snapped. He was on his feet and already unbuttoning the frock coat that made him so uncomfortable. "I won't be missed. I'll change and get on over there now."

"Sorry," Zach said to Jacie after Judd had gone into the cabin. He was turning his hat around and around in his hands. "Sorry about a lot of things, like you fallin' the other day. I shouldn't have let you do it."

"If it was anybody's fault, it was Michael's," Jacie told him matter-of-factly. "There's nothing for you to apologize for."

"He didn't see it that way."

She raised an eyebrow. "He didn't punish you, did he?"

He laughed. "What's he gonna do? Turn me over his knee and give me a paddlin'? He just run his mouth, that's all, and I want to thank you." His voice softened as he looked down at her and felt a heated rush to think how much he wanted her. "He told me you made him promise not to do anythin' to me."

"Well, I persuaded you to set those hurdles up and show me how to jump them, Zach, so it wasn't fair for him to take out his anger on you. But it's over now. Don't worry about it anymore."

He started to leave but had to tell her, "You sure are pretty, Jacie, probably the prettiest girl I ever saw in my whole life. And I want to wish you a happy birthday."

"Why—why, thank you, Zach." Jacie came and stood on tiptoe to impulsively kiss his cheek. "You're sweet to say that."

"Jacie. Get in here."

Violet had witnessed the scene and was furious. One of these days Jacie was going to get herself in trouble by being too friendly with people, and what could she be thinking, anyway, kissing Zach Newton, even if it was just on his cheek and to thank him for a compliment. Zach was a rowdy. Violet could tell. She could also tell he liked Jacie a little bit too much and needed to be put in his place. Jacie wasn't helping the situation.

"I have to go," Jacie said to Zach.

He swung himself up into the saddle. "You have yourself a nice party, Jacie."

"I will. Thanks again."

He rode away, and Violet bounded out of the cabin and down the steps. She was wearing a lovely gown too, a blue taffeta with a slightly scooped neck, the bodice crusted with little pearls. The sleeves were puffed all the way to the elbows, where more pearls sprinkled the fabric and then they tapered to the wrists. Her hair was pulled back in a snood. Michael had offered to send over one of the Negro girls who was especially good at fixing ladies' hair, but Violet had declined. She had worn her hair in a snood for years and was not about to be fussed over with a bunch of curling irons and combs.

"Are you out of your mind?" she lashed out at Jacie. "I saw what you did."

"I kissed his cheek," Jacie said quietly. "He's my friend."

"And he might take it the wrong way and get ideas about how maybe you aren't really a lady, and he certainly doesn't pretend to be a gentleman. What would Michael think?"

Jacie stiffened. Her mother scolded her for everything. Actually, the only time Violet ever talked to her at all was to fuss or give her a chore to do.

"Michael understands I show people I like them, Mother."

"He doesn't know how friendly you can be sometimes. You'll get yourself in trouble one day. And what are you looking at, anyway?"

A chickadee had landed on a branch of the mimosa tree and Jacie was staring up at it with an expectant look on her face, only to seem flooded with relief as it flew away. "Mehlonga told me birds can see into the future and if a chickadee perches on a branch near the house and chirps, it's an omen that you have a secret enemy plotting something terrible against you. I didn't want that kind of omen, today of all days. I'm glad it flew away without making a sound."

"Oh for heaven's sake. You listen to your pa and stay away from that old fool."

The carriage arrived a few minutes later and a groom, resplendent in a red satin coat and black satin pants, helped Jacie and Violet inside.

Violet settled back comfortably. She felt so at peace. Soon Jacie would no longer be her responsibility. Best of all, Jacie would not be around to intrude on the precious hours when Judd was at home. Violet would work harder to make him love her. There was still time; they were not so terribly old. She closed her eyes and dreamed of how wonderful it would be.

The carriage moved along the path beside the river and then onto the main road, turning finally into the long drive lined with the towering red oak trees that gave the vast plantation its name.

As they drew closer, they passed the gardens on one side, noted for their camellias, with pigeon houses covered in wisteria and honeysuckle. On the other side there was a statuary and a marble fountain. Everywhere the lawn was lush and green, sprawling all the way to the distant cotton fields.

Jacie's breath was always taken away by the sight of the great house—two-storied and tremendous in scale, with a hipped and dormered roof supported on all sides by huge Roman Doric columns, twenty-eight in number.

The guests spilled out onto the porch and the sweeping lawn, the women in billowing skirted gowns of every design and color imaginable and the men smartly dressed in their finest frock coats. Carriages were parked two and three deep in the circular drive in front of the house. A string ensemble played on a side terrace and servants moved through the crowd offering trays of cool drinks.

"Isn't it wonderful?" Jacie breathed as their carriage came to a stop.

"Yes, it is," Violet replied, equally impressed by the setting.

Impatiently, Michael pushed aside the groom to help Jacie alight. Then, oblivious to those watching, he kissed her on either cheek and pressed his lips to her ear to whisper, "My god, you are magnificent, and I've never loved you more."

Violet, taking the hand of the groom to step from the carriage, glanced about self-consciously as she always did to see if anyone was noticing the lack of resemblance between her and Jacie. Violet had seen it many times, the amazement of folks that anyone so plain could have such a beautiful daughter.

Then Violet noticed how one young woman was pushing her way through the crowd gathered around Michael and Jacie, not waiting her turn to be properly introduced. She was smiling, but only with her lips, for her eyes were grim.

Violet heard her say—too sweetly, she thought—"Michael, aren't you going to introduce me to the guest of honor? I've seen her at a distance when Mother and I have visited in the past, but we've never formally met."

He obliged. "Jacie, I would like for you to meet my cousin, Elyse."

That was all Violet heard before Olivia Blake appeared to politely greet her and squire her up the steps and inside.

No one noticed the chickadee as it perched on a branch near the house . . . and began to chirp its song.

# 4

*Elyse Burdette regarded herself* in the elaborate Louis Quinze filigree framed mirror and wondered not for the first time why her cousin Michael was not attracted to her. Other men certainly were; they liked her bright red hair and big blue eyes, framed by incredibly long lashes that she knew how to bat coquettishly. She had a shapely figure. She had also attended the best finishing school in Charleston and knew how to behave with impeccable charm and grace.

So why couldn't Michael see her in a romantic light?

"It's that white trash," Verena Burdette said as though answering her daughter's unspoken question as she breezed into the parlor of the guest wing. "She's put a spell on Michael, bewitched him somehow. He can't be in his right mind to want to marry a ragtag like her."

Elyse responded dully, "Cousin Olivia says Michael has fancied himself in love with Jacie since they were children. He's never had eyes for anyone else."

"You didn't push yourself hard enough." Verena glanced about at the opulent decor of the room. Accenting the blue and gold Empire sofas and chairs were Sevres and Dresden vases, hand-painted china figurines and brass cornices. Paintings in gilt frames hung on the walls. There was a bedroom to each side, with incredibly carved mahogany beds and lavish lace canopies. "Jasper Blake certainly spared no expense when he built this place, and he's probably turning over in his grave to think his grandson is going to marry a blacksmith's daughter. "You just didn't put your mind to it," she continued to nag.

"I don't know what else I could have done. Look at the gown I'm wearing. It's fancier than Jacie's, but Michael didn't notice."

Verena agreed the dress was exquisite, with tiers of shaded blue satin accented with lace and ribbons. She also knew how much it had cost, because she had paid for it. "We are not far from the poorhouse, Elyse. Everyone thinks your father left us a lot of money, but he didn't, and we've had to scrimp for the past three years to live on what he did leave. If you don't marry a rich man, and soon, I just don't know what we're going to do."

"Did you tell Cousin Olivia that you're selling the house?"

"She knows. She thinks it's only because I want a smaller place, anticipating you'll marry and move away soon. Maybe you will," Verena added hopefully. "You have beaus in Charleston—"

"But I don't want any of them. I want Michael, and

not for his money, either. That doesn't matter to me and never has. I've loved him since I was a little girl and I wouldn't care if he were poor as a church mouse."

"That's crazy," Verena scoffed. "Besides, you just might find out what it's like to marry a poor man, because none of those young swains beating a path to our door in Charleston has anything. All the rich bachelors married while you were pining away waiting for Michael. You'll have to take what you can get or be an old maid."

"Then I'll be an old maid. I refuse to marry anyone else."

"Well, it just makes me angry to think how I went and spent almost all the money we had left in the world to come here. Olivia never said one word in her letter about Michael getting married. I thought there might still be a chance for you, or we wouldn't be here."

"But now that we are," Elyse said with a gleam in her eye, "we're going to stay."

Verena agreed. "For a few months, at least. We won't have to worry about food, and maybe the house will sell in the meantime. We'll just settle down and enjoy ourselves."

"That's not what I meant. Actually I plan to use the time to do what I should have done years ago—make Michael realize I'm the one he should marry. You have a lot of influence over Cousin Olivia. She listens to everything you say, and I'm sure you can find dozens of excuses to convince her to make Michael postpone whatever wedding date they set. Tell her it's too close to Christmas, or Cousin Halsey's birthday. Anything. Just stall. Staying here in the house, being around him all the time, I'll find a way to make him want me instead of Jacie Calhoun."

Verena did not share Elyse's optimism but felt they had nothing to lose by trying. "I can guarantee you six months."

"That should do it." Elyse turned back to the mirror and pinched her cheeks to make them rosy. "I'll also make friends with Jacie. Good friends. That way she'll never suspect a thing about my feelings for Michael."

"Then stop wasting time by talking about it. He's probably asking her to marry him this very moment. As soon as she cut the cake, he took her outside."

Elyse, ebullient, followed after her mother. "I can do it, I know I can," she said, more to herself than to her mother. "I am going to be Mrs. Michael Blake."

Verena surely hoped so. She did not relish the thought of moving to the poorhouse.

Halsey Blake had found the red Georgia clay to be especially good for scuppernongs—the golden-green grape native to the South and named for the Scuppernong River in North Carolina. He had designated several acres for a vineyard but had so liked the green twining leaves and the fragrance of the grapes that he wanted to have a few vines closer to the main house. He had an arbor built, with latticework on the sides and top, and the vines grew hearty and secured themselves. The result was a lush tunnel of green leading to a gazebo overlooking the river. It was a private place, almost secret, for servants were not allowed to go there, only the gardener from time to time to prune. Olivia Blake did not venture there, fearing the garden spiders that liked the coolness of the arbor. But Michael and Jacie loved it, making it a special point of rendezvous, and it was there that Michael took her to propose.

Nature could not have gifted them with a more perfect night. Violin music wafted from the terrace as a full moon cast its silvery glow on the dark waters beyond. A gentle breeze set the draping fronds of the surrounding willow trees to dance in the cool night air scented with the sweet fragrance of gardenias and roses.

For long moments, Michael held Jacie close in the magical setting. Finally he said, "It's as if we're all alone in the world. I wish it could always be this way. Happy birthday, my darling."

"I can't remember one happier," Jacie said, not about to admit she had never experienced any kind of celebration before. Her mother never marked holidays because, she said, one day was no different from another.

"Did you like the cake? I had one of the best chefs in Atlanta come here to bake it."

"Everything was wonderful, Michael. It was like something out of a fairy tale."

"It *is* a fairy tale," he said fervently, "and you are a fairy princess. But I'm going to make you a queen. Oh, Jacie, you just don't know how much I love you. You can't possibly know, but one day you will. . . ." His words melted into a kiss as his mouth claimed hers.

She clung to him, enjoying the touch of his mouth against hers but feeling all the while strangely empty inside. Where was the voice Mehlonga had told her about, why couldn't she hear it? Michael was so good, so kind, everything a woman could want. Why couldn't her heart cry out with love for him?

She could feel his breath quickening, and his tongue parted her lips to plunge inside and meld against her own. Feeling a little wave of panic that he might be losing control, she broke free then to push him away and suggest, "We should get back to the party. Our guests will think we're rude."

"Not until I've given you this," he said, taking the necklace, which was wrapped in a square of pink satin, from inside his coat. He unfolded the satin slowly, watching Jacie's face all the while.

At the sight of the gems, so dazzling in the moonlight, Jacie cried, "Oh, Michael, I've never seen anything like it! It's the most beautiful present in the whole world."

He held the necklace up to her face and tenderly proclaimed, "No, it isn't. You are. And I was right. The amethysts pale next to your eyes." He fastened it around her neck as he told her how he had designed it himself, and that the lavender stones had come all the way from Brazil.

Though grateful and impressed to the tips of her toes, Jacie could not help blurting, "But it must have cost a fortune."

"I had to outdo my other gifts," he bantered. "Let's see. I believe the first present I ever gave you was on your sixth birthday. I carved a slingshot for you, and then you shot me with it and gave me a black eye."

"Because you pulled the tail of that little dog I had back then." She smiled at the recollection.

"Then there was the frog the next year."

"I really liked that one, but not as much as the

turtle you gave me a few years later. You tied a ribbon around his neck, and the poor thing nearly choked before I could get it off because he kept trying to pull his head back into his shell."

They laughed together, then fell silent for long, poignant moments as their gazes met and held. Jacie touched the jewels at her throat and whispered, "Thank you. I promise I will cherish it forever."

He gathered her close once more. "I hope you do, but not merely as a birthday gift. I want you to always remember I gave it to you the night I asked you to be my wife."

Jacie could not speak. She had anticipated the proposal but could not find the voice to respond. And what could she say, anyway? Yes, she would marry him, spend the rest of her life with him, but she was not sure she loved him because of what an old Indian medicine man had told her? He would be appalled, think her daft. All of a sudden she wasn't so sure about her sanity herself; she should be ecstatic instead of waiting for a silly legend to come true.

"Oh, God, how I love you," he said in a voice thick with emotion. "I want to spend the rest of my life with you, Jacie. Everything I have is yours. You'll want for nothing and I'll be so good to you. We'll have beautiful children, just like you, and every night of my life I want to fall asleep with you in my arms and awaken to find you still beside me. I've thought of nothing else for years."

Clasping her shoulders, he stood back so he could look into her eyes as he said, "You will marry me, won't you? Say yes, and we'll go back inside and tell everyone tonight. God, I want to shout it to the whole world!"

Jacie closed her eyes and swayed ever so slightly to think how he loved her, adored her. Of this, she was sure. And she had to love him back, didn't she? There had never been the slightest thought of another man in her life. Only Michael, her past, present, and surely her future. *Speak to me, heart,* she commanded in silent desperation, *speak to me now*. . . .

He gave her a gentle shake. "You're teasing me by not saying anything, aren't you?" His voice had a slight edge to it, as though he were starting to wonder if she would refuse him.

Jacie's eyes flew open and she drank in the sight of his dear face, so hopeful, so loving. "Michael, I—" she began, not sure of what she was going to say but knowing she had to respond. Then suddenly the sounds of someone shouting and calling her name made them spring apart, shattering the moment.

Michael drew her close again protectively. He recognized Zach Newton's voice, knew something awful had happened as he burst from the latticework bower, the moonlight touching his stricken face.

"Somebody said you headed this way," he cried, chest heaving from running. "You better come quick, Miss Jacie. It's your pa. He just keeled over in the shed. I'd gone to eat my supper and found him when I got back. I went to get your ma from the party, and Doc Foley was there, so they took off to see to him. She said to come get you."

Jacie tore herself from Michael's grasp so quickly he could only let her go. Taking the hand Zach held out to her, she ran beside him, but Michael caught up to pull her away and hold her hand himself as they hurried through the arbor, then skirted around the house.

Guests were spilling out onto the porch and lawn as word spread of what had happened. Elyse came running to ask Jacie, "Do you want me to go with you, dear? Oh, I hope he'll be all right."

Jacie was too busy trying to keep up with Zach to respond, and it was Michael who called back, "Tell Mother to clear the parlor and get the sofa ready. We'll bring him there."

The blacksmith's shed was situated a good distance behind the barns and stables as a precaution against fire, and as they approached, Jacie could hear the sounds of her mother's hysterical sobbing.

Some of the men had followed Violet and Dr. Foley and stood in the doorway watching. They stepped aside for Jacie and Michael.

Jacie saw her mother and the doctor kneeling near the roaring fire. All she could see of her father was his legs, his worn leather boots.

"Put out that fire," Michael snapped to Zach. "It's an oven in here. No wonder the man passed out."

Hearing Michael, Dr. Foley turned to convey with a look that it was much more than a fainting spell, then noticed Judd was starting to come around and quickly asked him, "Where does it hurt? Tell me, Judd."

Judd's face screwed up in pain. "My chest," he said weakly. "Feels like the anvil's sittin' on it. Hurts bad. Help me, Doc, please . . ." He began to cough and wheeze as he fought to breathe.

Dr. Foley noted Judd's flushed face, the cold sweat that beaded his forehead. It was obvious he was having a heart attack.

Just as he began to wonder why it was taking so long to get his medical bag from his carriage, someone pushed through the crowd to hand it to him. Taking out the stethoscope, he listened to the labored sounds of Judd's heart as the valves struggled to open and close. He slipped a nitrate pill under Judd's tongue but saw how his eyes were beginning to dilate and knew then it was almost over.

Violet knew it, too, and willed herself to stop crying long enough to minister to the only man she had ever loved. She slipped an arm under his head, raising him up a bit.

Dr. Foley did not try to stop her. He exchanged a glance with Michael that said there was nothing more he could do, then closed his bag and rose.

Michael went out with him, leaving Jacie and her mother their private moment, everyone else politely doing the same.

"Judd, hear me," Violet said shakily, rocking him gently in her arms. "I love you and you're going to be all right. I won't let you die. I need you. I've always needed you. There's never been anyone but you. I'd die in your place, if I could, but you can't leave me, you can't." She began to weep again, her tears splashing onto his face.

Jacie went to comfort her.

Suddenly Judd's eyes flashed open and he looked at her in pleased wonder, then held out his arms to her and cried, "I love you!"

Violet's heart slammed into her chest to hear, at last, the words she had prayed for through the years.

"I love you . . ." he repeated faintly.

She began to rain grateful kisses on his face, which had turned almost gray. "Oh, Judd, Judd, how I've longed for this moment. I love you too, darling. I always have, I always will."

"I love you . . ." He fought for one last breath. ". . . Iris."

And then he died.

Violet uttered a sound like that of a wounded animal and collapsed, while Jacie, struck with her own grief, could only watch and wonder what it all meant.

# 5

**The Texas Plains, 1858**

*The sounds of wailing echoed* through the warm and humid night as the Comanche women mourned the death of their chief, Great Bear.

The customary preparations for burial had been completed. The men had bathed him, painted his face, and sealed his eyes shut with clay. They had dressed him in fine clothing, then drawn his knees up to his chest, bent his head forward, and wrapped him in a blanket. Burial would be at dawn, when his body would be placed facing the rising sun on a scaffold made of poles.

Iris sat alone in the tepee she had shared with Great Bear. She had pulled back the bearskin from the opening to signify that visitors could enter without announcing their presence. But no one came; they left her to grieve in private.

Great Bear's death had been a shock to everyone, for

he was not an old man. Iris was approaching her forties, as best she could figure, and Great Bear had always seemed perhaps a few years older. He had not even been ill. In the middle of the afternoon he'd entered their tepee, lain down, and died without warning.

There had been nothing Iris could do, although the Indians of their small band had looked to her for a miracle. After all, she had been their medicine woman, their shaman, for a very long time, using the skills handed down from her father and developing others, while adapting her remedies to the herbs and plants available. But that day Great Bear was beyond help. He carried a white man's bullet in his body, he told her long ago. Perhaps that was what had eventually killed him, but there was no way of knowing. He was gone, and despite the tragic circumstances that had brought them together, Iris was saddened by his death.

She closed out the sounds of ritual wailing and allowed her mind to take her back to those early years. How terrified she had been in the wake of such tragedy.

The Comanche had taken her to their camp, where Great Bear had decreed she would nurse his son, who, for the time being, had been named Little Bear. At first she had resented the child and saw him only as a dirty little boy who ran around naked like the other boys. But gradually, as she had held him and nourished him from her own body, a bond had developed between them.

She had been ostracized by the other Indians, given a tepee all to herself. Iris had feared she would be raped by the warriors, who eyed her boldly, hungrily. Then she came to realize that it was a custom among the Comanche that sex was not allowed with a woman nursing a child. After that, she welcomed Little Bear, encouraging him to nurse as long as he wanted, knowing as long as he did so, she would be spared.

There were times, though, when Iris did not care what happened to her. She would cry until there were no more tears, praying to die so she could be with her husband and children. Sometimes Little Bear would come to her as she wept, and though he did not understand, he would try to comfort her as best he could, placing his little arms around her.

The bond grew deeper. After all, the boy was the only person in the world with whom she had real contact. Her food was left outside her tepee. If she ventured outside, she was watched lest she try to run away but otherwise ignored. When camp was moved, some of the men tore down her tepee and she doggedly walked behind the Comanche to their next destination. No one really had anything to do with her except Little Bear.

Then came the time when fever struck the tribe. Little Bear was one of the victims, and when the tribe's shaman could do nothing for him, Iris was allowed to use her medicine. Day and night she sat beside him, sponging his face with cool water and spooning her potion between his parched lips. Slowly, he rallied, and then came the poignant moment when Iris's status among the Comanche would forevermore be changed. Little Bear opened his eyes, looked at her and smiled, and said the magical, wonderful word "Mother."

From that day on, Iris was held in esteem. And something else happened as well. Great Bear saw her in a new light and began to court her in the Indian way. The morning she awoke to find a prize mustang tethered outside her tepee, she knew that Great Bear intended her to be his wife.

Iris had come to accept her lot, and the love she felt for Little Bear played a major part in her new life. But she also believed there was no reason for her to return to the white man's world since her loved ones were all dead. Despite the hardships, she realized, she had found contentment among the Comanche, and so she agreed to marry Great Bear.

Great Bear's first wife had been called Moonstar, for on the night he knew he loved her he had seen a distant twinkling in an otherwise starless night, near a mist-shrouded moon. When Iris was brought to him, there had been another bizarre incident: a lone star shone near a hazy sun, and recalling that on their wedding day, he named her Sunstar.

Great Bear had, to Iris's surprise, been a gentle and patient lover, but it was her first husband, Luke, who would forever possess her heart. She had named their first-born son after him and somewhere along the way, she could not remember exactly when, she had begun to call Little Bear by the same name, even though he was dubbed Howling Wolf after his vision quest was fulfilled.

Luke shared his innermost thoughts and feelings with the woman he loved as a mother, and he had told her about that fateful night, when he was nearly twelve. Carrying the customary items, a buffalo robe, a bone pipe, tobacco, and lighting materials, he had left the camp and gone to an isolated hill. Four times he had stopped to smoke and pray.

He'd had two visions—one of a wolf standing on the edge of a cliff howling wildly, and another of many white birds drifting in and about black clouds in an azure sky.

Iris had listened raptly, then, taking advantage of the Indians' superstitious nature, she had gone to Great Bear and given him her interpretation of Luke's dreams. "He is destined to be a peace maker." She had reminded him of how the Indians' world was changing as the white man moved ever westward and urged him to allow Luke to be properly educated to prepare him for the vision he had seen.

Great Bear had told her he would think about all she said, and he had—for five years. During that time, Luke became a strong and fearless warrior. Iris bit her tongue to keep silent when he returned from raids with many scalps, for she had learned to cope by trying not to see the primitive and savage side of her environment.

But then, without warning and to Iris's delight, Great Bear told Iris he would send his son to study with missionaries at a settlement just across the Mexican border.

Luke was gone for nearly three years. When he returned, he had changed in many ways. He could read and write and speak English fluently. He no longer wore his hair parted in the center and braided on either side. He had also stopped plucking his facial and body hair. With his civilized looks, Iris knew he could easily pass for a white man who just happened to have dark skin.

Iris also knew that Luke was still Comanche in his soul and always would be, for he loved his people and his heritage. That was why it came as a big surprise when he told his father that he felt their band should no longer engage in raids on the white man that resulted in bloodshed for both sides.

Great Bear agreed, and they concentrated on hunting buffalo instead of attacking the settlers and stealing from them. But then the government began rounding up Indians and sending them to reservations. Great Bear vowed never to surrender and, consequently, had been striving ever since to avoid the army.

Iris took the moving about, the running, in stride, for she kept busy. After realizing education had meant so much to his son, Great Bear had finally allowed Iris to begin teaching the children. Between instructing them and continuing to minister to the sick, she felt her life took on new meaning.

But now Great Bear was gone and she faced an uncertain future.

Suddenly a shadow fell across the opening of the tepee, and Iris gave a soft cry of joy as Luke entered. "You came, my son," she said, holding her arms out to him. "I was afraid you wouldn't."

He squeezed her hands, then dropped down to sit beside her. "We were on our way back when we saw the smoke signals and heard the drums. Tell me what happened."

Iris well knew how stoic warriors could be but she could see the grief in Luke's eyes. She related the tale of his father's death.

After a long silence, Luke nodded, relieved to know his father had apparently not suffered.

"His body has been prepared," she said. "The men were waiting for you to perform the other rituals." She quelled a shudder when she thought of how Great Bear's favorite horse would be shot.

Luke seemed to know what she was thinking and said, "I'll cut off the tail and mane of his horse and leave it on his grave. The tribe cannot spare a horse. Especially now."

Iris understood. After all, it was summer, and high hunting season for buffalo. The animals were fat and had shed their winter hair. Hides were at their prime, and Luke had been out with his band scouting for the vicinity of the herds. A communal hunt would begin soon, with temporary camps set up near wood and water. Iris had always looked forward to hunting season, for even though the hunts meant hard labor for everybody, it was a time for eating, rejoicing, and merriment, with dances held nightly around huge campfires. Iris thought of it as harvest time for the Indians. But now, there would be no celebrations as Great Bear was mourned.

Luke said, "I want you to know that even though I learned from the missionaries the foolishness of superstitions, I must honor the ways of our people. My father was a great man, and the tribe believes his ghost is even more powerful, so we have to move away from this camp by sundown. This tepee will have to be burned, along with any of my father's possessions that aren't taken with him to the scaffold."

"I'll start getting my things ready."

Luke was thoughtfully quiet for a moment, then said, "I have decided to set you free. You may go back to your own people. I'll send the others on ahead while I take you close enough to Clear Creek so you can go the rest of the way by yourself. You can take whatever you want that belonged to my father. Although it is the custom to destroy everything, I know he would want you to have—"

"No." She looked at him in astonishment and shook her head slowly. "I have no people to go back to. This is my home. And you are the son of my heart. Do you think I could bear to leave you? I had a chance many years ago, remember? And I chose to stay."

Luke smiled and put his arm about her shoulders. The memory was still vivid. She had wandered away from the camp just before a small cavalry unit attacked. The Comanche managed to flee but were forced to abandon Iris, who was found by the soldiers. Seeing she was white, they took her back to their post to hold her till family could be located. She kept telling them she had no family except the Comanche and wanted to return to them. The soldiers were horrified and refused to let her go, but she had managed to escape at just the right moment, because Great Bear and the warriors had been about to attack the fort and take her. She ran right into them, and together they hurried back to the wilderness. Iris had never had a moment's regret..

"Yes, I remember, all right," Luke said, able to laugh despite his sorrow over his father. "That was just before I became a warrior, but I went along with the men. I had my bow and my arrows, and I was ready to do battle with the blue-legged soldiers to get my mother back."

Iris was not laughing. "And now you want me to leave."

"No, I don't. But it's for the best. You need someone to care for you, and it's the custom for a widow to marry her husband's brother. I'm chief now. Do you want me to send you to Standing Tall's tepee? He already has three wives."

Iris clenched her fists, beating them on her knees as she declared, "No. And I don't need anyone to look after me, either. I can take care of myself. Besides," she said, lavender eyes sparkling, "you can take care of your mother since you don't have a wife."

"I can take care of you even then if you choose to stay, but I want you to know I'm willing to give you your freedom."

Iris felt she already had freedom of a sort—to teach the children and love them as though they were her own, to help the sick and wounded. She also felt blessed to belong somewhere, to have a reason for living. "There came a time when Great Bear would have let me go, had I asked him to," she said. "I've stayed because I love all of you, Luke. Please don't send me back now. I promise not to be a burden."

"You could never be a burden." He got to his feet. "I'm happy you want to stay. And don't worry. If you do not want a husband, I won't decree you should have one. You'll be a teacher, a medicine woman, and everyone will take care of you if need be."

Iris also stood. It was time she joined the others for open weeping, lest they be offended and think she did not truly grieve for her husband. She paused and turned to her son. "But what about you, my son? When will you take a wife? You need someone."

Luke did not lack for the company of women. Unmarried girls had been slipping into his tepee for years, but he had not slept with one yet that he truly cared about.

He took her arm as they left the tepee. "Don't worry about me. When I meet someone just like you I'll marry her. Till then," he said with a wink, "I prefer my freedom."

# 6

*Hearing Judd admit with* his dying breath what she had always known but sought to conquer, Violet felt she no longer had any reason to live.

She spoke only once, to ask that Judd be buried in his favorite spot beneath the mimosa tree. After that, she remained silent, not even acknowledging those who came to pay their respects as she sat next to Judd's coffin in the big room of the cabin.

Jacie, seated beside her, accepted the condolences for both of them and worried about her mother.

Violet had not shed another tear since the night Judd died whispering Iris's name. Everyone thought she was in a deep state of grief, when actually she was wallowing in self-pity and rage. All the years of trying to make Judd love her, waiting on him hand and foot, treating him like a king, feeling guilty about deceiving him—her sacrifices had come to naught. He had never loved her. Only Iris.

Now her life was truly meaningless.

When Judd was buried and the last clod of red Georgia clay had been packed down with the back of a shovel, Violet went inside the cabin, to the bed she had shared with him. She lay down . . . and she did not get up.

A few days after the funeral, Dr. Foley went by to see Violet at Michael's request and reported afterward that there was nothing he could do for her. "She's wasting away. She refuses food and hasn't uttered a sound since the night Judd died. She's obviously made up her mind she wants to die too, and she will eventually get her wish."

When Michael drew Jacie from Violet's bedside to share Dr. Foley's dire prediction, she said drearily, "I know. I beg her to eat but she just lies there, staring out the window at Daddy's grave and acting like she doesn't hear a word I say."

"I should never have agreed to let him be buried there."

"I don't think it would have made any difference. She's going to grieve herself to death because she wants to, and there's nothing we can do."

Michael frowned to note Jacie's appearance. She had not left her mother's side, snatching a few hours of sleep each night in a chair next to the bed. There were deep circles under her eyes, and her face was pale, drawn. The ordeal was taking its toll and he voiced his concern. "Jacie, this has got to stop. I'm not going to let you make yourself sick. I'm going to move you and your mother to my house. The servants can look after her, and you can get some rest."

But she declined Michael's invitation. "I don't think that's a good idea," she told him. "I'll just do what I can for her and pray she comes out of this."

"I don't approve, and if she's not better soon, I'm going to move you both over there regardless. Meanwhile, I'll leave Sudie here. You can send her to get me whenever you need me."

Jacie was in no mood to argue.

"Something else," he said. It was twilight, and he had coaxed her to the front porch. "I know you've got other things on your mind right now, but I've been thinking that we shouldn't wait to get married. Everyone will understand how you need someone to take care of you and your mother, so as soon as she's better, we'll set a date."

"I don't think—"

He pressed a fingertip to her lips. "Jacie, we've waited long enough."

Jacie was suddenly feeling smothered. "I don't know. I can't think about it right now." As good as he was to her, as comforted as she felt when he was near, Jacie just wished he would leave her alone for the time being. "I really should get back inside."

She turned to go, but he pulled her close. "Listen to me. Fate kicked us in the teeth the night your father died. For so many years I had waited for that special moment to ask you to marry me, and I refuse to let anything else stand in our way."

She could see the misery and desperation in his eyes, and he unconsciously dug his fingers into her flesh, he held her so tightly. His face was lined with tension, and she was about to attempt once more to make him understand that she could not now cope with thoughts of marriage, a wedding, but he suddenly could contain himself no longer and brought his lips down on hers in a kiss that was almost bruising in its intensity.

She yielded only for a moment before turning her head away to say, "I really have to get back inside."

Releasing her, he stepped back, rubbing at his temples with his fingers. He turned his back on her to stare at her father's grave beneath the tree, anger helplessly rising as he silently cursed Judd Calhoun for dying when he had. It wasn't fair, damn it . . .

He admonished himself for being so childish and whirled back around. "I'm sorry," he said wearily. Then, attempting to lighten the mood, "I want to see you wear the necklace again," he said. "I'll never forget how it looked on you."

Jacie thought of it, wrapped in a handkerchief and hidden beneath her mattress. "I will. Now I really do have to get back to my mother." She hated to seem ungrateful or cold, but too much was happening. Her mind was spinning.

He took her hand and pressed it to his lips. "I'll be back in the morning."

She went into the cabin to find Sudie standing in the middle of the room staring at her with frightened eyes. "Your momma's been talkin' funny," she said.

The child was obviously upset, and as much as Jacie longed to rush to her mother, she instead dropped to her knees in front of Sudie to clutch her shoulders and say, "There's no reason for you to be afraid. This means she's getting better."

"No, it don't, 'cause she's been talkin' to your daddy like he's still alive, but he ain't, so that means she's talkin' to his ghost."

"There's no such thing as ghosts." Jacie stared past

her into the bedroom. Her mother had likely been talking in her sleep. She gave Sudie a hug. "I'll go see about her now. I won't be long." Then Jacie entered the room quietly and eased into the chair beside the bed. Her mother appeared to be sleeping, but the chair squeaked ever so slightly and Violet's eyes flashed open.

"Jacie," she whispered feebly, raising a wan, beckoning hand.

Jacie leaned to clasp her fingers, alarmed at how cold they were. "Are you feeling better?" she asked anxiously. "Let me get you some soup. You need to eat."

"No. Listen. There's something I have to tell you before I go."

"Don't talk like that. You're going to get your strength back and everything is going to be fine. You'll see." Jacie forced a smile.

Despite her frailty, Violet was able to muster the strength to squeeze Jacie's hand almost hard enough to hurt her. "You have to listen. I don't want to live, child. I want to die, but first I've got to make peace with my Maker. I can't do that till I confess to you what I did. You have to know."

Jacie could only stare at her expectantly, and for some strange reason, fearfully as well.

"Now do what I tell you." Violet raised herself up to point to a dark corner of the room. "Go to my trunk, over there. Take everything out. There's a false bottom. Lift that up. You'll find a blanket there. Bring it to me." She sank back against the pillows.

Jacie did as she was told. The trunk was old. Her mother had had it as long as she could remember, using it to store linens. Jacie removed everything, then felt the bottom and realized it was indeed loose. Lifting it out, she found a soft bundle.

Her mother held out her arms for the bundle she had concealed for so many years. Jacie gave it to her and watched curiously as she ran her fingers along the blanket's hem.

Violet felt the telltale lump. From time to time in the past, as the thread had dry-rotted she had restitched the seam, but now she did not have the strength to break it. "Help me," she said.

Why on earth, Jacie wondered in alarm, was she wanting to rip open the hem of a blanket? Maybe she really was losing her mind. She started to take it from her, "This can wait till tomorrow. I'm going to get you some soup."

Violet held firm to the blanket. "No." Her eyes narrowed with determination. "Break the threads, Jacie. You have to see what's inside."

Jacie was bewildered. Leaning closer, she saw the bulge she had not noticed before.

"I couldn't tell you while Judd was alive." Violet felt herself becoming dizzier by the minute as the shadows were coming closer, reaching out for her. She prayed for enough time to tell her story. Only then could she die in peace, when her soul was at last cleansed of the sin of deceit that had tormented her for eighteen years.

"Judd would have been angry with me for not telling him the truth. He would have left me, and I couldn't let that happen, because I was foolish enough to think I could make him love me. I never stopped trying, and it wasn't till he died that I realized what a fool I'd been. He could never love anybody except her."

"My aunt Iris." Jacie wondered what her father's infatuation with her aunt had to do with the blanket and whatever secret her mother had kept from him.

"Help me rip the seam open, and you will understand."

Jacie decided to humor her. With a quick snap, she broke the threads and was surprised to see a locket and a small leather pouch inside.

"I never touched any of the money," Violet said, indicating the pouch. "I don't even know how much is there. I felt it belonged to you."

Jacie focused on the locket. Opening it, she gasped at her own likeness. "It's a daguerreotype, and it looks like me."

Just then, Sudie started through the door, curious to see if everything was all right. Before anyone noticed her she saw Miss Jacie holding up what looked like a tiny painting of a woman and heard Miss Violet say something that made her freeze in her tracks.

"That is your mother."

Backing away, Sudie went to stand outside the door. She knew it was wrong to eavesdrop but could not resist after what she had just overheard.

Jacie looked from the locket to Violet in astonishment. "No. It can't be."

"It is. She was your mother, not your aunt. And her husband Luke was not your uncle, he was your father."

Jacie shook her head. She could not grasp what was being said. Her mother had to be out of her head, yet, as Jacie continued to regard her own image, something told her Violet spoke the truth.

"You and I were spared when the Indians killed them and your brothers, so I told Judd you were his child. He never suspected anything, because he didn't know our own baby had been born dead a few days earlier."

"Why are you telling me this now? Why did you lie to me, and to Daddy, all these years?"

"Because it was like fate meant for me to, so I wouldn't lose him. Iris had given you to me to nurse that morning, because I still had milk for my own baby, and it was making me sick. I had to get rid of it. So I took you and walked away from the wagons and off into the bushes, and that's where I was when they attacked, and . . ." Harsh rasping sounds came from deep within her chest, making it difficult for her to talk. When she finally caught her breath, she begged, "You've got to understand that I only did it because I loved Judd so much, and I thought Iris was dead, so what good would it have done anybody for me to tell the truth? If Judd had left me then, how could I have taken care of you?"

Jacie's gaze had been fixed on the picture of her mother. Slowly, something terrible dawned on her. She looked up at Violet. "You said you *thought* Iris was dead. Didn't you know for sure?"

"I thought I did, then. You see, I fainted, Jacie. It was all too much. The last thing I remember seeing was your father being killed as he tried to protect your mother."

"But you didn't see her die?"

"No. And when the soldiers counted bodies after I told them how many people were in the caravan, a woman was missing."

Jacie was having difficulty taking it all in. "So she could actually have been spared."

Violet explained that the soldiers had not thought so then, and sadly, neither had she or Judd. "We figured maybe animals had dragged one of the bodies away, but then something happened about ten years ago that made me wonder."

Jacie tensed. "Go on."

"A man who was once a Texas Ranger with Judd came through on his way east to make a new life. Judd wasn't around, he'd gone off hunting, so the man talked to me. He wanted to tell us about something strange that had happened at a place called Bird's Fort. A white woman had been found living among the Comanche. The army rescued her, but she ran away, back to the Indians."

Jacie's eyes went wide. "What makes you think that could have been my—my *mother*?"

"She had lavender eyes like he'd never seen before. The Ranger remembered Judd telling about his sister-in-law's pretty lavender eyes, so he thought Judd should know there was a chance Iris might still be alive, living with the Indians, especially since they were Comanche, the same as attacked the caravan."

"Oh my God," Jacie breathed. "Why didn't you tell him? How could you keep it from him?"

Violet seemed to shrink into the pillows, pressed by the weight of her conscience as she defended herself. "Because there was no real proof, but that wouldn't have made any difference to Judd. He'd have gone to Texas anyway, and whether or not he found her, he would have hated me for deceiving him all those years. I'd never have seen him again. I couldn't risk that, don't you see? As for Iris, if she was that woman, she was obviously happy where she was or she wouldn't have run away to go back there. It was just best to leave it all alone."

"But you had no right to make that decision!"

Violet nodded feebly. "I know, child, I know. I've lived with the misery of knowing that all these years, but I did what I felt was right. Now I see I was wrong, and I had to tell you so you can do what you want about it, and I can die in peace," she finished lamely.

Jacie looked at the daguerreotype again. What should she do? If her mother were still alive, she knew she wanted to find her, but if Michael found out, he would try to convince her it would be futile to look for her now. He would insist it was best to leave the past alone. And of course his mother would have another attack of the vapors to think her son might actually be marrying the daughter of a woman who lived with Indians. None of that mattered to Jacie, not if there was even the remotest chance she could be reunited with her real mother, for now she understood so much and knew, at last, why the people she had thought of as her parents had lived together in such misery.

"Can you forgive me?" Violet asked pitifully, wretchedly. "In my way, I've loved you, tried to be a good mother to you."

Jacie took her hand. Now was not the time to condemn. "There's nothing to forgive. You did what you thought was best and I love you, too. You've got to get well and—" Jacie stared in horror to see that Violet's head had suddenly lolled to one side, and her fingers, which Jacie still held, had gone limp.

Violet's eyes glazed over while still fixed upon Jacie, as though frozen in a plea for understanding and pardon, even in death.

In the silence that followed, Sudie dared to steal a peek inside the room, then covered her mouth in terror and fled noiselessly out to the front porch. Miss Violet was dead.

She sat down in the swing and waited. Soon Miss Jacie would come and tell her she had to run get Master Blake from the big house. Oh, she felt so sorry for Miss Jacie to think how she'd just found out Miss Violet wasn't her real momma just before she died, and that her real momma didn't even know Miss Jacie was alive.

Sudie wasn't sure what it all meant but her heart sure went out to Miss Jacie.

# 7

*It had been nearly three weeks* since Violet's death, and Michael was becoming more concerned about Jacie with each passing day. He knew it had to be a terrible ordeal for her to lose both her parents within such a short period of time, but he feared if she did not snap out of her doldrums, she was going to grieve herself to death as her mother had done.

He had brought her to the house despite her protests, putting her in the guest suite opposite Verena and Elyse.

He had agreed, of course, to allow Violet to be buried next to Judd but did not like Jacie visiting the graves every day to sit and brood for hours. One afternoon after lunch he insisted she come to his study.

She sat across from Michael, who regarded her from behind his desk, and stared down at her hands folded in her lap as he went on and on about how she had to stop mourning so deeply. He expressed his sympathy and understanding but reminded her, ever so gently, that Dr. Foley had said her mother willed herself to die. "I don't want you to follow after her, Jacie," he said, frowning. "You hardly eat. You're losing weight and you don't look well at all."

With so much on her mind, she wished everyone would just leave her alone. "I don't feel like eating."

"That has to change. I called you here to tell you that I want you to stop going to your parents' graves so often. I think it's keeping you depressed and is probably one of the reasons you don't have an appetite."

"I won't stop!" she cried.

"It's for your own good."

"It's none of your business. Michael, I'm moving back to the cabin. I insist. I want to be alone for a while."

He was unmoved by her anger. "I won't allow it."

"You can't stop me. And I never should have let you bring me here after the funeral, but I didn't want to argue—then," she added pointedly.

"Jacie, darling, I don't like to seem dictatorial, but that cabin belongs to me and I decide who lives there. Now you're here in this house, and I want you to think of it as your home, because it is, and as soon as you are ready we will be married. You will move into the master suite with me. Forget the cabin. Life has to go on. I'm having your personal belongings brought here, because I'm going to let one of the other artisans and his family move into the cabin."

"You can't do that—not yet," she said so sharply that Michael was taken back. She was thinking of the trunk. She had returned the blanket, along with the locket and the money pouch, to the hiding place in the false bottom and had not been able to bring herself to take it out since her mother—no, her aunt Violet, she reminded herself—had showed it to her.

"Well, maybe we can wait a few more days," Michael conceded, seeing how upset she was and thinking how he would have to speak to Dr. Foley about giving her something for her nerves. "But I want you to promise you'll stop going to the graves so often. I'd like you to get your mind on other things. I'm going to be leaving for Charleston early tomorrow morning. Cousin Verena just received a letter from her lawyer saying her house has been sold, and she wants me to go with her to help take care of things. Mother is going, too. Elyse has very kindly offered to stay here and be company for you."

"That's sweet of her, but it's not necessary."

"She wants to get to know you better. I shouldn't be away for long—"

Olivia burst into the room without knocking, face flushed. She sank into the nearest chair and began to fan herself with her handkerchief as she wailed, "You've got to do something about that crazy old Indian, Michael. I heard he was at one of the slaves' cabins last night, handing out one of his potions. It terrifies me to know he's sneaking around here. I want guards posted. The next time he comes around, shoot the dirty savage."

Michael was aghast to hear his mother speak of such violent measures, but before he could utter a word, Jacie had leapt to Mehlonga's defense. "Don't you dare order him shot, and he's not a savage. He's kind to a fault, and he's only trying to help. Dr. Foley doesn't care if a Negro is sick. Someone has to look out for them."

"Oh, my . . ." Olivia's hand fluttered to her throat. She looked at Michael, her face twisting with anger. "Now do you see why I insisted you make her disassociate herself from that old fool? She is absolutely impudent, taking up for him. What will people think?"

"I'm not listening to this." Jacie got up and stalked from the room ignoring Michael's annoyed command that she return.

She knew she had to get away and be by herself for a while. When she had gotten only halfway to the cabin, she heard someone coming on horseback and knew it was Michael. She rushed into the woods, then made her way up through the hills to the secret place where she hoped to find Mehlonga.

He came, as always, and she poured out her soul to him, telling him everything she had learned the night Violet Calhoun had died. He listened quietly, absorbing every word.

"I know your heart bleeds to find out if your real mother is still alive. What are you going to do?" he asked her when she'd finished.

"She's probably dead. I know that. I only wish she could have known about me. She wouldn't have gone back to the Comanche once she was rescued. I don't understand why she did, anyway, when she was given the chance to return to civilization."

"Who can know what was in her heart? She had been living with them for many years. You must remember, you do not know for sure that the woman was your mother."

"No, I don't." Jacie stared up at the cerulean sky as

though she might find the answers to all her problems there.

Suddenly he asked, "Has the spirit of love spoken to your heart?"

She gave a dismal sigh. "No, but I would have accepted Michael's proposal that night."

"Because you thought you had no choice."

Jacie did not like thinking of it that way but knew he was right. "I suppose."

"And now?"

She gave a helpless shrug. "I suppose I still don't. He says he wants us to marry right away, because I need someone to take care of me. He's moving another family into the cabin, and I won't have a home, nowhere to go." She sighed again. "I really don't have any choice, Mehlonga. But I shouldn't feel that way. He'll be good to me. I know he will."

"What if you did have somewhere else to go?"

She looked at him sharply. "What are you talking about?"

"I have made the decision to leave here. I am getting too old to sneak around the plantations and risk getting shot. I do not move as quickly as I used to. It is time for me to go west and spend what time I have left with my people. I will take you with me if you want to go. I will see that you get to this place you spoke of in Texas, Bird's Fort. You can start your search for your mother there.

"And if you do not find her," he added mysteriously, "perhaps you will find something else."

Jacie was too excited to ponder his words. "I could do it, couldn't I? I have the money hidden in the blanket. I could go out there and look for her. Even though it's been ten years, surely someone would be around to remember a white woman who rejected freedom to return to her captors."

Though he knew what she would say, Mehlonga asked, "Will you tell anyone where you are going—and why?"

"I don't dare. Michael would never hear of it. He'd tell me to forget it and beg me not to say a word to anyone about it."

"So you will have to sneak away."

"Yes. I'll leave a note so he won't worry. He's going away tomorrow. It's the perfect time. We can be well on our way before he even knows I'm gone." She chattered on, making plans, thrilled to think how she was not only going to search for her real mother but would actually see the other side of those distant mountains at last.

Mehlonga listened to her talk for most of the afternoon. Finally, toward sundown, he quietly said, "Jacie, the Indians have a saying—be careful what you look for, you just might find it."

"I don't understand." She laughed, uneasy and not knowing why.

"You will, when it happens. But have you thought about what you will do if you are able to find your mother?"

"Why, bring her back with me, of course." What else would she do?

"And you think Michael Blake and his mother will welcome her into their home?"

"Yes," she replied, feeling even more apprehensive. She had not thought about that in the wake of the momentous decision she had just made.

"Do not be so sure. Think about it carefully, and make up your mind that you will be able to face the consequences should your search be fruitful. I leave you now. If you are not here at dawn, I will know you have decided not to go, and if we do not see each other ever again, I bid you farewell and a happy life, my child."

He left her, but Jacie stayed to consider her decision awhile longer. Michael was going to be hurt and angry when he found out she was gone, but she could not worry about that now. This was her one and only chance to reunite with her real mother; she could not lose it.

Deep in thought, Jacie lost track of time. Only when she heard an owl screech did she break out of her reverie to realize twilight was falling. She had to get back fast—Michael would be worried sick.

She hurried along the trail she knew so well. Night was closing in as she reached the clearing where Zach had set up the forbidden jumping hurdles.

"Miss Jacie! Lord, I've been lookin' all over for you."

She was relieved to see Zach as he came toward her on horseback from the path leading by the cornfield. "Mr. Blake is out of his mind, raisin' hell and demandin' every able-bodied man and woman at Red Oakes get out and look for you. Get on up here with me."

Jacie caught his arm as he reached down, and he easily swung her up to sit behind him. She put her arms about his waist and unconsciously rested her head against his back, succumbing to weariness. It had been a long hike, and she was exhausted from having made it so fast.

Zach reveled in the feel of her body pressed against him and felt a stirring in his loins. He could smell her hair, sweet like sunshine, and the sheer woman scent of her. He flexed his shoulders a bit, relishing how she melded against him. He did not know that she was merely tired and dared to think she was actually cuddling against him on purpose. But why shouldn't she? he reasoned. They had shared good times together when Michael was in Europe, laughing and teasing each other. And he'd never forget how she had kissed his cheek the night he wished her a happy birthday. Maybe she'd have kissed him right on the mouth if they had been anywhere but right outside the cabin, with her folks so close by.

Zach's imagination ran away with him as he thought how if it hadn't been for Jacie's daddy, she wouldn't have to marry Blake. But her daddy was dead now, and maybe she was having second thoughts and that was why she had run off that afternoon.

He thought he felt her press even closer, and was that a little squeeze she gave him with her fingertips, kind of shy like? Maybe it was just fantasy, but it was time he found out where he stood. They could even get something going right now. He could sneak her into his cabin over behind the barn without anybody seeing, because they were all out looking for her. Then if she did go ahead and marry up with Blake, Zach would already have his finger in the pie and be all set to taste it regular.

He pulled back on the reins to stop the horse, then, before Jacie realized what was happening, he twisted around to grab her, covering her mouth in a hot, wet kiss, one hand squeezing her breast.

Jacie came alive with a start, but before she could

react a shot rang out. She heard Michael's furious voice shouting, "Damn it, what's going on there?"

Zach let go of Jacie so quickly that she slid to the ground, landing shakily on her feet. She saw Michael running toward them down the border of the corn field with several of the field hands, all of them carrying torches against the pressing night.

Zach knew that from where Michael had spotted them he could not be sure he had actually seen him kissing Jacie. Trusting she would back him up, he lied, "I was bringin' her home. Hell, Blake, you scared me to death, firin' like that. I dropped her, and she coulda got hurt."

Michael reached them, face livid. "Are you all right?" He grasped Jacie's shoulders as he raked her with an anxious glance from head to toe.

She nodded, not looking at Zach, afraid her own rage would show on her face. If she told Michael what had happened, that Zach had kissed her, fondled her, he might kill him. It was best to let it go for the present and put Zach in his place first chance she got. "I'm all right," she said, trying not to appear upset.

Michael turned his fury on Zach once more. "What the hell were you doing with her? You were supposed to signal if you found her, fire your gun. I don't like this, you stubborn fool. I don't like it one damn bit when my orders aren't followed."

And Zach didn't like being cursed and flared back at him. "Now don't get your britches all twisted. I forgot about givin' any signal. I just wanted to get her home fast as I could. I knowed everybody was in an uproar to find her."

Michael shook his fist at him. "You've disobeyed

me for the last time. Get your gear and leave Red Oakes by noon tomorrow or I'll order you shot on sight."

"You ain't got no call to do that," Zach said tightly, his own fists clenching with the urge to pound Michael into the ground. "I told you, I just wanted to get her home fast as I could."

"I don't like you and I don't trust you. And I damn well don't have to put up with the likes of you."

Jacie put her hand on Michael's arm and brought it down to his side. "There's no need for this. Zach forgot, like he said. He had been worried too, and he wasn't thinking about what he was doing." She wanted no trouble, and Zach had been a friend in the past, however wrong he had been to kiss her. She would like to forget the incident and concentrate on her impending journey.

But Zach did not get her meaning, thrilled over how she had taken up for him, lied for him. He had been right, he told himself happily, despite the situation at hand. She did have a hankering for him. "You heard her," he retorted, "and you better think about it. I'm a good overseer and you know it. Your daddy knew it, too. That's why he hired me."

"My father is dead. I run things now, Newton, but you haven't been able to accept that. That's why I'm ordering you out of here."

"You got no call. Not like this. How about if you just give yourself time to calm down, and we talk about this in private tomorrow? You give me a second chance." Ordinarily, Zach knew he would have told him to go hell, but now that he was confident Jacie wanted him as much as he wanted her, he didn't want to leave Red Oakes.

"You heard me," Michael said grimly, taking Jacie's arm. "If you're anywhere on my land after noon tomorrow, you're a dead man."

He began to lead Jacie back toward the house, but they had only gone a few steps when she turned to look back at Zach and shake her head in pity.

Zach was shaking he was so mad, but it made him feel better that Jacie had looked at him like she had and thought what a shame it was it hadn't worked out.

Jacie Calhoun, he knew, would have been one delicious slice of pie.

# 8

*Michael gave Jacie time to* take a bath and change, then sent word she was expected to join everyone for dinner. He also asked her to wear the diamond and amethyst necklace, secretly hoping it would remind her of why he had given it to her and evoke tender memories to dispel the tension between them.

Jacie dreaded going but knew there was no way to avoid the gathering without a scene. Michael had hardly spoken on their walk back to the house, and she had found herself wondering if maybe he actually thought there was something going on between her and Zach. If that was the case, she was even more glad she had chosen to go with Mehlonga. It might be good for her and Michael to be apart for a while.

Sudie came to help her dress, and as she brushed her hair the girl told her, "You sure had everybody scared today, Miss Jacie. I ain't never seen Master Blake in such a dither, not knowing where you were."

Jacie could not resist teasing her. "Well, it's a shame you couldn't tell him like you did last time."

"I'm sorry," Sudie muttered.

"No, it's all right. You thought you were doing the right thing."

"I was afraid Master Newton would get mad, and I sure don't want him mad at me. He can be real mean, Miss Jacie." She lowered her voice to speak of the man all the slaves feared. "I's so scared of him."

Ordinarily, Jacie would never have confided such a matter to a servant, much less a child, but something made her want to put Sudie at ease. "It doesn't matter now. Master Newton will be leaving Red Oakes. Master Blake fired him today."

Sudie dropped the hairbrush to clap her hands in glee. "Oh, I'm so glad. Don't nobody like him, Miss Jacie. He's mean to the slaves when Master Blake ain't around. He even beat my pappy once, and my pappy had to wear a shirt, even though it was summertime, so the whip marks wouldn't show, 'cause he knew if Master Blake saw, he'd get mad at Master Newton, and then Master Newton might kill him. I sure ain't sorry to see him go."

Jacie was horrified. "Are you telling the truth, Sudie? Mr. Newton whipped the workers?"

Sudie knew she had said too much. "You won't say I told, will you?"

Jacie believed her, assured her she would say nothing, and in that moment made up her mind she no longer cared what happened to Zach. He might have been her friend once, but no more, not after she'd learned how cruel he was.

Everyone was already at the table when she entered the dining room. Taking her seat, she nodded politely to Olivia, who regarded her coolly. Verena was gracious and clucked about how glad she was that Jacie had been found safely, and Elyse smiled and said she too was relieved.

"Well, it's over now," Michael said with a flourish, signaling to the hovering servant to pour them each a glass of scuppernong wine. "Jacie is fine, and we'll have no more problems. As soon as I return from Charleston, we'll start planning the biggest wedding Georgia has ever seen."

Jacie focused her attention on the wine.

Olivia drew a sharp breath. She and Verena were in agreement that a wedding simply could not take place so soon after the death of Jacie's parents. "Not before spring," she declared firmly. "It would not be proper."

"I'm not concerned with propriety," Michael said. "Jacie is all alone now. She needs me to take care of her. Don't you agree, my dear?" He flashed a smile at Jacie.

Jacie was not about to join in the conversation, even though she was the topic. Spring was fine with her. That was when she planned to return from Texas, if not before, but she could not tell anyone that, could only bide her time till dawn. Hedging, she responded, "I really don't feel like discussing any of this tonight, Michael. I'm tired."

"Of course, you are, dear," Olivia said, feigning compassion. "By the way, what *were* you doing this afternoon to have made you so exhausted? That must have been a very long walk."

"I think we should change the subject," Michael said then. "She doesn't want to talk about it."

"Well, I was just wanting to make sure she wasn't with that dirty old Indian again. Did you do as I asked and order him shot on sight? We've put up with him far too long."

"Mother, there was too much else going on, and—"

"Don't you dare!" Jacie got to her feet, unable to stand any more. "You don't just order someone killed because they're tending sick people, Michael." She whirled on Olivia, "And I'm surprised at you for asking him to. You're always going on about manners and refinement, yet you demand the death of a harmless man. You should be ashamed of yourself."

"Well—well, I never. . ." Olivia sputtered indignantly.

Jacie bolted from the room, but Michael caught up with her as she was about to run up the stairs. "That was uncalled for," he admonished her. "You know Mother didn't really mean what she said. She's been demanding that old coot shot for years. Now I want you to come back to the dining room, apologize, and finish your dinner."

"And I want you to stop treating me like a child and giving me orders." She plucked his hand from her arm, lifting her chin defiantly. Even though he did not know she was leaving, she felt the need to let him know she had no intention of ever being subservient. "You are not my master, Michael. I am not your slave."

His face darkened. "But you are going to be my wife, and you will do as I ask, Jacie. As you will vow on our wedding day, you will obey me. Love, honor, obey. You can't say the words unless you mean them."

"I don't intend to," she fired back.

"Listen to me." He pushed his anger back. "I don't like it when we argue and I'm leaving early in the morning, way before dawn, because I want to take the first train for Charleston. We won't have another chance to talk, and I don't want us to part like this. Now please, come back with me and make peace. I'm going to do everything I can while we're away to convince Mother to give her blessing to our marriage right away, and it would help if she isn't angry with you."

"I just can't." Jacie could stand no more of his mother's criticism of Mehlonga. "Make my excuses, please. I am going to bed. Good night, Michael."

She went on up the steps, but she could feel him staring after her and knew he was hurt and miserable. She did not want to leave him that way and turned to tell him, "Everything will turn out for the best, Michael. You'll see." And she hurried to her room.

Michael wondered what on earth she was talking about. It worried him how strangely she had been acting lately, and he was concerned it might not altogether have to do with her parents dying so close together. He also did not like what he thought he had seen earlier; though he'd been a good distance away, it appeared that Zach was kissing Jacie, but she would not have lied for him . . . unless . . .

He gave his head a brisk shake. He would not allow himself to contemplate such a possibility. Jacie would never have anything to do with the likes of Zach Newton, or any other man but him. He was being silly, and once he got back from Charleston, everything would be fine.

He would make it so.

It seemed to Jacie that it took forever till the house became dark and still. She crept from her room and tiptoed downstairs to the study. There, after lighting a small lantern and making sure the door to the foyer was closed, she sat down behind Michael's desk and wrote her letter:

*My dearest Michael,*

*I am going away for a while, but please do not worry. There is something I must do. I cannot explain it to you now, but when I return in the spring, or before, I will tell you everything.*

*Affectionately,*

*Jacie*

Unfastening the necklace, she placed it beside the letter. She was not about to take something so valuable with her. It might be lost or stolen, or, God forbid, something might happen to her and she would never return.

There was a closet in the study that went through to the back hallway. Servants could move in and out, when summoned, without having to go through the main hall and foyer to enter. Absorbed in what she was doing, Jacie was unaware that the door to the closet had opened just a crack.

The letter finished, she took her satchel, which was empty, and let herself quietly out the front door, hurrying down the moonlit path to the cabin. She was wearing a simple muslin dress and would carry only one change of clothing, leaving room for the blanket. When it was packed, she breathed a sigh of relief that everything was taken care of. All she had to do was wait.

She went to the swing on the front porch and sat down, too nervous to sleep, and began to talk aloud to herself, whispering in the night. "I can't believe I'm going. Texas. Bird's Fort, Texas. I wonder how far it is. He said he'd see that he got me there. Oh, please God," she prayed fervently, "Let me find my mother. I know she's still alive. I just feel it, somehow."

She got up and went slowly to the graves. "I'm going to find her," she said to Violet's simple headstone. "So rest in peace. . ." Her head came up at the sound of twigs snapping in the darkness. It better not be Zack, she thought with a flash of anger. If he had seen her heading this way and followed, she would give him a piece of her mind.

"Who's there?" she demanded fiercely. "You come out right now. I don't like being spied on."

"I'm sorry, I'm sorry." Sudie burst from the woods to throw herself against Jacie. "I didn't mean no harm. I just don't like you goin' away, and I know you are, 'cause I seen you sneak out with a bag. Please don't go, Miss Jacie. I love you so much." She was not about to tell her she had followed her to the study, then hid in the closet and watched as she wrote on a piece of paper.

Jacie knelt to take her in her arms and explain, as best she could. "Yes, I am going away, but I'll be back in the spring. Now I want you to go home and go to bed, understand? And don't say a word to anyone."

Sudie sniffed a few times. Jacie gave her a hug and she turned back, shoulders slumped with worry. Actually, she had been there long before Miss Jacie heard her. She had seen her take the blanket out of Miss Violet's trunk again, then pull open the binding and take out that locket Miss Violet had showed her the night she died. Then Miss Jacie had cried a little, put it back in the hem of the blanket, and stuck the blanket in her satchel.

Sudie had no idea what was going on but knew she couldn't let Miss Jacie go off with nothing but that piece of jewelry that didn't look like it was worth much.

She took off toward the Blake house as fast as her little legs would carry her.

It was nearly an hour before Sudie returned to the cabin. She was glad to find that Miss Jacie had finally fallen asleep and that she had left the lantern burning on the table by the bed, because she would never have been able to find the satchel in the dark without making noise and waking her up.

Working quietly and quickly, Sudie opened the bag and took out the blanket. She ran her fingers along the edge as she had seen Miss Jacie do and found the opening. Then she stuck the necklace she had taken from where Miss Jacie had left it on Master Blake's desk and stuffed it inside.

Sudie was pleased with herself. She couldn't let Miss Jacie go off without the beautiful necklace. Now she had something to sell, if necessary, to get home on. Sudie didn't know why she had wanted to leave it anyway, but it didn't make any difference now. Miss Jacie wouldn't find it till she was too far away to bring it back.

Reaching the big house, Sudie hurried upstairs and into Jacie's room and closed the door, a little harder than she should have in her haste to get to her pallet in the dressing alcove. Tomorrow morning, she told herself as her eyes closed sleepily, when everybody started asking questions about where Miss Jacie was, she would pretend not to know anything. And come spring, Miss Jacie would be back like she promised, and everything would be just fine.

Elyse awoke to the sound of Jacie's door closing. She sat up, then reached for her robe at the foot of the bed, put it on, and padded across the floor. Opening her own door and peering out into the dark hall, she listened for any sound. All was quiet, but now she was wide awake, her curiosity piqued. She was positive it had been Jacie's door she heard, but what was she doing prowling around in the wee hours of the night? Maybe she was planning to see Michael off to Charleston.

Elyse heard the clock downstairs chime four times. Michael would be up soon and stirring about, along with her mother and Cousin Olivia.

Elyse knew she had to find out what Jacie was up to. She lit a small lantern and proceeded down the hall and down the stairs to the foyer. She did not hear anything but continued to look around. Then, seeing that the door to the study was open, she went inside.

Holding the lantern high to light the room, her eyes went to the desk . . . where she saw the letter. Quickly she sat down to read it, tingling with excitement to realize she was about to discover why Jacie had been prowling around.

The corners of her mouth lifted in a smile, which spread into a grin across her whole face as she realized with a happy lurch of her heart that this was the chance she had been waiting for.

Jacie was going away. No doubt she and Michael had been having more problems than anyone realized. But if she did come back in the spring, as she had written, Elyse was going to make certain Michael would not be waiting with open arms. Because by spring, Elyse planned to be his wife.

She hurried back upstairs to her room, anxious to think about all the details of what must be done to make her scheme work.

She took Jacie's letter with her.

# 9

*Mehlonga was waiting with* a horse for her, a beautiful brown mare. There was no saddle, only a woven blanket on the mare's back, but Jacie did not mind; she was a good rider.

"Are you sure of what you are doing?" he asked her. "You can still turn back."

"I can't go back until I find out what—if anything—is waiting for me out there," she answered, pointing west.

Michael had ordered breakfast to be ready, should anyone want it, even though he knew he would probably be the only one with an appetite at such an ungodly hour. He was surprised to find Elyse at the table. "What are you doing up? Didn't you say good-bye to your mother last night?"

"Yes, but I didn't say good-bye to you." She hoped

he did not notice her nervousness, for she was barely able to contain her exhilaration at the knowledge that Jacie had left.

He gave her a light peck on her cheek and sat down. "That's nice of you. Nicer, too, that you're willing to forego a trip home to stay with Jacie. I'm very worried about her, you know. If you could get her mind on something besides her grief, it would be wonderful. Perhaps the two of you can go riding. She loves to ride."

"And jump," Elyse said with a soft laugh, wanting to remind him of the incident Cousin Olivia had told her about and how upset he had been.

"There won't be any jumping. Besides, I fired Newton last night. He's leaving this morning. Now I don't have to worry about Jacie wheedling him into going behind my back to set up hurdles. I've also ordered the equipment destroyed."

He talked on about how reckless Jacie could be, but Elyse was no longer listening, because another idea was forming in her head. So far, all she had done was destroy Jacie's letter so that when Michael discovered her missing he would have no idea as to why. Now she saw a way to make him go into a rage and never want her back.

Before she could ponder further, Michael's words caught her attention. "Maybe I should talk to her again before I leave. Would you mind waking her and asking her to come downstairs?"

Elyse was panic-stricken that she would have to report Jacie missing. If Michael found out, he would go after her and probably find her, because she could not have gotten far yet. "I don't think that would be wise," she said finally.

His brows lifted. "And why not?"

Rapidly the lie tumbled out. "I heard her moving about till all hours. Obviously she couldn't sleep. She's probably exhausted, and we should let her rest."

Disappointed, he had no choice but to agree, knowing it would not be gentlemanly to request her presence after such a bad night. "I just wish I didn't have to leave her now," he said.

"Stop worrying, Michael. I promise you I'll take care of her." She patted his hand, thrilled, as always, at the chance to touch him.

As soon as the carriage rolled down the driveway in the early morning mist, Elyse hurried to the overseers' cabins, which were situated directly behind the stables. She worried that she would not be able to find Zach Newton but then she saw him leading his horse, saddlebags packed, out of one of the barns.

Zach recognized her as one of Blake's relatives and slowed, wondering what the hell she wanted as she came straight toward him. She was pretty and he liked red-haired women. She had a nice shape, too. He could tell by the dress she was wearing—the waist was tight, accenting her bosom.

"You're Mr. Newton, aren't you?"

"That's right." His gaze roved over her, and he hated Blake even more for running him off. There were lots of tasty morsels around Red Oakes, just waiting to be sampled.

"I'm Miss Elyse Burdette of Charleston," she informed him, then recited the story she had hastily invented. "I overheard Mr. Blake saying he had told you that your services are no longer needed here at Red Oakes."

"How does that concern you? Is he sendin' a woman to make sure I'm leavin'?" he asked, snickering.

She ignored his question. "Do you have another job in mind?"

"No," he replied slowly, curiosity piqued. "But I'll find somethin' around here. It's cotton pickin' time, and good overseers are needed. I do happen to be a good one, regardless of what Mr. Blake might think," he added with a little sneer.

That was exactly what she was afraid of, Elyse thought, that he would stay in the area, and she could not allow that. He could not be seen anywhere around, not if her scheme was to work. She handed him a folded sheet of paper.

He opened it and read as she explained, "That's a map showing you the way to the Owen Kernsby plantation in Beaufort, South Carolina. Mr. Kernsby was a close friend of my father. And here is a letter asking him to do me the favor of giving you a job. I am sure he will honor it. The last time I saw him he mentioned he was always in need of good overseers, because his plantation is quite large."

Zach took the envelope but asked suspiciously, "How come you're doin' this? How come you give a damn?"

She gave a careless shrug. "Mr. Kernsby needs workers, and you need a job. What other reason would I have?"

He grinned. "Well, now, that's real nice of you, Miss Burdette." He tipped his hat. "I'll just get on down that way, and I'm sure beholden to you."

She bid him a safe journey and was about to walk away when he said, "By the way, you tell Miss Jacie I appreciate what she did. She'll know what I'm talkin' about. And if she ever wants to find me, you tell her where you sent me, all right?"

Elyse stiffened to think he could be so brazen but was not about to annoy him with a tart response. Instead, she managed to say sweetly, "Why, you can be sure I'll do that, Mr. Newton. I know the two of you are good friends."

She hurried back to the house, waiting till she was out of his sight to start laughing aloud with glee.

It was time, she felt like shouting to the whole world, to discover that Jacie Calhoun had run away with Zach Newton.

**Texas**

Iris went with the others to meet the returning braves. And while wives and children greeted husbands and fathers, Iris held out her arms to the young man she loved as a son.

"Thank God, you're safe," she whispered against his broad shoulder as they embraced. She stood back to clasp his hands and drink in the sight of him. "You must be starved. Come. I will fix you something to eat, and you can tell me everything."

While feasting on roasted elk, Luke described the results of his scouting the past few weeks. He had left the hunters to see what was going on around the forts. "I'm afraid things are getting worse," he told her. "Ever since the Texas Ranger Rip Ford killed Iron Jacket and defeated his band in the spring, the soldiers get more daring. There is much bloodshed."

"And our band only wants peace," she murmured

sadly, daring to suggest, "Maybe we should turn ourselves in to the Brazos Reserve before they attack and kill all of us."

"No!"

She jumped at the fierceness of his reply.

His face was a thundercloud of anger. "I would rather die, and have my people die, than go there. The reservations are nothing but a living death. And something else—I learned that the reason the soldiers are able to make so many raids on the Comanche is because Rip Ford was able to convince over a hundred Tonkawa to scout for him after the Texas governor Runnels put him in command of all the state's forces."

Iris was aware that for the past three years, since 1855, the advancing line of settlement in Texas had tightened around the Clear Fork and Brazos reserves. Until his death, Great Bear had been forced to keep the tribe moving to avoid trouble, because they had found themselves caught between two fires: The Indians who wanted war with the white man despised them, and the whites didn't care which tribe was which; they considered them all savages.

"I had hoped," Iris said, "that when we moved after Great Bear's death we could settle in for the winter, but I have a feeling you're about to tell me that isn't possible."

"That's right. We have to move farther north. I stayed at Bird's Fort a few days and found out the Second Cavalry has been ordered to march into the Wichita Mountains of Oklahoma with four companies of cavalry and one on foot. They're setting up a base camp between the Canadian and the Red rivers."

"That isn't far from here," she said, alarmed.

"Not far enough for us to feel safe. I've made the decision to have the camp moved north of the Red, deep into Indian Territory. You will start tomorrow."

Iris and Luke were very close. She knew him so well and now sensed he was keeping something from her. "But there's more, isn't there? Something you don't want to tell me."

He was silent for a moment. He hated to worry her but knew she would fret even more if she thought he was holding back. "It's Black Serpent." He bit out the name.

Iris tensed. For a long time, there had been bad feelings between Luke and Black Serpent, caused by a young maiden named Singing Waters. Black Serpent had chosen Singing Waters for his wife and had followed the custom of giving her father a horse and other gifts. Singing Waters, however, had rejected Black Serpent, for it was her intent to marry Luke.

There was chaos then. When Black Serpent heard of the rejection, and the reason, he had challenged Luke to fight for the girl. But Luke was not interested in marrying her, even though Iris knew Singing Waters had been slipping into his tepee every night for several weeks. Many young Indian maidens went to him, but he never seemed to encourage any of them.

Great Bear had decreed there would be no fight, and Singing Waters's father decreed the horse and gifts from Black Serpent would be accepted and she would marry him, but Singing Waters refused and eventually married someone else, which only added to Black Serpent's humiliation. He blamed everything on

Luke, and Iris had always worried there would be trouble between them sooner or later. "What has he done?" she asked warily.

Luke described how they had come upon a small patrol of soldiers. The soldiers did not see them, so Luke, wanting to avoid trouble, signaled to his braves to stay hidden and let the soldiers pass unharmed. Black Serpent, however, had wanted to show off. He had also wanted to make coup. So he had attacked the four soldiers, who immediately ran from the advancing, screaming man. He had run one down, killed him, and taken his scalp.

Iris closed her eyes against the image of such horror. "Oh, Lord, why does it have to be this way? Why can't there be peace?"

"One day, perhaps there will be. Till then, we can only try to avoid fighting. That's why I have decided to take Gold Elk and Sharp Knife and keep an eye on things at Bird's Fort for a while, to try and head off trouble. We'll join you at winter camp later."

"And what about Black Serpent? With you gone, he'll try to take over our band."

"We don't have to worry about him anymore. I banished him."

"Oh, no. How many went with him?" She knew there were some men who sided with Black Serpent in his lust for blood.

"A few. But it's just as well. I don't want their kind, and I can't have a warrior who won't follow orders. To allow him to stay weakens me in the eyes of my people. I couldn't let that happen. He was just waiting for an excuse to take his followers and go off on his own."

Iris had been so happy to see Luke and listening so

intently to everything he was saying that she had not noticed how he was dressed. Now she realized he was wearing a skin shirt, which puzzled her, because the men went bare-chested in warm weather. Then she saw the dark stain below his shoulder and cried, "You're bleeding."

He shrugged it off. "A small wound. It's nothing."

"Let me see." She opened his shirt over his protests. With skilled fingers she removed the poultice of weeds and grass he had packed in the wound to try and stop the bleeding. Relieved to see it was not deep, she said, "Black Serpent cut you, didn't he? I'm surprised you didn't kill him."

"I gave him a worse fate—having to live with the scar my knife left on his face. You know how vain he is."

She knew, as everyone did, that Black Serpent considered himself very handsome.

"It's not serious, I tell you," Luke protested when she brought out her herbs and bandages to treat and dress the wound properly.

"And we will see that it heals, but it is going to leave a scar."

"To go with the others." He grinned. Through the years, Luke had had his share of injuries from combat with both man and beast. "You women are lucky your scars are few."

"Oh, some of us have many. But we carry them in our souls, where they aren't seen."

He became silent as she fussed over him, and when she was finished he put an arm around her affectionately and said, "I don't like to think of the scars you carry on your soul, Mother. I wish I could turn back time and take away the sorrow you've had to live with. It would never have happened if my people had thought then as they do now."

They had spoken of the terrible thing that had brought them together only rarely. It was something Iris had tried, without success, to forget. Now she wished she had not said what she had about scars within, for it triggered the painful memory for both of them.

"I don't like to think of how you came to me," he went on, "but I'm glad that you did. You've taught me so much. Without you, I would never have learned to cherish peace, because we both know my father only allowed me to go away to school due to your influence. Now I can't wait to take all my people there come spring. We're going to have a good life. You'll see."

"You know, if you keep scouting instead of spending time with the young women, you aren't going to find a wife. I shouldn't be the one to worry constantly about you and take care of you."

He laughed. "You don't mind. And as for worrying, you'd do that, anyway. Besides, why do you think I prefer the forts? The women there are all married to soldiers. I don't have to worry about losing my freedom."

"One day it will happen," she warned him happily, "When you least expect it. Love can be found anywhere, my son. You just have to open your eyes so you can see it."

Closing his eyes, he pretended to stumble around blindly. "Then I'll keep them shut, because the last thing I need is another woman telling me what to do."

She chased him from the tepee, all the while

thinking how the lucky girl he eventually chose for a wife would have herself a fine man—and how proud she was to have been a part of making him so.

# 10

*In the twenty years since* the forced march of the Indians that fateful winter of 1838–39, new trails had been forged by Cherokee slipping away to return to their beloved Great Smoky Mountains. Though skirting around impossible heights was necessary, as well as crossing unchallenged rivers, Mehlonga was determined he would not lead Jacie on the original and lengthy Trail of Tears. Mehlonga wanted to reach their destination before the onset of winter.

They raised few eyebrows when they passed through a settlement town, looking like a father and daughter traveling west. Jacie had convinced Mehlonga they could avoid trouble from Indian haters if he replaced the bandanna around his head with a straw hat. Reluctantly, he agreed, and nothing else about his costume gave hint he was Cherokee. He wore an old black coat, trousers and a dingy white shirt.

The weather was good most of the time, so they camped in the open. Rain drove them to seek shelter in caves or beneath rocky overhangs. Occasionally they happened upon Indian farmers, who welcomed them and gave them the chance to wash their clothing, sleep in a real bed, and eat a home-cooked meal.

But Jacie liked the camping nights best. During the day, riding behind Mehlonga, there was no opportunity for conversation. At night, however, after a meal of dried corn and, if luck was with them, a roasted rabbit or squirrel, Mehlonga would light his pipe and settle back, and Jacie would listen eagerly as he spun the tales she found so fascinating.

One night when they had been on the road nearly two weeks, Mehlonga recounted the stories that had filtered back from Indian Territory of how his people had joined four other tribes—the Creek, Chickasaw, Choctaw, and Seminole, all of whom had also been forcibly removed from the Southeast by the government in the 1830s.

Nearly fourteen thousand Cherokee had died, Mehlonga said. "So they should have been a broken people. But from all I have heard, they rallied, and they have built a prosperous society.

"We always felt we were cultured," he went on to say. "We lived in log cabins. We wore homespun clothes. We tended livestock and plowed fields with oxen. Some of our people even married whites, and tribal leaders could read and write English and comprehend the law. So it was not surprising to hear that the survivors of the march restored their way of government.

"Once"—he smiled with pride—"I even saw a newspaper they had printed at their capital in Tahlequah. It was in English, as well as our own language. It was called the *Cherokee Advocate.* They have schools there, too, for both men and women."

Jacie had eagerly learned what was known as the Cherokee syllabary, a script used for writing the Cherokee language. It had been devised by a half-Cherokee named Sequoyah and had spread rapidly. In a short time, she was able to write it fluidly but kept her knowledge to herself. Her parents would not have liked it, and neither would Michael. His mother would have succumbed to the vapors to know her future daughter-in-law was scholarly in the Indian way.

"What do you think you'll do when you get there?" Jacie asked.

Mehlonga stared into the fire for a few moments, then said with resignation, "Die."

"Don't say that."

"And why not? To die is only to go from one place to another. I have no fear of dying. No Cherokee does. But until the spirits call me, I will do what I can for my people with my medicine. And I will try to find my relatives. A brother may still be alive, and my sister. If they have gone ahead of me to that other place, then I will find their children. I will have family again. And so will you," he said with a confident nod.

Jacie's heart skipped a beat, like always, to think her mother might still be alive. "You think I will find her, don't you?"

"Not many have eyes like you. Not many white women live among the Comanche, at least not in favor. They make slaves of prisoners, but they must have treated the white woman well or she would not have returned to them willingly."

"Tell me what you know about the Comanche."

"They are fierce. And deadly. But there is a story about how they befriended the great Sequoyah. He was in their territory looking for a remnant of the Cherokee, and his party's horses were stolen by Tewockenees Indians, so they built a raft to cross a river. Comanche saw them, and because they were wearing caps, thought they were Texans and were going to kill them. Then someone noticed they had feathers in their caps. So they helped them, gave them food, horses, and sent them on their way. So the Comanche are not all bad. No man is," he added wisely.

"I want you to promise me something," he went on. "If there is no one at this place called Bird's Fort that will help you, I want you to go back. It is too dangerous for you to stay and search on your own."

"I won't make such a promise," Jacie said stubbornly. "I didn't make this trip to turn around and go back without doing everything possible to find out the truth, Mehlonga. You know that."

"I suppose I do. That is why I have decided to give you this." He drew a knife from inside his coat and held it out to her. "I will teach you to defend yourself."

Jacie stared down at the wicked-looking blade gleaming in the fire's glow. It felt heavy in her hand, and unnatural. She decided she was afraid of it, and her hand began to tremble.

"You will learn to hold it with a steady hand, just as you will learn to use it with skill and cunning.

Every night from now on when we stop to make camp, I will teach you. By the time we reach Fort Smith, I will not worry about leaving you to go my own way."

Jacie did not want to think about the time when they would part, but Mehlonga had made it clear that he would go no farther with her than Fort Smith, Arkansas. He would make sure she had an escort to take her on to Bird's Fort, while he continued on to the Cherokee capital known as Tahlequah, where he hoped to find whatever was left of his family.

"You will be as good as any warrior with the knife," he predicted.

"Do you think I will need it against the Comanche?"

"Be prepared to defend yourself against anyone who would do you harm, my child. Look not at the color of his skin but to his eyes, where the evil in a man's heart is revealed."

It was already dark, but Mehlonga showed her the way to grip the knife, how to strap it to her leg beneath her skirt to conceal it, and then how to whip it out at a second's notice. When she was skilled at that, he would teach her how to cut—and kill.

"I want you also to have this." He handed her a piece of soft deerskin that had been folded into a tiny square, hardly bigger than her thumb. Inside she found small seeds, hard and black.

"Seeds from the blue flower called the morning glory. Should you ever have enemies, they will make a nice potion to make them very sick. They will become dizzy and see visions, as well as vomit and be afraid. Since it would be hard to get them to eat the seeds whole, you must mash them into powder and then mix the powder in liquid for drinking."

Jacie was amazed. She loved morning glories. She had even planted some next to the porch at the cabin and enjoyed seeing their green vines grow to wrap around the posts, shading the porch with large, heart-shaped blossoms. But never had she thought they could be used to poison.

"As I told you," he said, "I want you to be able to take care of yourself when we are no longer together."

Looking from the knife she held in one hand to the poison seeds in the other, Jacie murmured, "I just hope I never have need of either of these."

"As do I, my child," he agreed solemnly. "As do I."

Jacie took her bedroll and lay down on the other side of the campfire, but she was too restless to sleep. After a time, she heard Mehlonga's even breathing and only then did she reach for the baby blanket she had not opened since they had left ten nights ago. Wanting to look at the daguerreotype once more, she felt along the hem for the telltale bulge, which oddly seemed larger and heavier than she recalled.

Her fingers crept inside, and she swallowed a startled gasp to find, along with the locket, the diamond and amethyst necklace. But she had left it on Michael's desk, next to the letter she had written. So how . . .

Sudie. She must have been inside the closet while Jacie was writing the note to Michael and must have seen her leave the necklace on the desk. She probably thought Jacie meant to take the jewels with her. She obviously sneaked into the cabin and hid it in the blanket, thinking she was doing her a favor.

Jacie could do nothing about it now. She snuggled down to rest as weariness washed over her. Sudie meant well; Jacie knew she would just have to be extra careful not to lose the necklace. After all, Michael was going to be angry enough as it was. He would never forgive her if she lost something so dear.

The trip had taken longer than Michael anticipated. He had figured the day-and-a-half train ride to Charleston, two days of business concerning the sale of Cousin Verena's house, then the return to Atlanta. Five days, six at the most. And now he had been away nearly ten days.

As the carriage reached Red Oakes and turned into the drive, Michael reveled in the sight of the cotton fields that stretched as far as the eye could see. White blossoms exploded like popcorn on a sea of green. Pickers stooped and worked their way between the rows, the big shoulder bags dragging the ground behind them.

The overseers watched from horseback. A few tipped their hats or waved as the carriage passed.

Olivia darted an anxious glance at Verena. The trip had been quite tense. As the days had dragged on, Michael made no secret of his growing annoyance. "See?" she pointed out, attempting to lighten his mood. "Everyone is hard at work. Red Oakes does not come to a standstill just because you aren't around, dear."

"That's right," Verena said in the chirpy voice Michael found so grating. "We didn't have to rush at all. Goodness, I hope I didn't forget anything, the way you were hurrying us to leave."

Michael's lips were a thin line of irritation. He did not trust himself to speak, for he did not want to be disrespectful to Cousin Verena. But it was her fault, damn it. If it had been left up to him, he'd have had workers pack everything in her house in one day, but she had insisted on supervising, picking and choosing what to store, give away or sell. Then there was her stomach upset that delayed signing the papers for two days. She had laughed it off, saying she knew collard greens sometimes didn't agree with her, but when her neighbor brought over a big bowl full, how could she refuse?

Shopping had also taken an extra day, as Verena said she had no idea when she would be getting back to Charleston and wanted her dressmaker to fit her for a few new gowns before leaving. Michael had really struggled for control then, yearning to tell her she could stay in Charleston if she liked. He wished she would, because he couldn't stand the thought of her living at Red Oakes indefinitely.

He had wanted to go on ahead, but his mother would not hear of it, so he'd had no choice but to stay and keep his mouth shut. But now he was home at last, and the second the carriage pulled to a stop he was out and bounding up the steps. The grooms could help the ladies. He could wait no longer to see Jacie.

Elyse had been watching from a window. Her mother had promised to keep Michael away from Red Oakes for at least ten days, and she had done so. There had not been time to explain everything before they left, only that Jacie had run away, and she needed time to come up with a plan to ensure Michael would not want her back. Verena had been only too happy to oblige, willing to do anything to help.

Elyse was wearing one of her prettiest dresses—a pale green taffeta that complemented her hair, the neckline dipping just low enough to be enticing without being obviously provocative. She had a nice bosom and knew Michael appreciated that fact, because there had been times when she had seen him looking at her when he thought she was unaware of it.

Michael was taking the steps two at a time as he called Jacie's name.

Elyse took one last look in the mirror, drew a deep breath, then walked out into the hall.

Michael was just reaching the landing, and despite his disappointment at finding Elyse waiting instead of Jacie, he greeted her warmly, unable to keep from noticing how fetching she looked and absently wondering why she had not married long ago. "You're lovely, as always," he greeted her. "I'm sorry you had to look after Jacie for so long, but blame your mother. You know how she is." He forced an indulgent smile to show that he meant no disrespect.

"Where is she? God, I've been so worried. Did you two go riding? Are her spirits better?" Michael called for a servant to go fetch Jacie.

Elyse bit her lip, her hands primly folded at her waist. The words had been carefully rehearsed. She knew them by heart. But it was important to wait until exactly the right moment. Meanwhile, she was trying to make herself cry. She thought about a little dog she had as a child, how much she had loved him and how hurt she'd been when he died. Then the tears came quickly.

"I'm sorry, Michael. Jacie isn't here."

"What do you mean? Where is she?.

He gripped Elyse's shoulders, and instead of wincing with pain as his fingers dug into her flesh, Elyse felt a delicious tremor at his touch. "She isn't here, Michael," she managed to say.

"What are you talking about? Is this some kind of prank the two of you are playing? I'm not amused."

She pulled away from his grasp, for he was squeezing harder and hurting her now. She hated this, despised having to cause him such anguish, but if that was what it took to make him her very own, so be it. Jacie did not love him, or she never would have left him, not for any reason. Therefore, Elyse reasoned, she did not deserve him.

"Oh, I see," he said. "She went back to the cabin to stay. Well, I might have known she would do that the minute I left. But you couldn't help it, Elyse. I know how headstrong she can be. There's no need for you to cry."

He turned to go.

"She's not there, Michael. She didn't go back."

He paused as a chill of foreboding crept over him. "Then where the hell is she?"

The words tumbled out, and Elyse no longer had to force herself to cry, so shaken was she by the way he was glaring at her, as though it were suddenly all her fault. "She's been gone since the day you left. I had the servants searching all over, but they couldn't find her."

He grabbed her again, and this time she tried to escape him, but he held tight, shouting, "Where did she go? Where *would* she go? Something has happened to her and you're keeping it from me. What is it, damn you. Tell me. . . ."

He trailed off as Olivia and Verena appeared. Olivia saw how he was holding Elyse and cried, "What is going on here? Michael, what are you doing to her?"

Michael waved the women back as they rushed toward him. "Stay out of this. Both of you." He gave Elyse a shake. "Are you going to tell me or drive me crazy?" He was almost hysterical as visions began to flash before his eyes—Jacie dead, her neck broken in a fall while trying to jump the hurdles, or dead from fever, sickness. If Elyse didn't tell him the truth, and soon, he was afraid he would have to put his fist through the wall to keep from beating it out of her.

"Let me go. You're hurting me," Elyse whimpered.

Verena threw herself between them and gave Michael a quick slap. "How dare you treat my daughter this way. I'll not have it, do you hear me?"

Michael's chest was heaving. He felt he was going to be sick. "Something has happened to Jacie," he said with a moan that came from somewhere deep inside. "And she won't tell me what it is."

Olivia began to sway. "For God's sake, Elyse, what is this all about? Tell us."

Elyse then threw herself against Michael sobbing wildly, "Oh, Michael, I'd rather die than have to tell you this." She took a deep breath, gathering her courage to tell the biggest lie she had ever told in her whole life. "Jacie has run away with Zach Newton."

Olivia fainted.

Verena fought to hold back a smile to think what a clever daughter she had.

And Michael pushed Elyse away from him to finally slam his fist through the wall.

# 11

*Michael was proud that he* had proved wrong the skeptics who said he was too young to take over for his father. He was also pleased to have earned the respect of some of the most influential people in Georgia, and there was even talk of his entering the political arena one day.

But in the wake of Jacie's running away, Michael Blake was a broken man.

It had been a week since he had returned to find Jacie gone, and all day, every day, he sat behind his desk and brooded. Elyse had taken to her bed, weeping with self-recrimination. Michael had tried to assure her that he did not blame her, but Elyse told him she felt she had let him down. He tried to make her see she could not have prevented what happened, but she refused to come out of her room and said she could not bear to talk about it.

Humiliation kept him from leaving his study, for he could not bear the pitying looks of his overseers. That first day, he had ridden out to the fields, pretending to be interested in how the cotton and corn harvests were going but actually wanting to escape his mother's wailing over such a scandal. But realizing the overseers knew about it, as well as some of the field hands, Michael had avoided everyone since. Eventually he would have to come out, but for the time being he wanted to be alone with his misery and heartache.

"Michael? Unlock this door."

He groaned to hear his mother's voice; she pounded till he had to let her in. "I don't feel like talking," he said brusquely.

"Well, I do." She sat down. "It's time we discussed that little doxy."

"She's not a doxy, Mother. She might have run away with Zach Newton, for God only knows what reason, but she's no doxy. And how can we know what she was thinking? She'd been friends with him for years and she was probably upset with me for letting him go. We'd had a fight the last night we were together."

"She was probably off with him that afternoon, making plans to leave."

"No, no, I don't believe that. She was angry with me. That's why she went with him. I shouldn't have left her at such a time. My God, she'd just lost both of her parents." He slumped into his chair, racked by torment.

Olivia Blake was unmoved by his defense of Jacie. "You can't make excuses for her, because there can be none for what she did. And the fact is she had been carrying on with him for some time, only we were all too blind to see it."

His head snapped up. "What are you talking about?"

"I hate to be the one to tell you this, Michael, but I've heard some of the servants' gossip. Jacie was sneaking out to meet Zach at his cabin behind the stables before her parents died. And after you moved her in here, she was seen meeting him at the gazebo in the middle of the night. Disgraceful." She wrinkled her nose and gave a shudder. "Not only did she behave like a wanton hussy, but her parents weren't yet cold in their graves. And the reason she wanted to go back to the cabin was so Zach could sleep there and you wouldn't know about—"

Michael slammed his fist on the desk and bolted to his feet. "That's enough, Mother. I won't listen to such filthy lies, and I'll have the heads of those spreading them. Who told you all this? I want their names."

Olivia shrank back in her chair. She had never seen him so angry. "Well, actually," she hedged, "I didn't hear it. Verena did."

"Verena!" He spat the name. "I might have known. She loves to stir up trouble. I wish to hell she'd go back to Charleston."

"They don't have a house there anymore, remember? She wants to find a smaller place, but with winter coming on, she wants to wait till spring to do anything. And she is your father's kin. I certainly can't ask her to leave. We've had enough impropriety at Red Oakes," she added pointedly.

Michael gritted his teeth at the thought of having to endure Verena for such a long time. "Well, if she's going to stay, she's going to have to keep her mouth shut and stay out of my business. I'm not going to have her upsetting you."

"Jacie has managed to do enough to upset me for a long time to come. Verena doesn't have to say a word. And by the way, I should think you'd be concerned about poor Elyse. She's making herself sick, she feels so bad about all this. She adores you, and it breaks her heart to know you're taking this so hard."

"I can't help it. I love Jacie and you know it."

"You're better off without her, and sooner or later you'll come to your senses and realize that. She was not of our class. I just wish we'd found out about her earlier. Then you wouldn't have made such a fool of yourself by giving her that necklace. I'll wager she and Zach get a pretty price for it, and they'll laugh at you the whole time they're spending the money—"

"That's enough!" Michael cried. His face turned ashen. The necklace, damn it. He had forgotten all about the necklace.

"Where are you going?" Olivia demanded as he hurried toward the door. The expression on his face was fearsome.

"To talk to the servants. I want to see how much they're willing to tell *me.*"

She got up to follow after him. "Forget them. Forget Jacie and say good riddance. It's Elyse you should be talking to."

The front door slammed on her words and Michael hurtled down the wide marble steps, taking them two at a time. Somebody had to have heard something, seen something. It was a big plantation, with hundreds of slaves, and they were the ones he could make talk. He had no intentions of demeaning himself by discussing his fiancée's infidelity with his overseers. The slaves were a different matter. And he'd dare them to gossip about his interrogation of them.

*Fiancée.*

The word rolled around in his mouth like bile and he screwed up his face in loathing.

Though he had not let himself dwell on it, Jacie had never said she loved him; but he had assumed she did. Just as he had assumed she would marry him, which she probably would have, if only for his money. Then she and Zach would have continued to be lovers behind his back. Only when her parents died and she had her greedy little hands on the necklace had she decided to take it and leave with Zach.

How could he have been so blind? Fuming, he rounded the house and entered the rear yards. Jacie and Zach probably became lovers while he was in Europe, and when he returned, distracted by grief and sudden responsibilities, it was easy for them to deceive him. Never had he suspected anything. Whenever Jacie seemed aloof, Michael thought she was just being coquettish. Now, with rage a hot fist squeezing the very life from him, Michael knew she had been thinking about Zach all the while.

And she could have him, he raged, but by God, he would be damned if she would have the necklace too. If he could find out in which direction they had headed, he was going after it.

The sky was a huge gray hand, reaching across the earth with rings of silver lightning and fingers dancing to the rhythm of thunder. Trees bowed in fear as the winds slashed and crackled like giant, punishing whips.

A bad storm was rapidly approaching, but it was

not only the threatening clouds that made those in Michael's path run for cover—it was the raw tempest in his eyes.

He passed the kitchen buildings with determined steps as the first drops of rain began to fall. The cooling rooms and smokehouses appeared deserted, but the washwomen scurried frantically toward the lines as the winds threatened to snatch the laundry and fling it into the sky.

The chicken pen was hidden behind a thick row of crepe myrtle bushes. Skirting around them, Michael walked with angry strides down the path leading to the whitewashed slave cabins.

Nearby, a tree was hit by lightning and went crashing to the ground. In the fields, cotton flew through the air like snow.

Michael was soaked within seconds, his hair plastered to his head. But storm or no storm, he was going to get some answers, and he was going to start with Sudie, whom he had not seen since his return. The girl was assigned to watch Jacie, so she might have seen or heard something but not dared to tell anyone.

By the time he reached the rows of shacks, the storm had exploded and the rains came down so violently he could barely see where he was going. Stumbling into the first cabin he came to, Michael yelled, "Find the girl named Sudie. Bring her to me here, and the rest of you get out."

They scurried to obey, a man, his wife, and two teenage children. Michael felt bad about the fear in their eyes, for he had never screamed at any of them in such a way, but he was desperate. His nerves were raw, and he feared he was reaching the breaking point.

He stumbled about the cabin, noting its bleakness. A large bed with a wooden bedstead stood in one corner opposite two smaller beds on the other side of the room. There was a table and a few chairs, hooks on the wall to hang clothes. The floor was dirt, and there was a crumbling stone fireplace for cooking and heating. No glass was in the windows, and the shutters had been fastened against the storm, which made the room stifling hot. He knew he should have been aware of the poor conditions but had let other matters take precedence. He made a mental note to see to it after he settled things with Jacie, then realized he was no longer alone.

Sudie was standing in the doorway, her dress plastered to her body, hair soaked and matted. She was shaking, but Michael knew it was not from being wet. He beckoned her inside and she came reluctantly. He went to the table, pulled out a chair and sat down, indicating she should sit opposite.

Sudie took a few more hesitant steps, then stopped, thinking that if she stayed close to the door, she could run if he tried to beat her.

"Sudie, I am not going to hurt you," Michael began patiently, "I just want to ask you a few questions about Miss Jacie. You are aware she has gone away, aren't you?"

Sudie mumbled that she was. Right then she wished she were anywhere but here, with Master Blake asking questions she did not want to answer. She had been afraid he would ask sooner or later, but when days passed after Miss Jacie took off and she wasn't sent for, Sudie figured she could rest easy—but not anymore.

"Before she left, you were told to stay with her in

case she needed you to do anything. Did you stay with her all the time, sleep in the room with her?"

"I slept outside her door on the floor when she was at her cabin, and when she moved to the big house I slept in that little place where she gets dressed. How come you're askin' me all this?" she suddenly became bold enough to ask.

Michael silently cursed, wishing he dared come right out and ask whether she had ever seen Newton sneaking in, or if Jacie had sneaked out and if they had sent messages back and forth. But Sudie was a child. She might repeat his questions despite his warning her not to. He could not take that chance.

Deciding to try another ploy, he got up and went to kneel before her. With his hands clamped on her little waist, he looked into her wary eyes and explained very gently, "I'm worried about Miss Jacie, Sudie. I don't know where she is and I hoped you could tell me something that might help me find her."

Sudie frowned, confused. She had seen Miss Jacie write Master Blake a letter and leave it on his desk, so why was he worried?

He attempted to trick her by adding, "She's all alone, and that's not good. She needs somebody to look out for her, so I think I'd better go see about her. Don't you agree?"

So that was it. Sudie suddenly brightened. Miss Jacie forgot to tell him where she was going, but she could put his mind at ease, because it wouldn't be wrong for her to tell what she heard Miss Jacie say aloud, because Miss Jacie didn't know she'd heard her, so Sudie hadn't had to promise she wouldn't repeat it. And she certainly didn't have to give away the secret about how Miss Violet wasn't Miss Jacie's real momma, 'cause he hadn't asked her nothing about that.

"Can you think of anything that might help me find her?" he prodded.

"You ain't got nothin' to worry about, sir, 'cause I heard her talkin' to herself and she was sayin' how some man was gonna take her to Texas. But she told me she'd be back in the spring," she added happily.

Sure she will, Michael thought grimly. She had her lover, the necklace. She would never come back, knowing he'd be waiting to wring her neck if she did. He forced a smile. "Well, I can't wait till spring, Sudie. I'm still worried something will happen to her. Now, where in Texas was she going? Did you hear her say?"

Sudie tried to remember the name.

Michael ran a hand across his eyes in frustration. He was wasting his time. It was hopeless. He couldn't just strike out after her. Texas was a big place, and why the hell had they gone there anyway? But he would be damned if he would give up, not when she'd had the nerve to keep his engagement gift. That was a slap in the face he could not tolerate. He was going to find them, even if it meant swallowing his pride by questioning the overseers. One of them might have heard something. Maybe after being fired, Zach could not resist bragging about how he was taking the boss's fiancée with him. According to his mother, the servants were gossiping, so eventually he would find a clue that might point him in the right direction.

"What's a fort, Master Blake?" Sudie asked all of a sudden.

Michael felt hope surging once more. "It's a place

where there are soldiers, Sudie. Why? Did Miss Jacie say she was going to a fort in Texas?"

"Uh-huh."

"Think hard." He tried to keep the excitement from his voice so as not to scare her. Already his mind was whirling, making plans. He would hire some men out of Atlanta to go with him. He wanted strangers, paid to do their job and then forget about it.

"I can't remember," she said, disappointed, because she did want to help him. If he was worried about Miss Jacie, then so was she.

His heart was pounding. "Did she say Fort Worth? Or Fort Clark?" Offhand, those were the only two he could think of.

Sudie had been so proud to think she could help Master Blake bring Miss Jacie home, but now she felt bad not to be able to remember the funny name and could only tell him, "It came before."

Michael mustered all his patience, because he wanted to grab her and shake it out of her. "*What* came before, Sudie?"

"The name of the fort. Feathers."

He ground his teeth together, told himself to keep calm. "Fort *Feathers?*" He swallowed hard, feeling foolish.

"No. It makes me think of feathers. I'm tryin' to remember."

"Think very hard, Sudie. I'll see that you get a real doll," he added impulsively, noticing the toy made of corn shucks that she clutched to her bosom.

"That would be real nice."

A faint squawking sound made them suddenly look out the front door in time to see a small sparrow caught up in the wind before it was swept helplessly away.

"A bird!" Sudie cried, her memory suddenly jolted. "That's it. I heard her say a bird's fort in Texas. What kind of place is that, Master Blake? Is it far away?"

*Bird's Fort.* Michael had no idea where it was, just as he had no idea why Zach had taken Jacie there.

But, for sure, he would find both answer and reason.

Sudie watched him as he bolted out into the rain, disappearing into the swirling gray mist, and wondered if he would remember his promise to get her a real doll.

# 12

*By the time Jacie and Mehlonga* arrived at Fort Smith, Arkansas, at the edge of the eastern border of Indian Territory, Jacie was quite skilled with her knife. It was concealed and strapped just above her right ankle. She could stoop in pretense of lacing her shoe and have the weapon in her hand, ready to strike within seconds. Not only had Mehlonga taught her close combat, but with his guidance she'd become expert at throwing the blade. She could hit dead center any target as far away as thirty feet.

Mehlonga had also endeavored to share all of his knowledge of herbs and potions and was satisfied she could match wits with any shaman or medicine man.

"I will not worry about you," he told her confidently, then added in one of his rare attempts at humor, "only those foolish enough to challenge you."

At a trading post along the way, they had met a Cherokee girl who was married to the owner. Mehlonga persuaded her to sell Jacie one of her own skin dresses, telling Jacie how the deer hide would be much more comfortable than her muslin dress. The girl also included a beaded headband, to keep Jacie's long hair out of her face.

Jacie quickly discovered Mehlonga was right about the native clothes. They were more suitable for long hours of riding, and by then she had learned it made no difference whether those they passed thought they were Indian. But before they arrived at Fort Smith she changed, fearing the soldiers might not be so ready to help her in her quest to reach Texas. With her skin bronzed by long hours riding in the sun, she could easily be mistaken for an Indian.

When finally they reached the fort, Jacie found it difficult to say good-bye to the man who had become so dear to her. "But we must part," Mehlonga told her solemnly. "We have separate paths to follow in this life."

She was close to tears. "I won't ever see you again, will I?"

"In another world. Till then, go in peace." He placed a firm hand on her shoulder and looked deep into her eyes as he said huskily, "Be still and listen, my child, so that when your heart speaks, you will hear it."

Mehlonga had sought and found a young Cherokee working at the post as a scout. His name was Tehlwah, and when Mehlonga asked him to take Jacie to Bird's Fort, he was reluctant but agreed out of respect for the shaman.

There was much trouble in that area, Tehlwah

said. They would have to ride hard and fast, keeping out of sight as much as possible, because the Comanche were on the warpath. Jacie assured him she could keep up.

As Tehlwah predicted, the near two-hundred-mile journey was arduous. Halfway, they traded horses, so they could continue without resting the animals. And though Jacie was exhausted, she dared not ask to stop but was always grateful when Tehlwah did so. But they slept only a few hours at night, because he knew the way even in the dark and wanted to reach their destination quickly so he could retreat from the dreaded Comanche country.

Jacie kept a wary eye as they rode through the rolling and rugged land, by mesquite groves that crowded spiny cactus. The weather was warm, even though back home in Georgia it would be fall, cool and crisp.

Home.

Jacie felt the lump in her throat whenever she thought about the life she had left behind. Despite having an escort she was lonely and afraid.

She was relieved when one evening near sunset they reached the Trinity River at last. Tehlwah pointed upriver and said, "The fort is that way. Perhaps a half day's ride. We sleep now."

He gave her a few strips of beef jerky and she ate ravenously. They had been riding steadily for nearly a week, and jerky, fruit, and nuts had been their diet, and not much of it. Tehlwah had refused to make a fire for cooking small game they could have caught, explaining that smoke would draw the enemy right to them. So Jacie would eat what she was given, then spread her big blanket on the ground and fall asleep at once, despite the hungry rumblings of her stomach.

But that night by the Trinity River, Jacie was so hungry she felt gnawing pains. She commanded herself not to think about food. The trip was almost over. The first thing she planned to do when she got to the fort was eat the biggest meal she could get, because the past few days she'd felt herself growing weaker.

When she slept she dreamed about food. Visions of tasty meals at Violet's table blended into memories of the scrumptious summer barbecues on the sprawling lawns of Red Oakes. She dreamed she was feasting on crispy fried chicken and thick slices of ham and sampling huge helpings of vegetables fresh from the garden—snap beans, butter beans, peas, and tangy sliced tomatoes. Chunks of crispy golden corn bread spilled from baskets, and everywhere there were cakes and pies of every kind.

But it was the hickory pits that made her mouth water, and the smell of the slowly roasting pigs. She could actually feel the heat rising from the glowing embers, blistering her face. So hot. But should it be so hot? She had always heard barbecuing had to be done slowly, so the meat would be done through, tender and . . .

She awoke with a start.

It was not the heat from her delicious dream of barbecue that scorched her face; it was the sun, the midmorning sun, blazing down mercilessly to heat her skin.

Scrambling to her feet, she looked about wildly for Tehlwah but knew instinctively she would not find him. Always they started out while it was still dark. The sun being so high in the sky could mean only one thing—he had abandoned her.

Her first thought was that he might have stolen her horse, but the mare was right where she left her, and she chided herself for being suspicious. Tehlwah had brought her within a few hours' ride of the fort and then for whatever reason had decided not to go farther. He would not steal from the charge of a shaman of his people. So she did not bother to examine the small blanket where her treasures were hidden.

She resolved there was nothing to be done but make it the rest of the way on her own. After a quick bath in the river, Jacie put on her one good dress, brushed her hair till it was dry and shiny, and then set out, following along the banks of the Trinity. Rounding a bend at midmorning, she breathed a sigh of relief to finally see the fort just ahead and urged the horse into a gallop, eager to reach her destination at last.

She waved heartily at the sentry who appeared at the gate. He was wearing a uniform like the ones she had seen back at Fort Smith—blue pants with yellow stripes down the sides tucked into knee-high black leather boots. His shirt was a darker shade of blue, and a yellow bandanna was tied around his neck. The rim of his felt hat shaded his face, but she could still see his astonished expression and how his mustache twitched as his mouth dropped open in surprise at the sight of her.

The sentry had a difficult time concentrating on what Jacie was saying. All he could focus on was the fact that here was a beautiful young woman where women were a scarcity. Her excited babbling about coming all the way from Georgia to find her mother was lost on him as his gaze swept her comely figure.

A real treasure to be sure, he was thinking, snapping back to harsh reality as a soldier of higher rank appeared to push him aside.

After repeating her story to several different soldiers Jacie was ushered across the parade ground and up some steps and into the office of the post commander.

"Actually, I am not the regular post commander," Captain James Logan explained. "But the colonel, unfortunately, is suffering from the gout and has taken to his bed, putting me in charge for the time being. So what can I do for you, Miss Calhoun?" Like every other man at the fort who had seen her, he could not help staring in fascination.

Again Jacie repeated her story, only to realize the man was not listening to a word she was saying as he stared at her with an odd sheen to his eyes and a silly grin on his face. "What is wrong with everyone around here?" she demanded irritably. "I'm trying to tell you why I came all the way out here and you act as if you don't hear me. I came all this way to find my mother, and I need your help. Don't you believe me?" She slammed her hands down on the desk in exasperation.

Captain Logan licked his lips unconsciously and blurted, "Miss Calhoun, I presume you aren't married. Otherwise you wouldn't be traveling alone in such dangerous territory. So would you—" He drew a sharp breath, held it, then plunged ahead. "Would you do me the honor of becoming my wife?"

Jacie reeled as though he had slapped her and could only stutter, "What—what on earth do you mean? Have you lost your mind?"

"No. Quite the contrary, Miss Calhoun, I'm thinking

very clearly by asking you before someone else does. In case you didn't know it, unmarried women are scarcer than hen's teeth in these parts. I'm surprised you haven't already had a proposal between the gate and here. Most women are taken within an hour of arriving at a post, and even the homeliest are married in less than two weeks.

"And you, Miss Calhoun," he added with an ardent smile, "could never be regarded as homely."

She began to squirm uncomfortably in her chair. "This is the most ridiculous thing I've ever heard of. I was at Fort Smith last week and I assure you I received no proposals, for heaven's sake."

"Fort Smith has no shortage of women, I hear. But we do, and I repeat, I'd be honored if you would allow me to court you."

He rose and hurried around his desk intending to drop to his knee before her in formal proposal, but Jacie quickly stood and snatched her hands away as he reached for them. "Captain Logan," she said crisply, "I will thank you to restrain yourself. I have no intentions of marrying you or any other man on this post. I have a fiancé waiting for me back in Georgia."

To cover his feeling of humiliation at her blunt refusal, he sneered and said, "Well, I would like to know what kind of man would allow his fiancée to travel alone. And why didn't he come with you to aid you in your search?"

"I don't want to talk about my fiancé," she replied, ire rising. "Now, are you going to help me find my mother or not?"

He returned to his chair, realizing she was not the sort to be pushed. But he had all the time in the world, because he was not about to let her go. The best thing to do, he reasoned, was stall while pretending sympathy and willingness to assist her. "Forgive me," he said, mustering a tone of sincerity. "Suppose you give me all the details concerning your mother and I'll see what the army can do for you."

Jacie sat down and started over. She was gratified to see he was all business now, making notes of everything she said.

When she was finished, he looked at her in wonder. "You realize, of course, that we have no proof that the woman who ran away from here is your mother."

"You can ask questions. Surely there's someone around who would remember."

"It's possible, but not likely. A story like that would be passed along, and I've never heard it."

"Do you know of any soldiers who might have been stationed here at that time?"

He shook his head. "None of them have been here over two years at the most, including the colonel. But I'll ask around."

"And so will I." She started to rise, but he motioned for her to remain seated. She did so, frowning in anticipation of his repeating his proposal.

"Let me tell you something about our life here, Miss Calhoun. It's stark, and we hunger for any reason to have a social. Not many of the men who are married have brought their wives out here. In fact, there are only ten wives, but they are constantly trying to find ways to break the monotony for all of us. They put on plays and musicales, charade parties, a dance now and then." With a chuckle, he added, "I've even seen my soldiers so desperate for recreation that they dance with each other."

"Well, what does all that have to do with me, Captain?" Jacie asked suspiciously.

"Word spreads quickly, and I'm sure even as we speak, the wives are planning a ball in honor of your arrival. So what I want you to do is concentrate on that and forget about your mother for the time being. Let me make some inquiries. It will take some time, but I can assure you I'll do anything I can to help you find her. How's that?"

"That would be fine," Jacie responded woodenly, "except that the only clothes I have with me are this bedraggled outfit I'm wearing and a buckskin dress. I hardly think your men would want to dance with an Indian."

He laughed. "Don't be so sure. And don't worry about your clothes. Necessity makes our ladies resourceful. They try to stay in fashion by copying Paris gowns from old magazines, only to find themselves sadly outdated when they go back east, but it doesn't matter here. They always manage to look lovely, and I'm sure someone will be able to loan you a gown. Lieutenant Cogdale's wife is about your size, I believe."

Jacie attempted protest. "Thank you, but I didn't come all this way to dance, Captain."

"No one is suggesting that you did, but surely you can reason that if the men feel sympathy for you, they'll be motivated to help you in your plight. You must be compassionate toward them, as well. So how can you deny an evening's pleasure to men like myself, who are starved for the company of a beautiful woman?" He flashed his most beseeching smile.

She knew she had no choice. "Very well, but I want to begin the search right away—"

He bolted to his feet again. "You say it's been ten years since a woman you think might have been your mother has been seen. A few more days won't make any difference, and you need some rest." He held out a hand to her and this time she took it. "I'll have you shown to comfortable quarters and your lunch delivered. By this afternoon you will feel better, and I'm sure the wives will be inviting you to take tea with them so you can get acquainted and make plans for a ball."

Jacie gritted her teeth. The last thing she wanted was to socialize, but if it meant the army's cooperation, so be it.

The buildings of the fort formed a U inside the surrounding wooden fence. The hub of activity—the offices, mess hall and dining room, infirmary, and a small chapel—was situated in the bottom of the U. On one side were the barracks for the unmarried soldiers, and opposite, accommodations for officers and those who were married.

Jacie's escort wore the two yellow chevrons on his sleeve that denoted his rank of corporal. He led her to a sparsely furnished room at the very end of the officers' side of the post. There was a double bed, a washstand, a table with two chairs, and a bookcase with limited reading material. Nonetheless, it was cheery, with yellow ruffled curtains framing windows looking out on the parade ground, and the bed was covered with a quilt of bright red, white, and blue squares.

The corporal apologized about the door being to the rear, rather than in front like the doors of the other rooms, explaining, "This was the arsenal before somebody had sense enough to realize it was dangerous to have it so close by. So a new one was built out back, and the ladies of the post decided to turn this into guest quarters—not that we have many guests," he added with a grin. "Who'd want to visit a godforsaken place like this?"

"I do," she said plaintively, "if it means finding my mother."

"Yeah, I heard about that." He took off his hat in a gesture of respect. Like everyone else who had been avidly discussing it, he was sure Miss Jacie Calhoun had come a long way for nothing. Looking about the room, he asked, to change the subject, "Can you think of anything that might make you more comfortable? The captain said to give you anything you want."

"Information." She looked him straight in the eye, not about to let him go so quickly. "Have you heard the story about a white woman running away from this fort to go back to the Comanche?"

He wished he had, because he thought Miss Jacie Calhoun was about the prettiest girl he had ever seen in his whole life and knew then and there he was in love with her. "The wives will probably have a dance for you. Would you save a place for me on your dance card, Miss Calhoun? I can't remember the last time I held a woman in my arms and never did know one as beauteous as you."

Jacie stifled a sigh. She did not want to hurt his feelings but neither did she wish to encourage him or any other man on the post. "I'll see what I can do," she said, then, aware she'd get no information from him, decided the best thing to do was get rid of him before he, too, proposed. Guiding him to the door, she bid him good day.

She was too excited to be tired, and when the

promised lunch tray came, she ate ravenously, then set out on her own to explore the post and begin her own inquisition of everyone she met.

She started at the livery stable, where she noted several uniformed men who stood away from the others. She could tell by their long black hair and copper-colored skin they were Indians working as scouts. Undaunted by the fierce way some of them looked and the fact that they seemed to be ostracized, Jacie intended to question them as soon as she finished speaking with the regular soldiers milling about. After all, she reasoned, Indians in these parts would probably know more about a white woman living among their kind than the soldiers at the fort.

But Jacie did not get that far.

She did not even have time to question the soldiers, because the moment she was seen leaving her room, it was reported to Captain Logan. Immediately, he dispatched Mrs. Cogdale to fetch Jacie to take tea, also requesting that the ladies of the fort keep her occupied so she'd not be free to roam about.

Jacie was not at all pleased to be squired away, but Amy Lou Cogdale was so sweetly persuasive she could only yield to her invitation.

As the two women walked away, one of the scouts shrank back from the others, drawing his horse with him in preparation for leaving. A Comanche, his name was Gold Elk, and the soldiers of the fort had no more regard for him than they had for any of the Indians employed to track other Indians, but he seemed more civilized than the rest, somehow. Peaceful, someone had observed.

In reality Gold Elk was peaceful, for he was one of Luke's most trusted warriors, and it had been his turn to be at the fort working as a scout in order to overhear any news that might be important. Now he was sure he had heard some, because Luke was going to be very interested to hear about the young woman who was claiming to be the daughter of Sunstar.

# 13

*There were times when Luke* was tempted to go to the commander of Bird's Fort and tell him about the vulnerability of the post.

True, the gate was secured, with sentries around the clock, but a weak point existed to the rear. The fifteen-foot wall made of two-inch-thick upright logs was mostly left unguarded there due to the clear-cut area beyond. It was not considered a threat that Indians would dare swoop down and attack from such an open area, for their approach would be seen by the sentries at the gate as they regularly looked in that direction during the day.

At night, soldiers marched up and down along the wall every so often, alert for any sound or sign of movement.

But what was not known, and what Luke had no intention of confiding to anyone, was that there was a spot in a far corner where someone could slip through by moving aside a log that had been deftly cut toward the bottom. All an intruder had to do was wait for the soldier to make his passing round, then slip inside.

Luke kept the secret for several reasons. Most of all, he liked having undetected entry and exit should he need it, but he also knew how starving Indians had made the passageway in the first place, so they could sneak in and steal food—not enough at one time for it to be missed but enough to satisfy their hunger till they could find other sources.

So it was through the wall that Luke sneaked on the night of the ball held in the white woman's honor. He could have dressed in his uniform and entered through the front gate like any scout, but the soldiers never completely trusted the Indians. They watched their every move, and Luke knew they would never have let him lurk about the dining hall, where tables and chairs had been pushed aside to make room for dancing. If he wanted to get a good look at the woman claiming to be Sunstar's daughter, he knew he would have to call on all his cunning to avoid being detected as he spied on the festivities.

It was a dark night, the moon hidden behind thick clouds as a light drizzle fell.

Luke waited till the soldiers made their rounds, then slipped inside, crouching and moving swiftly, silently along the wall to a rear window. Raising up cautiously, he peered inside. He had spied on socials before and knew what to expect. The ladies, their fancy gowns a rainbow of color, huddled together when they weren't dancing with their husbands, while the men gathered around a table where food and punch was served.

But this night, he saw at once that things were different.

The women were clustered together but not conversing with one another. Instead, they stood almost in a straight line, staring across the room at the menfolk, who were not hovering about the refreshments but instead were gathered around something. *Someone.*

Then he saw her.

Black hair piled in ringlets on top of her head, a few long tendrils curling down to her bare shoulders, she wore a soft pink gown of material he knew was called satin.

Luke's eyes narrowed as he tried to absorb her every feature from such a distance.

She was beautiful, and he could see that every man in the room obviously thought so, too—especially the one escorting her to the dance floor. Luke recognized him as Captain James Logan, a man he was not particularly fond of, known for his hatred and mistreatment of Indians.

Music from a small band drifted through the window to catch on the night wind and serenade the wilderness beyond, but Luke focused only on the woman. He knew she had to be the one Gold Elk was talking about.

"I heard her with my own ears," Gold Elk had told him. "She knew all about how Sunstar came to be with us, how she ran away from the fort to return to us. Now she has come to find her, to take her home."

Luke told him that was crazy, that she had to be looking for someone else. All of Sunstar's family had been killed, something he did not like to think about. But that was long ago, when his father's band was warring against the white man.

Gold Elk had been worried nevertheless. "But if it is so, Sunstar would want to go away with her. Then who would heal our people? Many would die without her, for there is no one else. Our number grows smaller."

Luke had been forced to agree that that was true and reminded him they were needed at camp to help with preparations for winter. Figuring they would have heard if the soldiers were planning any kind of maneuver in their direction during the coming months, he knew it was a waste of time to hang around the fort any longer. Still, he was curious about the woman. So he had instructed Gold Elk and Sharp Knife to return to the camp but warned that they should not repeat the story to Sunstar. Gold Elk gave his word and they were off.

Now, as Luke watched Captain Logan dance the woman closer to the window, he searched for a resemblance to Sunstar but could see none. That didn't really mean anything, because he couldn't remember what Sunstar looked like when she had first come to them so many years ago.

But he was not concerned with the possibility the girl might be telling the truth.

He just wanted to hear her story, then tell her himself that she was crazy and send her on her way before the drums of gossip reached Sunstar's ears.

He settled down to wait.

"You have to marry me," James Logan said fervidly as he held tight to Jacie's arm.

They were outside the door to her room, and he knew protocol was being strained by his standing in the dark with an unmarried lady, but competition for her hand was fierce, and he was desperate for a wife.

"We won't always have to live here," he rushed on. "I hate it myself. I've already asked to be transferred back east. I thought I wanted to make the army my career, but I don't. Not anymore. My father has a store in Boston. We'll live there after I'm discharged and—"

"And I thank you," Jacie cut him off, "but it's out of the question." Her head was still spinning to realize how frantic the men were for wives. She had received five proposals in the last three hours. When she confided her amazement to Amy Lou Cogdale, Amy Lou had assured her it was all quite normal, admitting that her husband had proposed to her within twenty minutes of their first meeting, and she had accepted.

"I'm not going to give up," Captain Logan warned, forcing a jovial tone as he fretted over how to make her change her mind. He reasoned her fiancé back in Georgia could not mean much to her, else she would have insisted he journey with her.

"And neither am I," Jacie replied sweetly. "I'm here to find my mother, not to be courted, Captain Logan. So I would like to talk with you first thing in the morning about how the search is going to be conducted. I'm getting tired of waiting."

James Logan prided himself on being a gentleman as well as an officer, but casting all thought of decorum to the wind, he put his arms around Jacie to draw her close. "The only thing I want to talk to you about is how good I'll be to you if you will marry me."

He attempted to kiss her, but Jacie twisted away. She did not want to anger him, lest he refuse to help her, but neither was she going to allow him to take any liberties. "Sir!" she gasped with proper indignation.

"I'm sorry. I shouldn't . . ." He shook his head, wiped a hand across his brow and stepped back. "Forgive me. . . . and good night." He hurried away, feeling foolish but knowing he would try again tomorrow.

Jacie let herself inside. She started to close and lock the shutters but decided Captain Logan would never dare crawl through the window, and she did want the cool air because the room seemed stuffy.

Undressing and carefully folding the gown Amy Lou had loaned her, Jacie put on a borrowed nightgown and got into bed.

Luke waited until all the lights of the post were out, save for the lanterns burning at strategic points about the parade ground and near the gate.

It was pitch dark behind the row of buildings, but due to his inherent cunning, Luke crept to the guest quarters without making any noise.

Jacie had not fallen asleep at once, tossing and turning as she stewed over her newest dilemma. She would have to keep Captain Logan and all the other would-be suitors at bay, while enlisting their cooperation. It was not going to be an easy task, she knew.

But finally she had dozed off, only to awaken with a start of horror to realize a hand was mashing down on her face. Jacie was sure it was Captain Logan, terror gave way to fury that he could do such a thing as sneak into her room in the dead of night to press his pursuit. She fought and thrashed but was held down on the bed, her angry cries muffled.

"Don't scream," Luke said into her ear. "I won't hurt you."

Jacie panicked to realize it was not James Logan's voice and really began to fight. Luke managed to catch her wrists with one hand and yank her arms above her head as he tried to reason with her. "I won't let you go till you calm down. I told you I meant you no harm. I came to hear the story about your search for your mother."

Hearing that, she froze.

"Will you promise not to scream?"

She nodded.

Cautiously, Luke lifted his hand.

"Who—"

He clamped it down again. "I'll be shot if I'm found in here, damn it. Keep your voice down."

"Who are you?" she whispered as he hesitantly released her.

"I'm a Comanche."

"Dear God—"

He grabbed her again. "How many times do I have to tell you I won't hurt you? Now answer me." He gave her a gentle shake. "Why have you come?"

Jacie was not sure she could ever find her voice again. She could not see his features, but he was almost on top of her, and she could feel his naked chest, the sweep of his long hair against her cheeks. He was a large man, she could tell, with powerful arms.

When she made no move, no sound, he let her go again. One of her hands absently dropped and brushed the rock-hard flesh of his bare thigh. With a stab of panic, she wondered suddenly if he were completely naked but hoped she did not find out. "I came to find my mother. She—"

But then he was clamping a hand across her face again, and she was about to think it had to be some kind of maddening game when light suddenly flooded through the window. At the same instant she heard voices just outside.

"Them damn horses was spooked by a coyote," a man grumbled. "I tell you, there ain't no Indians around here. They don't attack at night. They're scared if they get killed their spirits can't find their way to heaven in the dark."

"Tell that to the captain. He says as long as them horses are stompin' and snortin', we gotta patrol this wall."

"Yeah, well, if you ask me, he don't know what he's doin', not since he laid eyes on that woman. . . ."

The sound faded as they went past, and Luke wondered what could have upset the cavalry horses. Certainly not him. He had been inside the fort for hours. It had to be something else. He only knew that he had to get out of there fast before they started waking up the entire fort to alert everyone to possible danger.

"Listen to me," he said, holding her captive still. "I want to hear about your mother. That is the only reason I am here. I'll come back, but only if you don't tell anyone I was here."

He got to his feet, prepared to bolt and run should she scream.

But Jacie did not scream, for in that brief instant of light, she had seen his face, his piercing but warm eyes, the strong lines of his jaw. Fine features. Handsome, maybe, in a rough kind of way. But besides that, she had sensed in that crystalized moment that he really did not intend to harm her and assured him, "I won't tell a soul. But why do you want to know about her? Can you help me find her?"

"I'm not sure. Not till I hear everything you have to say." Luke had no intention of telling her about Sunstar, even if he discovered she was actually her daughter. He did not want Sunstar to leave their people. Not now. Not when he knew how much good she did with her medicine. This girl was a stranger. "I will be back. We will talk then. But remember. Don't say a word, or you will never see me again."

She reached out for him in the darkness, sensing he was moving away. "Please. Tell me why you want to know. You wouldn't be here if you didn't know something about her. . . ."

But he was gone, as quickly and silently as he had come.

Jacie lay awake for a very long time, pondering the strange visit, daring to hope it meant she would find what she sought.

But she knew she would keep his visit a secret, praying all the while he would soon return.

The moon slipped from behind a cloud, and the renegade Comanche known as Black Serpent motioned for his men to halt. They were far enough away from the fort that they no longer had to move cautiously and quietly. "Next time," he said, "we will leave our ponies farther away. Their ponies heard ours and the guards were alerted."

Culojah, the warrior riding beside him, agreed. "Nothing must go wrong. Tall Tree was able to tell us about the temporary storage of the guns and ammunition in a shed near the hole in the wall, but the soldiers will not leave them there long. We must move fast to take them."

"Yes, but not only for the guns. I want to see Sunstar's daughter for myself." He knew of the raid many years ago when Great Bear's woman, Sunstar, had been taken by the soldiers and how she had fled them to return to the band. He had only been a boy then but remembered well his people's wonder over what Sunstar had done, and how after that they had accepted her as one of them. But he had never cared for her, because she had belonged to Great Bear. He hated the chief and thought him weak for his talk of peace with the white man.

But Black Serpent hated Great Bear's son, called Luke, even more.

"You do not know that it is so," Culojah said. "Tall Tree might not have heard right. We need to get the guns and leave quickly, not waste time on the woman."

Black Serpent glared at him. "I say what we do. Not you."

"I mean no disrespect. But what difference does it make if she is Sunstar's daughter? We left her and the others. Why should we care?"

"Fool," Black Serpent sneered. Daily he was reminded why he was the leader; the others were strong and brave warriors, but they were stupid. "Don't you realize it would be my ultimate revenge on Luke? I will take her and make her my slave. And when Sunstar hears what has happened to her daughter, she will grieve, and her pain will be Luke's. And when I am done with her, I will send her body to their camp, and Sunstar will blame Luke for incurring my wrath and causing me to take vengeance in such a way. And all the others will hate him, too, for making Sunstar grieve. He will be ruined. They will no longer want him for their chief."

Tall Tree nodded. Thinking of it that way made sense. "So we will go back tomorrow night. I will lead the way to the guns. You take the woman."

"Not that soon. The guns will not be moved for several days, but the soldiers will be uneasy for the next few nights. There will be extra guards. We must wait."

Black Serpent touched his face and felt the still open wound from Luke's blade. Now the maidens would not talk of how handsome he was. But Luke would pay. With his life. This, Black Serpent had vowed on the grave of his father. "We will wait," he said fiercely, "but I will have her."

# 14

*"Miss Calhoun, Jacie,* if I may," Captain Logan began, "we can make inquiries among the scouts and other peaceful Indians we come in contact with, but that's really all we can do after ten years."

They were seated in his office, and with barely concealed impatience Jacie had waited for a soldier to serve them coffee and cake before getting to the point of her early morning visit. But now her forbearance was exhausted. "That's not enough. You must send out patrols to look for her."

"Patrols?" He leaned back in his chair and laughed. Then, seeing her icy glare, he said soberly, "I'm sorry. I don't mean to make light of the situation, but you don't understand. We are at war with the Indians. When we see them, we shoot them. It's that simple. We don't go knocking on their tepees asking if they know of a white woman living among them who might be interested in knowing her infant daughter wasn't killed eighteen years ago."

"I am wasting my time here."

"No you aren't. Give us a chance." Give me a chance, he thought, panic rising to think she might leave. "A week, at least. You'll be surprised how news spreads out here. I've already ordered that the scouts be apprised of the situation so they can begin making inquiries among their people. Wait. Please."

"Very well." After all, she reasoned, beneath her perplexity was the smoldering hope that the Comanche would return that night and speak the words she longed to hear—that he knew where her mother was and would take her there.

"Wonderful. And now that that's settled, let's talk of something else." He reminded her of the tea the ladies were having for her that afternoon and how much he was looking forward to the special supper the Cogdales were hosting for just the two of them.

But Jacie did not care. All she wanted was for the hours to pass till she could retire for the night and wait for her visitor. And if he did not come, and a week passed with no encouraging news, then she would have to think of a way to conduct her own search.

She managed to get through the day but by dark was afraid her anxiety would show and arouse suspicion. It was all she could do to make polite small talk during the evening, being careful not to tell the truth about where she was from or mention any names that could be linked to Red Oakes. In the back of her mind she feared that when Captain Logan finally realized she had no intention of accepting his proposal, or of giving up her quest, he might send word back east for someone to come and get her.

Finally, when the hour grew late and she could stand it no longer, Jacie pretended to stifle a yawn and pleaded sleepiness. She could see James's disappointment, and he took his time walking her back to her room. Outside her door, he tried everything to keep her lingering, and finally she had to be almost rude to make him leave.

At last alone, she left the door unlocked, the shutters open, and tensely waited.

But the hours passed, and when the first faint light of dawn crept through the window, Jacie knew the Comanche was not coming and feared he never would.

Another grueling day passed. The officers' wives decided that to entertain Jacie they would present last season's Christmas chorale, even though it was hardly autumn. Jacie gritted her teeth and went to the social, again counting the minutes till she could once more anticipate her nocturnal visitor.

Again she waited, and again she was disappointed as the night wore on and he did not appear. Finally, she left her vigil and moved to the bed, where exhaustion carried her away to a deep sleep.

Luke entered soundlessly. He crept to the bed and stood staring at her shadowy outline. He had not wanted to come. In fact, as she had waited in vain the night before, he had been on his way to the winter camp, convinced it was best to leave well enough alone. She would never find Sunstar. The soldiers would not know where to start looking. Eventually she would give up and go home, which would be best for everyone.

But as he had ridden steadily onward, Luke had felt a strangeness gathering within him. Perhaps it was the idea that the girl might actually be Sunstar's flesh and blood. If that were so, it would explain why he was drawn to her. At least that was what he wanted to think, for he did not like to contemplate the feeling of warmth that had spread throughout him at just her nearness.

He had told himself to keep on going. Not to look back. But by midday, he knew he would never know peace until he heard her out.

Lowering himself gently to the side of the bed, he put his hand over her face once more to stifle any cry from her at being awakened so abruptly. But awareness came fast and she did not struggle. He released her and gently commanded, "Tell me everything."

She was eager to do so but first had a few questions of her own before confiding in a man many would consider savage. "How is it that you understand and speak English?"

"My father sent me to study with missionaries."

"And why do you want to know about my search for my mother?"

"I won't know that until you tell me everything."

And she did so.

When she had finished, Luke was even more torn, because with each word she spoke, he knew she could very well really be Sunstar's daughter.

"Do you know my mother?" She asked him. "Can you take me to her?"

He could hear the desperation in her tone but told himself that Sunstar was better off where she was. In the white man's world, she would be shunned and mistreated. "I know of no one such as you describe," he lied.

Jacie bolted upright. "Then why did you come here? Why did you want to hear my story? Did you want to torture me by making me think you could help me?"

"I promised you nothing," he said defensively, experiencing a heated rush as her hands clutched his shoulders. She was wearing a nightdress of some sort, and the material was thin. He could feel the rise and fall of her bosom, her nipples grazing his bare chest ever so lightly. She was dangerously close and all too appealing.

In an attempt to escape the torture, he fastened his hands on her waist to move her away from him.

Jacie did not notice as she continued her angry tirade. "Then answer me. Why are you here?"

"I'm not sure," he said, more to himself than to her. "Maybe I thought I knew someone. Now I don't think so."

"A white woman?" Hope sprang in Jacie's heart once more. "You know of a white woman held captive by the Indians? Then take me to her, please." Again, she caught his shoulders; later she would be frightened by her boldness but at the moment was not thinking of anything except convincing him to help her.

"A lot of white women have been taken by Indians. You think you can find every one?"

She could not see his taunting sneer but sensed it. "Only the ones who fit the description of my mother."

"You are wasting your time. Go home." He stood. The woman smell of her was arousing emotions he did not want, just then. And there was something else he sensed in her that ignited his desire—spirit.

He could tell she possessed the same strength and spirit that Sunstar had shown once she had come out of her deep depression and embraced his people. Coincidence, he told himself. Two women could have the same traits without being related, and somehow, some way, he was going to make himself believe that these two were not related, because he did not like feeling guilt over keeping them apart.

But Jacie was undaunted. She bounded to her feet, stumbling against him in the darkness. "And you can go to hell if you won't help me," she said hotly. "You sneak in here and get my hopes up, then refuse to help me. Oh, what's the use? Just go. Please."

She turned away, wiping fiercely at her eyes and cursing herself for being so weak as to cry. But it seemed the whole world was collapsing around her. Captain Logan had one thing on his mind—persuading her to marry him. The officers' wives welcomed her as an excuse to have socials. The soldiers didn't care. And now a flesh and blood Comanche had appeared to hear her out and then laughed in her face and told her to go home. It was suddenly all too much.

He spun her about. "I did not mean to hurt you. I am sorry. I shouldn't have come." He cursed the needles of pleasure assaulting him as he felt the softness of her. His naked thighs touched hers through the filmy gown. And was it his imagination or had her nipples become hard as they teased his chest? Could she likewise feel desire?

Jacie's pulse began to race as she wantonly allowed her mind free rein to envision how it would be to succumb to him, to fall into his embrace—dear God! She gave herself a mental shake and moved away from him. What was she thinking?

"If you won't help me, then go," she repeated curtly. "Get out of here."

"I will," he said, equally gruff and lashing out in his own misery over emotions he could not deny. "And if you are smart, you will give up your foolish search. You aren't going to find your mother. You aren't going to find anything except danger."

All the heartache she had endured the past weeks exploded in her next words: "Oh, damn you to hell! Just leave me be. . . ."

But he was already gone.

She flung herself across the bed and allowed the wretchedness of the past weeks and months to burst forth—the heartbreak of learning her parents were not her real parents, the anguish of envisionng her true mother's suffering all these years, confusion about her feelings for Michael, the hardship and exhaustion of the trek west. She had endured it all, only to have a stranger reduce her to sobs of near hysteria.

But when she had cried until there were no tears left, Jacie wiped her face, lifted her chin, took a deep breath, and acknowledged that she suddenly felt much better. She resolved to try and sleep the rest of the night; in the morning, she would make her plans to leave the post despite Captain Logan's protests.

There was a settlement nearby, she had learned, called Fort Worth. She would go there and seek help. She would not give up.

And she would forget all about the Comanche and the strange sensations he had evoked in her.

Finally, she slept.

Deeply.

And when she awoke once more to find a hand

over her face, she thrilled to think he had returned and lay very still to let him know she was neither frightened nor angry.

Black Serpent was puzzled by how the white woman did not fight him. Perhaps she was frozen in fear, like an animal knowing it was about to die.

Slowly, hesitantly, he moved his hand, ready to press down should she try to scream but was further bewildered to hear her excited whisper, "You came back. You're going to take me to her, aren't you? Bless you."

Black Serpent could not believe what he was hearing but then instantly realized what had to be happening—she thought he was Luke. Luke had been here, and now she thought he had returned to take her to Sunstar.

With a surge of triumph, Black Serpent knew abducting her was going to be much easier than he'd thought. "Yes," he murmured in reply, not wanting to say anymore than necessary, lest she discover the truth by his voice. "Come. Now."

"Wait outside. I have to change."

It was all he could do to keep from laughing out loud as he left, this time going through the door.

Jacie knew they had to leave fast, so there was no time to pack what belongings she had.

Shaking with excitement, she took off Amy Lou's borrowed nightgown and reached for her muslin dress. All the while she was thinking how she should be terrified to be stealing away in the middle of the night with a Comanche Indian, but she could not let fear stop her. Not now. She had come too far and reasoned if he had meant her any harm, it would have come to her before now. The only possible motive he could have was to take her to her mother, and that belief gave her all the courage she needed.

Grabbing up the satchel with the blanket and its secrets inside, she rushed out into the night to meet her destiny.

It was nearly dawn when Luke nestled down to sleep among some rocks, hidden from view all around.

He knew he needed to join his people but could not get the woman out of his mind. He told himself it was because he owed it to Sunstar to look out for her if she was indeed her daughter.

Maybe he would never know for sure.

Perhaps it was not important that he did.

He just knew it could do no harm if he stayed close to the fort for a few more days to keep an eye on her.

She was obviously disgusted with the army, having gotten no help from them, so it would probably not take much longer for her to heed the wisdom of his words and give up.

He settled down to rest a few hours before changing into his army scout's uniform and returning to the fort.

# 15

*Jacie knew, too late,* she had made a fatal mistake by daring to trust the Indian.

Grabbed and quickly gagged and bound the instant she stepped out the door, her struggles were futile.

"Ah, you brought me your treasures," Black Serpent gloated as he realized she had a small satchel. He wound the ropes that secured her wrists through the satchel's handle, then threw her over his shoulder.

Terror stabbed Jacie like a thousand needles as he ran with her in the dark.

"Hey, what—"

The startled voice rang out directly in front of them. Instantly there came a sickening thud as blade violated flesh and, with a thick grunt, the soldier who had happened upon them fell to the ground.

His yell, however, had been loud enough for the sentry atop the gate to hear, and he fired his rifle to sound the alarm. At once, shouts rang out amidst the clatter of people running.

Jacie heard other voices speaking in a strange, guttural language she did not understand, which meant more Indians. She was shoved through the hole in the fence, and then slung up on her captor's shoulder again. Jostled and bounced, she continued to try and scream against the foul-smelling gag.

In the scant moonlight she was able to see horses, and men hastily tying things onto the animals' backs, and she knew the Indians had stolen from the fort. Probably weapons, she thought, cringing at the thought of army weapons in their hands.

She was lowered to the ground but left for only a moment before being hoisted to sit astraddle a horse behind the Indian who had abducted her.

Repulsed by the feel of his bare flesh, the sweat and smell of him, she shrank back. He laughed, and when he spoke she knew for sure he was not the one who had first come to her room. "So, you do not want to touch me? That is too bad, because I have no intentions of letting you fall. You are Black Serpent's woman now. Scream and you die," he warned, and removed her gag.

All around them, the others were busy loading the horses. Jacie seized the time to dare plead, "Let me go. The soldiers will be after you and I'll only slow you down."

He pushed against her, his back rubbing against her breasts. At the same time, he squeezed her thigh and said huskily, "You will make me hurry to where I am going so I can see what you look like. If you look as good as you feel, then I have a bigger prize from the fort than guns."

Swallowing against hysteria, Jacie told herself that all she could do was wait for a chance to attempt to get away from him. For the moment, it was best to make him think she was too terrified to do anything. But all the while she pretended to be a whimpering mass of fear, she longed desperately to get her hands on a knife.

Someone called out in the Comanche language, and Black Serpent snapped the horse's reins, setting him into a full gallop.

As they raced through the darkness, Jacie knew she was in terrible danger, for she had overheard stories of Indian atrocities. But even as the horror of her plight coursed through her veins like a mountain river run wild, she was able to keep her senses about her, ready to seize any opportunity of escape.

They rode into a creek, water splashing about them. She could feel Black Serpent's knife against the inside of her right forearm. It was tucked at his waist. All she had to do was twist her bound hands sharply to the side, then jerk backwards, grab the knife, yank it out and plunge it into him. She would have but one chance and one chance only. If she failed, he would kill her.

Over and over, Jacie played the scene in her mind but could envision no other ending except him falling off the horse and taking her with him due to how her arms were tied around him. There was nothing to do but wait until later, when they were alone.

The night wore on. They left the water, and Jacie wondered if they were ever going to stop. At last she felt them slowing just a bit and dared hope they had reached their destination, but great shadows hovering on both sides told her otherwise. They were apparently going through some kind of ravine that seemed to be bordered by rocky outcroppings. Soon it was necessary to ride single file and allow the horses to pick their way over the rocky terrain.

The last thing Jacie wanted to do was fall asleep, but with the horse walking so slowly, almost rhythmically, and her exhaustion, she could not help herself. Her head fell against the Indian's back, and she went limp.

He smiled. It was good that she slept. He was also tired. They would camp soon and count their loot before resting. But he would keep the woman from the others, for he was not about to share. She was his. He would not take her for a wife; he had more pride than Great Bear and would never make a white woman his wife. She would be his slave, do his bidding, and he would teach her a thousand ways to please him in his blankets.

At last the Indians, outlaws from their own people, arrived at the campsite, where they could feel safe. Situated among rocks, there were many little caves and overhangs where they could take refuge. Black Serpent untied Jacie's wrists, grinning as he whipped about to grab her in his arms and take her with him as he dismounted. With the sun having leapt from the horizon he could see her face and noted she did look something like Sunstar, but he would think about that later. His comrades were shouting happily to each other as they began to unpack their pillage from the fort. Rifles, pistols, ammunition; it was a bountiful harvest.

Hoisting Jacie over his shoulder again, Black Serpent carried her to his favorite place—a big cave in the face of a rock, far away from the others. He had taken women there before and known many hours of pleasure.

As he lay his newest prize on the ground, he paused to run his hands over her breasts in delicious anticipation. "Soon," he promised, "I will have you again and again."

Fiercely, bravely, she dared to plead, "Why have you done this to me? If you are a Comanche, I beg you to hear me out and help me. My mother—"

"Your mother," he spat. "Forget your mother. Forget everything about your old life. You are mine now, I say."

He walked away, and she thought it just as well, knowing it was useless to beg. Now she focused on the fact that he had not retied her, probably thinking she was too scared to think of running out into the wilderness.

She started to rise up to investigate her surroundings, but then she heard someone coming and lay very still, pretending to have fainted. Watching through lowered lashes, she saw one of the Indians throw her satchel down and walk away. No doubt he had looked inside but found only the blanket and decided there was nothing worth stealing.

When all seemed safe, she crept out to peek over the rocks and watch as the Indians danced around, whooping and hollering and waving some of the newly stolen guns. She hoped to spot the one who had come to her earlier, wanting revenge against him as well for making her believe she was in no danger, but she did not see him.

One of them was searching through a box and suddenly let out a shriek that drowned out all the others. He held up a bottle, and as the Indians began to push and shove to get at it, Jacie saw they had found a cache of whiskey. Perhaps a soldier had hidden it, sneaking drinks when no one was looking. But it made no difference how liquor had gotten into the arsenal, all Jacie knew was that now the Indians had something that would make them really crazy and even more dangerous.

She watched as the bottle was snatched back and forth between them, each man gulping long and deep. The merriment continued, and Jacie settled back in the cave to wait. As she did so, she contemplated her situation. It was grave, but she had a chance, and Mehlonga had taught her that as long as there was a chance to survive, then there was hope of succeeding.

She was certain the Indians would not be awake for long. They had been awake all night, riding hard, and with their senses numbed by the whiskey they were guzzling they would sleep deeply and long. If she could slip away without being seen and take one of the Indian ponies, she could be far, far away before they woke up and discovered she was gone.

For the time being she was not going to worry about which way to go. Mehlonga had taught her how to read the stars for direction, and she knew Fort Worth was up the Trinity River at the confluence of the Clear and West forks. When she was sure she was not being followed, she would head that way.

The sounds of revelry grew louder.

Jacie chanced another look and saw that Black Serpent was right in the middle of it all, slapping his hand against his mouth and emitting a strange, yodeling kind of whoop. He stomped about in circles, lifting his legs up and down frantically, knees almost reaching his chest.

She took a good look at his costume, as well as those of the others. Mehlonga had told her as much as he knew about Comanche garb—the trouserlike garment they wore, edged with beads and nickel rivets, was called leggings. And the apronlike cloth with fringes and tassels at the end was a breechclout. The faces were painted red, and their hair was parted in the center and braided on each side, with a scalplock at the top of the head. A few had a single yellow or black feather stuck in their scalplocks, but she saw that Black Serpent had donned a headdress with buffalo horns.

She counted sixteen Indians dancing and decided Black Serpent was definitely the most ominous-looking of the bunch. Ever so often he would whip his knife from his breechclout and make vicious motions as though striking out at an invisible enemy. He was also large, with a barrellike chest, shoulders like shank hams, and forearms like hocks. The long jagged scar on his face made him appear even more fearsome, and Jacie cringed to think of him touching her. She had to get away, she thought, biting into her lower lip. Dear God, she just had to.

Finally, their dancing grew less spirited. A few were stumbling, and one fell flat on his face. But Black Serpent was still jumping about, apparently able to hold his liquor better than his followers. Holding a bottle, he continued to drink.

Soon, everyone else had passed out. Black Serpent staggered forward a few steps, lifted the bottle to his mouth, then apparently changed his mind as he belched and hiccupped, trying again to walk, lurching from side to side.

"Just hang on to that bottle, my horn-headed friend," Jacie muttered under her breath as she parted the leaves of a shrub to see him coming her way. "Just hang on to it, and don't drink it all, because I've got something to make it a little more potent."

She was clutching the pouch containing the morning glory seeds. She had already beaten them into a powder with a flat rock, but there had not been time, or facility, to soak them or strain them. She would just have to find a way to get them into the bottle Black Serpent was carrying—and pray he was so drunk he would not know what he was drinking.

# 16

*Black Serpent stumbled* into the clearing, which was ringed on three sides by rock.

Jacie was trapped.

She had backed as far as she could, holding the powdered seeds behind her, wondering frantically how she was going to get them into the bottle. He was still holding on to it, a bit of liquid sloshing around in the bottom.

He looked her up and down hungrily, his tongue darting across his lips. "I did not at first want to learn the white man's language," he said, voice slurring. "But now I am glad, because I can tell you how to please me." He set the bottle on a ledge and commanded, "Take off your clothes."

She could only stare at him in horror.

His hand snaked out to clutch her throat. "Do as I

say or I will punish you with pain as you have never known."

Jacie squirmed in his grasp, hardly able to speak. "Don't do this. Have mercy, please . . ." she whispered.

A dark, brooding hatred flashed in his black eyes. "Mercy?" he echoed with deadly menace. "When have your people ever shown mine any mercy?" He yanked her against him, and she could feel the hard heat of his chest. She fought to keep her hand behind her as he bent her head back. Her eyes locked on the red, raw scar that swept across his cheek, and she could not control the shudder of revulsion that shot through her.

With a shriek, he slapped her. "So you cannot stand the sight of my face? My scar sickens you? Perhaps you would like one of your own, then you will know what it is like."

She had staggered from his blow, but he grabbed her again, only to slam her head back against the rock so hard she felt a dizzying pain and had to fight to hang on to consciousness. From out of nowhere came the knife; he held it ominously above her. Jacie closed her eyes and prayed as she had never prayed before, sure that any second she would feel the cold steel slashing into her flesh.

"Answer me!" he screamed. "Would you like a scar so you will not find me ugly?"

Jacie opened one eye and later wondered how she could have been so bold as to taunt, "I would find you ugly without a scar, damn you."

He laughed at her bravado and returned the knife to his belt. "No. You would find Black Serpent the most handsome warrior of the Comanche, like the girls who crept into my tepee night after night. They taught me well, as I will teach you. And it will make no difference that you cannot bear to look upon my face. You will look upon my body, instead, for it is still glorious as a man's should be. And I will look upon you. All of you."

Jacie's arm ached terribly, bent back against the rock, but still she clung to the seeds, hoping he would pass out. His eyes were getting bleary, and he seemed to be having difficulty staying on his feet.

"You want me to tame you, little she-wolf?" he taunted. "Is that what you want? I have ways to make you obey me and no one cares about your screams . . ." He trailed off, suddenly unable to ignore any longer the annoying pressure from all he had drunk. He would have to relieve himself before taking his pleasure.

Spinning about, reeling as he did so, Black Serpent turned his back on her, directing himself toward a clump of bushes as he lifted his breechclout.

Jacie knew she had but one chance. Snatching up the bottle, she opened her hand and released the powder. She gave it a quick shake, wiped the residue from the rim, and set it back down.

He turned back around, annoyed to feel so heavy-headed, so sleepy. Perhaps another swallow of the firewater would make him feel better. But where had he left it? The world was spinning. And then he saw the bottle. With a grunt of satisfaction, he lifted it to his mouth.

Jacie felt an excited rush.

He drained the bottle, then sent it crashing against the rocks. "Now I will have you," he yelled, beating on his bare chest with his fists.

He lunged, and she ducked and tried to dart under his arms but was not quick enough. Grabbing her hair, he yanked her back, but she fell against his legs, knocking him off balance, and he went down, taking her with him. He caught her wrists, rolling to the side to pin her beneath him. "You will beg to die before I am through with you, bitch," he vowed with a snarl of menace. "And you will never refuse me again."

He was all over her, fingers digging, mauling, tearing at her clothes. She screamed again and again, horror searing wherever he touched. She managed to free one hand and brought her nails raking across his cheek. With an oath, he whipped out the knife to press against her throat and threatened, "I will take you after you are dead if you keep fighting me."

Jacie caught her breath and held it, her struggles ceasing. She had put a heavy dose in the bottle but had no idea how long it would be before it took effect. Combined with the whiskey she hoped it would work more quickly than usual and dared believe her hunch was right when she saw his eyes begin to roll back in his head.

He dropped the knife, his hands clawing first at his throat, then his stomach, as he made a thin whining sound. Then he dropped to his knees, still holding his belly, and pitched forward onto his face.

Jacie wasted no time. Grabbing up her satchel along with Black Serpent's knife, she made her way quickly down from the rocky alcove and on past the other Indians, who appeared to be sleeping deeply.

She went to where the ponies were tethered and selected a pinto that looked a bit stronger than the rest, leading him a short distance before throwing a blanket over his back. Tying on the satchel, she walked him farther from the camp before mounting and riding away.

The sun was high in a cloudless sky and seemed

to melt into a shapeless bed of golden flame as it stretched to touch the faraway mountains. Jacie shielded her eyes and tried to figure out where she was. The Trinity River ran from northwest to southeast; she knew because she had asked Tehlwah its course when they had made camp that last night. She did not know why she wanted to know, except that since leaving home, she had the need to have some idea, at all times, of where she was. It made her feel less apprehensive, somehow, about constantly being in new surroundings.

Jacie made a mental note of when they had crossed the river, estimating they had ridden an hour or more after doing so before entering the shadowed ravine. She had dozed after that but guessed it had been another hour's ride before they got to the camp. Several times she had glanced upward to find the north star and suspected that they had gone through the ravine to keep parallel to the river so they would not pass directly by the settlement of Fort Worth, which was where she wanted to go.

Her stomach rumbled. Many hours had passed since she had eaten at the fort. She was weak and weary but plodded onward, knowing that when the Indians finally woke up to find their leader drugged and sick, they would come after her. She had to get to the settlement as fast as possible or they might overtake her—and God help her if they did.

Back in Georgia, Jacie knew, signs of autumn would be everywhere, the hills and ridges burning with red and yellow and orange as the leaves offered a spectacular farewell before falling to the ground. But here the earth shimmered with waves of heat. Her dress, soaked with sweat, clung to her, and her hair hung limp and damp. She could feel her skin burning from the relentless sun.

She tried to push thoughts of food from her mind but wondered how long she could go without proper sustenance. She felt herself growing weaker as the day wore on, and it was getting harder and harder to stay on the pony's back. She would feel herself slipping, would be about to fall but would mercifully rally at the last instant to wrap her fingers in the pony's mane and haul herself back into position.

To get her mind off eating and the heat, and the seriousness of her situation, Jacie tried to turn her thoughts to Michael, and how perhaps she should have told him everything. No. She shook her head firmly. She had to do it her way. Still, she drifted to think how protected he made her feel when he held her in his arms, and the sweetness of his kisses, and what a comfort it had been to hear him vow that she would never have to worry about anything ever again in her whole life once they were married. He would always take care of her. She'd not have to worry her pretty little head, he would laugh and say, because he would do everything for her. To be sheltered and cherished, that would be her life as Mrs. Michael Blake.

Jacie could not help laughing aloud—a weird sound in the barren wilderness—to wonder what Michael would think if he could see her right then. She had journeyed all the way from Georgia to Texas with a Cherokee medicine man only to be abducted by a Comanche Indian and threatened with rape and death. Now she was weak and racked by hunger and, God help her, completely lost. But she was still alive, undaunted and determined to survive. Hardly the image of a genteel planter's wife in ruffles and lace. Michael would be amazed. And surely he would be impressed by her courage. She was certainly impressed with herself, and when it was all over, she would tell him and describe it all in detail, and he would know her for the strong woman she was and surely respect her all the more for it.

Her head began to loll. It was getting harder and harder to sit on the pony. He was moving slowly. She dared not urge him into a faster gait for she could never hold on then. She could see green in the distance, a cluster of trees. If she could make it there, she would rest, if only for a little while. But then she felt herself falling again. This time, she was unable to rally in time to hold on . . . she was unconscious by the time she hit the ground.

Luke knew something had happened when he came in sight of the fort. The gates were wide open and a patrol was riding in, met by one headed out. He could see a hubbub of activity inside and could actually feel an air of tension all around him.

Riding toward the departing soldiers, he recognized Sergeant Major Ward Stackhouse and hailed him to ask what was going on.

"Damn Injuns made a hole in the southeast corner of the fence and broke in to raid the arsenal. They got away with a hell of a lot of guns. Ammunition, too."

Luke's teeth ground together to think of what it meant. "Any idea which tribe was responsible?"

"Comanche," Stackhouse said flatly, aware some of his men were casting hostile glances at Luke.

While they knew he was a good scout, they were wary of him, especially now, after what had happened.

"How can you be sure?"

"Hell, Luke, I know a Comanche when I see one. We caught one as he was scrambling through the hole."

"Is he still alive?"

"No. Had to shoot him. He wouldn't surrender. Kept swinging a tomahawk. He's Comanche, all right. And it's worse than just stealing, by the way," Stackhouse added. "A soldier was killed. Stabbed."

Luke reined his horse in the direction of the fort as Stackhouse called out, "Hey, aren't you gonna ride with us to try and track them devils?"

"You won't find them, and I've got business to tend to."

Stackhouse was about to tell him that a woman had been taken, but Luke rode away before he could do so.

Luke hurried on to the fort, hoping the Indian's body had not been disposed of. It hadn't, and his suspicions were confirmed when he recognized one of the young bucks who had chosen to follow Black Serpent. Now he knew beyond a doubt who was responsible for all the trouble.

Hearing Luke was at the fort, Captain Logan sent for him to tell him he wanted him to head up the next patrol going out. "You know those bastards better than anyone else. They're your people. You know what to look for."

Luke frowned. If he was off on patrol, he couldn't keep an eye on the woman. Maybe last night's trouble had scared her into wanting to leave. "I hear there is a white woman here who thinks her mother is living among the Comanche."

Logan paled to think how it was bad enough that under his command the fort had been robbed by Indians without the added humiliation of having a young lady abducted. With marks like that against him, he would never get his transfer back east and would likely wind up being sent to the least desirable post in the west. Maybe he would even be stripped of his rank. He didn't want to think about it and had made up his mind, during the tortured hours of the night, to whitewash the situation as much as possible, but he saw no reason to discuss it with an Indian, for heaven's sake. "That's no concern of yours. I gave you orders. Be ready to move out with the next patrol."

Luke noticed the captain's unease. "I want to know what is to be done with her. Is the army going to help her in her search?"

"Hell, no!" Logan cried, exasperated, then tested the lie he had conjured to paint a less grim picture of what might be considered the dereliction of his duties. "The Comanche themselves are going to help her. She went with them willingly last night." He knew that could not be so but was clutching at straws.

Luke knew it too but felt as if he'd been slammed in his gut to hear she was now in the hands of Black Serpent. "I want to know her name," he said through tightly clenched teeth.

Logan did not like the almost maniacal gleam in the scout's black eyes and decided maybe if he answered him, he would leave. And what difference did it make if he told him, anyway? "Her name is Miss Jacie Calhoun."

"And what makes you think she would go with the Comanche willingly?"

"Oh, hell, I don't know. All I do know is that she didn't scream or make any sound. Nobody heard anything till the guard that got stabbed hollered out. But all that's got nothing to do with you. Now get out of here. You've got your orders." Logan bolted to his feet and pointed to the door. If the bastard made one move toward him, he would draw his gun and shoot him.

"You don't think she went with them willingly at all," Luke said quietly, coldly, all the while wondering if the woman could actually have been lured out after mistaking Black Serpent for him. But Logan could not know that. He was just trying to make the situation less embarrassing personally.

He turned on his heel and left.

Logan did not protest, because as badly as he needed Luke to try and track down the Indians, the expression on Luke's face had chilled him to the very marrow of his bones.

He was glad to have him go his own way.

# 17

*Jacie did not want to wake up,* but something was nudging her foot, hard. She forced her eyes to open, then instantly shrank back in horror.

The man was framed by the setting sun, a flaming red and gold halo streaming around him. He stood with fists at his hips, legs wide apart as he stared down at her.

Horrified to think Black Serpent had found her, his name instinctively escaped Jacie's lips, but when the man spoke, she knew it was her original nocturnal visitor.

"I am not Black Serpent. My name is Luke. And you needn't be afraid. I won't hurt you."

Her panic lessened but only a little, because she was still scared out of her wits. She thought of the knife she had stolen from Black Serpent, which she had tied to her ankle, but realized he must have seen it, for her skirt was tangled up about her knees.

He stepped to one side, and the sun was suddenly blinding in her face. She raised her hands to shield her eyes, then held them out to fend him off as he dropped to one knee beside her. "Don't touch me," she said hoarsely, angrily. "This is all your fault, anyway. If I hadn't thought Black Serpent was you, I'd never have walked out that door so trustingly."

"I can't help it if you mistook someone else for me. Now drink. You need water." He raised her head and held a canteen to her lips. She drank eagerly, but he withdrew after she had taken only a few sips. "Too much will make your stomach hurt. Now tell me how you escaped."

Suspiciously, she said, "You're one of them. Why should I tell you anything?" Then she noted how he was dressed. Though bare-chested, he wore army trousers tucked into knee-high boots. His hair hung all the way to his shoulders. An Indian in stolen clothes, no doubt. "Did you kill a soldier to get that outfit?" she asked sharply.

"Get something straight, Miss Calhoun. I'm not one of Black Serpent's followers. I'm an army scout . . . sometimes. And you can trust me. I swear it."

"And how is it that you know my name?"

"I asked Captain Logan. But that's not important. I want to know how you were able to get away from Black Serpent."

"There was whiskey in some of the boxes they stole from the fort. They got drunk and passed out." She was not about to confide she had drugged Black Serpent. That was her secret, and just because this man said he could trust her didn't mean she would do so.

"So you stole a pony and rode away," he said, admiring her courage.

"Yes, I rode all day, but I must have passed out from hunger and the heat. It's a wonder they didn't find me before you did."

"I've seen Black Serpent and his friends when they drink too much. They probably don't feel like coming after you and may not bother anyway, since they got what they were really after—guns and ammunition. But I'm not taking any chances." He allowed her a few more sips of water, then stood and held out his hand to her. "We need to get out of here." He felt sure Black Serpent had not told her about Sunstar, or she'd have been screaming to high heavens, demanding to be taken to her.

Jacie raised up on her elbows. "I don't want to go back to Bird's Fort. Captain Logan isn't doing anything to help me find my mother. I'd rather go to Fort Worth."

"I'll decide what to do with you later when we get a chance to talk. Right now, we're getting out of here."

Jacie allowed him to help her up but stood her ground when he started walking toward his horse, a huge white stallion. "Mister, I can't see that we've got anything to talk about. You know why I came here in the first place, but you don't want to help me, so the least you can do is point me in the right direction."

He turned to sweep her with an amused gaze of scrutiny. She had spunk. Spirit. He admired that. Another woman probably would not have managed to escape Black Serpent in the first place, much less stand up to a stranger in the wilderness. But he was losing patience. He had seen the Indian on horseback watching from a distant rise and thought he recognized him as one of Black Serpent's men. He had turned back, no doubt to report what he had seen, and Luke wanted to get the hell out of there. If they caught up with him, he would have to face a dozen men by himself, and he had to consider the safety of the woman.

"Well are you going to help me get to Fort Worth or not?" She was annoyed by the way the corners of his mouth quirked in a smile, as though he found her an amusing child. "If not, then I'll manage on my own somehow."

She looked around for her pony and saw that he had maneuvered himself up to a rocky ledge to nibble at a patch of wildflowers. She was relieved to see the satchel was still tied on, and she lifted her skirt to climb up, then saw that her knife was no longer strapped to her leg.

In response to her accusing glare, Luke said, "I figured it was asking for trouble letting you keep it."

"I'd like it back, please. If I'm going to be traveling alone, I need some protection."

"You would only hurt yourself." He clambered up quickly to grab the pony's reins and bring him back to level ground before adding, "Besides, you aren't going to be traveling alone. Like it or not, you're coming with me."

"And just what do you plan to do with me? I told you, I'm not going back to Bird's Fort."

"And I never said that's where I was taking you. Now are you going to get on your pony or do you want me to throw you on him?"

He would, too; she could tell by the smug way he

was watching, waiting for a chance to make good his threat. She swung up onto the pony's bare back. "Some soldier you are," she lashed out at him, "refusing to help a lady."

"I never said I was a soldier, and I haven't made up my mind that you're a lady."

"I'm very much a lady, but the behavior of others forces me to forget that sometimes. You needn't concern yourself with me any longer. Good day." Jacie dug her heels into the pony's flanks and popped the reins to send him into a swift gallop. She would find her own way, by God.

Ahead loomed mountains, in between were rock formations. If she could get far enough, maybe she could hide from him, and—her heart turned over at the sound of the thundering hooves coming on strong. She was a fool to think the little pony could outrun the stallion.

In seconds Luke was upon her, reaching out to grab the reins and snatch them away from her, bringing both mounts to an abrupt halt. "You try that again and I'll hog-tie you and throw you across his back. Now just calm down, because I don't have time for your tantrums."

Her mouth twisted with scorn. "I'm not going anywhere with a damn heathen Indian—"

"You're too pretty to be using such language." He grinned, which only further infuriated her. "And I'm not a heathen. I'm very well educated, thank you."

"Black Serpent spoke English. Am I supposed to believe he's educated?"

He laughed. "I taught him. I also learned Spanish at the mission school, and I speak the languages of all the Plains Indians. I consider myself civilized and peaceful, like the rest of my band. Forget Black Serpent. He's no longer one of my people. That's all you need to know for now."

Jacie was annoyed by his arrogance and pushed aside any admiration she might have felt to discover how learned he was. "You still haven't told me why you won't help me."

Still holding her reins, he kneed his horse into a gentle trot, keeping the pony right beside him. "I *am* helping you."

"You refuse to take me where I want to go."

"I might change my mind later." He noticed the lavender flowers blooming among the rocks they passed and thought out loud, "Your eyes are the same color."

Jacie could have told him how she came by her name but didn't. It was none of his business. Besides, she was beginning to fear she was no better off than when she was with Black Serpent, and that she must again be ready to seize any chance of escape.

Luke was struck to think how there might actually have been a survivor of that long-ago massacre; the girl could have been the infant for whom Sunstar's milk was intended. But there was no time to ponder the situation now.

He took a strip of dried buffalo meat from a saddlebag and gave it to her. "This will have to do till we make camp, and then I can fry up some bacon and beans. You're nothing but skin and bones. I don't know why they even wanted you, but at least they led me to you."

He nodded skyward with a crooked smile, and

Jacie also looked up to see large gray birds circling in a giant sweeping pattern. "Vultures," he said.

Jacie shuddered and began to chew the buffalo meat with a vengeance.

He gave her back the reins, confident she would not be so foolish as to try to outrun him again.

When they came to a stream, Luke led them down the middle for quite a distance. Finally leaving the water, Jacie watched as he used a knife, not hers, she noted, to hack two large branches from a scrub brush, securing one to each horse's tail. She saw that any tracks made in the dirt and sand were obliterated by the sweeping motion.

"That's smart," she said, as though she really didn't think so. "But tracks won't be seen at night anyhow."

"They would be in the morning, and that's when Black Serpent will begin his search. If he got as drunk as I think he did, he'll spend today screaming with his head pounding." She felt like telling him it was probably worse than that but decided not to.

They rode for a time in silence, layered veils of pink and orange misting around them as the sun sank lower in the west. Then shadows began to creep from rocks and brush and soon they were surrounded by darkness. "We're going to get lost," Jacie said uneasily. "How much farther do we have to go?"

"Indians don't get lost, and you'll know when we get there."

She knew he was being sarcastic and could not resist snapping at him. "You say you want to talk to me before you decide if you'll help me, but all I get from you is foolish banter. Can't you be serious?"

"Being serious sometimes means being unhappy,

something I do my best to avoid, but if you insist, start talking and I will try to restrain myself."

Though she was not about to let him know it, Jacie found him fascinating, despite how vexing he could be. She could tell he was quite intelligent and she also found him attractive—but not like Michael. Michael was charming and polished, never a hair out of place, except for the one unruly curl forever toppling onto his forehead, she recalled fondly. Michael was handsome in an almost pretty kind of way, with long, dusty lashes framing incredibly soft blue eyes, lips that were perfectly sculpted, smooth skin with never a shadow of a beard. Always impeccably groomed and manicured, he was a gentleman through and through. Luke, by comparison, was ruggedly handsome. She found herself drawn to his dark, almost black eyes and the penetrating way he could look at her as though seeing all the way inside to know what she was thinking.

His body was that of a warrior, hard-muscled, rawboned, trained for combat and survival. He probably had the cunning of an animal and feared neither man nor beast, and though she had known him but a short while, Jacie realized she felt safe—safe from others. But she was still leery of what he planned to do with her once they bedded down for the night.

Suddenly she was swept with a little tremor of guilt to realize that the first time she had thought of Michael since Luke found her was to compare the two. Something told her it would be best if her time with Luke went swiftly. She actually found his raw and rugged good looks vastly appealing and chided herself for such nonsense. He was the enemy. Michael was her fiancé. The sooner she completed her mission and returned to Georgia, the better.

She decided to try and come to some understanding with him. "You said you wanted to talk before deciding what to do with me, and since this night seems to go on forever, why not do it now?" she asked waspishly.

"I thought you might want to wait till you've eaten and had some rest."

"I'll rest easier if you promise to take me to Fort Worth tomorrow. Now just what is it you want to know?"

"You told me you had reason to believe your mother lives with the Comanche, but I have a feeling you didn't tell me everything."

"Are you sure you don't know of her?" she asked suspiciously.

Luke braced himself, knowing he had to be careful what he said, because more and more it looked as though she could be Sunstar's child, and he was not about to reveal that to her. "A lot of white women have been taken by Indians. Most of them were killed. What makes you think she would still be alive?"

She had told him about her mother running away from the fort but not how she came by the information. "A man who was once a Texas Ranger heard about it, and when he was passing through Georgia he told my aunt."

"You say that was over ten years ago. Why is there just now a search for her? Why hasn't someone come before now?"

Jacie did not want to confide Violet's deception but saw no other way. "My aunt didn't tell me till right before she died. Till then, everyone thought I was her daughter, including me. Even her husband thought I was his child. I know it sounds crazy, but she had her reasons, I suppose. All I know now is that I have to find my real mother and let her know I wasn't killed with the rest of my family. I believe the only reason she ran away from the fort to return to the Indians was because she felt she had no other world to go back to, but now she does, and I have to tell her that. Don't you see?" She looked at him beseechingly but could not see his face in the darkness.

Luke did not know what to say. If the two were actually mother and daughter, he knew he had a lot of thinking to do before deciding to allow them to meet.

"Have you heard of a woman like that?" Jacie prodded.

"I hear many things, but there is nothing I can tell you." He reined in his horse. "We will camp here for a while."

She wanted to ask him more, but he was dismounting, and she quickly did the same. There was scant light, but she could see yet another rushing stream with rocky banks. He pointed to a screen of scrub brush. "There is a hollow in the rocks beyond those bushes with room for the horses. We will take them there with us to sleep for the night after they've had water and grazed a bit. You go and tend to your personal needs while I make a fire." He took her knife from where he had tucked it into his belt and held it out to her. "There are snakes around that give no warning before they strike. Take this—though I doubt you know how to use it."

"Keep believing that," she muttered under her breath as she went into the bushes.

When she returned, a fire was burning. He had taken a pan from his saddlebag, and the smell of bacon sizzling made her mouth water.

She sat down but kept her distance. "I want you to know I'm grateful to you for helping me hide from Black Serpent and feeding me but I have to say you seem to enjoy making me miserable by not helping me in my search for my mother."

"Maybe I am helping you avoid more misery."

"And what is that supposed to mean?"

"If I did know of a white woman who fit your description of your mother and I took you to her, it might only cause both of you grief."

"But you'd have to give us a chance to find out. You would have to."

"I did not say I knew of such a woman for sure," he hedged. "I only said if I did, it would be cruel to get both your hopes up for nothing."

There were no plates, and Luke took his time laying the bacon on a rock to cool. "Eat. Then we will sleep. We are both tired."

Jacie bit back the urge to beg him to tell her more, positive that he knew something he was not telling her but felt it best to bide her time and coax it from him bit by bit.

She ate ravenously, and so did he. Then he left and returned with her satchel. "In case you need anything inside," he said, setting it at her feet.

"As a matter of fact I do." Jacie opened it, reached inside for the baby blanket, and took out the locket and handed it to him. "Look at this and tell me if there is a resemblance to any white woman that you know."

Curiously, Luke stared at the locket. He had never seen anything like it. Jacie opened it for him. Then, seeing what she explained was called a daguerreotype, he had to admit to himself it did look something like Sunstar and definitely resembled Jacie.

"That is my mother. Her name is Iris Banner. She looks like me, doesn't she?"

"I suppose." He closed the locket with an angry snap and gave it back to her. Sunstar's name had once been Iris, and now he felt a burning pain inside to think he might lose her. And it was not fair. She'd had a chance at freedom once and refused. Now this upstart of a girl was going to tear her life apart, tear apart the lives of all his people. They loved Sunstar, and they needed her. If Sunstar left with Jacie, it would be like going to live with a stranger. And she would go, Luke was certain of that. She would feel bound to do so, because Jacie was her own flesh and blood. He would just have to protect her from herself, he decided fiercely. He would not let her make such a fatal mistake as to try and return to the white man's world now. She had been Comanche too long.

He started to turn away, but Jacie reached out and caught his arm. "Listen to me, please," she said in desperation. "Awhile ago you said *if* you knew a white woman. I think you do know one. Please tell me about her. We have a right to know each other, Luke—"

"Yellow hair," he cut her off. "The white woman I have heard of has yellow hair. Not black. And she is too young to be this woman." He nodded at the locket, which Jacie clutched with trembling fingers. "So there is no need to take you to her. Now make your bed and sleep."

Jacie stared after him as he disappeared into the shadows. She was disappointed that he knew nothing of her mother, but grateful to realize he had no illicit intentions toward her. Perhaps he had a bit of gentleman in him after all, which gave her hope she might eventually persuade him to take her where she wanted to go.

Curling up on her blanket, she tried to dream of Michael . . . but thoughts of the Comanche known as Luke kept getting in the way.

# 18

*Jacie's first thought on waking* was that she had been deserted. Luke was nowhere to be seen. The campfire was a pit of cold black ashes. Her pony was still tethered nearby, but not the stallion. Suddenly she felt more helpless than when she had escaped Black Serpent. At least then she could hope to eventually stumble onto the river and follow it back, but now she had no idea where she was.

Wilderness surrounded with sandy ridges and rock formations amidst clumps of sagebrush, cactus, and stretches of saw grass, some of it knee-high. It was early morning, with not a cloud in the dazzling blue sky, which meant the heat would be unbearable by midday. She wondered which direction to take, all the while fearing the same thing would happen—she would succumb to exhaustion and faint, only this time there might not be anyone to find her before the vultures did. She also had nothing in which to carry a supply of water, no canteen, as Luke had.

The more she aimlessly walked about stewing over her plight, the angrier she became. If he had planned to desert her, why had he brought her so far from where he found her? Why didn't he just leave her be? He could claim to be civilized all he wanted, but to forsake a woman in the wilderness was cold and remorseless.

"Savage," she muttered, pounding the air with clenched fists as she circled about the clearing. "No better than a wild animal. Dirty, rotten savage. I hope the vultures get him."

"They won't."

She whirled about to see him crouched on a rock above her, dark eyes twinkling, his face spread in a wide grin of amusement.

"Unlike some people I know, I don't get lost." He dropped to land flat-footed in front of her.

Flustered, Jacie covered her embarrassment with indignity. "You scared me to death. I thought . . ." She trailed off as she realized he was no longer dressed in army trousers and boots. Instead, he wore the garment known as a breechclout and nothing else. His legs were bare and so were his buttocks, and the sight of his hard, corded thighs and the firm, sculpted flesh of his hips made her ill at ease. "You . . . you changed clothes," she managed to say, instinctively retreating a step. She had never seen a man so nearly naked.

"I'm more comfortable this way when I'm hunting bison."

"Bison?" she echoed. "Around here?"

"Or buffalo. Whichever you want to call them, and

yes, around here. My people rely on them, not only for food but for other essentials, like clothing, weapons, tools, tepees. Normally a hunt is a big task, with a lot of men involved, but then buffalo usually travel in large herds, around fifty in number. I was out scouting for some food this morning and saw only a few grazing together. I came back to change and get ready to go after them."

"That sounds dangerous," she said uneasily.

"I don't have any choice. I couldn't find any other game or berries. You ate the last of my pemmican and jerky yesterday. There's no more bacon. I didn't take time to pack enough supplies, so Buffalo steaks will make a nice meal." He was not about to confide that he welcomed the time-consuming task, for it would give him a chance to try and figure out what to do with her.

She pointed at the stream. "We can catch fish, maybe birds." She did not like the idea of helping clean the carcass of a huge animal and knew it would be expected. Maybe he even thought she would do it all. From what Mehlonga had told her about how hard Indian women worked, Jacie was of the opinion they did the dirty tasks while the men gloried in the kill.

"The Comanche do not eat fish or wild fowl. Neither do we eat dogs," he added, "in case you think otherwise."

"Well, I never said you did." The idea was revolting.

"Some Indians do. Not my people."

"I still don't think we need a whole buffalo. I'm not that hungry. Besides, when we get to Fort Worth–"

"I am hungry now, and what we don't eat, I will take to my people."

She followed after him as he walked back around the rock and saw he had left his horse there. The saddle was on the ground nearby. A trailing rawhide thong was tied around the stallion's neck.

He saw her looking at it and explained, "That's all I need, so I can grab hold if I fall and slow him down by dragging my body and then pull back up. I need both hands free for these." He held up a three-foot bow and a quiver of iron-tipped arrows and pointed to a sheath knife tucked in his belt.

"Why not a gun?" Jacie asked, still dubious over what seemed a formidable task.

"I prefer these. All I have to do is single a buffalo out and hit him three times just behind his last rib to make his lungs collapse."

He swung himself up on the horse's back, and Jacie was helplessly rocked once more by the sight of hard muscles and bare flesh. Glancing away self-consciously, she said, "I wish you'd forget about this."

"You can watch."

Jacie looked in the direction he pointed and saw the great hulking beasts framed against the horizon.

"Climb up on the rocks and I'll run them in this direction so you can see."

Jacie did not share his optimism that bringing down a buffalo single-handed would be an easy task. "Maybe you'd better point me in the direction of Fort Worth in case you get killed. There's no need in both of us feeding the vultures."

"You'd never make it, little one." The horse was pawing the ground, anxious for the chase to begin. "But don't worry. I've done this many times."

She clambered up the rocks to watch him ride slowly toward the distant buffalo.

Luke glanced back, and she waved. He felt only a mild twinge of guilt over the decision not to take her to Sunstar. He had lived in the white man's world after attending the mission school. He had worked with vaqueros in Mexico, then drifted for a time, taking odd jobs on farms and ranches, and he had learned how cruelly some whites treated Indians, the contempt and scorn they inflicted. He had no doubt that Sunstar would be looked down on after living so many years among the Comanche, and her suffering would be far too deep for the love of her daughter to heal.

Sunstar's welfare was his only concern, and he knew she was looking forward to the move to Mexico in the spring. The white man was taking over the west, coming in great numbers, and no matter how many were killed, more would take their place. Nothing could stop them. And if the Indians did not bow down to them, then the Indians would be destroyed. Sunstar knew that, as Luke did, and while they urged peace, more and more hotheaded young bucks like Black Serpent were taking off to form renegade bands. So it was time to make a new life somewhere else.

Now the young woman had arrived to complicate things. He had watched her for a long time last night as she slept and could not deny the deep stirring in his loins that she provoked. But it was not altogether physical, this drawing he felt. Something was tugging in his heart, a feeling he'd not had since those wandering days after mission school when he had been sorely tempted not to return to his people at all. He had never told anyone about it, but Sunstar, in her uncanny way, had suspected something had happened and that it had to do with a woman. That was when she had begun to urge him to take a wife, as though she feared he would return to the white man's world—and the woman he would not talk about, who'd stolen part of his heart and torn it to shreds.

Her name was Amelia Prescott, and Luke had been dazzled by her heart-shaped face, her hair the color of a sunrise. When she smiled, she had dimples in her cheeks, and when she laughed it was like hearing little silver bells ringing in the breeze. Her father, Will Prescott, was a wealthy ship owner in Galveston, and the family home was situated right on the bay. Luke had taken work at the docks, and from the very first day he was aware of how she watched him from her front porch. She became bolder and at the end of a week had sauntered down to the dock, saucily twirling a lace parasol and wearing a fetching blue gingham gown with a tight bodice and a dipping neckline that accentuated her breasts.

Luke had been instantly taken by her beauty as well as her coquetry, and it was not long before her delicate subtlety gave way to brazen intent. She asked him to meet her for a moonlight walk, and he was waiting at midnight when she sneaked out of her house to meet him on the sandy beach. Before the sunrise began to bleed onto the waters of the quiet, silent bay, Luke had discovered new ways to please a woman, because Amelia was only too eager to teach him.

But he made a mistake. He foolishly let himself fall in love with her. Other men working with him, who were not blind and knew what was happening, warned that she was poison. She would never marry a lowly dockman, much less an Indian, and if her pa found out, Luke would be a *dead* Indian, they grimly predicted.

Luke had not listened. The romance had continued on through the summer. He was completely bewitched, and when he finally got up the nerve to speak of a future together, she had given no indication she did not share his dreams, as she moaned and thrashed wildly in the sand beneath him.

Luke kept it all a secret, how she had agreed to be his wife and go with him to Mexico, where they could live in peace. There he did not feel their union would be so frowned upon, and he did without things, starving himself sometimes, to save what meager wages he earned for their future. Luke knew he would break his back, if need be, to take care of her.

Then one day, when Luke was unloading a ship that had just docked, shadows fell on his happiness. Amelia appeared, all dressed up, accompanied by her parents and her three older brothers. She very carefully did not look in Luke's direction, and the other workers noticed and teased Luke about how she pretended not to know him.

He watched in misery as a smartly attired man came down the gangway and the Prescott family swarmed around him in greeting, including Amelia, who threw her arms around his neck. But Luke told himself that was what she had to do. No doubt the man was an important business associate of her father's. So he went about his work, filling his mind and heart with thoughts of the passion to come later that night.

Only that night she did not come, and Luke stood outside the Prescott house with fury mounting to see how the family fawned over their guest. And later, when Amelia drew the stranger out to the porch and went into his arms and pressed her mouth against his, Luke had exploded with rage. He had lunged from the darkness, forgetting how he had vowed to turn his back on his heritage and become part of the white man's world. He had screamed the words of the Comanche counting coup as he tore the stranger from the embrace of his beloved.

Will Prescott and his sons heard and charged out to drag Luke off of him, but Luke had turned savage, and he gave them a fight they would never forget. It was only when one of them ran back into the house for a gun that Luke retreated. But he froze at the sound of Amelia's voice screaming hysterically, "Shoot him. Shoot the crazy Indian!"

Amelia's brother fired once, striking Luke in the arm. But Luke did not run. He stood where he was, meeting Amelia's glare while Will Prescott snatched the gun from his son and cried, "He's not armed. No need to kill him if he'll get the hell out of here now."

Still, Luke did not retreat. Instead, he drew a ragged breath from the very depths of his soul and looked straight into Amelia's furious eyes. "You said you loved me."

"Love you?" she trilled incredulously. "I don't even know you." She whirled on her brother. "Kill him. He's out of his mind. He's dangerous."

Luke had left then but had not sought help for his wound. He had kept on going and did not stop until he reached his people and the woman he called mother. She had tended him, and the damaged arm had healed—but not his heart.

His mind snapped to the present. He was upon the

buffalo without realizing it. He had let his concentration wander, a deadly mistake, because a bison bull whirled around, nostrils flaring. Beside him was a cow, and Luke knew there was nothing more dangerous than an ill-tempered bull intent on rutting.

The beast charged.

In a flash, Luke had the bow in place and pulled back on the string. The arrow shot through the air, striking the bull on target, right below his rib, piercing his lung. But the bull did not falter and kept right on coming.

Luke's horse did not have to be told what to do. Cutting to the side, he avoided the first charge, and Luke was able to get off a second shot, also on mark. The bull was weakened but his rage of pain kept him coming. Luke fired again but the arrow was high, hitting muscle. Mustering nerves of steel, he was ready with yet another arrow, but suddenly the horse cut too sharply. Luke felt himself falling and grabbed for the rawhide thong just as his back struck the rocks below.

Ignoring the anguish, he called on every bit of strength he possessed and pulled himself up. Just as he was clearing the ground, the bull was upon them, and Luke felt a hot, sharp stab as he was gored in the shoulder. Teeth digging into his lower lip, it was all he could do to hang on to the thong, but he knew if he dropped it and fell back, it was over. The mighty bison would charge again, killing him.

Luke screamed at the horse in Comanche, urging him to go faster. Blood was pouring from the hole in his shoulder and torture was a great fist choking his entire body. He knew he could not cling much longer. Behind him he could hear the thundering hooves of the crazed bison in heated pursuit—but was the anguish now filling his ears, obstructing his hearing? Miraculously, it sounded as though the bison was actually slowing.

Luke managed to twist his head, realized it was so and felt first a thrust of joy, then a stupendous burst of strength. He managed to dance his legs in front of him, digging down with his heels as he yelled to the stallion to stop. At last he was able to let go, and he slumped to the ground, the fist clenching about him ever tighter and finally squeezing him away to merciful oblivion.

Jacie came to life. She had frozen in terror as the macabre scene was played before her horrified eyes but now she scrambled down from the rocks to race toward him, all the while praying she could remember everything Mehlonga had taught her.

Captain Logan looked at the soldier standing before his desk. "Are you sure?" he asked tensely.

"Yes, sir." Sergeant Buckham had hated to be the one to bring the news. Everybody on the post knew Captain Logan was plenty upset over the Indians taking the woman. The latest development would only make things worse.

"What did you say this man's name was?"

"Blake, sir, Michael Blake. He comes from Georgia and he's got some other men with him."

Logan groaned inwardly. Jacie had told him that her fiancé's name was Michael Blake.

"He told the guards at the gate he was looking for her and a man by the name of Zach Newton, because he was told they were heading for this fort."

Logan seized on that. Jacie had been traveling alone. Could it be she had originally run away with another man? There had been so much about her story that was mysterious.

At once Logan decided to let Blake think she had been abandoned by her lover and unfortunately seized by Indians. Logan certainly didn't want Jacie's fiancé to think he had been stalling her search for her mother so he could court her. Perhaps Blake didn't even know about her mother. If not, he would certainly not be the one to tell him. "Has anyone else on the post talked to this man?" he asked with narrowed eyes.

"Just the guard at the gate. And the minute he found out it concerned the woman, he sent me to tell you."

"That was wise. Now you go and bring this man to me, but you keep your mouth shut, and spread the word that if anyone gives him more than the time of day, they'll find themselves on a suicide patrol into the heart of Comanche territory. The last thing I need right now is civilians raising hell about army business. Do you understand me, Sergeant?"

Sergeant Buckham assured him that he did.

When he was gone, Logan leaned back in his chair and took a cheroot from the box on his desk. He lit it and inhaled deeply. It relaxed him to smoke, and he certainly wanted to appear calm as he described to Mr. Blake what had happened—how tragic it was that Miss Calhoun had been snatched from her bed in the guest quarters. Search parties had not been able to find a trace, but he would keep sending them out daily, and, no, there had not been a man traveling with her. She had been alone, separated from her companion, he had assumed, but she'd been so weak when the guards found her staggering toward the gate that she'd been allowed to rest, promising to tell her story the next morning. Only the next morning she was gone. So sad.

Logan smiled as the blue haze of smoke clouded his face. He would send Mr. Blake on his way, with regrets and sympathy, of course. He would explain how he wished he could offer the hospitality of the fort, but security was tight, what with all the Indian trouble. It was best Mr. Blake just go back home and await word as to Miss Calhoun's fate, if it were ever known.

Logan was confident he would have nothing else to worry about. Even the women of the fort would keep their mouths shut if they didn't want to become widows. Eventually it would all be forgotten, like Jacie, because, regretfully, he was sure she would never be seen again—alive.

The Indian scout listened with interest to the five white men who stood talking animatedly just inside the gate of the fort. He did not understand all the words but heard enough to know they were talking about the white woman Black Serpent had taken with him the night he and his men had robbed the arsenal.

The scout had wished he could have been a part of it all, for he hated working for the pony soldiers, but he had been caught stealing from his people and the chief had banished him. No other band would have him.

The Indian, known as Two Trees, knew how dangerous it would be in such bloody times to roam about alone, so he had taken the job at the fort, where he was given food, a place to sleep, and meager wages.

But Two Trees was not satisfied and wanted to be a part of Black Serpent's war party. And now he was optimistic that Black Serpent would at last agree to let Two Trees join him when he heard this latest bit of information.

# 19

*Several days had passed* since Luke was injured, and, except for rallying long enough to sip the water Jacie offered, he had slept.

He had been bleeding badly from his left shoulder when she had reached him. She had immediately begun to tear strips of cloth from her petticoat to pack the wound, and when they were gone, she started ripping at the hem of her dress. He had come to long enough for her to help him stand. Then, with his good arm across the horse's back for support, his other over her shoulders, they had made it to the campsite.

The first thing she had done was to rub sticks together and get a fire going. Along with the herbs and potions Mehlonga had given her, there was a lump of pine tar that had to be melted in order to pack it into the wound.

She was relieved when he passed out again, sure he would protest her treating him. She also knew it had to be terribly painful for him as she ran the needle threaded with boiled horse hair through the torn flesh to stitch it back together.

Finally, it was done. The pine tar would stop the oozing while the skin mended. Using the remaining material from her skirt, she had finished with a compressing bandage. Since he was strong, apparently fit and hearty, she was hopeful he would heal quickly.

But now she decided it was time to wake him up and coax him to eat. When she had searched his saddlebags in desperation for something to ease her own hunger, she had found some beef jerky tucked in the bottom that he had overlooked, but that was gone, and both of them needed food.

Mehlonga had told her how to catch fish by lying on her stomach at water's edge, face inches from the surface, and remaining very still. When the wily fish happened by, she had only to plunge her hands down to catch it and twist about to fling it out and onto the bank.

She removed the buckskin dress. She had found it tucked in the bottom of her satchel and did not want to get it wet, since it was all she had left to wear. She had destroyed her other dress making bandages for Luke's wound.

Wearing only her drawers and chemise, she got in position, but after a while she realized it was not going to be as easy for her as it had been for Mehlonga. Three times she grabbed for a fish and each time the fish escaped with a saucy flip of its tail. She wished there was something else to eat, but fish would be the easiest to cook. She could clean it and skewer it to roast over the fire. Later, she would go out and look for other sources of food that Telwah had told her she might find on the plains—the fruit of the prickly pear cactus, and prairie turnips. But for the time being, she did not want to wander too far from Luke, lest he wake up and think she had abandoned him.

She lunged and at last caught a big fish but was unprepared for the slimy, slick feel of it. It wriggled mightily and she gave a soft scream of surprise and made ready to throw it far back from the water so it would not flip-flop its way back in and escape.

She rolled quickly, raising the fish over her head, but at the sight of Luke sitting up and grinning at her she was so startled she dropped her catch, and with a loud splash it was gone.

"How—how long have you been watching me?" she stammered.

"From the time you first rolled onto your belly and stuck your pretty little bottom up in the air. Please continue. I told you Comanche don't eat fish, but I'm hungry enough to forget that. Besides, I have to confess there have been times I have tasted forbidden fruits." He winked.

His grin was infuriating, and Jacie was suddenly washed with embarrassment to realize how she must have looked, wriggling around on the ground in her undies. Scrambling to her feet, she quickly pulled on the buckskin dress as she asked irritably, "Just how long have you only pretended to be asleep these last few days while I made a fool of myself?"

"Long enough to be impressed by your skills as a medicine woman. But most of the time I was asleep. I knew I had to rest to get my strength back after losing so much blood. But tell me, where did you learn all that? You knew exactly how to close my flesh with the needle and horse hair."

Jacie was astounded. "You were actually awake while I was doing that? But you never moved a muscle. You didn't even twitch."

"The first thing a Comanche learns is how to endure pain. That was nothing, anyway. But where did you learn it?" he asked again.

"A Cherokee taught me."

"Did he also teach you to make that dress you have on?"

"No. We got it at a trading post on our way out here."

"Your skin has darkened from being in the sun so long, and with your black hair . . ." He trailed off, thinking that if not for her eyes, she would look like a real Indian—like Sunstar.

The way he was looking at her made her suddenly uncomfortable. Treating him, touching his almost sculptured body, had made her feel uncomfortable. And now, with him sitting there with knees bent, the breechclout barely covering him, Jacie felt a warm flush begin to creep over her entire body.

Luke settled back against the rocks. His wound did not hurt so badly and he knew once he ate, he might even feel like riding, maybe even be so daring as to go find the damn bull bison and take his revenge so they could have meat for supper. He could shoot a gun or throw a spear or knife with either hand, so his injury would not render him helpless. However, he did not want to move just yet, preferring to watch Jacie.

Despite his intent to take her back to civilization and be rid of her as soon as possible, he knew he wanted her. Watching her as he had when she was trying to catch the fish, her drawers pulled tight across her gently squirming buttocks, had aroused him deeply. He had felt desire for her before, but the closeness of her body to his as she had tended him had made it worse. Now images began to come to mind of how it would be to hold her naked in his arms, to touch and tease her into a frenzy of submission. He could close his eyes and picture what it would be like. . . .

"When do you think you will feel well enough to take me to Fort Worth?"

Her voice cut into his thoughts, and he came crashing back to reality to realize he had broken out in a sweat fired by his feverish longing. He was breathing deeply, heavily, and for the moment could not speak, nor did he want to. She was kneeling in front of him, a beseeching look on her lovely face. Her eyes shone with warmth and hope in the golden glow of the fire.

She reached out to press cool fingertips against his forehead, then drew back to gasp, "You have a fever. I was afraid of that. You have to be careful—you shouldn't be sitting up." She was scrambling to her feet, hurrying to get his blanket as well as her own.

Returning, she helped him to lie down, and he let her, pretending to be suddenly weak. It was all he could do to keep from smiling, but he forced his mouth to set in a firm, grim line as she fussed over him. And when she began to gently pat cool water on his face with her fingertips, he longed to pull her against him and feel his lips on hers while his hands caressed her all over till there was no turning back.

Jacie hoped he could not feel her tension, the strange emotions coursing through her body. What was wrong with her? She was supposed to be feeling revulsion, fear, for this savage who stared up at her with dark, piercing eyes in a way that set her heart to pounding. She could feel her own fever rising as unaccustomed but delicious emotions began to twist her insides about. She knew so little about sex, about what a man and woman did together once they were married, but something told her she was teetering on the edge of a dangerous precipice here, because this man, this strange and feral man, was making her wonder what it would be like if he were her husband and showed her what it was like to be his woman, his wife.

But perhaps what disturbed her most, Jacie realized, was the reality that never, even when he had held her, kissed her, had she felt this way about Michael.

Suddenly frightened by what she was feeling, she drew back. "I'd better see about catching another fish."

Michael shook his head at the bottle of whiskey Pete offered. The temptation was great to drink away the misery, but he was determined to resist. Liquor would keep him from being able to think clearly, and God knew, he needed all his wits about him now, because he had never had to face anything as terrifying as the thought of Jacie in the hands of Indians.

Somehow, some way, he knew had to find her, or at least try.

Even if she had run away with another man, Michael would never know another moment's peace if he left her fate to savages. And where was Newton? Why had he deserted her? And when? Just how damn long had she been wandering around by herself before she stumbled onto the fort? It was a wonder she had not been found by Indians or outlaws before then.

The others sat warily watching him in the glow of the campfire. They were camped for the third day in a row in a grove of cottonwood trees, away from the fort, which could still be seen in the distance.

Michael blamed the army for what had happened to Jacie and was furious at Captain Logan's refusal to allow them to go along on the daily patrols. Logan said they would get in the way and told them to go home, that there was nothing they could do. But Michael refused, and every day he and his men tagged along after the patrol, angering the soldiers and accomplishing nothing, for no trace of the Indians was found.

"Why don't we just head on back, Blake? We're wastin' our time," Pete Harkins mustered the nerve to suggest, prodded by meaningful looks from his three companions.

Doggedly, Michael said, "I'm not leaving till I find her, or at least find out what happened to her. I'd feel as if I was deserting her, because the army doesn't give a damn." He had stopped caring about getting the necklace back and realized that had only been an excuse anyway. He knew now it had always been in the back of his mind to try and persuade her to come back to him.

Silence hung heavy. The others were leaving it all up to Pete to speak for them. Finally, he said, "Look, we done figured out she was really your woman, and that story you told us about your foreman stealin' somethin' was just made up. That's all right, 'cause we understand, and we know it's tough for a man to take when his woman runs off with another man. But it's over, Blake. There's nothin' you can do. Them Indians got her, and you ain't never going to see her no more, and it's best to go home and try to forget her, hard though it'll be. Hanging around here is only gonna make it all hurt that much worse."

The others chimed in to agree.

Michael knew he was probably right but said, "I still can't go. But I don't expect you all to stay, and there's no hard feelings. I'll write a note for you to take back to my banker so you'll get your money."

And then the idea struck, and he hastened to add, "But if any of you will stay on, I'll pay twice what I promised. No"—he swept them with an excited gaze to see they appeared to be interested—"I'll pay you three times what we agreed on. I swear it. I'll even go ahead and write the note for that amount now, so you'll have it should anything happen to me."

The men looked at each other. It was a lot of money, and they were tempted to agree but still leery. Pete was their spokesman again. "My scalp is worth more than that, Blake, and that's damn sure what I'm riskin'—what we're all riskin'. There's five of us and no tellin' how many Comanche. We wouldn't stand a chance against them."

"I'll hire more men," Michael offered.

"How many more?" Joe Clyder asked.

"As many as it takes. There's a settlement upriver,

and we'll go there and round up our own army, by damn."

"And you'd pay us three times what you said you would?" Sterne Walters wanted to confirm. It would be more money than he had ever seen in his lifetime. Maybe he could even buy some land and settle down and farm and give up being a hired gun. "You'll promise that much money in addition to hirin' as many men as it will take, so we won't be committin' suicide? You swear?"

"I swear. I'll send back east for whatever it takes to run down those redskin bastards. And I'll hire scouts so we can track them down no matter how far they try to run, and—"

"You will not need them."

They whipped about, startled to see the Indian step from the shadows and into the fire's ring of light. Big and heavyset, he was naked except for a small apron attached to a tasseled belt. Long plaits of coarse black hair hung down to his hips. And when they saw the lowered rifle he carried, they did not dare reach for their holsters.

The Indian held up a hand in greeting. "My name is Two Trees. I am Comanche. I will not hurt you unless you make me. I come in peace to talk with you about the white woman you are seeking."

Michael slowly got to his feet. The others began to edge away, sure he was about to get himself shot, because his face had turned to a mask of rage, and his voice, when he spoke, was trembling with fury. "You have her? You have the woman? You're one of the devils who took her from the fort?"

"Do not come any closer," Two Trees warned him as he glanced about anxiously to make sure no one would be so foolish as to challenge him. He was swift with gun and knife, confident he could kill all five of them and flee before the pony soldiers heard the shots and screams. To Michael he said, "I was not among them. Then. But that is not important, because they no longer have her."

Michael unleashed a guttural snarl and reached for his gun, but Pete's hand shot out to grab his arm and keep him from drawing. "Don't do nothin' foolish," he whispered urgently. "He wouldn't have come here to tell you they killed her. Now just simmer down and see what he wants. And he's probably not alone, anyway. The woods are probably full of the bastards."

Michael fought for calm, but hatred for the man standing before him was searing his insides. Through clenched teeth, he ordered, "Tell me what happened to her."

"She was stolen by our enemy, a man named Luke, and—"

"You mean a white man has her? Who—"

"He is Indian," Two Trees was quick to assure him. "Comanche. And I do not know why he has a white man's name. I was not told. It is not important, but our leader, Black Serpent, despises him and wants revenge."

"Well, so do I," Michael cried, bewildered that the man had dared come to him. "I want revenge on all you bastards. Now what's the reason you're here?"

"We know you have come a long way seeking her, and we are willing to let you take her if you will join with us in our vengeance." Two Trees smiled. He liked the plan Black Serpent had thought of when he had been told Luke was seen with the woman some days ago. But Black Serpent had made all of his men swear not to tell how the white woman had escaped on her own, for he felt shame to have gotten so drunk that he allowed it to happen. And also he had been enraged to think she might have dared to attempt to poison him, for never had he been so sick, he had confided. So now Two Trees told the tale that Luke had sneaked into the camp to steal her for himself. Two Trees would never say otherwise. He was too grateful for having been taken into the band of renegades.

"What the hell are you talking about?" Michael was demanding.

Pete still held on to his arm. "Go easy. Hear him out," he urged. "If he'd wanted us dead, we already would be. He's up to somethin'."

"We have scouts out looking for them, but they have disappeared. No one has seen them. No one can find them. We only know our enemy has her, and we have many ears listening for the drums to tell us which direction they are going when they are found, but we believe sooner or later he will take her to his people. When he does, we will follow. You will go with us with your men and your guns. We will kill them all, for they are all enemies of the great Black Serpent. Then you may take your woman. We will count coup."

Michael looked at Pete. "What the hell is he talking about—count coup?"

"They get points for how many enemies they kill, as well as the way in which they do it. It's like a game."

"No game," Two Trees corrected. "High coup make

high warrior. Mighty warrior." He struck his chest with a fist.

Michael lashed out at him. "Listen, I don't give a damn about your coup or your mighty warriors. All I'm interested in is getting the woman back. If you want me and my men to help you kill the ones who have her now, we'll do it, but I warn you, once it's over, don't try to stop me from taking her."

"We want our enemies more. You have my word."

"Then let's go." Michael started toward where the horses were tied but stopped at the Indian's next words.

"Not now. At dawn you will follow the pony soldiers as you have done every morning. Let them get far ahead of you, and when the time is right, our warriors will find you and the search will begin."

"And how do we know you won't lead us away so you can count us as part of your damn coup?"

But Two Trees did not answer, because he had already disappeared as quickly and quietly as he had come.

Michael stared after him in the darkness, aware that his men were watching, waiting. He turned to face them. "All right. I know I may have spoken prematurely. You haven't said you'd stick it out with me, and I don't blame any of you if you want to turn back, but I don't have any choice except to hope I can trust them."

Joe Clyder had taken out his pistol and sat gripping it tightly. More to himself than anyone else, he muttered, "We coulda taken the bastard. There was one of him and five of us. We coulda killed him."

"Sure we could," Pete agreed. "But you were thinkin' like the rest of us, Clyder, how there might have been more of them hidin' out there. It was best to sit and listen, 'cause we're still alive."

"It'd be crazy to trust them," Sterne Walters put in.

Ethan Terrell said, "Well, I know a little bit about Indians, too, and it's true that most of the time when they give their word, they'll keep it, unless you turn on 'em. And he came to us. And like Pete said, we're still alive. So maybe he's makin' a genuine offer, and they really do want us to help 'em kill their enemies."

Sterne shook his head. "I don't know. It's still risky."

"Do what you want. All of you," Michael said sharply.

They all looked at him.

"You're forgetting the one thing I care about. Jacie is alive, and I intend to do everything I can to free her, even if I have to do it alone."

"I still think it would be takin' a chance," Sterne said. "They could use us and then scalp us."

Ethan again argued, "And I say the bastards have a sense of honor."

"Well, what's it going to be?" Michael was impatient to know their decision. "I said I'd triple what I originally promised you."

The others looked at Pete once more. They would go along with whatever he decided.

When Pete had heard Michael Blake was hiring a sort of posse to head west to run down somebody that had stolen from him, he had asked around and learned that he was quite wealthy, and he knew Michael could afford to more than triple their pay. "It's like this," he said, "If you're willin' to risk your life to try and get your woman back after she ran off with another man, that's your business. But if you want us to risk ours, it's going to cost you ten times what we agreed on."

The other men looked at each other incredulously. It was more money than any of them had ever dreamed of having.

Michael did not bat an eyelash. "You've got it. And I'll do what I said—make sure you get it no matter what happens."

"I'll drink to that." Pete lifted the bottle, took a swig, then passed it to the next man.

Michael declined the toast and got up and walked away. He wanted, needed, to be alone. Finding Jacie was all that mattered now, making sure she was safe. And no matter if she had run away with Zach, he knew he would swallow his pride and take her back.

After all, the thought of ever loving—or marrying—any other woman had never occurred to him.

Always and only, it had been Jacie.

# 20

*It was almost dark, and Luke* was again leaning back against the rocks, watching Jacie as she rinsed the cooking utensils in the stream. His warriors teased him about using white man's tools, but during the time he had lived among them, he had discovered small things like frying pans and tin mugs that could easily be packed and taken along and saw no reason not to have them. He had also learned to like the white man's food, like bacon and steak, which he ate every chance he got. But now there was only fish. Jacie managed to catch some every day, and he was tired of it. He might have gone hunting for deer or rabbits but secretly enjoyed her ministering to him, so he continued to appear weak. Actually, the wound wasn't as deep as he'd thought at first and was healing nicely, thanks to Jacie's skills.

He knew he needed to get rid of Jacie and go back to his people to help make ready for the cold weather ahead. Why then, he chided himself, was he pretending to be worse? He was only torturing himself and wished he could muster the willpower to turn away from her, because his desire increased with every moment they were together.

It was a cool night, with a gentle breeze blowing, and a full moon beaming down to bathe the earth in silver. Jacie returned from the stream, and in the dying firelight, Luke noted the determined look on her face. She had very carefully avoided him since the night he had almost kissed her, keeping her distance except for changing the dressing on his wound, and then doing so quickly. Now, however, she sat down to face him and said, "It's time we had a serious talk. I saved your life, and you owe it to me to do as I ask and take me to Fort Worth."

"Fort Worth," he said mockingly. "That's all you think about."

"I'm willing to go anywhere to get help. I just thought that would be the closest place I might find it."

"Why don't you go back where you came from?"

She gave a stubborn shake of her head. "Not till I find out what really happened to her. And Fort Worth is the nearest settlement, isn't it? So that's where I want to go. Surely there will be someone there who'll help me, as soon as I buy a new dress, so I won't look like an Indian—" She caught herself. Now he would suspect she had money hidden away and try to steal it. Quickly she attempted to cover. "I mean, I'll have to get a job of some sort so I can buy new clothes."

He could tell she was nervous and suspected the reason. "I know about the money you have hidden away inside the small blanket you keep tucked in your satchel. I also know about the necklace made of diamonds and a stone the color of your eyes, but you don't have to worry about me stealing from you."

A gasp of surprise melded into one of indignant anger. "So you've been going through my things. You've no right—"

"I was curious about the herbs and potions you have, and I happened to feel a lump in the hem of the little baby blanket and discovered your hidden treasures. I don't care about them, but what I do want to know is why you have poison."

"Poison?" she echoed, swallowing hard and pretending not to know what he was talking about.

"I recognize the seeds of the trumpet-shaped flower that grows on a vine, and I am aware that when they are ground into a powder and put in drink they can make a person very sick, even kill him if the dose is too strong. Why would you need something so evil?"

"Mehlonga, the Cherokee who taught me his medicine, gave them to me should I need to defend myself against an enemy."

"And have you thought of giving them to me?" He watched her keenly as he spoke, seeking the truth in her face, in her eyes.

"No. You would have harmed me that first night if you were going to, so I felt no threat from you, even though you're still my enemy"—she tensed, remembering—"because you are a Comanche, the same as the ones who killed my family and stole my mother and made her suffer ever since."

Luke could have told her that while Sunstar had endured the same hardships as other Indian women, she had never been mistreated. But he kept silent as Jacie unleashed her resentment.

"I think I hate all of you," she said quietly, bitterly. "And if I do find my mother still alive, I'm going to take her home as fast as I can."

"And what makes you think she would want to go? Maybe she's managed to find peace, happiness. The Indian loved his life before your people came to bring disease, kill our buffalo, steal our land. Maybe before the misery came, she learned to love the Indian's world, too. But tell me," he went on, curious, "Don't you have other family? A husband? A lover perhaps?"

"No." Michael could not be considered her lover, and Luke had not asked if she had a fiancé. And the engagement was never made official, anyway, she reasoned in order to quell her suddenly nagging conscience. His proposal had been interrupted that night, and she had never officially told him afterward that she would marry him.

"But you must have some family," he prodded.

"They're all dead now."

"Then where would you take your mother if you found her and she agreed to go with you? Your money won't last long."

Jacie flared, "We'll get by."

"You showed me the locket with the likeness of your mother inside, but what about the necklace? Did that also belong to your mother? You were foolish to bring something that valuable with you, anyway. Others might not be as honorable as I am."

"Not that it's any of your business, but I didn't

intend to bring it. Someone put it in the blanket without my knowing about it. I suppose they were worried I might run out of money and need to sell it to get home." She saw no need to tell him about Sudie.

"But you said you have no family." His persistence was becoming annoying. His brows rose, and there was the play of a smile on his lips. "You mean you have a friend rich enough to give you jewelry to sell in case you need the money to get home, but this friend isn't willing to help you in the way you need it most—to come out here with you to search for your mother. I think I want nothing to do with your friends, Jacie. I prefer my people, who are there for me when I truly need them."

She was really starting to get angry. "Listen, the person who gave me that necklace didn't know I was leaving, because I didn't ask for his help. Someone else put it there."

Luke seized on that. "You mean a man cared enough for you to spend so much money on a gift, and you didn't feel close enough to him to share something so important?"

Truly flustered, Jacie stammered "He—he didn't know about my mother—my real mother, I mean."

"Why didn't you tell him?"

"I just didn't." Oh, why wouldn't he stop?

"I think you were ashamed for anyone to know your mother had been living with Indians all these years."

"That's not so," she cried, infuriated that he was able to make her feel so guilty. "He . . . he wouldn't understand, that's all," she said lamely.

"You would want to take her back to live among

these people who don't understand? People who will look down on her for having lived with Indians? And this man who gave you the necklace, he was more than a friend, wasn't he? He had to have been, to give you such an expensive gift."

She felt the color rise in her cheeks. "He asked me to marry him." There. She had told him and was glad, hoping now that it was out in the open it would somehow dispel the tension surging between them. By day she had tried to ignore him, but at night her dreams betrayed her, as he filled the darkness with the light of his kisses and caresses. And always she awoke in a tremor of hunger and longing, cursing herself for being unable to control the fantasies of her mind.

Luke cut into her brooding. "And how do you think he will like having a mother-in-law who's probably more Comanche by now than white?"

"He will accept her because he loves me," she said despite her doubts.

"And do you love him?"

"Of course, I do." Jacie answered weakly. The conversation was making her more and more uncomfortable, and this was not what she wanted to talk about anyway and said so. "My personal life is not your concern. Now I remind you again, I saved your life, and you owe it to me to do as I ask. Take me back to civilization where I can find someone compassionate enough to want to help me." Her voice had risen with her frustration.

He grinned lazily. "I saved your life, too, so I'd say that makes us even."

"Oh, damn you." Jacie got to her feet. "And to hell with you. I'll find my own way."

He cocked his head to one side, thinking how she was even more fetching when she was all riled up, eyes sparkling, cheeks flushed, her bosom rising and falling and the slight twitch to her hips. "You aren't going anywhere, Jacie, so calm down."

"You certainly can't keep me here day after day to slave for you. You're able to take care of yourself. You don't need me, and I damn sure don't need you."

"Oh, I'm not going to keep you," he said easily. "In a day or two, I'll—"

He froze.

He saw the flash of steel in the moonlight but never caught the lightning movement of Jacie's hand as she whipped out her knife. There was no time to dodge. Only one heartbeat was between him and death as he braced himself.

He actually felt the stinging heat of the blade as it brushed the side of his cheek, and realizing with a quick rush that she had missed, he bolted to his feet to lunge and knock her backward to the ground, pinning her with the full weight of his body as he cursed. "God damn it, woman, have you lost your mind? You kill me and you'll die out here. You'd never find your way back. . . ."

He fell silent to see how she was looking at him with heated gaze, her lips parted ever so slightly, and to note how she did not struggle, though he had to be hurting her. Instead, she seemed to be yielding, taking him with her to fall into the softness of her.

"I did not try to kill you," she whispered. "Look."

Without letting her go, he twisted around to see the snake. Copper-colored, with bold reddish-brown crossbands on the midline of its back, it lay scant inches from where he had been resting, its head neatly severed by Jacie's knife.

"It's one of the snakes you spoke of that doesn't rattle," she said in a tiny voice, overcome by the heady feeling of his nearness.

"It's called an Osage copperhead, and it's deadly," he said, turning his gaze to meet hers. There was no mistaking the desire he saw in her sensuous lavender eyes. "But not nearly so dangerous as what you make me feel in this moment, little one. I am going crazy with wanting . . ."

His mouth came down on hers softly, tenderly, but as her lips parted in submission, the kiss became fierce, possessive. She welcomed his tongue, melding against hers, and at the same instant felt his hips undulate ever so lightly, enough that his hardness pressed into her.

Jacie knew in a few seconds there would be no turning back. Though his mouth was bruising she could still twist away from him, scream for mercy, perhaps bolt and run to hide in the shadows till his passion cooled. But what of her own need, the driving pulse of desire she could no longer hold back? What she wanted she could not be sure of, for she had no knowledge of what it was like to mate with a man. There had been kisses, but none like this, and there had been tingles of delight, but never, no, never had there been endless waves of longing rolling over her again and again.

She felt caught in the tide of passion, unable to move, not wanting to, powerless to tear herself from his arms, to fight her way to the surface of reality. This should not be happening. But she did not care. In that moment in time, she could more easily have stopped breathing than deny this wonder, this awe, this new and wonderful thing that her body had become, that he was making her become. She wanted him, and if she regretted it later, so be it. This was here and now in God's wilderness of truth, where there could be no pretense, no denial.

Twisting her hands ever so slightly, he let them go, and they moved upward to clutch the hardness of his shoulders as she opened her mouth yet wider so he could drink the nectar of her acquiescence.

He rolled to his side, taking her with him, reaching to cup her breasts and squeeze with tender possession. She was molded against him, and time seemed to stand still, but then he was rising, taking her with him, leading her, his gaze locked hypnotically on hers in the streaming moonlight, to the blankets spread on less rocky ground. There, he held her away from him, reveling in the serene beauty of her face illumined by the kissing light sent from heaven above. Slowly he reached to lift the hem of her dress, sliding it up to her waist, then on upward, and she raised her arms so he could easily remove it. Flinging it into the shadows, she stepped from her drawers, then helped him with the fastenings of her chemise. The buckskin garment was not meant to be worn with undergarments, but Jacie had been shy—till now.

And then she was naked before him, and he ran his hands up and down her back, liking the feel of her, the tight curves of her buttocks, the trim firmness of her thighs, marveling at her tiny waist. He trailed his fingertips around to once more touch the fullness of her breasts, to pinch ever so tenderly the hardness of her nipples.

She was close against him, aware there was very little left between them now, only the breechclout, and his desire was evidenced there. He was a head taller, and she could not stop looking at the rugged handsomeness of his face, the granite lines, softened with lust as he smiled ever so slightly. His hair hung about his massive shoulders, which she clutched as though too frightened to let go. But then she yielded a little more and left her innocence further behind her as she dared to trail her hands lower—first to savor and squeeze the corded muscles of his arms and then to caress the sinewy hardness of his chest.

As though with a mind of their own, her fingers played onward, smoothing across his rocklike belly, then boldly going to explore rigid hips . . . the lines of brawny thighs.

He kissed her again and held her so close their hearts seemed to beat as one. When they were breathless, he moved to trail his lips down her throat, and she threw her head back in divine submission.

Downward he went, savoring, suckling each nipple, evoking delicious sighs from deep in her throat as he thrust her bosom forward to take yet more.

Luke dropped to his knees, burrowing his face in her belly, cupping her buttocks and pulling her tight. And when Jacie thought she could stand no more, when she was sure she would die if he did not take her where her body screamed to go, he drew her down with him to the ground.

"It is your first time," he murmured hotly. Not a question but a statement, for he was sure she had never had a man before. "It will hurt a little, but I will be gentle."

Jacie could not speak, for she was too caught up

in the enchanting aura of passion gone wild. Easier it would have been to turn the wind to blow away the moon than try and resist the surge of her body's craving to satiate the hunger unleashed. She allowed him to spread her legs, and bend her knees, and wrap her about him. And when he entered, slowly at first, she cried out, but only a little, for quickly the pleasure of their coupling smothered any discomfort or pain. She gave herself to him freely, clutching his back to hold him tighter against her as he rocked to and fro.

His movements quickened, then slowed, for he was not about to take his pleasure before giving hers. He stopped, staying inside her as his hands caressed her breasts, her face, his tongue touching hers in exquisite joy. They were locked in time.

Jacie dug her nails into his shoulders, dizzily aware of his wound, trying not to touch it. But if he felt discomfort, he gave no indication. She pressed against him, eager for more of this strange new world he had taken her to and never wanting to leave it.

He could feel her cresting and he took her then, thrusting mightily until both of them were sated and lay in each other's arms, awed by the splendor of the moment.

For a long time, Luke did not speak, nor did he want to. He was savoring the sweet afterglow and the realization that never, after more women than he could count, could he remember anything so pleasurable. No one else had ever given him so much of herself, and Luke was awed to think that a part of her would somehow be with him forever more.

Jacie lay with her head snuggled against his shoulder, lost in wonder at what it all meant. And she too silently acknowledged that nothing in her life would ever be the same. No matter where fate led her, she would never forget her first lover, her Comanche lover . . . nor did she want to.

Somewhere a coyote howled, and Jacie instinctively wriggled even closer. Luke smiled and tightened his hold on her and said, "Don't worry, little one. You saved my life again, so now I suppose I am honor-bound to protect you."

Reality was like cold water in her face. This cannot be, Jacie told her rapidly pounding heart. I cannot let it be. It's a warm, sweet interlude between two people, alone together in the wilderness. That's all it is, and all I'll let it be, and I've got to remember why I'm here.

She pulled away from him and sat up, drawing the blanket over her to cover her nakedness. "I don't ask you to protect me, Luke, only to take me where I want to go. This shouldn't have happened, and it can't happen again," she said tremulously.

Luke was also hurtled back to reality but was confused by what he was feeling for her, which made him respond coldly. "It only happened because you wanted it, too. And that's the only way it will happen again. As for taking you where you want to go, I don't think you even know where that is." He got up and walked toward the stream.

Jacie stared after him, thinking, despite her resolve, how magnificent his body was in the moonlight.

He has to take me, she thought desperately, and soon, because if he doesn't, God help me, I might not want to go. . . .

# 21

*Jacie awoke from a restless sleep.* Luke had bedded down on the other side of the scrub brush, and when she pushed through it, she found he was already up and saddling his horse. He was dressed in army trousers once more and wearing boots. As she faced him, she felt a warm rush to recall the way he had held her, kissed her, and hoped her face was not flushed.

"Are we going somewhere?" she asked.

Luke gave a curt nod. He had lain awake all night, angry with himself for what had happened, madder still to admit he cared for her. A hell of a lot. And not just for the pleasure they had shared. Something was stirring in his heart, causing an inner battle that he was losing. And it wasn't anything like what he had felt for Amelia. He had eventually come to realize that that had only been a melding of the flesh, but with

Jacie it was different, in a way he did not like to think about.

Toward dawn he had made the decision it was best to get her out of Texas, out of the west, and send her back to the man waiting to marry her. "Get your things," he said, a little gruffly. "We're getting out of here."

Jacie was puzzled by his tone but too happy that they were leaving to dwell on it. He probably wanted to forget last night as much as she did. Surely they would part soon, and then they'd never see each other again, which was best, she tried to tell her aching heart.

They rode out into the early morning sunshine, and Jacie drank deeply of the fresh, crisp air, making an attempt to ease the tension. "This is my favorite time of year back home. Buckeyes and oaks and poplars and black gums are dripping with gold and blazing against the sky. It's good-eating time, too." Her stomach gave a hungry growl. "Apples and pumpkins and raspberries. My—my aunt," she said, having to correct herself again, for it was still hard to think of Violet as anything except her mother, "would make apple butter in a big kettle over a hickory-fed fire, and I'll never forget how good it smelled. Mehlonga showed me how to cook lots of things too, like a soup made of parched corn."

"Did this Mehlonga also teach you to throw the knife?"

"Yes. He wanted me to be able to protect myself."

"I would never have given it back to you if I'd known you had a warrior's skill. He taught you well. Tell me, when you return home, will you be a medicine woman there?"

Jacie was glad for the chance to talk, because when there was silence, there was also an awareness, and she wondered if he was recalling last night's splendor, as she was. "No. A planter's wife has a lot of responsibilities. Michael has a big house and many servants working there. I'll eventually be in charge of them, as well as of planning socials. He might run for political office one day, you see, and—"

"I don't care about him." He cut her off suddenly, sharply, to ask with contempt, "These servants you speak of—they are actually slaves, aren't they?"

Jacie felt uneasy. "Well, actually the Blake family never refer to their Negroes as slaves. They're treated quite well, you see."

"Can they leave if they want to?"

"I—I don't think so," she stammered, but rushed to add, "but they have no place else to go, no way to earn money for food and shelter, clothes. The Blakes take care of them. It's the way it's always been."

"They are still slaves, and it is wrong, but maybe you disagree. Maybe you think it's all right to hold a man against his will."

"No, I don't."

"But you will marry a man who does."

Jacie fell silent for a moment, choosing her words carefully in hopes of making him understand. "He can't help it. He has thousands of acres of land and he could never afford to hire Negroes to work it. And he inherited the plantation, as well as most of the workers, who were bought by his grandfather when he first came to this country."

"It's still wrong. A man should be free for all of his life. That is what my people are struggling for—

freedom, and the land that's rightfully theirs. Your people want to take it away. I think they'd make slaves of us too if they could."

Jacie, resentment bubbling, fired back, "Well, you have no right to criticize. I'll remind you that if my mother is still alive, she's been a slave of your people for over eighteen years."

"She's not—" Luke caught himself. He'd been about to say Sunstar was not a slave, that she had been revered not only as the wife of a chief but eventually respected as a shaman. Damn it, he needed to rid himself of this woman who filled him with lust and confusion, before she found out he was hiding the truth from her.

Jacie was watching him with eyes narrowed. "She's not what?" she said slowly, quietly. "It sounds as though you know something about my mother after all."

"Not your mother," he lied. "The yellow-haired woman I told you about. She was married to a chief, and she learned to love his people as much as they came to love her. She was very happy."

Grudgingly, Jacie said, "Well, if she fell in love with someone, I guess I can understand that."

"Can you?"

"Yes, because I believe that when you love someone, it doesn't matter who or what they are."

"And you feel this way about the man you are going to marry?" Luke wanted to bite his tongue. Oh, why couldn't he let it go? If he didn't get rid of her soon, he was going to make a fool of himself, say the wrong thing and make her really suspicious that he was hiding something about her mother. And he didn't want that. He wanted her to go home and not look back, never to wonder what she might have discovered had she stayed to search relentlessly.

But then he realized she was not responding to his question and was instead staring at something scurrying among the rocks. Deliberately changing the subject, she asked what it was, and he seized the opportunity to also get his mind on other matters. He explained that the small, fat, reddish-brown animal was called a prairie dog. "When he sees an enemy, he'll sit up on his haunches and make a yapping sound like a dog to alert others of his kind in the vicinity. Actually, they're a good source of food, but small. My people like them as a change from buffalo meat, and the young boys learn the rudiments of stalking game with bow and arrow by hunting them. They're quick and wiry and . . ."

He fell silent and reined to a stop, holding up his hand to signal she should do likewise.

Jacie had been listening with interest but realized something had caught his attention and followed his gaze to the rocks overhanging. At once she reached for her knife, but Luke had anticipated what she would do and caught her arm and held it.

"Don't," he said sharply. "There is no need."

Jacie did not share his optimism. The huge cat was staring down at them emitting low, ominous growls and looked as though it were going to spring any second. "Shoot him," she whispered thinly, noticing Luke had not reached for a weapon. He's going to attack."

As though able to hear and comprehend the death sentence Jacie decreed, the cougar opened its mouth to display lethal fangs as it let loose a scream that went to the very marrow of their bones.

But still Luke made no move. Instead, he fastened the cat with a steely gaze and began to speak to it in the Comanche language.

The rope reins were cutting into Jacie's hands, she was squeezing them so tightly in her terror. To her amazement, however, the growls subsided, then the great cat became quiet as it surveyed them warily with its shining golden eyes. Finally, with an annoyed swish of its tail, it turned and disappeared among the rocks.

Luke saw how she had paled. "See? It isn't necessary to kill everything you fear. Sometimes it goes away on its own, in peace."

"And he understood what you said to him?" Jacie was stunned.

"Who knows?" Luke kneed the stallion and started him moving again. "Maybe it was the tone of my voice. He sensed I was no threat unless he attacked. So he left. In peace," he added with a smile.

"But it doesn't always work that way."

"No. Sometimes you have to kill what you fear, to save yourself."

As they rode on, Jacie concentrated on the world around her, asking questions, not only because she wanted to learn, but to steer conversation away from anything personal. Hard as it was not to look at Luke and remember the ecstasy they'd shared, she was determined to try and forget. She even attempted to think about Michael, but try as she might, it was difficult to dwell on him when images of Luke's lovemaking lingered. Washed with guilt, she wondered whether Michael would be able to tell that she had been with another man, and if so, whether he would still want her. It was going to be difficult enough for him to hear the truth about her parents without thinking of her in the arms of another man. She would have to pretend it had never happened and somehow make herself believe it hadn't.

But deep inside, a voice taunted that it would be futile to even try, for no woman could ever forget being made love to by a man like Luke.

She saw her first porcupine, along with mice, gophers, toads and lizards. They ate their fill of prairie plums, hard and green but tasty. Then Luke shot a prairie chicken with an arrow, and they cleaned it together beside a rushing stream to skewer and roast for their midday meal.

As they rested in the shade of a cottonwood grove, bellies full for the first time in days, Jacie ventured to ask, "Where have you decided to take me?"

"To a place called Nacogdoches, where I have a friend who works for a stagecoach line. He'll see that you're put on a coach heading east." He watched her face for her reaction and did not miss how her eyes suddenly danced with tiny dots of red among the lavender hue.

"You can take me anywhere you want to, but I won't go back now."

"Lord, you are one stubborn woman," he said, irritation boiling over. "What's it going to take to make you realize it's best for you to forget this nonsense? Hell, even if you did find her, that man waiting for you wouldn't want you bringing her back—if you thought he would, you'd have asked him to help you find her in the first place. Forget it, Jacie. If she's alive, she's better off where she is than in your world, living in misery."

They were sitting side by side, and she leapt to her feet, hands clenched into tight fists. "You only feel that way because the only life you've ever known is that of a savage. You might have gone to school in Mexico, but so what? That didn't tell you anything about my people."

"Oh no?" He laughed bitterly and rose also, towering angrily above her. "I know plenty about your people." He felt a wave of bitterness to recall the prejudices he had known whenever he crossed the line between red and white. The army might respect him for the expert scout he was, but he was ever aware of the shadowed contempt. The only way he had ever been accepted was to dress like a white man, wear his hair like one, and pretend to be everything he was not. Luke did not like living that way and passed for white only when necessary.

Jacie was staring at him warily. The way his face had turned to granite, his nostrils flaring ever so slightly in his fury, she was not sure she wanted to continue the debate. Better to be on their way and part company as soon as possible. She got up and started toward her pony, but his next words stopped her dead in her tracks.

"Yes, I know all about your world, Jacie, but you know nothing of mine."

"Nor do I want to," she said coldly. "And I told you before—we are even now. You saved my life. I saved yours. You got what you wanted last night. You have no more need of me, so let's be on our way. The sooner I'm rid of you, the better."

He reached her in quick strides to grab her by her shoulders and spin her about. "No," he said, face ashen, eyes flinty. "You're wrong. *You* got what *you* wanted last night. I would have stopped any time you wanted me to, and you know it. But you didn't want to stop. You wanted to see what it was like to mate with someone you think of as a savage, didn't you?"

She slapped him.

He saw the blow coming and could have ducked or caught her hand but didn't, because he wanted her to lose her temper, to get mad. Anything to head off the emotions he had sensed smoldering beneath the surface all day.

Jacie braced herself, unsure of what he would do. He could snap her neck with one squeeze of his strong hands, but he merely glared at her with icy black eyes.

After what seemed forever, he said, "Let's go. We won't reach Nacogdoches by night, but don't worry. I won't touch you."

"Well, that's fine, because I—"

He held up a hand. "Silence. Don't move." Hurrying to his horse, he took his rifle, and motioning again to Jacie to stay where she was, he disappeared among the thick trees.

Jacie drew her knife and quickly dropped to her knees behind a clump of plum bushes, praying there were not other Indians around who might be Luke's enemies. If they killed him, she shuddered to think of what they would do to her, but she also knew she did not want anything to happen to him. No matter that he had made her mad, no matter how she argued within herself, she knew she cared for him deeply.

Long, torturous moments passed. She could stand it no longer and was about to creep out and see for herself what was happening but heard footsteps approaching and stayed where she was. Only when she heard Luke's voice speaking his native tongue did she dare rise up, then shrank back to see he had two Indians with him.

He saw she was alarmed and called, "It's all right, Jacie. They're friends."

She peeked out. Scalplocks fell from the tops of their heads, and one of them had tucked a single yellow feather into his. The other's braids were wrapped in what looked like animal fur. But it was their faces that startled her the most, for they were painted with bright red streaks.

"They won't harm you, because you are with me. They're members of a Comanche band called the Honey Eaters."

"What . . . what do they want?" She had to strain to speak, because the way they were looking at her was terribly unnerving.

"There's a wounded child. A boy. Too young to be a warrior, and they didn't know he had followed them until it was too late. They ran into some trouble with renegades, and he was shot in the leg. They're on their way to their medicine man, but the boy is bleeding badly. Can you help him?"

Jacie did not hesitate. She ran to grab her bag from where it was tied on the pony and followed Luke out of the cottonwood grove—and stopped short. There were at least twenty more men on horseback, all of them staring at her with narrowed, suspicious eyes.

"I showed them my wound," Luke said. "I told them how you helped me, so they will let you tend him."

She saw him then, the small form held in the arms of one of the mounted warriors, blood flowing from the child's leg. She started toward him, but one of the warriors screamed out, and she hesitated. Luke spoke to him, then gave her a gentle push to indicate she should continue.

Grudgingly, the Indian holding the boy handed him down to Luke, who laid him at Jacie's feet. A piece of doeskin torn from someone's leggings had been wrapped around his leg below the knee. Jacie removed it, did a hasty examination, and was relieved to see the bullet had apparently passed through the calf of the leg and had not hit bone. If she could stop the bleeding, she was confident he would heal.

Luke followed her directions, getting a fire going and bringing water so she could cleanse the wound properly. Jacie melted the lump of pine tar, which would be packed into the wound. For a bandage, she tore strips from her blanket, finally able to advise Luke, "Tell them he'll be fine. Their medicine man will know what to do from here on."

He translated the message, and they took the boy and left with slight nods of gratitude in her direction, giving a sack of fresh deer meat to Luke.

Luke and Jacie did not talk as they rode onward, each lost in private thought.

They stopped for the night near a small waterfall, the pool beneath dancing with pink and purple shadows from the setting sun over the rise beyond. Serene and peaceful as it was, Jacie felt a whirlpool of emotion within to see how Luke was ignoring her as he set about to prepare their food.

They ate in silence, and afterward Luke went

beyond some bushes to bed down, and Jacie spread her blanket near the dying fire.

An unseen hand flung thousands of diamonds to sparkle in the velvet cloak spread overhead. Somewhere a coyote gave a mournful howl. Jacie was no longer frighted by such night sounds, but loneliness was a vise, squeezing tears that stung her eyes as she prayed sleep would come soon to take her away from her miserable ponderings, for she was starting to think maybe Luke was right. Perhaps it would be best for her to go back and leave well enough alone.

She tried to focus on thoughts of Michael. Her heart had still not told her she loved him, but that no longer seemed important. What preyed upon her now was how she felt a desperate need to get as far away from Luke as possible, and she hoped by dwelling on Michael and the security he had always offered, she could find solace in an otherwise shaky world.

But it was not working.

Over and over she relived in her mind how she had felt so drawn to Luke, almost from the moment they met. It was as though they had known each other their whole lives. And their coming from two different worlds had not seemed to matter as they had so eagerly struggled to bond and become one unto the other, in spirit as well as flesh.

Like the night wind's cooling kiss soothing her heated face, the thought came to her—if tomorrow their time together ended, then what harm would there be in having one last night to remember forever and always?

Afraid that if she hesitated she would lose her courage, Jacie got up and went to him.

He was not asleep, she knew. He lay on his back, arms folded behind his head, staring at the curtain of night, deep in reverie.

She sat down next to him and touched her fingertips to his hard, flat belly and felt him start, but he made no sound.

And then she voiced the decision she had not realized she had made until that precise moment: "I'm going home, Luke. I'm giving up. I'll always wonder whether I would have found my mother and what the outcome would have been, but I'll just make myself believe that if she is still alive, she's better off not knowing about me."

"And you go home to marry the man who waits for you?" he asked quietly, painfully.

"He will make me a good husband. I will do all I can to make him a good wife. That's my world. But for tonight"—she drew a deep breath of resolve—"I want to be a part of yours."

He knew what she meant, and he wanted it too. He sat up and gently drew her dress over her head, and she helped him to render her naked, their eyes locked in feverish anticipation all the while.

He stripped off the army pants, then drew her down beside him.

Slowly he ran his hands up and down her body, and she murmured with a shy kind of pleasure. How easy it would have been for him to fall upon her like the cougar upon a rabbit, to devour her and feed his great hunger. But Luke held back, wanting to savor each morsel of her body, to delight in every touch, every caress.

Her fingers began to play across his chest, her touch inflaming him, and when her hand traveled lower, to gently caress and stroke his hardness, it was only by mustering every shred of self-control he possessed that he was able to keep from entering her then and there.

Jacie could feel how he wanted her, could feel her own desire quickening within her. He began to suckle at her breasts, cupping her bottom and pulling her to and fro gently, sliding himself between her thighs, and suddenly she could stand no more. She caught him by surprise, reaching to take him in her hand and guide him into her softness.

Luke was pleasantly stunned, and he rolled onto his back, taking her with him, so she could straddle and gently ride him. He allowed her to set her own pace, rocking with her, his hips grinding against the ground beneath.

She arched her back and caught her hair with her hands, flinging it to whip about her face in the playful breeze, moaning deliciously as every nerve in her body screamed with joy.

He held her by her waist as he thrust in and out, and when he began to feel the tiny shudders within her, he knew she was ready.

Rolling her onto her back, he braced himself with his hands on the ground, arms straight, while he rocked against her, for he wanted to see her face in the moonlight as he took them both to divine fulfillment.

And when it was over, when they lay with arms about each other, her head on his shoulder, Luke pressed his lips lovingly against her forehead, then reverently whispered, "Tonight, for a little while, heaven traded places with the earth. . . ."

# 22

*Everyone's patience was* wearing thin, and Michael's men were growing more restless with each passing day. It had been nearly a week since three Indians had quietly appeared to lead them on an arduous two-day trek north. Finally, beside a swiftly flowing creek, they were told with grunts and gestures that they were to camp there until their leader came.

"How much longer?" Pete grumbled as they drank the last of the coffee. "We're almost out of everythin'. One more day of beans, and then we starve, unless we want to start eatin' lizards or whatever it is those bastards up there survive on. Damn, it gets on my nerves, the way they're always watchin'." He cast an angry glance at the Indian perched on a rock above them.

"Simmer down," Michael said, tossing down the rest of his coffee. He was tired of waiting, too, but thoughts of finding Jacie and getting her out of this madness kept him going.

Joe Clyder, sitting beside Pete, nudged him with an elbow, and Pete spoke for all of them. "Blake, we been talkin', and we've decided we should forget all this and go home. Despite the money—and God knows, it's a hell of a lot to turn down—we're gettin' more and more leery of gettin' in the middle of an Indian war. There's only five of us, remember."

"I can count," Michael snapped. "I also remember we had a deal."

"Yeah, but we don't like all this waitin'. It's gettin' on our nerves. I don't like it."

"Then go," Michael waved a hand. "Take the men and go. "I'm sick of your whining, anyway."

Joe started to get up, but Pete motioned him to stay where he was, asking Michael, "What about you? You're comin' with us, aren't you?"

"Not without Jacie."

"But that's suicide. Those damn Indians will be so furious when we take off they'll shoot you for the hell of it. What good is one man to them anyway? You've got to go with us. You'll die if you stay."

Michael shrugged. "It doesn't matter. Without Jacie, I don't have a life, anyway."

The others murmured among themselves, but Pete exclaimed, "Hell, no woman is worth dyin' for. Damn it, she left you for another man. She—"

Michael lunged for him, grabbing him by the throat and knocking him backward to the ground. "I won't listen to that kind of talk, you hear? Now go on and get out of here. I don't need you. I don't need any of you cowards." He got to his feet, feeling how fast his heart was pounding with his rage.

The Indians, watching from above, looked at each other and wondered why the white men were fighting.

"You'll get your money," Michael said. "My banker in Atlanta will pay you. But there will be no bonus. Just what we agreed on in the beginning. Now go." He stalked away, head bent, shoulders slumped, hands stuffed in his pockets.

"He's crazy," Sterne Walters declared. "If he wants to die, I say let him. I'm ready to get out of here right now."

Joe Clyder and Ethan Terrell muttered their agreement, but Pete was staring after Michael, thinking how he had to love that woman a hell of a lot. "I'm not so sure I can desert him."

Sterne's eyes bugged out. "What are you sayin'?"

"I don't think I realized till now just how determined he is. And we came this far. It wouldn't be right to walk out on him now. Besides, we're talkin' about a lot of money. I'm not sure I want to walk out on that either."

"But we might die," Ethan cried.

Pete shook his head. "I don't think so. We're good shots. All of us."

"But we don't know how many Indians are comin'," Ethan argued. "Besides, we talked about it last night, and we all agreed on turnin' back."

"Yeah, but I thought he'd go, too. He won't stand a chance without us. That and the money makes me think we ought to stay."

"Pete's got a point," Sterne chimed in. "Maybe we ought to hang around another day. If somethin' doesn't happen by then, he'll probably be ready to give up."

"And if he isn't, we'll hog-tie him and make him go with us. Agreed?" Pete glanced around for confirmation.

But Joe Clyder was not listening, and his face had gone pale as he suddenly realized there were no longer just three Indians standing on the rock staring down at them. Now he counted an even dozen, faces painted with streaks of red and yellow paint. "Looks like the waitin' is over," he said thinly.

The others followed his gaze, each man feeling a tingling up and down his spine. But when one of the Indians, a big man wearing a headdress adorned with buffalo horns, started toward them, they went to stand with Michael, hands close to their holsters in readiness for trouble.

"I think it's their leader," Pete whispered.

Black Serpent looked them over cryptically. Their eyes reflected fear, which was only natural since they did not know what to expect, but he also noted courage as they stood in readiness to draw the fine weapons they carried and defend themselves to the death. "I am Black Serpent," he said, pressing his fist against his broad, bare chest. "Leader of my people. Which of you claims the white woman held captive by my enemy?"

"That would be me." Michael looked him straight in the eye, unflinching. "And I've got a question I want answered before we go any further. Why are you asking our help in rescuing her when you're the bastards who took her in the first place?"

Black Serpent was not impressed by his show of nerve and challenged his self-control by gloating, "That is true. And if not for my enemy Howling Wolf—who has taken the white man's name of *Luke*," he added with a sneer of scorn, "she would be my woman now. I would be the one she would pleasure each night. Not Howling Wolf."

Michael knew he was goading him, trying to see how far he could go. He replied coolly, calmly, "Then it would be you I would be hunting down to kill."

Black Serpent threw his head back and laughed. "So. You want revenge. That is good. You will make a fine warrior when we raid the village of my enemy."

"How do we know you aren't using us to get her back for yourself?"

Black Serpent snorted. "You think I taste the leavings of Howling Wolf? I do not want her now. What I want is for Howling Wolf's blood to flow into the ground. I want him and his followers to die in disgrace by the hands and guns of white men. Then I will have honor. Peace. You will have your woman. This I promise."

Michael looked at Pete, and Pete looked at the others, who all indicated they would keep their bargain. "Then we will ride with you," he said.

"We start at dawn. It will take us several days to get there." Black Serpent held up his fist and bit back a grin of triumph. Soon the sky would be filled with the language of the smoke, telling the tale of how he, Black Serpent, had avenged the death of the son of Great Bear and the other Comanche by slaughtering the white men who had dared attack them. And there would be only one survivor, the white woman, whom Black Serpent would take for his slave. Many coup would be counted, and his name would forever more be spoken with reverence and awe. Most of all, he would not be condemned by other Comanche for killing his own kind.

"Wait a minute."

All eyes were on Pete.

"You want us to kill them all?" he asked. "Are we talkin' about women? Children?"

Black Serpent's eyes narrowed. "Women will kill if given the chance. They will run from their tepees and cut you with a knife. Their children will grow into warriors and kill you when they can. They must die. All of them."

He turned on his heel and walked away.

Pete stared after him as he scratched his beard thoughtfully. "I can't stomach the idea of slaughterin' women and children. I think once we find the woman we should high-tail it out of there and not do any unnecessary killin'." He looked at Michael.

Michael assured him that he agreed, which satisfied everybody. What he did not say, however, was that there were two killings he considered quite necessary, and he intended to carry them out himself.

Black Serpent would be the first, because he was the one who took Jacie from the protection of the soldiers.

Then Michael would glory in gunning down the one who now held her captive—the warrior known as Howling Wolf.

They had made love all night long, and when dawn kissed the dark away, they lay with their arms wrapped about each other, each held prisoner by thoughts too intimate to share.

Jacie did not want to leave Luke and knew a part of

her never would. But she also knew she must go before they reached a point of no return. Michael waited, with all his love and goodness, and now she wished she had never left him, had never tasted the wonders that would haunt her forever, and she prayed that he would never sense that she longed for another.

Turning to look into Luke's pensive eyes, she could see he was locked in musing over his own emotions just then. "What is going to happen to you?"

He shared his plans for going to Mexico in the spring. "It's beautiful there. Tall mountains with much game, and cool, green forests, and enough land that we can plant crops and farm and settle down. Most of all, we can find peace there to raise our children, educate them. The life we knew here no longer exists. We must make a new life, in a new land—or perish. I won't lead my people to a reservation."

"Or into a battle they can no longer win," she murmured.

His smile was tender, and he reached to lovingly brush her hair from her face. "All of life is a battle that can't ever be won, Jacie. We all die in the end. It's how we survive in the years before that count. We have to live them as happily as we can."

"Happy . . ." Jacie spoke the word almost dreamily, allowing it to roll about in her mind as revelation dawned. "I realize now that never in my whole life have I asked to be happy. I just didn't want to be *un*happy."

Luke told himself to hold back, not to ask the question that smoldered in his heart like coals in a fire, but he could not refrain. "Is that how you will be with your husband? Not unhappy?"

"I suppose." She rested her head against his shoulder once more, not wanting to talk about it.

Luke rolled onto his side, sliding his hand up and down the curves of her body, enjoying the feel of her. "Why did you come here, Jacie?" He asked suddenly, soberly.

She was surprised by such a question. "To find my mother, of course. What other reason would I have had for leaving the only home I've ever known to come to a wilderness?"

"The Indians have a saying. A person should be careful what he looks for, because he might find it."

She was jolted to remember how Mehlonga had said the same thing and told Luke that, adding, "I still don't understand what it means."

"You will. When your heart is ready to understand. Till then, it means nothing." He brought his mouth down to hers, kissing her deeply. The world seemed to stand still, and Jacie prayed that it always would, that this wondrous moment would never, ever end.

Clutching him tightly against her, she thought how it would be heaven to wake up every morning of her life in his arms. No matter they had not been together long. She knew that what they shared could not be easily found, not in this lifetime. And with tears of regret stinging her eyes, she mourned the reality of knowing she would never, ever experience it again.

When at last he raised his lips, he took her hand and placed it against his chest, then put his against her breast. "You have to return to your world, and I must go back to mine. And though we will never see each other again, our hearts have touched. I will never forget you."

"Nor I you . . ." She pulled his face down for another kiss that left both of them shaken, and she then scrambled to her feet so he would not see that she was crying.

But he knew, yet could not offer comfort. True, he could tell her about her mother, ask that she stay and live with her, with him—and then fear that one day she would regret having done so. No. He shook his head solemnly as he made ready to leave, allowing Jacie time to wander off and calm herself. He would not ask her to stay, for to do so meant committing his whole heart. All he had been able to bring himself to do was allow her to briefly touch it.

They rode into the day, Jacie sitting in front of him as he held her tightly, the pony trailing behind. They hardly spoke. There was nothing left to be said. It was over.

She was returning to a world she should never have left.

And Luke would go back to the one he could never leave.

As the earth became shadowed with misting hues of red and gold, they topped a knoll overlooking the Angeline River and the settlement of Nacogdoches came into view. Luke pointed to a fortlike structure made of stone. "The stagecoach leaves from there. I can see it is dark and closed now. You can find a room for the night at the hotel, but go there tomorrow and ask for a man named Howard Carson. Tell him you are my friend, and that I will see that he gets paid for your passage east. He will take good care of you."

"I have some money." She was fighting tears again and anxious to be on her way lest she break down.

He did not dismount but helped her slide to the ground. He did not want to look at her and stared straight ahead. "Do as I say. You might need your money along the way for food. Take the pony. Leave him with Carson as security for your ticket. Go now, before it gets any darker."

"Thank you," she managed to say around the lump in her throat. "I wish you a long and safe life, Luke. Be well."

"Go and do not be"—he could not resist looking at her one last time—"*un*happy." The smile he offered was sad.

Through a veil of tears, she watched him disappear into the purpled night.

It would be a long journey home. Maybe the stage would not leave for a few days, giving her time to rest, to buy some new clothes. She hoped so, and she really did not care how long it took to get back to Georgia, because she was not looking forward to facing Michael and having to tell him the truth about everything—everything except Luke. That was the secret she would carry in her heart all the way to her grave, the secret longing for what was, what could never be.

Wiping her eyes, Jacie rode into town. A few men were still out on the street, and they stared curiously at the sight of what they took to be an Indian girl, all alone. But in her misery, she was oblivious to anything around her—until someone yelled in an ugly tone, "What're you doing here, squaw? We don't want no squaws here."

She looked at him with disdain, then saw she was right in front of a sign that read ROOMS. She dismounted.

"I said . . ." The man came running over, his face twisted with anger. He was followed by two others. "I said we don't want no squaws here. Now you just ride back out of here, and there won't be no trouble."

"No, there won't be," she said frostily, "because I am not a squaw. I am white. Now I am going to go into this hotel and get a room, and have a bath, and then I will find a store somewhere that will sell me a dress. Then I will look white. Will that make you happy?"

"Well, yeah, sure," he said uneasily, then stiffened. "But how come you're dressed in that dirty skin dress if you ain't no squaw?"

She laughed shortly. "I don't see where that's any of your business, mister."

"I'd say it is. I think you're a breed."

"No. Both my parents were white," she said sweetly, all the while thinking what an ass he was.

"Then you been livin' with Indians. Is that it? You been livin' with them savages, and if you have, that makes you one of 'em."

"If I have, it's still none of your concern," she said, dismounting. She hitched the pony to the rail and started up the hotel steps.

His friends snickered at how she had stood up to him, which made him even madder. "Well you just go get yourself cleaned up, and then we'll decide whether you can stay."

She was halfway up the steps but whirled about to stare at him. "But if I look like an Indian, I can't? Why is that?"

"We don't want redskins in our town." He struck the air with his fist. "Dirty, stealin', no-account murderin' redskins. The only good Indian is a dead Indian." His friends cheered in approval.

Jacie realized that this was what Luke had meant when he said if she found her mother and took her back she would be miserable. Prejudice was everywhere. Cold, cruel, mean.

All of a sudden she did not want to go inside the hotel. She went back down the steps, untied her pony, and led him down the street and back out of town, the laughter of the men echoing behind her. She would camp in the woods and tomorrow morning would seek the man Luke had told her about, Howard Carson. If he were friends with Luke, he would not be rude. He would help her get back to . . . what?

She stood frozen in the darkness.

What exactly was she going back to? And what, exactly, had she been looking for when she came west?

Had it really been her mother?

Placing her hand against her breast, she was stunned to feel the warmth radiating. It was as though Luke were actually touching, caressing, her heart, her soul. Was he thinking of her in that instant?

And that was when she heard the whisper from deep within, warmth spreading throughout her body, coursing through her veins, as her heart began to actually burn with the intensity of the love she was feeling . . . for it was the message she had longed to hear—but not what she had expected, for it spoke not of Michael.

Instead, her heart was whispering of love for Luke.

In that moment, as the moon slipped from behind a silver-tipped cloud in the magenta sky, Jacie knew she had, indeed, been looking for something besides her mother—and she had found it. It was called happiness, the one thing she had never sought before, fearing it was beyond her grasp.

But did she dare reach for it now?

And was she willing to fight to hang on to it if she did?

It would not be easy to enter the world of the Comanche, but her own mother had done so, had actually chosen that life over the one she had been born into when given the chance to return to it. And even though Jacie could not be completely sure she was able to do likewise, she knew she had to try. To turn her back now would leave her with an emptiness inside never to be fulfilled, and that would not be fair to Michael, who certainly did not deserve to have a wife who secretly pined for another man.

And didn't she owe something to herself as well?

Wasn't it time she stopped robbing herself of true joy by attempting to avoid misery? Already, only minutes after parting from Luke, Jacie felt as though a part of her was missing. What would it be like in the years to come?

She did not want to know.

She mounted the pony and urged him into a gallop in the direction Luke had gone.

Night wrapped about her, and with the moon slipping in and out of the clouds, it was hard to see anything.

What if she could not find him?

What if he were gone to her forever?

*Don't let it be too late,* she prayed, every nerve screaming as desperation surged. She called out to him, the sound echoing forlornly in the night. . . .

Finally, surrounded by empty darkness, she knew it was hopeless.

He had ridden away, hard and fast. Now it really was over, and God forgive her, in that moment she did not want to live. . . .

But then the clouds parted once more, and she gasped at the sight of him. Bathed in moonlight, he was sitting on the stallion on the rise just ahead.

Luke saw her and gave thanks he had not been able to force himself to ride away just yet, hoping against hope she would come to him.

Leaping to the ground, she began to run toward him, sobbing his name over and over, her arms outstretched.

Luke jumped from his own horse and ran to meet her, grabbing her and swinging her up and around and around. Then he gently lowered her to her tiptoes and searched her face in a frantic attempt to assure himself she knew what she was doing.

"It's the point of no return, Luke," she whispered raggedly, fervently. "I can't go back. I know now it was you I was looking for all along, because my heart has spoken to me at last. It tells me . . . I love you." Pressing her head against his chest, she hugged him with all her might.

"Are you sure, little one?" he asked softly.

She twined her arms about his neck to pull his face down to hers. "I've never been so sure of anything in my life."

He kissed her then, long and hard, and they clung together as Jacie reveled in the knowledge that Mehlonga had been right.

Her heart *had* spoken, and thank God, she had listened.

# 23

*They rode north across land* that seemed monotonous. A cloud sending a shadow to earth was comfort for their burning eyes. The soil was gray; the vegetation sparse. Scattered sagebrush, Spanish dagger, prickly pear cactus clumped here and there.

Along the way they spotted herds of buffalo, and Jacie teasingly warned Luke not to dare think of trying to bring one down. He said there was no time, because he was anxious to reach his people. But he pointed out to her how the bulls had shed most of their long hair, and she could see how fat the brown calves were as they trailed at the cows' flanks.

They did not lack for food. Luke killed a deer, so they had fresh meat for a few nights. Jacie had little trouble coaxing him to catch fish when they passed a stream, and they munched on hard, green prairie plums, which were plentiful.

It was a relief to finally reach the Red River and the cottonwood trees growing along its banks like giants. Their whitish-gray furrowed trunks were bigger than Luke could reach around, and they towered above with rustling leaves to offer the respite of cooling shade.

Still, Luke did not tarry, explaining he needed to get to the winter camp to help prepare for winter.

They talked constantly as they rode, eager to learn as much as possible about each other.

One day, as Jacie rode astraddle in front of Luke, the pony trailing behind them, he began to talk about his father. She was impressed to hear how Great Bear had changed from a warlike chief to one seeking peace for all of his people. But she was sickened and horrified when Luke described his life prior to his conversion. He admitted to taking part in raids on white settlements, to killing people, burning their homes, stealing horses, livestock. "I'm not proud of those days, Jacie," he said. "But you must understand I knew no other way of life then. Once I went to the missionary school, I knew I could never again take a life except to save my own."

"I'm surprised your father let you go. He didn't know any other way, so why would he want you educated, knowing it would probably change you completely? And what made him change himself and want peace?"

Luke chose his words carefully. To explain fully meant telling Jacie about Sunstar and her influence on his father, which he was not ready to do. "He was a wise man. He realized the world was changing and the way of the Indian could not continue."

"Then he was afraid your people would eventually be defeated by the white man's settlement of the west."

"No. That was not his thinking. The Comanche were defeating themselves. We had already been tested by a century of warring with Spaniards and enemy tribes and had been victorious. Every man was a strong warrior, wily, intelligent, courageous even to death. We knew the land intimately and fought when and where we chose. Texans feared and hated us. No." He shook his head for emphasis. "My father did not fear the Comanche as a whole could be defeated. It was only when they began to fight among themselves that they started getting weak."

"You're talking about warriors like Black Serpent and his men?"

"Partially, but you see the Comanche divided into a number of self-governing bands with no real unified leadership, which made them incapable of sticking together to fight either a tribal or a national war. Instead of attacking with organized armies, they had nothing but angry war parties. It's still true. That's why they will eventually be beaten, and why I plan to take my band to Mexico. We've always been nomadic, another weakness. It's time we settled down."

"In Mexico," Jacie said with a shiver of anticipation at the thought of the new life awaiting, so different from anything she had ever known before. Then apprehension crept over her once more, and she asked, "What is going to happen when we get to your camp? How are your people going to feel about your bringing me there?"

"At first, they'll consider you my captive."

"Does that mean I will share your tepee as your . . . wife?" She realized he might already have one. Maybe several. Mehlonga said it was not an uncommon practice among Indians, and she'd not thought of it till now.

Luke decided to tease her. "Actually a Comanche can have more than one wife. He inherits his wife's younger sisters, and he can always steal women from enemy tribes. Then there's the custom we also practice called the *levirate,* when brothers lend one another their wives."

Jacie asked uneasily, "Do you have brothers?"

"No." Luke was having a difficult time keeping a straight face. "Do you have any sisters?"

"No." She twisted sideways then and saw the twinkle in his eye. "And you don't have any other wives, do you? If you did, you wouldn't be bringing me back, because you know I'd never agree to being part of a harem."

"Harem?" Luke repeated, unfamiliar with the term.

"That's when a man has many wives, concubines they're sometimes called, another word for lovers, mistresses, a group of women a man takes turns bedding."

"Well, I don't have a harem. Or a wife. But you'll have to sneak into my tepee after everyone has fallen asleep. It's the custom."

She laughed. "I'll do nothing of the kind. Making love out here on the trail is different. No one knows about it. But sneaking around like that, chancing someone might find out, well, that's something a woman of ill repute would do."

"Not if it's a custom they were raised with. Sexual

relations before marriage aren't encouraged by my people, but they aren't punished, either, because a man doesn't marry at an early age. He has to gain a reputation as a hunter and warrior, first, because that puts him in a good position to take the girl of his choice for his wife. So boys and girls slip around to be together."

"And you expect me to do the same thing?"

"You have to, as long as we aren't man and wife. I'm not supposed to come to you. It isn't the custom."

Jacie decided to change the subject. He would learn soon enough she had no intentions of sneaking around at night and crawling into tepees, for heaven's sake. "Is your mother living?"

"Yes," he said. As far as he was concerned, Sunstar was his mother, so it was true.

"What will she think of me?"

He wouldn't let himself consider an honest answer, that Sunstar would be delirious with joy. He hedged, "She never questions what I do." That was a lie, he smiled to himself to think. Unlike other Comanche mothers, she did not shy away from voicing disapproval when she felt it was warranted.

Jacie relaxed a little. "What is her name?"

"Sunstar."

"That's pretty. Do you look at all like her?"

"No. She's not my real mother. My real mother died. My father took Sunstar as his wife when I was still a child."

"And they had no other children?"

"None." Luke was starting to feel uncomfortable. Spotting a rabbit, he seized the chance to end the conversation by quickly dismounting to pursue their dinner.

They camped that night out in the open, and after their passion was spent, Jacie lay on her back staring up at the theater nature had provided for their entertainment. A star careened across the velvet curtain, and she exclaimed with delight. Never had she been able to witness a star's journey for so long, but then she'd never been afforded the backdrop of such a broad highway.

Luke lay beside her, smiling at her joy, as well as at his own. Her exuberance was infectious, and he was going to like the experience of teaching her all the wonders of that part of the earth that was theirs.

Jacie did not mind the tedious ride as they traveled north, for they did not run out of things to talk about. She asked the name of every plant, insect, or animal she saw. Luke wanted to hear more about Mehlonga and all she had learned from him. He was also eager for her to tell him about the way she had lived before, but he carefully avoided the subject of her fiancé. So the hours passed slowly but sweetly, in that special wonder-of-you-and-me time enjoyed and savored by those in the throes of falling ever more deeply in love.

Then late one afternoon, Jacie was startled to see smoke spiraling from beyond a distant ridge. "Does that mean Indians?"

"No. It means settlers, and they're friends. The Turnage family. My men and I saved them from the Tonkawa once, and now they live in peace, because they're friends to all the tribes and everyone else who passes by here. We're only a day away from my camp now, and we'll stay here tonight. Maybe Mrs. Turnage will loan you a clean dress."

The thought of a bath, clean clothes, maybe even a real home-cooked meal was thrilling, and Jacie urged him to go faster.

They topped the ridge, and no sooner had the cabin come into view when people began to come out on the porch. Luke called out, and they started waving. Two little boys and a girl ran down the steps. A man in overalls and a plaid shirt stood with his arm around a woman in green calico, both of them smiling broadly to see a dear and treasured friend. Beside them were two teenage sons and another daughter, who appeared to be the oldest.

"Praise God, Luke. It's been a long time," the man said when they rode into the yard, but his eyes narrowed at the sight of Jacie. "Who you got there with you?"

"Don't get the wrong idea, Silas. She's not a prisoner. She's with me of her own will. This is Jacie. Jacie, meet Silas Turnage and his wife, Martha. I can't remember all the names of their offspring."

Martha recited their names, which Jacie knew she'd have trouble remembering, and then came to give her a hug of welcome as she dismounted. "Welcome, child. Any friend of Luke's is a friend of ours. He's a fine man. Saved our lives, he did. But where did you come from? And look at you." She held her at arm's length for scrutiny. "Why, you even remind—"

"Martha." Luke spoke so sharply that all eyes were upon him, startled, and he realized he had reacted in a way that might raise suspicion, but he knew Martha had been about to comment that Jacie had eyes like Sunstar, and that would not do. Forcing a smile, albeit nervously, he said, "I was hoping you'd help

Jacie get a bath, loan her a dress. That is, if we can impose on your hospitality for the night."

"Why, don't be silly. Of course you're stayin'. Jacie can bed down with the girls, and you can sleep in the barn, like you always insist on doin'."

Martha had started to lead Jacie inside, but Luke moved quickly to wave to the oldest daughter and say, "You go with her. I need to talk to your ma."

Jacie was too excited to notice how Luke was behaving. She went with Myra, the fifteen-year-old, and as soon as they disappeared inside, Luke pulled Martha and Silas aside and told them everything.

When he had finished, Martha had to dab tears from her eyes with a corner of her apron. "Lordy, Luke, Sunstar will be so happy. To think after all these years she's goin' to see the baby she thought was dead. I wish I could be there to witness the look on her face. Praise God."

"Now, I can't be positive it's so," Luke pointed out. But the evidence is strong,"

"I would say so," Silas agreed. "Sunstar may have copper-colored skin now like the rest of you after all the years in the sun, and she looks wore out like all of us, but when I looked into that girl's eyes, I saw Sunstar. No, there ain't no doubt about it. She's her young'un all right."

"But Jacie isn't to know anything yet, understood? I want to talk to Sunstar first and prepare her."

Martha said she thought that would be wise, adding, "Oh, she's goin' to be so happy to see both of you. Your people came by here a while back, you know. We gave them something to eat, like always, and Sunstar was tellin' me how glad she'd be when you caught up to them. She surely loves you, Luke, and it's goin' to be wonderful for all of you to be a family, unless—" She hated to ask but had to know. "Does Jacie want to take her ma and go back wherever she came from? I know you wouldn't like that. Neither would your people."

He was proud to be able to tell her, "Jacie is going to be one of us, Martha."

Martha cried a little more but got hold of herself before going inside to help Jacie prepare to be introduced to the mother she had no idea she was about to meet.

Jacie was impressed by how friendly everyone was, and she was also fascinated by the construction of the cabin. The walls were made of roughly hewn logs, with dovetailed corners. The large chinks were daubed with mud. The chimney was put together from mud-plastered sticks, and the roof was made of clapboard and anchored by weighted poles. Hard-packed mud provided the floor. There were two separate rooms connected by a roofed, open corridor like a breezeway, which Martha explained was called a dogtrot.

The wide porch in front provided storage space for harnesses, tools, kegs, and saddles, and there was a lean-to shelter on one side. The kitchen was connected by another porch running along the opposite side.

It happened that Jacie and Myra were the same size, and Myra obligingly loaned her a dress of soft peach muslin. It took Luke's breath away when he saw her all fresh and scrubbed. Her hair, like black silk, hung soft and loose about her glowing face, and he could hardly tear his eyes from her. Martha and Silas exchanged knowing looks. They could tell Luke was smitten by her.

During a dinner of fried prairie hen, stewed turnips, boiled corn, and hoecakes, Luke shared his plans for taking the tribe to Mexico in the spring. Afterwards he and Silas went out to the porch to enjoy cigars and some mulled cider, while the women cleaned up.

Martha chattered away about how civilized Luke was, and how it was hard sometimes, especially when he dressed like an army scout, to remember he was a Comanche. But she very carefully avoided talking about his stepmother, and winced when Jacie brought up the subject by saying, "I hope his people will accept me. Especially his mother. You mentioned her when we first got here. Do you know her well?"

"Oh, yes, yes, I do." Martha said as she vigorously scrubbed a pot that was already clean. "An extraordinary woman. She knows a lot about medicine. They rode by here one fall when my youngest, Billy, was sick with the croup. She knew just what to do. She had some pokeberry leaves in her pouch and boiled them for tea, and she made a poultice out of camphor berries. Smart, she is, all right.

"Well, now." She gave an exaggerated sigh and hung up the dish towel. "Let's go join the men, shall we?" And she hurried from the kitchen, anxious to avoid more questions.

Jacie stared after her. Was it her imagination or had the mention of Luke's mother upset her? Maybe Martha knew Sunstar wasn't going to like him bringing a woman home. Maybe she even had a wife picked out for him.

Folding her dish towel, Jacie decided there was no need to worry about it now. She would just try every way she knew how to make Sunstar like her once they met.

Joining the others on the porch, she watched Luke in the lantern's glow. He was engrossed in what Silas was telling him, his face an angry mask as he learned that a northern band of Comanche had been attacked while on their way home from a friendly council with government officials.

"They were camped near a Wichita village situated near Rush Springs," Silas recounted. "The Second Cavalry under Captain Earl Van Dorn, along with over a hundred Indians from the Brazos Reservation—Shawnes, Delaware, Wichita—hit without warning. Over fifty Comanche were killed, three hundred horses taken. The survivors scattered."

"Damn him." Luke got up and began to pace angrily about on the porch.

Martha also stood. She did not like such upsetting conversations and had already sent the children to bed. Now she moved to go inside, motioning for Jacie to go with her, but Jacie pretended not to notice, wanting to hear everything. If she were going to be living as an Indian, she felt she should know as much as possible about what was happening to them.

"Van Dorn should have known about the band's recent council with the government," Luke raged on. "Things like this only enforce my people's belief that the white men can't be trusted."

Silas drew deeply on his cigar. "Well, he was wounded. So was Ross, the one leadin' the Indians from the Brazos. Two of the survivors came by here in the night. Martha, she treated their wounds best she could and fed 'em. They said things were getting real bad, that the Comanche will raid or starve now. I tried to tell 'em that's only goin to make the citizens of Texas even more hostile. But they won't listen. There's just too much goin on, especially on the reservations. And if it weren't for the army, mobs of white men would be attackin' them. There's talk now of movin' them up to Indian Territory or to the Wichita Reservation near Fort Cobb."

Luke slammed a fist into his open palm. "It won't happen to my people. Come spring, we move south. We will not go to a reservation."

Martha cleared her throat, a signal to let Silas know she did not like the tension and wanted the evening to end. He obliged by saying good night to their guests and followed her.

Martha was no fool and had all ideas Luke and Jacie had been sleeping together like man and wife out on the trail, but she maintained a Christian home and had no intention of allowing them to carry on under her roof. But in all fairness, she knew neither of them expected it and gently called to Jacie, "Come along now, dear. You can bed down with the girls in their room across the dogtrot."

Jacie responded politely, "Yes ma'am. I'll be right there."

Martha gave them a moment alone, and Jacie went to Luke to place a comforting hand on his shoulder. "Maybe you should think of going to Mexico right away. If things are getting worse, it might not be safe to wait."

"We have to," he said, irritable, but not with her. It was the situation that made him bristle. "We have to dig in for winter. I'm going to bed now. When the others are asleep, come to me. I'll be in the barn. You can slip back inside before it's light."

He bolted down the steps to disappear around the corner, with Jacie staring after him. She had no intention of sneaking out. What if the girls awoke and found her gone? And what if Martha or Silas heard her leave? Jacie would take no chances on making them think ill of her.

Besides, she thought with a determined lift of her chin, it was time Luke found out that she was not going to be at his beck and call when it did not suit her.

# 24

*Martha was beside herself* as she made breakfast, frying thick slices of ham and baking huge, fluffy lard biscuits. She was trying not to think about what a joyous day it was going to be for Jacie, because she did not want to appear nervous. But she had never seen Luke so somber, and she was not about to ask him what was wrong. She and Silas had talked long into the night about how hard it might be for him, because no matter what he thought, Jacie might not want to stay. They had not been around her long enough to decide whether she was really in love with him and had the makings of an Indian wife. But, Martha thought as she broke eggs into the skillet and began to scramble them, it was his life, and she and Silas weren't about to interfere.

After breakfast, they all gathered in front of the cabin to say good-bye. "Remember the smoke signals

I taught you how to send should you have any trouble," Luke told Silas. "I will take the men and get here as fast as I can."

Silas clasped his hand. "I know you would, but we've been here long enough now for every Indian around to know we only want peace and that they can always find food and shelter here. You just look after yourself, and your woman." He grinned at Jacie.

Martha hugged Luke and whispered in his ear, "I hope everything turns out the way you want it to."

He did not respond and stepped quickly from her embrace.

They forded the river and rode doggedly north. When Luke made no attempt at conversation, Jacie assumed he was angry because she had not gone to his bed the night before, and she decided to ignore him.

She had no way of knowing he was so deep in thought over the poignant reunion ahead that he was unconcerned with anything else.

She rode on the pony so they could travel faster. Luke wanted to reach camp by nightfall. Martha had packed a bag with ham biscuits from breakfast and cold prairie chicken from dinner the night before. They ate as they rode, stopping only to water the horses and tend to their own needs.

The sun began to set, bathing them in shadows of sherry and gold. Luke had spoken only to point out precarious spots along the trail. Annoyed, Jacie was starting to wonder if this was how he would behave when she didn't obey his command. Finally, weariness making her cranky, she could hold back no longer and demanded, "Would you mind telling me how long you intend to pout because I didn't go to you last night?"

"I'm not pouting," he said tonelessly.

"Then if you aren't mad, why have you ignored me all day? Is something wrong?" Suddenly she started to worry that maybe he was actually beginning to feel he had made a mistake. After all, it was going to take a lot of patience and understanding between the two of them, as well as from all of his people, for her to adjust to such a totally foreign way of life. Or maybe that was not it at all. Maybe an Indian girl was waiting to marry him, and he was wondering how she would react.

He cast a sideways glance at her and saw how her brow was furrowed with anxiety. "I just have a lot on my mind, Jacie. It has nothing to do with you," he lied, wanting to put her at ease. "But I was disappointed you didn't come last night," he added.

"I was afraid someone would hear me sneaking out."

"Someone might hear you tonight, but don't let that stop you. I miss having you sleep in my arms." His smile was warm.

She was not sure she could do it, was not sure of anything right then.

Luke could see she was still tense. "Many things are going to be different, Jacie. We both know that. Your new life isn't going to be easy, I'm afraid. But don't worry. I'll help you every step of the way. I don't intend to ever let you go."

Her eyes began to shine to think of all the tomorrows they would share, and the uneasiness left her face as she said, "Luke, I can look back now and see my old life wasn't easy, because I was trying to make myself believe in a love that was not meant to be. I've found my true love, and I don't intend to ever lose you."

His breath caught in his throat to see the love mirrored on her beautiful face. "Come here," he said huskily, reaching to take her reins and pull her pony close beside his stallion.

Their lips met and held in a searing kiss of silent avowal of love, and she clung to him and felt the familiar shudderings of desire begin. Forcing herself to pull back, she warned him in a shaky voice, "If we don't stop this, we won't reach your camp till morning."

"You just come to me when you can." He kissed her once more and somehow knew she meant what she said, that she would never leave him.

Digging his heels into his horse's flanks, Luke set him into a full gallop.

It was time to end one journey . . . and begin another.

Iris stood at the cooking bag, which she had made by tying the ends of the stomach lining of a buffalo to four poles. It was new, freshly made, and would last three to four days before it became soggy and soft from the heat. Then it too would be eaten. Meanwhile, she was cooking stew and had started the water to boiling by dropping in hot fist-size stones. Then she added meat and prairie turnips.

She was not hungry herself but was helping cook for the other women, who were busy working with the game the hunters had brought in the day before.

There were deer to be skinned and cut for drying, and buffalo, the hides to be treated for tanning to make clothing and blankets. It was a busy season, and they had to work fast, because the men had set out again and would be returning in another day, bringing more trophies to be readied for the cold months of winter ahead.

Iris was about to sample the stew when she heard Gold Elk, who'd been left to guard the camp, calling out to her as he ran from his lookout post. "He is back, Sunstar. He is back."

She set aside the wooden tasting spoon and wiped her hands. Now she could rest easy. Always when Luke was away, she worried, but now he would be home for the winter. But seeing the look on Gold Elk's face as he reached her, Iris was not altogether sure she should relax just yet. "What's wrong?" she asked anxiously. "Is he hurt?"

She started by him, intending to climb to the rocky perch overlooking the trail to watch Luke's approach, but Gold Elk held her back. "He is not hurt."

She laughed, relieved. "Then why do you look so upset? You should be happy. Like me." She started by him again, but he continued to hold her. She was getting annoyed. "What is wrong with you? Let me go."

"I should prepare you. I should tell you he is not alone."

"He has men with him? Some of the renegades have asked to come back into our fold?" She could think of no one else.

Gold Elk hated to tell her, for he was afraid of what it might mean for Luke to return with the woman, sure she was the one from the fort. Like the others, Gold

Elk felt deeply for Sunstar and would be sad if she went away. "It is a woman."

Iris began to smile. She was not surprised. It was time for Luke to take a wife. And she was sure she would love her as he did. "Can you tell what band she is from? She is Comanche, isn't she?"

Some of the women had gathered to hear what Gold Elk was saying, and they gasped as one when he announced, "No. She is white."

Iris struggled with her own reaction. Dear God, surely Luke had not taken a woman captive. He would never do such a thing, not since his education at the mission school. She could not imagine his doing something so barbaric as to abduct anyone, man or woman.

Several of the younger woman, unmarried and daring to dream they might be chosen for the wife of their leader, began to wail. "Take them away until they can calm themselves," Iris said, snapping her fingers. She had enough to cope with without having to listen to them.

Gold Elk pointed. "Here they come."

Jacie now rode behind Luke on his stallion, clinging to him, arms about his waist. Peering timidly over his shoulder, she saw the women staring curiously, noting that while their hair was hacked off raggedly, their faces were meticulously painted, with red lines above and below their eyelids, some of them crossed at the corners. Their ears were painted red inside, and both cheeks had been daubed with a solid circle of orange and red. They wore drab, plain dresses of buckskin, and ankle-high moccasins.

But one of them, Jacie noted curiously, stood out and apart from the rest. She was wearing a beaded and fringed blouse of buckskin, a skirt with an uneven hemline that fell to her ankles, and low-cut moccasins. Unlike the others, her eyes were lined in yellow, and the painting on her cheeks was in the shape of a triangle. She heard the woman call out to Luke hesitantly and asked, "Is that your mother?"

"Yes." Luke dismounted, leaving Jacie where she was. "Stay here." He started toward Sunstar.

Iris could see the girl was indeed white, and also that she appeared to be quite pretty, her dark black hair framing a heart-shaped face, but she was too far away to tell anything else about her.

"Oh, my son, don't tell me you have taken a captive," Iris said worriedly when he embraced her. She steeled herself for his admission that he had when he did not step back but kept his hands firmly upon her shoulders.

"She came of her own free will, Mother."

A sigh of relief escaped her lips, and she chided herself for ever doubting him. Then the myriad of questions bubbled out: "Where did you meet her? How did you meet her? And what is her name?"

Luke glanced over his shoulder long enough to make sure Jacie was obeying him and staying put. Then he took Iris's arm and steered her far enough away from the others that they could not be overheard. He could see Gold Elk anxiously looking on and knew he had figured out who Jacie was.

Iris was feeling apprehensive again. "What's wrong? Why aren't you introducing me to her? I want to meet her—"

"And you will." Luke cupped her chin, forcing her to meet his steady gaze. "But first I want to tell you her name."

His demeanor was making her uneasy. "Go on," she said.

"Her name is—" He drew a ragged breath and held it for a second, then said, "Jacie."

He tensed for her reaction, but she merely stared at him. The name did not register. It had been a long time, and there was no reason to make any connection—yet.

"That's a lovely name. And she's a lovely girl, as best I can tell from here. Take me to meet her. I'm happy for you, Luke. I really am, though I'm afraid there are a few who don't feel the same." She nodded toward the sound of young girls weeping over crumbled dreams.

Luke could feel Jacie's eyes boring into his back and knew she must be wondering what was going on, why he was taking so long, how his mother was reacting to the news. "Her name is Jacie," Luke repeated, more firmly this time, firing the words like bullets, wanting to get it all said as quickly as possible, "She came here from the east to look for her mother, who was taken by Indians more than eighteen years ago. Her father and her brothers were killed. Only she and her aunt, her mother's sister, survived. Her aunt raised her as her own child. Her aunt's name was Violet; she died not long ago. . . ."

But Iris was listening no longer. His hands fell away from her, and she stepped back as if in a trance. *Jacie . . . Violet . . .* The names fought to rise above the great roaring within her, as she walked toward where she sat on the stallion, staring so bewilderedly. And in that crystallized moment, everything around Iris faded like the mist at sunrise, and in its place, the past came rushing back, bold and bright—her precious baby, given to her sister to nurse. They had walked away from the wagons to disappear among the rocks and waist-high saw grass. She could see it all so clearly once more. And then came the screams . . . the awful screams . . . the gunfire, the hacking of tomahawks and knives and the shrieks of the dying amidst the fire and smoke. A nightmare of long ago, only now it was back but different than before, because all was not lost. And with a great halo of realization bursting all around her, Iris Banner knew that her world had not ended at that scene of carnage all those years ago, because she had only to look into the young girl's eyes to know that she was actually looking inside her very own soul.

"My baby. Oh, dear God, it's my baby . . ." She was barely able to speak past the swelling of her heart that filled her bosom and squeezed her throat. She held out her arms, tears streaming down to smear the painted red triangles on her sun-bronzed cheeks. Her lips trembled, sobs bursting forth as she cried hoarsely, "Jacie, my baby. It is you. Oh, my precious darling, you're alive. You didn't die. You didn't die."

Jacie blinked, shock momentarily imprisoning her in a velvet cocoon. But then she came alive, and with a scream of joy scrambled from the horse and leapt upon her mother to wrap her arms about her. "I don't believe it. Sweet Jesus, I don't believe it. This can't be so. . . ."

And then they were clinging together, crying together, and Luke motioned to the other women to go back to their tasks, to grant Sunstar and Jacie privacy in their golden moment.

He went to where Gold Elk stood frowning.

"Why did you bring her here?" Gold Elk asked accusingly. "She will take Sunstar away."

"Neither of them are going anywhere," Luke was pleased to be able to assure him.

Gold Elk's brows rose sharply. "You are going to make the young one stay? She will be kept against her will?"

Luke gave him a hearty pat on the shoulder. "You ask too many questions. You're worse than a woman. Now go help the men with their hunting and tell them to hurry, because there's going to be a wedding."

Gold Elk let out a loud whoop of joy and ran to his horse. Placing his hands on the animal's rump, he vaulted onto its back, then took off in a cloud of dust. He could not wait to tell the news. Not only had Sunstar found her daughter, but their leader had found a wife.

Still clinging to Jacie, crying unashamedly, Iris started to lead her to the privacy of her tepee, but Luke took Jacie's hand and said, "Mother, let me have a word with her first, please."

Drawing her to one side, he quickly explained why he had lied to her before. "It was selfish, I know, but I love her, too, Jacie, and I didn't want her to be taken away, only to be hurt back in your world."

Jacie could understand that but was hurt herself to think he had planned to send her back without her ever knowing the truth. "It will take me some time to forgive you for that, Luke," she said with candor.

He laughed then, playfully tweaking her nose. "Why do you think I was out there waiting for you, little one? If you hadn't come back, as I was hoping you would, the settlement of Nacogdoches would have had a one-man Indian raid that night, because I assure you I would have turned savage and ridden in there to find you. Then my mother would have been mad at me for taking a white woman captive. Don't you know now I couldn't let you go, Jacie?" he asked tenderly.

She felt warm all over, glowing with more happiness than she ever dreamed possible. She wanted to throw her arms around him and kiss him again and again, and he was likewise having difficulty holding back from embracing her, but neither dared with the women watching from a distance.

"Go now," he told her, their locked gaze conveying secret messages of desire. He wanted her and Sunstar to relive the past eighteen years as quickly as possible so they could begin the rest of their lives—together.

Some of the women obediently and hastily erected Luke's tepee for him, then brought him food and drink. He ate his fill of deer stew and turnips, then wearily sank onto the bed of thick blankets of soft rabbit fur and fell asleep, dreaming of how good it would be to awaken later with Jacie beside him.

In the mellow glow of the small campfire burning outside the open door of the tepee, Iris drank in the sight of Jacie and thought surely she had to be dreaming. Holding the locket and its daguerreotype, she listened to her daughter's story, then said, "I can understand and forgive why Violet did what she did. She and Judd hadn't been getting along, and she was afraid he wouldn't want to stay married to her once he found out the baby they had both wanted for so long was born dead. With no one to know any different, I suppose it was all too tempting not to go through with such a deception.

"But how were you able to find me?" she went on to ask incredulously. "You had nothing to go on except the story of how I ran away from the fort all those years ago."

"Enough about me," Jacie said, laughing. "Tell me why you did run away. No one could understand."

And Iris obliged, explaining that she had felt she had no reason to go back, and how she had come to feel she belonged with the Comanche, loving Luke as her own son, and yes, she admitted, she had begun to care for Great Bear as well.

They talked on, the hours slipping away. Jacie told all about Mehlonga, how he had made sure she got to Bird's Fort, and finally about the horror of being abducted by Black Serpent.

Iris's face went cold. "Did he . . . hurt you in the a way a man can hurt a woman?"

"That was his intention, but I poisoned him before he could."

"But how?"

Jacie described what she had done with the morning glory seeds, how Mehlonga had taught her about them along with other herbs and potions.

Iris was impressed. "You must take after my father and me, with your interest in medicine. And there's so much more I can teach you, but . . ." She fell silent to think how they had talked of nothing but the past, with no mention of the future. She did not want to speak of that just yet and asked, "What about your life back in Georgia? I want to hear everything. As beautiful as you are, you must have many beaus. Maybe even a husband?"

"No husband," Jacie said.

"But a beau?"

Jacie nodded and told her all about Michael, intending to finish by explaining how she now knew why she had never been able to tell him she loved him, but her mother interrupted, "If he had asked you to marry him, why would he let you come on such a dangerous journey by yourself? Why didn't he come with you?"

Jacie lowered her eyes. "I didn't tell him."

"I see," Iris said quietly, at once understanding how Jacie had known Michael would not have condoned her search, and, no doubt, would not want anyone to hear of such a scandal, much less about her mother living with Indians.

Jacie suspected her mother was afraid she was going to ask her to go back with her and sought to allay her fears. "None of that matters, because—"

But Iris would not let her continue, deciding to settle the matter once and for all. "Listen to me, my child," she said in a rush. "I am glad we found each other, but do not ask me to return with you, please. These are my people now. I don't belong back there. But you do. So I want you to stay for a visit, as long as you like, and then Luke can take you to a settlement to begin your journey home. But let's just enjoy each other for now and not waste time arguing about my leaving, all right?" Oh, she hoped Jacie understood. Leaving was out of the question, and never would she expect Jacie to give up her own life for her mother.

"Mother," Jacie tried again, "you don't understand. I just told you how I realized that I could never tell Michael I loved him because I didn't, and I never will, and—"

"And he sounds like a wonderful man," Iris cut in again, smiling to show she approved. She held up the diamond and amethyst necklace Jacie had shown her. "He gave you this. A man who gives a woman something so fine has to be generous. You will learn to love him. He will make you a good husband."

"I'm sure he would, but—"

"He's probably worried sick about you. And why did you bring this, anyway?" She admired the necklace. "You might have lost it."

"I didn't know I was bringing it, Mother," Jacie said quickly, wanting to take charge of the conversation so she could tell her about Luke. "A child put it in there without my knowing, thinking I could sell it if I didn't have the money to get back home, but that isn't important. You have to listen to me. I'm not leaving you—"

"Yes, you are," Iris insisted. "Now please, let's don't spoil our time together arguing about it."

"Mother, please. Be quiet and hear me out."

She spoke so sharply Iris's eyes went wide.

"I'm trying to tell you something very important," Jacie said, heart full to bursting. "I'm not leaving you, not ever—*because I'm not leaving Luke.*"

It dawned then, and Iris felt fresh tears welling.

"I love him," Jacie went on, "and I believe he loves me. Don't you see? He didn't tell me about you, afraid I'd try to take you away, so he took me where I could make my way home, but I knew I couldn't go. I stopped thinking about finding you then. All I wanted was to be with him. He knew then it was meant to be, just as I did."

Iris knew Jacie meant every word she spoke. She knew also that Luke would never have allowed her to believe he loved her unless he did. Still, despite the glow on her beloved daughter's face, Iris had mixed emotions over Jacie embracing the Comanche world, for she remembered the difficulties she had experienced. And she did not know her daughter, could not be sure she had the mettle necessary to endure.

Jacie could see her doubts and beseeched, "Please be happy for us."

"I am, my darling, I am," Iris assured, "but so much has happened, I am dizzy to think. Let's sleep and talk in the morning. I want to hear what Luke has to say."

Iris made her a bed of buffalo skins at the rear of the tepee. With yet another hug and kiss, they said their good-nights.

Jacie settled down to dream of even more happiness to come. She dared not sneak out to find Luke, did not know where to find him anyway, and, finally, wearily, she slept.

She did not hear the knife as it sliced through the skin wall of the tepee, was unaware of what was happening until the warm hand pressed down on her face to smother any sound she might make and strong arms reached for her to render her helpless in the darkness.

# 25

*Terror bowed to a thrilling* rush as Jacie heard Luke's husky whisper against her ear, "Be quiet. I don't want to wake anyone." Lifting her, he carried her quickly through the opening he had cut in the tepee wall.

Jacie clung to him, arms around his neck, as he moved swiftly in the night. Only when they were inside his tepee, set back from the others at the edge of the camp, did she scold, smiling as she did so, "Mother isn't going to be happy about what you did."

"I'll mend it tomorrow." He set her on her feet. "Besides, I had no choice. I couldn't just storm through the door, and I knew you wouldn't know where to find me even if you did muster the nerve to sneak out.

"And this night, little one," he added, "I knew I had to have you." Gently, he drew her body close to his and began to caress her wordlessly. He could feel her flesh start to quiver before she pressed her head against his bare chest and rendered a small sigh of surrender.

Jacie closed her eyes to shut out any thoughts of the dazzling events of the day. Later she would marvel at the miracle of reunion with her mother, but this was here and now, and she wanted only to languish in the bliss of being possessed by the only man she had ever loved—the only man, she now knew, that she ever would.

It was uncanny, the strong, irresistible bond that had grown between them. Not only of the flesh but mind and heart as well. When he drew her down beside him, as he was doing now, deftly, quickly removing her clothing, his clothing, till naked flesh clung to naked flesh and desire burned hotly, brightly, every sense, every nerve, became raw with yearning. But there was more. Much more. And albeit subtle, it was there all the same, that driving need for each other, the hunger for contentment found only when they were close again.

He planted light kisses along her cheek and neck, pausing to nibble at her ear in a way that made her undulate her hips with pleasure, delighting in the feel of the soft rabbit fur against her bare skin as she did so.

Mellow light filled the tepee from the glow of the watch fire just outside. How beautiful she was, Luke reflected, feasting upon her bronze-gold body, the magnificent black cloud of hair, so thick and lush, like curtains on each side of her face as she gazed up at him with the radiance of desire in her mysterious lavender eyes. To realize that this woman, of all he had known, possessed the power to hold him a captive of her heart was overwhelming. He knew now, beyond all doubt, that he could not live without her. From the moment of their first meeting, Jacie had crept every so subtly, secretly, into the core of his being, until without warning, he knew he was helplessly in love with her.

Her perfectly formed breasts rose and fell with her quickened breathing, and he bent to take a nipple between tongue and teeth and bite gently, inflicting only sweet pain that caused her to gasp out loud and press her fingertips on the base of his neck, urging him on. He began to suckle, gently at first, then taking as much of her into his warm, eager mouth as possible, while one hand slipped down to cup her buttocks and pull her tight against him to feel the hardness of his desire slide between her thighs in promise of ecstasy to come.

The burning within her loins was a hunger not to be denied, and she thrilled to feel his muscles, his nerves, vivify as she touched him there, glorying in her power to invoke the diamantine state of his manhood. She closed her hand about it, smiled to feel the eager throbs, then moved slowly, gently, ever downward to cup the rest of him, thrilling to hear the soft cry of pleasure escape his lips as he continued to devour her breasts with abandon.

He could stand the sweet torture no more, but was not ready yet to take them both to the heights of glory, so he rolled onto his back, taking her with him so that she was above him, stretched the length of him. Then, hands at her waist, he held her as he bathed her in the warmth of his smile and said, "I don't think our mother would approve of your sneaking into my tepee every night. Like I told you, only experienced girls do that, and I don't think she would like to think of you as having that kind of past."

"*Our* mother." Jacie laughed to say the words. "I still can't grasp everything that's happened. Neither can she. At first she thought you just brought me here to find her, and she started talking about how I should go home and marry and settle down, but then I told her I had no intentions of leaving—because of you." She planted a kiss on the tip of his nose.

His brows rose. "And what did she say to that?"

"She's happy for us but worries I won't be able to cope with the hardships. She says it was different for her, because she had nothing else."

"But you do, and she worries you'll miss it. Maybe so do I," he added, searching her face for any sign he might be right.

She responded earnestly, fervently. "The only thing I would ever miss is you if you left me. But I don't intend to let you out of my sight."

"Then I guess we're going to have to do something about making sure she doesn't get upset with our spending our nights together. Which means I have to marry you."

"*Have* to?" Jacie pretended affront, even though her heart was hammering so hard he could surely hear it. Cocking her head saucily to one side, she teased, "Well, I wouldn't want you to be forced into doing something you don't want to. Maybe I'd better go back to my own bed, and you stay in yours, and we'll just give ourselves time to think about all this."

"And you talk too much." He gave a mock growl and grabbed her roughly, possessively, to roll her once more beneath him. And when he was on top of her, pinning her down, devouring her with hot, hungry kisses, he paused only long enough to avow, "I am going to marry you because I want to, Jacie, and because I love you."

He took her then, spreading her thighs to enter her as she yielded, hooking her heels into his buttocks. His mouth was pressed against her neck, and she twined her fingers in his long, dark hair, her gasps in cadence with his rhythmic thrusts.

They soared together to the moon, to swing upon the stars and orbit the earth in celestial bliss, both awed by the wonder of their ecstasy.

Afterward they lay together, bodies slick with perspiration. Jacie's head was upon Luke's shoulder, and he wrapped his arms about her possessively. For a long time neither spoke, both yet locked in the splendor of their love. Then Luke told her how they would plan to marry when the hunters returned in a few days, for he wanted all of his people to share in their happiness.

They talked also about the beloved woman they both called mother, about how happy they were all going to be. Dawn was nearly tinging the sky when they finally began to succumb to weariness.

"Later this morning," Luke said sleepily, "I'll show you where to find prairie apples, just outside camp to the west. We'll pick enough so that Mother can make her delicious apple flapjacks."

"I should go back to my own bed now. She shouldn't wake up and find me gone."

He pulled her closer. "Stay a little longer. I don't want to let you go. . . ."

Jacie listened to his even breathing and soon knew he slept. But she was too keyed up to be still. She wanted to tell her mother they were going to marry soon, and she was also anxious to meet the other women in the camp, eager to communicate how she wanted to be friends with them. "So much to do," she whispered to herself as she quickly put on her clothes. And first she wanted to surprise Luke by finding those prairie apples by herself, so that when he awoke, his flapjacks would be ready and waiting for him.

She slipped out of the tepee and stepped into the rose and peach mist as dawn kissed a new day hello.

Black Serpent's men hung back, but he had taken his horse to the peak of the hill overlooking the camp and then dismounted, crouching to look for any sign of early morning stirrings. All was quiet. The campfires had long turned to ashes. It appeared everyone was still sleeping. And the fact that they had not come upon a guard, and that there were only a few horses grazing, told Black Serpent that what he'd dared hope was actually so—the men were out hunting. Howling Wolf, when he had ridden in late the day before, had probably sent any braves remaining to join the others.

And, oh yes, Black Serpent knew exactly when Howling Wolf had arrived. He'd had his enemy's every move watched on the trail for the past two days. Black Serpent had not, of course, let on to the white men that Howling Wolf and the woman had been sighted. They had no need to know anything till he gave them their orders to attack.

Now, seeing only Howling Wolf's white stallion, and realizing the other men were out hunting, was luck Black Serpent had not counted on. When they returned, they would find all their women and children dead, with Black Serpent claiming to have happened upon the carnage but not in time to save them, only to avenge their deaths by killing the white men. Howling Wolf would also be dead, unable to tell the truth and soon forgotten, while Black Serpent would be forevermore hailed as a great Comanche warrior.

Black Serpent would also count many coup, but the best would be in making the white woman wish for a quick death as he took his revenge for how she had tried to poison him. She would die only after slow and painful torture.

Michael and his men watched from a short distance away.

"I don't like this," Pete said uneasily. "I don't know anything about Indian villages, but it appears to me there's no braves around in this one. I count maybe forty tepees but only one horse."

Joe Clyder said, "They're out huntin', getting ready for winter. Ain't nothing down there but women. Children. I don't know about the rest of you, but I didn't bargain to kill women and children."

"Fact is," Sterne Walters cut in, "as best I recollect, when we left Georgia we didn't bargain to kill nobody."

"That's right."Ethen Terrell said. "We don't even know your woman is down there, Blake, so how come we're goin' to ride in and gun down innocent people?

I don't like the looks of this a'tall. I say we get out of here—and fast."

Sterne and Clyder mumbled in agreement, but Pete held up a hand for silence as he asked Michael, "What do you want to do? I agree with them, but if you think she's down there . . ."

"She's down there."

His reply was like the crack of a whip, swift, lethal. Following his almost mesmerized gaze, they saw her then, a girl with long, dark hair wearing a dress that looked like anything but Indian garb. She was walking from the camp toward a thicket of bushes at the edge.

Black Serpent also spotted her and turned to gauge Blake's reaction. Hurrying to where they stood, he said, "We will attack now. She is out of the way. Mount your horses and make ready to shoot and kill them all."

He was about to signal to his warriors, but Michael reached out and seized his arm. "No," he said through tightly clenched teeth. "There's no need to kill anybody. We'll ride down and get the girl, and if you and your men want to shoot up the place, do so. But we're getting out of here first."

Black Serpent's face became a thundercloud of rage. "We made pact," he hissed, fists clenched. "You agreed to help us kill our enemy, kill Howling Wolf, the one who took your woman."

"No," Michael said again evenly as he drew his gun. "You're the one who took her from the fort. If not for you, she wouldn't be here."

A shot rang out, and Michael's attention was diverted just long enough for Black Serpent to seize the chance to lunge for the gun. The shot had been fired by Ethan Terrell, who had seen one of the Indians lift a rifle and aim at Michael. Struck between the eyes, the Indian fell to the ground, but the others were raising their weapons, preparing to fire.

Michael was grappling with Black Serpent, falling to the ground and rolling downward, while his men dove behind rocks for cover as the bullets started flying.

Jacie had frozen as the first explosion split the stillness, but only for an instant. Turning, she started running back toward the camp to alert Luke and everyone else, when suddenly, right in front of her, two men hit the ground, pummeling each other with their fists as they cursed and grunted mightily.

"Oh, my God!" Her hands flew to her mouth at the recognition first of Black Serpent, then Michael, but there was no time to wonder over the why of it, because Michael had suddenly landed a blow to Black Serpent's chin that knocked him unconscious. Scrambling to his feet, he grabbed her hand and took her with him as he to lunged for cover behind a rock. He had dropped his gun during the scuffle, and they were helpless as the others rapidly exchanged gunfire.

"Michael—how . . ." Jacie stared at him in shock, but then he pulled her against him to shield her, pressing her head beneath his chin and holding her tight.

All around were the zinging sounds of the gunfire, the stench of sulphur, and from beyond, the screams of the women and the cries of the children as they awoke in terror to the bedlam.

"Stay still," Michael ordered as she struggled

against him. "My men are good shots. I see Black Serpent's men going down like flies." He spoke more to himself than to her, preoccupied with the hell exploding all around them. He winced to see Joe Clyder hit, knew he was dead before he hit the ground as blood spurted from his eyes and nose. But the Indians were falling faster, as he saw Pete take three with successive shots.

It seemed to be ending. Michael dared think that it was. Still holding Jacie—tighter than he realized, for one hand had gone about her throat—as he got slowly to his feet, taking her with him. She was having difficulty breathing.

"Let her go."

Michael froze. A man was coming toward him, and he had a gun. His hair was long and wild about his face, which was a mask of rage. His nostrils flared, the nerves in his jaw twitching as his lips curled back ominously.

"I said let her go, damn you," Luke repeated, the clicking of the gun's hammer an ominous sound in the stillness.

Above, Pete had seen what was taking place but could not fire, because Michael and the woman were in the way. "Move, Blake. Now," he screamed.

Michael did so, still holding Jacie, but he leapt in the direction of Black Serpent, who had only pretended to be unconscious and had managed to get his hands on Michael's gun, which he now held beneath him, waiting for the right moment to fire.

And he thought it was upon him—but that was in the precise instant that Michael fell to the ground beside him, hitting his arm to knock his aim off. The bullet went wild, but Luke was quick to react, firing his gun to hit Black Serpent in the forehead, killing him.

But before Luke could move to shelter, Michael's hand shot out to grab Black Serpent's and point the gun in Luke's direction. Squeezing the dying Indian's finger, which was still curved about the trigger, Michael fired the weapon, and Luke went down.

The scream was ripped from Jacie's throat, and with strength she never knew she possessed, she tored herself from Michael's grasp to propel herself to her feet and run to where Luke lay unmoving. She was oblivious to Michael's frantic shouts amidst the cries and shouts of his men as they scrambled down the hill toward her.

"No, God, no." Jacie dropped to her knees beside Luke. Blood poured from the wound in his neck. She dared not try to lift him but bent to place her trembling hands on his face and pat gently, rocking to and fro as she whispered in anguish, "Please, God. Don't let him die. Please . . ."

Michael came to stand behind her uncertainly, ignoring Pete's anxious voice at his ear telling him, "They're all dead, so's Clyder, and we got to get the hell out of here, and fast. We don't see any men in the camp, but somebody will go for them. Hell, they might even be close enough to have heard the shootin'. Let's ride." He squeezed Michael's arm, hard.

Michael was jolted by Jacie's reaction. The dead Indian was her captor, yet she seemed to be slipping into shock from grief, and he did not know what that meant, was not sure he wanted to know. He attempted to draw her away. "We have to go now. Come along. It's over."

"Don't touch me!" She whipped her head about to scorch him with a reproachful glare, then swayed with relief to see her mother running from the camp and called frantically, "Hurry. Luke's been shot. He's bleeding bad."

"Jacie, we'll all be killed if we don't get out of here right now," Michael yelled fiercely.

Iris dropped to her knees on the other side of Luke, panic boiling. She had no idea who the men were or why they were here, had recognized Black Serpent and assumed he and his warriors had all been killed. She did not care about them, nor was she concerned with who the white man tugging at Jacie was. All of her attention was focused on Luke, who was losing a lot of blood. As best she could tell on hasty examination, the bullet had gone completely through the side of his throat. If she could get him back to her tepee and treat him, stop the bleeding, there was a good chance he would live, but she dared not say so, fearing the men hovering around would finish him off then and there.

"Can you help him? Can you save him?" Jacie begged.

Michael saw Pete and the others were already on their horses, waiting with his, impatient to go. He knew they were getting ready to leave without him. He grabbed at Jacie and gave her a rough tug. "I said let's go, damn it."

"And I said I'm not leaving him, Michael," she wrestled against him as he tried to pull her away.

Amidst the horror surrounding, it suddenly dawned on Iris who he was—the man who had asked Jacie to marry him. Iris also knew that after traveling so far to track her down, he wasn't about to go back without her. She knew time was of the essence. If she did not start ministering to Luke at once, he was going to die, but she could do nothing while the men remained. If they knew Luke still lived, they would doubtless finish him off. She knew she had but one chance to help him, and God forgive her if it was wrong, but she had to take it.

Scrambling to her feet, Iris stepped around Luke to tear Jacie from Michael's feverishly clutching hands and hold her close and whisper the lie that might save Luke. "He's dead. And there is nothing here for you any longer. Go with this man who has come so far to claim you, Jacie. He loves you. He'll take care of you. Forget this happened. Forget me. Please. You have to do it. The warriors will be coming. I sent one of the older boys on Luke's horse to find them. They'll kill Michael and his men when they get here. Don't let anyone else die. Go. Now." She gave her a gentle shove.

Jacie shook her head and flung herself against her mother. She was having difficulty thinking amidst the choking grief. Luke was dead. Her life, her love, was over. But she still had her mother. "I won't leave without you!" she cried. "Come with us. I'll take care of you."

"No." Iris pressed a finger against Jacie's lips to silence her plea. "This is my world. I will never leave it. Go back to your own and never look back."

Jacie felt a daze descending over her. Michael was drawing her away from her mother's arms, and Jacie allowed him to, for the expression on her mother's face told her it was no use to argue.

It was over.

"Blake, come on," Pete yelled from where he sat his horse, holding Michael's by the reins.

Michael took Jacie and ran with her to his horse, lifting her up and then swinging up in front of her. She waved one last time at Iris, who stood beside Luke's body. "Dear God," she whispered brokenly to herself, "to find her after all these years and then leave her, it's not right. It's just not right." She crammed her fist against her mouth to keep from screaming.

Michael was hell-bent on getting out of there. Later, he would want to hear everything, like why she was so damn stricken over the Indian's death, but for the moment, there wasn't time, except that he could not resist asking as he set the horse into a gallop, "Who are you talking about, Jacie?"

And her next words nearly jolted him right out of the saddle.

"My mother," she said quietly, painfully. "I'm talking about my mother."

# 26

*Michael managed to* convince himself that Jacie had, for the time being, gone daft. That was also what he told his men. She had been through so much the past months—it was enough to make anyone go crazy. The thing to do was to leave her alone, except to urge her to take food and water, and get her home as quickly as possible. Then there would be time for talking. For now, she could only withdraw and dwell on the horror she had endured, and when she was ready, she would put it all behind her.

But despite his pretense of confidence, Michael was an inner cauldron of turmoil. The image of Jacie's grief and hysteria over the dead Indian was burned in his mind. What had she been thinking? The man was a barbarian. He had taken her from another of his kind, yes, but that made him no less evil, for he had held her against her will . . . hadn't he?

Jacie had not been relieved to be rescued. In fact, Michael had had to force her to leave.

And who was that squaw who had come running, whom Jacie had clung to in tears? In her delusion, Jacie had thought she was her mother, which only reinforced his assumption that she had temporarily lost her mind.

As they passed through settlements on their journey east, they stopped overnight. Michael wanted to give Jacie a chance to have a bath, sleep in a real bed, and taste civilization again in hopes of hastening her recovery. He bought a wagon and a team of horses, so she would be more comfortable traveling. He also purchased new clothes for her in an attempt to make her feel better. But still she paid no mind to anything or anyone around her, locked within the tentacles of her deep and abiding sorrow.

After what seemed forever, they arrived in Atlanta. Michael first made sure Jacie was comfortable in a hotel, and then he went with Pete to see his banker. Withdrawing the promised bonus, he handed over an extra portion, explaining, "I want you to give this to Joe Clyder's family, if he has any. If not, divide it among the three of you. It's not right that he should die for nothing."

"He has a mother in Gainesville. I'll see she gets it." Pete shook his hand, started to walk away, but then turned, yielding to the curiosity he and the others had harbored all the way back. "Call me a nosy son of a bitch, Blake, but me and the boys want to know what the real story is about your woman. Was she with them Indians 'cause she wanted to be? She sure as hell went all to pieces over that buck you shot. And what happened to the man you said she left with? There's just something funny about all this, and since we'll probably never see each other again, I figured there won't no harm in asking."

"No harm. But I can't tell you, because I don't know myself, and I'd appreciate it if all of you would forget everything. Frankly, it doesn't make any difference to me. It's finished now. I love her, and I'm going to marry her, and the less people know about what went on, the better. Do I make myself clear?"

Pete respected Michael and would do as he asked. "Count on me. And I speak for the boys, too. We wish you well."

Michael hurried to the hotel. He had waited long enough to ask questions, and he intended to get some answers, because everything had to be settled before he and Jacie went to Red Oakes.

He knocked on Jacie's door, but when she did not respond, he let himself in, for he had no concern for propriety at the moment.

It was a pleasant room, the walls covered in a blue floral wallpaper, white chintz curtains at the windows and a pink woven rug covering the pine floor. The bed had a lace canopy, and there was a skirted dressing table and a carved armoire. He had asked the desk clerk to see if fresh flowers could be found, and a huge vase of chrysanthemums stood on the bedside table.

There was also a marble fireplace, and a warm, cozy fire burned in the grate. Jacie was sitting in front of it on a brocade divan, staring into the crackling flames with a haunted expression. She was wearing the blue silk dressing robe Michael had bought at the dress shop just next door. He noted with relief that she had at last washed her hair and brushed it down about her face. Perhaps it was a sign that she was finally coming out of her doldrums.

He went around in front of her, then dropped to his knees. "Jacie, we have to talk," he said quietly.

She did not look at him or acknowledge his presence. He took her hands and squeezed them until she winced. "Stop. You're hurting me."

Dropping her hands, he leaned forward to put his head in her lap and murmur plaintively, "That's the last thing I want to do. You're my life. You're the reason for every beat of my heart. If I don't have you, I will die."

Jacie had tried throughout the journey home to hate Michael for killing the only man she would ever love. But she could not, forced to admit he had believed he was rescuing her. He'd had no way of knowing the truth. Neither would he ever have imagined she could have fallen in love with a Comanche and want to spend the rest of her life with him. So she could not despise him. His only sin was loving her too much.

When she did not respond and made no move to touch him, he straightened to stare at her miserably and cry, "My God, Jacie, talk to me. Tell me what went wrong. You don't know the hell I've been through, worrying about you. To think you'd run away with any man never entered my mind, much less that you'd take off with the likes of a scoundrel like Zach Newton—"

"Zach?" She did look at him then, incredulously. "What makes you think I left with him?"

"Didn't you?"

"No. Who told you that I did?"

"Sudie. When you disappeared, I was out of my

mind, but I finally managed to get enough out of her that I could figure out where you'd gone, and she said you left with someone."

"And you assumed it was Zach?"

"What else was I to think? There was gossip about the two of you, but I didn't hear about it till after you left, and good heavens, I was out of my mind, not knowing what had happened to you. I came back from Charleston to find you had just dropped out of sight. Elyse went all to pieces, blaming herself. You don't know the hell you put all of us through, Jacie."

"What about my note? If you read that . . ." She fell silent to see his surprise, then realized what had happened. "You didn't find my note, did you? Sudie must have taken it when she took the necklace, because it was lying right next to it."

"Sudie took the necklace?"

"Yes, and she put it in the blanket with my other things. I guess she thought I might need it to sell for money to get home on."

Michael pulled himself up to sit beside her on the divan. "Maybe you'd better start at the beginning and tell me everything." He was not about to confide that if he had not believed she had taken his engagement gift, he would not have gone after her. It would only make the tension worse, for she would think it wasn't her at all that he cared about, though nothing could be further from the truth. But men had died, and he could not let her think that his motivation had been anything but his deep, abiding love and desperation to get her back. "Please," he begged.

She began with Violet's deathbed confession and ended with how she had finally found her real mother. She described little of the events between.

Michael was stunned. After several moments of awkward silence, he was able to say, "God, I'm sorry. It had to have been awful for you. Oh, why didn't you come to me? How could you have gone off with that old fool Indian? I could wring his neck for deserting you," he added, furious.

"He didn't desert me. He saw to it that I got to Bird's Fort. What happened there was unfortunate, but it doesn't matter now. I found her. That's what's important. But tell me, what would you have done if I *had* come to you, Michael. Would you have encouraged me or told me to forget it?"

"Probably told you to forget it," he admitted. "There's been nothing but trouble. And I still don't believe that woman is your mother," he said crossly.

"She *is* my mother. Didn't you get a good look at her?"

"Frankly, I was too shocked by how you were crying over that Comanche, Jacie." He was trying to hold his temper, because he was imagining all sorts of things. "Who was he, anyway?"

"He was my friend," she said coldly. That was all he needed to know.

"He must have been a close friend"—he sniffed with disdain—"the way you were carrying on."

"She was my mother," Jacie repeated, wanting to turn the conversation away from Luke. Thinking of him was agony beyond description. "I only wish I could have convinced her to come back with me."

"Come back to what?" Michael cried. "God forgive me for saying it, Jacie, but the truth is, she was wise not to want to. She's had over eighteen years of living with those savages, and she knows she could never fit into society again. She would be looked down on, resented. She'd live a miserable life, and so would you, because you'd be devastated by how others treated her."

"And how would you have treated her?" she challenged him.

Wearily, he said, "I would have tried my damnedest to accept her, because I love you. I would have done my best to make both of you happy, but it would have been extremely hard all the same, because people like my mother don't change. It would have been rough on all of us, so be glad she stayed where she is, and though I know it's difficult, you've got to make yourself try to forget she exists."

"She has the necklace."

Michael shrugged. "It doesn't matter. I can always have another one made."

"It was in the blanket Violet kept all those years. I didn't have time to retrieve it. I didn't even think about it."

"And I told you it doesn't matter."

Jacie had only to look at him to know he spoke the truth. "Maybe she can sell it to buy food and things for her people. They want to move to Mexico in the spring and make a new life, find peace, and . . ." Her voice cracked as she thought of the dreams Luke had, dreams she had wanted to share with him.

Michael touched her shoulder hesitantly, and when she did not rebuke him, he put an arm around her. "I understand your pain, but you have to put it behind you. We can't mention any of this ever again. My mother doesn't know the real story. No one does. And we'll keep it that way. When we get to Red Oakes, we'll say you left with Mehlonga because you were upset with me for being jealous of Zach, and you were tired of all the lies and gossip about the two of you. But Mehlonga went off and left you, and you got lost. I went after you and found you, and you wanted to come back with me, because we love each other and refuse to let anyone or anything come between us."

Jacie doubted people would believe such a tale but did not really care. Luke was dead, and all the joy in her life had died with him. Nothing mattered anymore.

"Jacie, I want to marry you as soon as possible."

"It wouldn't be right. Not now. Not when—" She had been about to tell him that she did not love him and never would, that her heart belonged to another, and though he was gone forever, his spirit remained inside to lock out any feelings she could ever have had for Michael. But Michael would not let her speak, because he was afraid of what she might say.

"I won't take no for an answer," he said adamantly. "And I won't talk about it. You are going to marry me, Jacie, and even if you don't think you love me now, I swear before God Almighty that one day you will. You will realize how I adore you, and you'll see how happy I'm going to make you every day for the rest of your life, and sooner or later it will happen." He forced a smile he did not truly feel just then. "I'll hear you say you love me."

He stood, drawing her up with him. "Now, I believe that dress shop also sent up a lovely gown that should fit you, and if it doesn't, you can send for the seamstress to come up and make alterations, because I'm taking you out to dinner tonight. We're going to celebrate a new beginning."

"Michael," she began in protest.

"You can, and you will. I've waited long enough." He cupped her chin in his hand, fervently avowing, "We're going to forget yesterday and think about today and tomorrow, because that's all that counts."

But she was not ready to put it aside, suddenly feeling disloyal to Luke's memory to hide what she had felt for him. "Michael, there's something else you should know, about that man you killed."

"He was going to kill me. I'm not apologizing for anything," he snapped defensively.

"Luke wouldn't have killed you. He was a wonderful man. My mother raised him. That's why the Indians took her in the first place. She had milk intended for me. His mother had just died."

"I don't care about that," he said irritably.

"He found me when I had escaped from the other Indians," she went on, ignoring his growing anger. "We were together, and Luke saved my life. Then later, I saved his, and—"

"Stop it, I say!" he exploded, covering his ears, for he could not bear to hear the tender way she spoke of the Comanche. Suspicion and jealousy slammed him in the gut, and he waved his hands wildly as he cried, "Why do you want to keep talking about it? We can't forget if you keep talking about it. Can't you just stop it?" He began to pace around the room, aware he was behaving like a child in the throes of a tantrum but unable to stop himself. He was no fool. He had already figured out during his miserable musings on the trip back that she had been romantically involved with the Indian. But as long as she did not put it into words, as long as she did not confirm it, then it would not be fact. They could pretend it was not so.

He whirled on her then to cry, "For God's sake, don't you know I don't want to hear you admit to anything? He's dead. And if you tell me you cared for him, if you dare admit it, I'm not sure I can forgive you. So let it go, Jacie. It's over."

Jacie knew he was right. It was over. With hands folded in her lap, she lowered her eyes and nodded her assent.

"Good." He let his breath out in a rush, unaware he'd even been holding it, in fear she would keep talking and ruin everything. "I'll leave you now, but I'll be back soon, and we will toast to the future and all the joy I promise to give you the rest of your life."

He brushed his lips against hers, softly at first, then, when she did not resist, he kissed her with passion, reveling in the sweetness of her mouth and the poignancy of the long-awaited moment. Whatever she had shared with the Indian called Luke was as dead as he was, and Michael swore silently there would be no ghosts. He would fill her life with so much bliss she'd have no time to think of anything else.

At last he let her go, laughing softly as he warned that their wedding night could not come soon enough for him. "As soon as we get home, we'll start making plans to be married."

When he was gone, Jacie remained before the fire to let the memories torture her one last time. Staring into the dancing red and golden flames, she lived again the glory of burning in Luke's strong arms.

All too soon, only embers remained. And as the last wisps of smoke disappeared up the soot-blackened chimney, Jacie closed her eyes and said good-bye to what was, what could never be. . . .

* * *

Iris watched in torment as Luke tightened the cinches of the saddle. She had cried and begged, but he would not listen. His mind was made up. He was going to Georgia to find Jacie, and nothing Iris could say would change his mind. "You're too weak," she said, trying again to focus on his condition. "It's too soon for you to travel."

"I'm fine, and you know it. It was a clean flesh wound. Went straight through without hitting any bone. You stopped the bleeding with ground sumac and honey, and I've rested almost a week, and it's time for me to go. They've got a big head start on me, and I've got to do some hard riding; they'll probably still reach their destination before I can catch up with them." He patted the horse's rump and stood back to make sure he'd forgotten nothing. Saddlebags were in place with supplies of pemmican and jerky. He had his canteen. There was a blanket roll for what little sleep he would allow himself. He intended to ride as long as there was daylight and on into the night if there was a sufficient moon.

Iris blinked back the tears of worry and frustration. The only time an Indian woman was permitted to cry was when there was a death, but she had not quite learned to control her emotions so stoically especially where the man she loved as a son was concerned—and now her daughter as well. "Leave well enough alone, Luke. Let her go. She told me about this Michael Blake, how rich he is, how much he loves her."

"And she also told you how much she loves me, didn't she?" he challenged with a dark glare.

Iris could only nod.

"That's right," Luke said, as though that settled everything.

"But she would never be able to adjust to this way of life."

"You did," he reminded her.

"Only because I thought I had no choice. Don't you realize that if I had known my baby survived, I would never have stopped trying to escape and get to her? Your father might have wound up having me killed, but I would never have given up."

"That's right," he agreed fiercely, "and right now Jacie is feeling like you did—defeated. She has no spirit. She's willing to take anything life hands out to her, because she thinks I'm dead, but I intend to give *her* a choice, by damn. I'm going to let her know I am alive, and then if she still wants to marry Blake, so be it. I'll accept it and leave. But *she will have that choice.*" He jabbed a finger in the air for emphasis.

"And you think she can adapt to this way of life?"

"Probably better than you did, because she will have come to it willingly."

"Luke, I hope you're right, for your sake and for Jacie's. And mine, too," she added. Having both Luke and Jacie with her would be happiness nonpareil, but not if it was at the expense of Jacie's well-being. She also prayed that Luke knew what he was doing and would not be hurt, either in body or spirit. There was always the chance that once Jacie got back to the comfort of civilization and the luxury of the privileged, she might decide that was what she wanted. And Michael Blake would never give her up without a fight, not after traveling so far to find her, even if she did choose Luke.

"At least take Gold Elk and some of the braves with you," she urged.

"No. They're needed here. And it's my fight, not theirs. Now, are you sure you know where they were going?"

"Yes. I asked her specifically where Red Oakes was, because I wanted to find out how close it was to where I was raised. I was curious about how things have changed after all these years. Just find Atlanta, Georgia and then the Oconee River, and follow the river as it winds northeast. She said Red Oakes is the largest plantation in that part of the state. You'll find it."

"I know I will." He put his hands on her shoulders and smiled down at her. "And don't you worry. I'm going to bring her back. For both of us. And come spring we've a new life waiting in Mexico."

He kissed her cheek, then mounted and took up the reins. "I'll be back as soon as I can. One moon will pass, maybe two. Surely no more."

"Luke, take this. Whether she returns or not, it's only right that Michael Blake gets the necklace back."

He took the worn blanket; then, seeing she had also included the daguerreotype, asked, "Are you sure you want her to have this too?"

"Yes. If I never see her again, at least she'll have it to remember me by." Her voice caught on a sob, and she brushed at her eyes and glanced away, not wanting Luke to see her cry.

"It's all right," he told her tenderly. "It's all right to cry. But she's coming back with me. You'll see. The spirits have spoken to both our hearts. We can never love anyone except each other.

She watched him till he was out of sight, then went and hid from the others of the camp to surrender to her tears.

# 27

*Verena was enjoying her* ritual of afternoon tea when Elyse came into the parlor and threw herself on the sofa to wail, "I don't know how much more I can stand of this waiting. Michael should have been home by now. He's been gone for weeks with no word."

Verena added a generous dollop of cream and two lumps of sugar to her tea before responding. She was accustomed to Elyse's moaning. "We've talked about this before, dear. There's no need to fret. He'll be back, and he's not going to find her."

"But why would she go to Texas? That's all Cousin Olivia could get out of him before he left—that Jacie had gone to Texas. He wouldn't even tell her how he found that out. It might not even be so, and then he's gone all the way out there for nothing."

"Oh will you stop it? So what if he has? It will only make him all the madder to spend so much time on a wild goose chase, which is what you want; he'll despise her all the more." She lifted the Meissen china cup and drank, then reached for one of the frosted sugar cakes she ordered baked fresh daily and popped it into her mouth greedily. "What you must remember, dear," she advised around the delicious morsel, "is that he won't find her, which means there will be nothing in the way of all this becoming ours."

With a grin, she spread her arms to indicate the opulent surroundings. *Trompe l'oeil* artwork decorated the walls and ceiling with elaborate plaster moldings, and there was an iron fireplace with a grape design. A Burmese rug accented the parquet flooring, and drapes of deep purple velvet hung at the Venetian glass windows. Objets d'art had been carefully chosen to compliment the furniture, which was all done in pastel brocade, befitting the ladies' parlor.

"You will be queen of this house, and I"—she touched her fingertips primly to her lips and made a smacking sound—"will be the queen mother."

Elyse did not share her mother's optimism that the dream would come true, and she never had. "Michael doesn't want me. It was always Jacie. He might be so brokenhearted he won't want to marry anybody."

"Oh, fiddle-faddle. That's ridiculous. Do I have to remind you he didn't go running after her to bring her back, anyway? Olivia said it was only when he realized she'd taken the necklace he gave her. He wasn't about to let her keep it. That's why he went—to get that. Not *her*.

"And by the way," she added, and reached for another cake, "do you think Zach Newton told any of the other overseers he was going to South Carolina? I'd hate to think of anyone saying something about it to Michael. He might decide to go chasing off down there too."

"I'm certain he didn't. If I'd been a minute later getting to him that morning, I'd have missed him. He was on his way then, and he kept on going after I talked to him and gave him the letter for Mr. Kernsby. I even turned around before I got to the house and saw that he was already at the main road, so he didn't talk to anybody."

"Good. We can't let anything interfere once Michael gets back. You've got to get him to marry you. And fast. That little tart got him in the first place by throwing herself at him, and you're just going to have to do the same thing, if that's what it takes. Coax him right into your bed, if you have to. Get him in a compromising situation so he'll be honor-bound to marry you. I'll get involved and demand he do so, if need be."

Elyse's mouth dropped open, aghast to hear her mother speak so brazenly. "Surely you don't mean that."

"Surely I do," Olivia mimicked, screwing up her mouth haughtily. "We can't keep on living here indefinitely, and we've nowhere else to go, and by Christmas I intend for you to be Mrs. Michael Blake, understand?"

Elyse understood, all right, and she wanted that to happen even more than her mother did, but for different reasons, and endeavored to tell Verena that. "All you care about is his money. I love Michael, and I'd rather know he was marrying me because he loves me too."

"Oh, don't be silly. Love has nothing to do with it. You give him babies and live a genteel life of luxury, and he'll take a mistress, maybe even go to the Negro wenches for his pleasure, and if he does, be glad. You'll tire soon enough of his animal lust."

Elyse did not think so. Thoughts of having Michael hold her, kiss her, made her warm all over. She would never tire of him coming to her bed for loving. She was sure of it. Her mother was wrong.

"Is that a wagon coming up the road?" Holding her cup, Verena got up and went to the window, eyes narrowing with annoyance as she said, "It certainly is, and it's coming right up the main road instead of taking the path around back. I tell you, when we're running this house, there'll be some changes made. I'm going out there myself and give whoever it is a piece of my mind, and—"

The expensive Meissen cup fell to the floor and shattered.

Elyse bolted to her feet and ran to the window to see what had caused her mother's distress and felt the blood drain from her face. "Oh, God," she cried in sweeping horror, "it's Michael! And Jacie is with him!"

Just then Olivia breezed in to greet them happily. "Ah, I see we have those lovely little cakes again. My, my, Verena, you are so good at handling the servants. They jump to please you. I was never able to . . ." She paused. "Good heavens, you two look as though you've seen a ghost. What is it?"

Olivia came to where they stood frozen at the window. Glancing out, she gave a barely audible cry—and promptly fell to the floor in a dead faint.

Michael murmured a hasty exchange of greetings to a waiting groom, then steered Jacie up the stairs and into the house. Relinquishing her to a wide-eyed housekeeper standing inside the door, he gave orders that she was to be taken to her room, where she would rest the remainder of the day. He also directed that a dinner tray be delivered to her.

She accepted Michael's light kiss on her lips and went docilely with the servant. They had agreed previously it was best she be sequestered until Olivia got over the shock of her return.

Michael did not have to wonder where everyone was as he stepped into the foyer, for there was a great commotion coming from the parlor. He walked in to see Verena and Elyse kneeling beside his mother, who was on the floor. He hurried to lift her in his arms and place her on the divan, demanding, though he suspected he already knew, "What's wrong with her?"

"She saw you with that woman." Verena could hardly speak, she was so mad. "It was more than she could bear, to think you'd dare bring that hussy back to this house."

Michael held back a scathing reply because a maid had come into the room and he wanted to avoid any more gossip. "Bring ammonia," he said curtly. "And water."

Verena sniffed. "She needs a doctor, that's what she needs. It's probably her heart, poor thing. Michael, how could you?" She stamped her foot.

Michael summoned all his patience and managed to say evenly, "Cousin Verena, my mother always has an attack of the vapors when she's faced with situations she wants to avoid. She's been like that her whole life, so I'm not going to worry about it, and neither should you. In fact, I would appreciate it if you would stop worrying about anything that goes on in this house, because it's no concern of yours. Have I made myself clear?" He glared at her.

The color was back in Verena's face full force; it had turned bright red with indignity. "How dare you regard your mother so callously?" she lashed out at him. "That's what cavorting with the lower classes does to a person."

Elyse knew her mother was going too far and attempted to stop her. "Mother, please. We've no right to interfere."

"That's right—you don't." Michael nodded gratefully to Elyse and even managed a smile.

Silence fell awkwardly, tensely. Elyse tugged at her mother's arm to try and make her leave, but Verena stood where she was, tight-lipped and furious. Finally the maid came with the ammonia, and the instant Michael held it beneath his mother's nose, her eyes flashed open. She began to cough, pushing the flask away.

"Are you all right now?" Michael asked, no trace of concern in his voice.

"Yes, yes." She looked about the room wildly, then clutched Michael by his coat and begged, "Tell me it was a bad dream. A nightmare. That I only imagined you brought Jacie back."

"You didn't imagine anything, Mother. I've brought her back to be my wife."

Olivia gave a soft whimper, and he warned sternly, "Now don't faint again, Mother. There's a few things you are going to have to understand, like how Jacie did not go away with Zach Newton. She was intending to ride part of the way with Mehlonga as he headed west to join his people. She was upset with me for being so jealous, when there was no reason. Then she got lost on the way back."

"Oh Lord. That crazy old Indian. I might have known. He hasn't been seen since she left. But that's even worse. Oh, God. She ran away with an Indian." She covered her face with her hands.

"Hmph," Verena grunted. "I think you're making that up. You just don't want to admit she was with that overseer. How did you find her, anyway?"

"Verena, you're really starting to annoy me," Michael said tightly. "I'd like you to leave."

"Oh don't take it out on her," Olivia moaned. "I don't know what I'd have done without her all these weeks. And sweet Elyse, too. You just don't realize the grief your insane devotion to that girl has caused this family, Michael."

"That's true." Verena folded her arms across her bosom. She was not going anywhere. "It's a good thing your father isn't alive to hear you treat your kin so disrespectfully and he'd never stand for that trollop being in his house."

"That does it." Michael drew himself up, about to remove her from the room bodily, if need be.

Elyse, biting back tears, realizing she had lost Michael forever, saw the explosion coming and grabbed her mother's arm and managed to coax her out.

Upstairs with the door closed behind them, Verena spent the next half hour ranting and raving, telling Elyse over and over that they had to do something. "We cannot let him marry her. We cannot."

Elyse cringed, because Verena kept getting louder and louder. "Mother, someone will hear you."

"I don't care. Let them. I want all the servants to gossip about him marrying that little whore. And that's what she is—a whore," she declared forcefully.

As she walked toward Jacie's room, Sudie paused to hear such a nasty word coming through the door. She was carrying a tray with ham biscuits and a pot of tea, so excited that Miss Jacie was back and anxious to see her, but now the glow was dimmed as she overheard Miss Verena say, "Olivia cannot allow him to bring the strumpet into this house. All the servants believe she ran away with Zach Newton. What will they think of their master marrying a whore?"

Sudie could take no more. She might get a whipping, but there was just no way she was going to stand for that woman calling Miss Jacie a whore. And she knew what it meant. She listened when the womenfolk talked and heard them sometimes call other women ugly names.

She set the tray on a nearby table, then, lower lip trembling with fear at what she was about to do, rapped sharply on the door.

Verena snatched it open. "Oh, what is it?"

Sudie marched right in. "I heard what you said about Miss Jacie, and it ain't so, and I know it ain't."

Verena advanced toward her, eyes narrowed in menace. "You little snot. I'll take a whip to you for being so insolent."

"Mother, don't," Elyse protested. "She's just a child, and she was always fond of Jacie."

"That's right." Sudie's head bobbed up and down as she inched farther into the room to get closer to Miss Elyse, since she seemed to be taking up for her. "And I know she didn't do what you said she did. She didn't go with Master Newton. I heard her talkin' to herself, heard her say some man was takin' her to Texas, but she didn't say who. I knew later, when Mehlonga didn't come around no more, that it had to be him. She wouldn't go away with Mr. Newton, not after I told her how he beat the slaves."

Verena wondered why she even bothered to argue with the child and resolved that she would definitely see Sudie got a whipping. "She went away with a man. That makes her a whore. Now get out of here."

"That don't make her no whore." Sudie clenched her fists at her sides, tears beginning to stream down her face. "Not when he was takin' her to find her real momma."

The two women looked at each other in wonder, and it was Elyse who rallied to probe, "What are you talking about, Sudie? Miss Jacie's mother died. You know that."

"No ma'am," Sudie said firmly. "Not her real momma."

Eyes suddenly glittering with interest, Verena went to the door and closed it, then gently asked, "Tell us about it, Sudie, dear."

Sudie was anxious to make them see Miss Jacie had done nothing wrong, and the words poured forth. "Miss Violet wasn't her real momma. She was her real momma's sister. She just pretended to be Miss Jacie's momma. Miss Jacie's real momma, she was taken by the Indians when Miss Jacie was just a little baby. She and Miss Violet was the only ones left alive, so Miss Violet made Master Judd think Miss Jacie was his young'un and raised her like she was, only the night she died, I reckon she was feelin' guilty over pretendin' all them years, 'cause she told Miss Jacie the truth, and Miss Jacie couldn't stand not knowin' about her real momma, so she took off to find her.

"And I know this is so," Sudie finished proudly, "'cause I was standin' outside the door and heard every single word.

"She knowed I knowed she was goin'." Starting to lose some of her nerve beneath the skeptical stares of the two women, Sudie went on. "And she told me not to tell, but Master Blake was so worried I had to tell him so he could fetch her back. You ain't gonna tell her I told, are you?" She looked from one to the other fearfully.

"No, not if you won't tell what you heard us saying about her," Verena said sweetly.

Sudie shook her head. "Oh, no ma'am. I won't do it, 'cause it would hurt her feelin's real bad, and there ain't no need to do that, 'specially now that you know it ain't so and won't say it no more."

Verena licked her lips in delight to know Jacie's secret. "Of course we won't, dear. But did you also tell Master Blake why Miss Jacie went away? Did you tell him she had gone to find her mother?"

"No. There wasn't no need. She must not have found her, nohow. You ain't gonna tell him, are you?" she asked suddenly, eyes going wide. "I don't want Miss Jacie mad at me, and I done said too much already."

"Don't you worry. This is between us. Why, we'll forget we even had this little talk." Verena ushered her to the door.

"And I won't get no whippin'?" Sudie asked.

"No whipping," Verena assured her.

With the door again closed, Elyse braced herself for her mother's tirade but was instead surprised to see her smiling quite contentedly. "Now you know what you have to do," Verena said. "Not only for yourself, but for Michael, to save him from himself. He has political ambitions. What if one day Jacie's real mother, a nasty Indian squaw"—she wrinkled her nose in disgust—"were to show up here at Red Oakes? It could ruin him. You can't take a chance on letting that happen. And think of the family name. It's our family, too, you know.

"No," she said adamantly, swinging her head from side to side, "you aren't going to let it happen."

"I'd like to know what you think I can do about it." Elyse looked at her in wonder. "If cousin Olivia can't make him change his mind, I certainly can't."

"Olivia won't know about it, you little fool. Do you think he would dare tell her? No. You heard what he said in the parlor, the lie he concocted about Jacie riding off with Mehlonga and getting lost. He's not about to tell the truth, because he knows there is absolutely no way he could expect Olivia to be even remotely civil to Jacie if she found out such a deplorable scandal about her family. He knows how she despises all Indians."

Elyse went to stare wistfully out the window at the sprawling plantation she would soon be forced to leave—to go where? She had no idea and at the moment did not care. She loved Michael and wanted to be his wife, and if that were not to be, nothing else mattered.

"This is our chance," Verena gloated.

"I suppose you want me to be the one to tell Cousin Olivia," Elyse said tonelessly. "Well, I won't. Michael would hate me then. He'd never marry me."

"Oh, I know that. Olivia finding out wouldn't stop him, anyway."

"Well, I suggest we just forget about it, hard though it is. If Michael loves her enough to want her despite everything, then perhaps we should just stay out of it. We can go back to Charleston. Surely some man will want to marry me."

"With us living in the poorhouse?" Verena hooted. "No man from a decent, wealthy family would court you, and I'll not see you wed anyone who can't afford to take care of me as well. You are going to marry Michael, and that is final."

Elyse leaned her head against the windowframe and closed her eyes. Her mother could rant on all she wanted. Sooner or later, she would realize the futility of it all.

"I want you to send a message to Zach Newton."

Elyse's eyes flashed open. "What kind of message?"

"Tell him you want him to get Jacie away from here. It doesn't matter what he does with her, just so she's never seen in these parts again."

"I don't believe what I am hearing."

"You will write him a letter and tell him he can have revenge on Michael for firing him by coming to Red Oakes and abducting Jacie. You will also tell him he will be paid a thousand dollars for his trouble."

Elyse laughed. "And where would I get a thousand dollars?"

"I'll tell Olivia I need to borrow it. She'll let me have it, no questions asked. Especially as distraught as she is now."

Elyse chewed her lower lip nervously. "I don't think I can do it."

"Do you love Michael?"

"You know I do," she said miserably.

"Then you must. There's no other way. Otherwise, Michael is going to marry Jacie as soon as he can throw a wedding together. He's bewitched by her. He's not thinking straight."

Elyse was not convinced the plan would work. "What if Zach gets the money, keeps it, and never shows up?"

"I've already thought of that. You will send five hundred with the letter and tell him where to find the rest of it when the deed is done. But I'm not worried about that," Verena said confidently. "He'll want revenge on Michael more than the money. You know there is no way that Zach has the working conditions in Beaufort that he had here. He probably curses Michael every day for kicking him out."

"I still don't know," Elyse murmured.

"It's the answer to all our prayers and problems," Verena went on to emphasize. "Olivia will never know you were responsible for keeping her son from marrying white trash, but she would love you to death if she did. And you'll also be ensuring a good life for me, as well, dear, and you owe that to me.

"But," and she bent her head to kiss each cheek in turn, "you owe it to yourself most of all, if you truly, truly love him as you say you do."

Elyse was still uncertain about doing something so dastardly and cruel, and all in the name of love.

Verena said brightly, "I'll get paper and a pen. We have to move fast."

* * *

That night no one in the household appeared at the dinner table.

Jacie remained in her quarters, locked in a grief that would not let her go, and grateful Michael had given her time to be alone.

Olivia had taken to her bed to try and absorb the earth-shattering events of the day, as well as Michael's insistence on marrying Jacie as soon as arrangements could be made.

Verena and Elyse retired to their individual boudoirs, having trays of food brought in. Neither wanted to face Michael just yet with all that was on their minds.

And Michael just did not want to be around anyone, because even though he was overjoyed to have Jacie home and to know they would soon be married, there were still demons within to be conquered. He could not erase from his mind the image of how she had clung to the Indian, how stricken she had been, and though he told himself over and over he must not let it haunt him, he could not help wondering what had gone on between the two of them.

Lights went out in the house earlier than usual, and all was still. No one was up or about to see the servant, who had been sworn to secrecy and threatened with having the flesh ripped from his back if he ever dared reveal his mission, as he rode away from Red Oakes.

He was on his way to Beaufort, South Carolina, and he carried a letter addressed to Mr. Zach Newton.

Luke rode doggedly, stopping only when utter darkness closed in, continuing at first light.

The wound in his neck still throbbed with pain, but he ignored it, as was the way of a warrior.

He had but one thought in mind, to find Jacie. If she chose not to return with him, so be it. But he would let her know he was alive. He would not allow her to endure the same mental anguish her mother had experienced, could not bear the thought of Jacie miserably accepting her lot in life believing there was nothing else for her.

When he found Red Oakes, Luke would strip off the army pants and boots and ride in as what he was, a Comanche.

Though Luke wanted no trouble, he knew that Michael Blake would not give up Jacie without a battle.

But by God, Luke thought fiercely, this time he would know he had been in a fight.

# 28

*Olivia had never known the* house to be so lavishly decorated. Not even for her own wedding, she thought jealously.

Michael had had the servants working day and night for the past five days. The greenhouse had been stripped, and flowers were everywhere—golden chrysanthemums, white winter roses, and early poinsettias. Gold satin ribbons twined the spindles of the stair railing, and more ribbons and greenery tufted about the crystal chandeliers.

Delicious smells wafted from the dining room, where the results of all the baking that had been going on for days were already displayed. Olivia shook her head in amazement over the lavish concoctions—pies, cakes, and pastries of every color and flavor, as well as hand-dipped chocolates.

Her mouth watered despite her disapproval over

the entire affair. Michael was making a terrible mistake. He could lie to her and everyone else, and maybe he could even make himself believe that Jacie had not had a tryst with an overseer, but Olivia was not fooled. Verena had told her about the gossip, the scandalous tales of Jacie being seen sneaking out at night to meet Zach Newton. And if a woman would betray her fiancé, she could not be expected to be a faithful wife.

Michael was letting himself in for heartbreak, Olivia was sure of it. But that was not her sole reason for opposing the union. Michael would eventually pay the price for his folly, but she was worried over the scandal sure to come when Jacie misbehaved and showed her true colors.

Couriers had delivered invitations to those fortunate enough to be on the guest list for the Saturday night celebration and Sunday afternoon wedding. But it would be a few hours yet before people began arriving, and Olivia had suggested a little supper for the family be served in her parlor, as there would be little time for host and hostesses to eat while mingling and making sure the guests enjoyed themselves.

Absently running her finger along the edge of a pumpkin cream cake and sampling it, Olivia frowned to think how hard she had tried to persuade Michael to at least wait awhile before marrying Jacie. But his mind was set. Now she was faced with having to endure the weekend without letting anyone be aware of her feelings. The few times she had been around Jacie, she had managed to be polite. Thank goodness, the house was large, and she could usually avoid her, except at mealtimes, of course, which Olivia could manage due to her refinement and good breeding. Otherwise, she wanted nothing to do with Jacie and intended to make that clear to both her and Michael.

Verena came into the room, looked around, and made a clucking sound of disapproval. "My heart goes out to you," she said consolingly, giving Olivia a brief embrace. "Michael is a fool, and he will learn that soon enough."

"I know, I know. Bad enough he's marrying someone other than Elyse. Such a sweet thing. If only he had taken the time to get to know her all these years you've been coming to visit, he'd have seen for himself how perfect she is for him."

"Well, the wedding hasn't taken place yet. Who knows? Maybe Jacie will change her mind again and run off to find that Newton fellow."

"But Michael swears she didn't leave with him," Olivia hastened to point out, "and I want so badly to believe that's true—that she did go off with that old Indian instead and got lost trying to come home. It wouldn't be as bad as her running off with a young man."

Verena shrugged. "Well, I happen to believe what the slaves say. They see and hear everything. I think what happened is that she and that overseer had a fight about something, and he went off and left her, and Michael just happened to find her trying to crawl back to him. You haven't seen the necklace, have you?"

Olivia had to admit she hadn't. "No. I asked Michael about it, and he said Jacie lost it somewhere."

Verena snickered. "She lost it, all right. To Zach Newton." Verena wondered what had really happened to the expensive piece but did not dwell on it, glad it was gone, for it reinforced the story that Jacie had actually left with Zach.

"Oh, I don't know what to believe," Olivia said fretfully. "I just hope I can get through this dreadful weekend without an attack of the vapors."

"Well, you certainly look lovely." Olivia admired her gown. "Even if you insist on continuing to mourn unofficially, you are simply elegant in black silk, and I love the dainty silver embroidery on your skirt."

"If this wedding takes place, I'll probably always be in mourning," Olivia quipped gloomily.

Elyse heard their voices. As she entered the room, Olivia and Verena gushed over her costume—a breathtaking creation of blue satin bordered at the shoulders with white fur, the neckline of the beaded bodice dipping just low enough to display her ample cleavage. The smooth skirt was accented with beaded embroidery in iris designs, and she was wearing elbow-length kid gloves, with thick pearl bracelets at each wrist. Her hair was caught high and held with a crusted pearl tiara, curls trailing provocatively to her shoulders.

"You are absolutely gorgeous," Olivia breathed in awe. "Oh, if only Michael weren't so blind."

"Oh, I'm not blind," Michael declared jovially as he joined them. "And if my heart hadn't been stolen by another years ago, I'd have been begging for your hand, Elyse—if I'd thought you would have me." He bestowed a light kiss on her cheek.

"You will have every unmarried man at the party drooling," he added, then dismissed her as he went to inspect the food.

Elyse hoped he had not noticed how she had

shivered at his touch. Her face felt warm, and she prayed she was not blushing.

Verena asked sharply, "Well, Michael, where is our guest of honor? Seems to me she'd be hovering around, making sure everything is to her liking. Especially since she's no doubt looking forward to taking over the household," she added to goad Olivia and knew she had succeeded when she saw the flash of disapproval on her cousin's face.

Michael had promised himself not to let Verena get under his skin this night. "Jacie is looking forward to many things, Cousin Verena, the least of which is taking over this house when and if my mother decides she wants her to. As for where she is, I asked her to stay in her room till I send for her. Sudie will take her a tray. I want her to make a grand entrance down the stairway when all the guests have arrived." He turned to his mother to inquire, "Did she like the dress I had sent from Atlanta? And her wedding gown? She was too tired to choose one herself, so I asked the couturiere to make the selections."

"I have no idea. One of the servants took everything up to her." Olivia couldn't care less what Jacie wore, much less whether or not she liked it.

Verena could not resist asking, "Will she be wearing that exquisite necklace you gave her at your *other* engagement party?"

Michael saw how Verena's eyes were glittering and decided to put her in her place before she went too far. "I'm sure my mother told you Jacie lost it, so why are you wanting to make trouble by bringing it up? Besides, I've already ordered another one made," he added to irritate her.

At that, Olivia cried, "Oh dear heavens. You spend money like it grows on magnolia trees. I'm going to the parlor and have a glass of sherry for my nerves."

"So am I." Verena was right behind her.

Elyse was suddenly ill at ease to find herself alone with Michael, yet she could not make herself leave him. The precious times when she could be with him would soon come to an end.

"Don't you want sherry for your nerves too?" Michael asked with a soft laugh.

"No. And I apologize for how my mother meddles in your business, especially when you've been so nice to let us stay here as long as we have."

Michael had never had a problem with Elyse but looked forward to her mother leaving. "It's been a pleasure," he said glibly, adding, "but I suppose the two of you will be going back to Charleston soon to find a place of your own."

"I would like that, but Mother hasn't said anything. Would you like us to leave, Michael?" she asked bluntly.

"Well, I—I . . ." he stammered, taken aback, for he had not expected her frankness, finally recovering to say with equal candor, "I suppose it would be nice to have things get back to normal as soon as possible, and I'm sure you would like to settle down somewhere and think about marriage yourself. You can't do that hiding away here," he added with a wink, pretending jollity.

"Yes, yes, I suppose." She turned away, tears smarting and not wanting him to see. "Maybe I should join the others."

"And I need to see to the barbecuing going on out back. I'll be along soon."

Elyse stood in the hallway and watched as he disappeared into the rear of the house, thinking how devastatingly handsome he was, so elegantly dressed in a blue velvet waistcoat, ruffled white silk shirt, and tight fawn trousers. It made her sick inside to think how, unless a miracle happened, he was lost to her forever.

But miracles *did* happen, her mother had told her earlier in the day when she had found her crying. Jacie could change her mind, she said, reminding Elyse that Jacie had been acting strange since her return, depressed, as if she were in mourning. And everyone had noticed how delicately Michael treated her, as though she were about to break down any second. There was something going on they did not know about, Verena had decreed suspiciously and had urged Elyse not to give up hope.

But Elyse could feel no hope—only pain.

Jacie stared glumly at her reflection in the mirror. The gown Michael had bought for her was pretty. Made of lime green taffeta brocade, the skirt had hand-embroidered nosegays sprinkled all over. The sleeves were elbow-length and puffed, and the neckline was straight and modest. A thin satin ribbon was the only adornment at the narrow waist. She wore satin shoes to match.

Sudie had done her hair in high ringlets, caught and held with a cluster of white roses. Then she had stood back to exult over her creation, declaring Jacie the most beautiful woman in the whole world.

But Jacie did not feel beautiful. The truth was, she did not feel anything. Nor did she care about anything. The past refused to leave her, clinging to torture and needle, and she had withdrawn within herself, finding solace only in her memories, refusing to be a part of anything going on around her. She felt as though she were slipping away from reality with no will to resist.

Jacie did not hear the man as he stepped through the window.

She was unaware of his presence until he loomed up behind her in the mirror.

But by then it was too late to scream, for he quickly stuffed the kerchief into her mouth to muffle any sound she might make.

Zach Newton's evil laugh sent rivulets of terror up and down Jacie's spine as she struggled futilely against him while he pulled her arms roughly behind her back to bind her wrists with the rope he had ready. "Well, well, you got all dressed up for me, did you?" he taunted, warm lips against her ear, making sure to speak softly, lest anyone passing by outside the room overhear.

"That was sure nice of you," he went on, "but the fact is, what I want is to have you *un*dressed. I want to see all the delicious morsels you've been dangling in front of me all these years. But we'll have time for that later. Right now I want to get my money and get out of here. Not that I wouldn't like the opportunity to do your pretty-boy fiancé in, but he might scream for his slaves before I got done with him, and they'd love to gang up on me. I don't intend for that to happen. So I'll just be happy knowin' what a kick in the balls it's goin' to give him to find you gone for good, little spitfire."

After binding her ankles, Zach lowered her to

the floor, then glanced about the room wildly, anxiously. The letter had said the other five hundred he had coming would be hidden under a clock, and, with a rush of joy, he saw one on the mantel on the wall opposite. Snatching it up, he breathed in triumph to find the money, as promised. For a time, he had worried it would not be there, afraid he would arrive too late. The letter had said he was to come at once, and he had, only it took time to get all the way from Beaufort, South Carolina, to Red Oakes. And he hadn't expected to see the place all gussied up for a big party, either. But no matter. He had done it. He had his revenge on Michael Blake, and soon he would have his fill of Jacie after wanting her for so long.

He lifted her up and slung her over his shoulder and left as quietly as he had come, all the while with an ache in his loins to think how bad he wanted her, only right now it was more important to distance himself from Red Oakes as fast as possible.

But he could muster the willpower to wait, he told himself with a grin. After all, he intended to keep her for a long, long time.

Maybe forever.

Because she just might prefer being his legal wife to having her neck wrung like a chicken, he cackled out loud to think, which is what he'd do to her if she refused him.

Olivia was having her third glass of sherry and wondering what was keeping Michael. Darkness was falling, and already servants were lighting the torches lining the driveway. People would be arriving soon, and he should eat his supper but was probably staying away fearing she would nag him about buying another necklace. Either that or he did not want to be around Verena. Well, that was too bad, because she did not know what she would have done without Verena's shoulder to cry on these miserable past weeks. Verena kept saying he would come to his senses, and Olivia wanted to believe that but knew she had to resign herself to the sad reality that it just wasn't going to happen.

Seeing Elyse so downcast, Olivia felt sorry for her. She knew the girl loved Michael, and nothing would have made Olivia happier than to have her for a daughter-in-law.

"So there you are," Verena said with a tiny sneer as Michael appeared. "It's a good thing we didn't wait for you, or the food would have got cold. Yours is, by the way," she added with a curt nod toward the little table that had been set up.

Paying her no mind, Michael said, "I thought Jacie might be here. She's not in her room."

Olivia gave an irritated wave. "Oh, she's probably ignoring you. She acts so strange all the time."

"That's right," Verena chimed in. "I've knocked on her door several times, trying to be friendly, but she didn't answer."

Worriedly, he said, "I used the passkey and unlocked her door, but she's not there."

Olivia's hand flew to her throat at the thought of her son daring to enter a lady's boudoir in such a manner, but Michael had already turned on his heel and left. Reaching for her sherry glass, she murmured, "Maybe it's best he does go ahead and marry the girl before he forgets all manner of decorum."

"Well, she's certainly not going to remind him," Verena sniped.

Michael returned a little while later, visibly shaken. "She's nowhere in the house. I've got the servants searching the grounds. I questioned Sudie, but she hasn't seen her since she took her tray up."

Verena saw how Elyse was glaring at her in warning to stay out of it, but she could not resist. Besides, it made no difference anyway, for she had given up on a miracle happening. "Oh, for heaven's sake, Michael, you're letting yourself get all upset over nothing. As your mother said, Jacie is strange. There's no telling where she went. Goodness knows, she might have run away with some man again."

Elyse cried, "Mother, that's not a nice thing to say."

"It's not a nice thing to *do,* dear," Verena said.

Michael was struggling to hold back his temper as he bit out the warning, "Cousin Verena, I will not have you speak of Jacie that way. As long as you're in my house, you will hold your tongue. I'm fed up with your sarcasm and meddling."

Verena gave her head a haughty toss. "I am here as your mother's guest, not yours. And it's a good thing I've been here to console her, because heaven knows, you seem to be doing your best to send her to an early grave by insisting on bringing a little tart into this family."

Even Olivia gasped at that bold insult, and Michael could contain his ire no longer. "That does it. I'll ask you to leave my house as soon as the necessary arrangements can be made."

"Michael, no," Olivia protested. "She didn't mean it. We're all upset and on edge because of the tension you've brought into this house. Now Jacie has done something else to tear our nerves up, disappearing right before guests are supposed to start arriving. She has no consideration. And you're taking it out on your family. I won't have it. Oh dear." She set down her glass and crossed her hands over her bosom. "I think I'm having an attack." She fell back against the sofa and began to take deep, rapid breaths.

"I'm sorry, Mother," Michael said curtly, meeting Verena's angry glare with one of his own, "but I'm fed up with her interference. I want her out of this house as soon as possible."

Verena screeched, "Interference, you say? It's not my fault that that little whore ran away with another man, and it looks to me like she's done it again."

"Don't you dare call her a whore," he warned.

Elyse was on her feet. "Mother, stop it. You've no right to say such things to Michael."

Verena was beyond restraint. "You feel the same way. You've said the same things. You hate her too."

"That's not true. I don't hate her."

"She's marrying Michael when you're in love with him. That's reason to hate her and wish her dead. I hope she *is* dead. Maybe then Michael will come to his senses and marry you, and then I wouldn't have to wind up in the poorhouse, and—oh, dear God." Her hand flew to her mouth, and her eyes went wide.

Elyse turned away on a broken sob, not noticing her mother's panic-stricken face as she whispered, "Mother, how could you?"

"Yes, Verena, how *could* you?" Olivia angrily admonished her, the attack of vapors forgotten. For Verena to embarrass Elyse in front of Michael was unconscionable. And now it dawned on Olivia that Verena had only pretended to care and comfort in order to stay at Red Oakes indefinitely, because she was destitute. "When I think of how—"

"Didn't you see it?" Verena shrieked, pointing to the window with a trembling finger. "It . . . it was the most frightening thing I've ever seen."

Michael stood clenching and unclenching his fists, wishing Verena were a man so he could punch her in the mouth for saying such things about Jacie, as well as humiliating Elyse. And now it looked as though once again what was supposed to be one of the happiest times of his life was going to be ruined. "Oh, what is it?" he demanded harshly, irritably. "I've no time for your foolishness. I've got to go help look for Jacie."

Verena had begun to shake from head to toe, her knees growing weak. "I've never seen one, but I've heard what they look like, and I swear"—she swallowed against the knot of terror in her throat—"it was *an Indian!*"

# 29

*The window exploded.*

Luke had grabbed the frame above for leverage, swiftly swinging back and propeling himself into the parlor to land feet first in a shower of glass.

Amidst Verena and Elyse's screams, Michael froze in shock, but only for an instant. "You! What the hell are you doing here? I thought—"

"You thought you killed me," Luke finished. "It's good you're a lousy shot . . . when using the finger of a dead man," he added to goad him.

"How did you find me?" Michael asked as he looked about wildly for anything that could be used as a weapon.

Luke also scanned the room. Two of the women were insane with their fear and no threat to him, and there was another on the sofa who had apparently fainted. No other men. No guns. But he knew it would not be long before people came running in response to the noise.

He had left his horse hidden in the woods and crept to the house on foot to peer into windows until he spied Michael and the women. He would have liked for Jacie also to have been present but could not wait for her to make an appearance. A celebration of some sort was clearly about to take place, and Luke wanted to present his case and be on his way—with Jacie, he hoped. Forced to leave his rifle on the porch, he was armed only with the knife tucked in his breechclout, but he made no move to draw it. He did not want any violence.

Holding up his hands to Michael in a conciliatory gesture, Luke said, "Despite what happened back at my village, how you shot me, I come in peace. I know you thought I meant to harm Jacie, but I could never do that, and you have nothing to fear from me. I am sorry about the window and frightening your women, but I didn't think if I knocked on your door that I would be invited in," he added sarcastically.

Verena and Elyse continued to make fearful moaning sounds as they stood with arms wrapped tightly around each other, staring at Luke in terror, sure that any second he would kill them.

Michael was likewise afraid but pretended not to be. "State your business and go."

"I must speak with Jacie."

"That's not possible. How did you find me, anyway?"

"Jacie told her mother where she lived, and since Sunstar once lived in this part of the country, she was able to tell me how to get here."

Michael shot a glance at Verena and Elyse, but

they were too stricken to realize what the Indian was saying. His mother was unconscious, thank God. There was still a chance he could keep things quiet—if he could get rid of the son of a bitch. But where was the butler, damn it? Surely someone had heard the glass breaking and all the screaming. "Listen, damn you," he said shakily, "I want you to get out of here before I have you killed. Just go. I'll forget this happened."

"It doesn't work that way." Luke stood with fists on his hips, legs apart, his eyes locked on Michael's and every bit as fiery. "You left me for dead, and Jacie thinks I am, and I'm not leaving here till she knows different."

Michael could not help a chuckle. "Do you really think you can come in here and take her? I realize you're nothing but a savage, but this isn't the West. It's Georgia. And we don't put up with things like that. You try it, and I promise my men will gun you down before you reach the main road. I'll never let you have her, you fool."

Luke's nostrils flared as he fought to hold back his temper. Getting mad would not solve anything. He was determined to try to reason with the man. "I'm no savage, Blake, but I can turn into one real quick when I get riled, and I'm about to do just that if you don't quit jawing and send for Jacie. I didn't come here to force her to go back with me, but I intend to give her the chance to make up her own mind."

Michael all but snarled, "You aren't talking to her. You've no business with her. Get the hell out of here while you still can."

Luke went on as though Michael had not spoken. "You see, I want her to know she's got another life besides staying here with you. You can't understand how important that is to me, or to her, and it's not necessary that you do, but I do intend to give her a choice. Now, call her in here, and there won't be any trouble. She'll see I'm still alive, and then she can make up her mind what to do about it. I'll accept her decision."

Michael endeavored to stall. Surely someone would come soon, he thought nervously. "You mean you actually want her to choose between me and *you*?" he sneered with contempt.

"That's right. And if you are a man of honor, you will agree to that."

"That is absurd, and besides, her trip out west was nothing but a farce, anyway. She knows now she never should have gone. And the very idea of that stupid Indian squaw claiming to be her mother is absurd."

Verena came alive then, drawing away from Elyse to snap, "Oh stop lying, Michael. We know the whole story. You can't hide the truth any longer. We know all about Violet Calhoun's deathbed confession, and how Jacie took off to try and find her real mother, and from what this Indian is saying, she found her, only you went and got her and made her come back, and that's why she's been acting so strangely since you did. Now for the love of God, tell him the truth, before he goes crazy and scalps all of us."

Luke decided it was best to let her keep thinking that was a possibility. "Listen to her, Blake. Don't cause me to do something you will later regret. Go get Jacie. If after she finds out I'm still alive she tells me it's you she wants, I will go in peace. But not before," he warned.

Luke's fingers inched toward his knife to show them that he meant what he said, and when Verena saw the movement she yelled, "No! Wait. He doesn't know where she is. She's gone. Nobody knows. We think she ran away with another man, like she did before. You'd best go on and do like he says and get out of here."

Luke regarded her coldly. "I think you are lying. And you are also making me lose my patience. Now, where is she?"

"It's true, it's true!" Verena cried, her head bobbing up and down as the words tumbled out of her. "She went away. She'll never be back, ever. Now you just go on and get out of here before anybody gets hurt. I swear it's the truth. She's not here."

Suddenly Luke reached out and caught her neck in the crook of his arm as he pulled her against him. Whipping out his knife, he held it against her cheek and told Michael, "I am going to search this house until I find Jacie. I will kill this woman if anyone tries to stop me."

"She isn't here," Michael said in panic. "My cousin is telling the truth. There's a search going on for Jacie right this minute. I don't know where she is. I swear it."

Luke stared at him uncertainly. Something told him he might be telling the truth. But if Jacie were not in the house, where was she?

Elyse had been watching in stricken silence as her mother's words sank in. Michael wasn't really listening, thinking her mother was too distraught to actually know what she was saying. But Elyse knew, all right, and her blood ran cold.

The Indian had his arm so tightly around her mother's throat she could not speak. Only faint whimpers of terror escaped her trembling lips. Her face had turned ashen, and Elyse feared she was going to join Cousin Olivia by fainting at any second. "Let her go," she said, surprised to hear the firmness in her voice. "Let me talk to her. I think she knows where Jacie is."

"Elyse, stay out of this." Michael reached to pull her behind him, lest the Indian slash out at her with the knife.

She shook her head solemnly. "No. He has to let me talk to my mother, Michael. She knows where Jacie is—don't you, Mother?" she asked sharply, going to stand before her.

Luke loosened his hold enough to allow the woman to speak, but her words were not what he wanted to hear.

"No, I don't. I just think she went away, that's all."

Neither was it what Elyse wanted to hear. "You're lying Mother. You wrote that letter after I refused, didn't you? That's why you're so sure Jacie is gone—Zach Newton has her this very minute, doesn't he?"

"I—I don't know what you're talking about." Verena's denial was barely audible. She could see the glint of the knife's blade, mere inches from her face. "I'm guessing, I tell you."

"What letter?" Michael demanded. "And what does Newton have to do with any of this? He's been gone for months. I know he's not working anywhere around here, because I've made inquiries, and nobody has seen him. And I know he didn't have anything to do with Jacie leaving before, despite the servants' gossiping."

Luke listened intently. He had no idea what they were talking about, nor who Zach Newton was, but evidently it had something to do with Jacie's whereabouts, and he was convinced now she was not in the house.

Misery and humiliation washing over her, Elyse attempted to explain. "It's my fault you ever thought she ran off with him in the first place, not the servants'. Forgive me, Michael, but I made it all up. I had no idea where she went. I just wanted to make sure that if she came back, you wouldn't want her." She turned away, unable to face him.

He yanked her back around, forgetting for the moment there was a Comanche standing in the middle of the parlor with a knife at the throat of his cousin. "Damn it, Elyse. You aren't making sense. What did you do?"

"I tore up the note she left you the night she left. She didn't say where she was going, only that she would be back in the spring."

Verena yelped, "You'd better shut up, Elyse. You'd better shut up right now. You're going to ruin everything."

Michael shot her a glare of menace, then turned back to Elyse. "So Jacie left me a note, and you tore it up, then schemed to make me believe she ran away with Newton? How could you do such a thing, Elyse? How could you?"

"Because I love you. Can't you see that? I think I've loved you all my life, but you never looked at me, because you were mesmerized by Jacie. When she ran away, I didn't know she'd gone west to look for her mother. I didn't know any of that until a short while ago. All I knew or cared about was that I finally saw a chance to turn you against her by making you think she was involved with another man. But I forgot the necklace. I forgot you would be so mad over her taking it that you'd go after her."

Luke had been trying to keep up with the conversation and figure out where the hell it was all leading. "She didn't intentionally take the necklace," he said then. "She told me a child sneaked it into her satchel, and she didn't find it till later."

Michael paid him no mind, instead giving Elyse a shake, sensing she was on the verge of hysteria and knowing that if she lost control he wouldn't find out what the hell was going on till it was too late. "None of that matters now. Where is she, Elyse? Why did you say Newton has her?"

"Because he must have received Mother's letter and come for her," she whispered raggedly.

Verena twisted in Luke's grasp. "I told you to keep quiet. It doesn't matter about Jacie. She's gone. Now get this Indian out of here before he cuts my throat."

"What letter? You aren't making sense. Please. We're wasting time." Michael felt like screaming.

"When you came back with Jacie, I just gave up," Elyse continued. "But Mother was desperate. We're out of money, you see. We've nowhere to go. My marrying you meant she would be taken care of the rest of her life—but I swear to you money was never my motive . . . only my love.

"Then Mother came up with the idea of my writing to Mr. Newton and telling him he could get revenge on you for firing him by coming to take Jacie away. But I refused. Now it looks as though she went ahead and did it."

"And how would she know where to find him?" he asked incredulously, dread creeping through him as all the pieces began to come together.

"I sent him to Beaufort, South Carolina, to work for a family friend." She looked at her mother again. "Did you also pay him the thousand dollars you were going to borrow from Cousin Olivia to entice him even more?"

"Oh my god!" Michael slammed his palm against his forehead. "I gave Mother a thousand dollars out of the safe that night I returned with Jacie. I had too much on my mind then to wonder why she wanted it, and I had forgotten about it since.

"Damn you to hell!" He whirled on Verena, fists clenched as he fought to keep from yanking her from the Indian's grasp and killing her himself. "You did it, didn't you? He's got her, and it's your fault. Now where is he? Where did he take her?"

Luke released Verena and stepped away. Let the two fight it out between them, he decided, and he would listen to every word, and as soon as he got some idea of where the man called Newton had taken Jacie, he'd be on his way.

But just then the door to the parlor burst open and Michael's overseers rushed in. There were four of them, all carrying guns leveled at Luke.

"It's about time," Michael roared, motioning to them to take Luke. "If he won't drop the knife, gun him down."

Luke knew he didn't stand a chance. He was also afraid that if there was a fight, the women would be hurt, and he didn't want that. He had never intended to kill the fat noisy one he'd been holding, had only wanted everyone to fear that he would. He had meant what he said—he only wanted Jacie, but now it appeared she was lost to both of them, unless . . .

"Hear me, Blake," Luke said as his arms were

yanked behind him, his wrists quickly bound. "I'll help you. They can't have been gone very long. I can track them. I know how. You don't. We'll slip up on them, take him by surprise. If you go after him, he'll hear you and hide, and then you'll never find him. You've got to let me help." He knew he was taking a risk. They could use him and gun him down later, but he had to save Jacie—even if it cost him his life.

"What do you want us to do with him?" Bart Ballough, the head overseer, asked Michael.

"Hang him."

Elyse screamed, "You can't do that! Listen to him, Michael. What he says makes sense. Jacie can't have been gone over a couple of hours at the most. But Zach won't take the main road. He probably knows the countryside better than you, and he'll know how to keep to the woods and streams so you can't follow him. And he won't take her back to Beaufort, anyway, because he can't be sure Mother wouldn't eventually admit what she'd done, and then you would go there looking for him. So there's no telling which direction he'll head."

Bart drew Michael away from the others. "Look, boss," he said quickly, "I don't know what's goin' on here, but it sounds to me like you've got a mess on your hands. If what your cousin says is true and Newton does have Miss Jacie, you got a problem, because the lady's right, he knows the back trails better than any of us. But the Indian could track him. They got noses like bloodhounds, I hear."

"I don't trust him."

"What can he do with guns on him? Give him a chance. Hell, we can kill him after he finds her. It's worth a try. And we're wastin' time," he reminded

Michael. "This place is goin' to be fillin' up with folks within the hour."

"All I want is to find Jacie."

"Then let's go," Bart urged. "Give the Indian a chance."

Michael studied Luke, bound and helpless. He knew now that his suspicions were correct. For him to have come so far, to have been so all-fired hell-bent to let Jacie know he was still alive, it could only mean the two had been lovers.

Michael felt like he'd been kicked by a horse.

His mind was spinning furiously as he tried to figure out what he should do.

Jacie believed Luke was dead, and Michael would prefer she continue to do so. He did not want her to be tempted to return west, fancying herself in love with the Comanche and remembering how the mother she had just found out she had was also there. Still, all things considered, what Bart had dourly said was true. They stood only a slim chance of locating Zach without Luke's tracking ability.

"What's it goin' to be, boss?" Bart prodded.

Elyse sobbed, not caring who was listening, for she was beyond shame now. "Please, Michael. Go after her. If I can't have your love, at least don't give me your hate. You will never forgive me if you lose her. Let the Indian help you, please."

Verena, who had retreated to a far corner, suddenly wailed, "You little fool. We could have had it all. Zach would have taken her where nobody would ever have seen either of them again." She glowered at Luke. "What the hell did you have to show up for? None of this would've happened if not for you."

"Oh, yes, it would," Elyse said with fervor. "I had my suspicions, and as soon as I made up my mind you were responsible, that you had sent that letter to Zach and that he really had come and gotten her, believe me, I would have told Michael everything.

"I watched his face while you were talking tonight," she rushed on. "I could see his misery growing with every word you spoke, how he was thinking to himself maybe she really had run off with a man, and it was killing him, and it was killing me to see him suffer. God knows, Mother, when you love someone, you don't want to cut his heart out. I couldn't have lived with myself knowing what I'd done to him."

"Fool," Verena repeated with a sneer. "Think about that when you're a spinster in the poorhouse."

Despite the turmoil going on all around them, Michael could not help feeling compassion for Elyse. Even though he could have wrung her neck for what she had already done, he would never have learned the truth if she hadn't confessed. And how could he condemn and despise her when she loved him so much? "I don't think Elyse has to worry about being a spinster," he said quietly. "A man will come along one day who sees her for the gem she is. As for you, dear cousin, I think it's time *you* took up residency at the poorhouse." He motioned to one of the servants. "See that she's packed and out of the house within the hour. Have a carriage take her to Atlanta tonight and leave her at a hotel. I never want to see her again."

Hearing her sentence, Verena screamed and ran from the room, but Elyse stayed where she was to plead with Michael, "Let her stay till morning, please. I'll have to go with her, and I don't want to leave till after you've found Jacie. I want to know she's all right, and I want to try to apologize to her for all the grief I've caused."

"Very well," Michael dismissed her, despite feeling so sorry for her. It was time to go. He went to where Luke was being held and said tersely, "You're going to lead us. We'll follow your orders, but I promise, if you try anything, you'll be dead before you hit the ground."

"I didn't come here to kill anybody, Blake. I told you, I only want Jacie to know I'm alive."

"You aren't going to try and take her back?"

"Only if she wants to go. Will you agree to let her make up her own mind?"

"Yes," Michael lied, feeling no guilt to make a promise he had no intention of keeping. Jacie was his. It was the way it had always been, the way it would always be.

He told Bart to take Luke to wherever he'd left his horse, and he would meet them at the stables. Then, when he and Elyse were alone, with his mother still unconscious on the sofa, Michael began, "Look, I have no right to ask you to do this . . ."

"Anything," she was quick to assure him. "I'm willing to do anything to try and make up for what I've done."

"Despite what's happened tonight, my guests are going to be arriving, and they can't know about any of this. I want you to be hostess for me. Explain that my mother has fallen ill, and Jacie and I are sitting with her. I'll try to get back as quickly as I can and put in an appearance. If I don't, you will have to make my apologies, and everyone can think Mother took a turn for the worse. You will have to confide in Dr. Foley, however, because he'll insist on looking in on her, but he won't tell anyone else."

"I will take care of everything. Don't worry."

"I'll have the servants carry Mother upstairs and have someone stay with her. As for *your* mother, I'm leaving orders she's to be locked in her quarters."

"And I don't blame you. Now hurry," she urged.

He started out of the room but turned at the door to tell her, "I appreciate your owning up to what you did. If you hadn't, there wouldn't be any chance at all of my finding Jacie. I will always be grateful."

And I will always love you, she vowed silently, watching him go.

# 30

*Zach was tired. He had ridden* like the devil from Beaufort, with hardly any sleep. Now it was starting to rain, the wind blowing like crazy, and Jacie was making choking sounds as he held her in front of him on the horse like she was having trouble breathing. He decided it was time to stop for the night. It had to be after midnight, anyway, and he was so damn deep in the woods, Blake would never be able to find him.

He yanked the gag from her mouth, and she began to cough and gasp. He could have removed it hours ago but didn't want to listen to her screaming and was not about to now. "I'll leave it out as long as you keep your mouth shut." he warned. "I don't want to hear your bitchin', understand?" Her chest was heaving, and Zach liked the feel of the rise and fall of her breasts against his arms as he held the reins.

"Why are you doing this?" Jacie asked hoarsely. Her throat was sore and raw from trying to shriek against the gag. "We used to be friends—"

"Friends!" He guffawed. "You can't fool me, Jacie, girl. You wanted more than that, and you know it. And now you don't have to pretend no more, because you aren't ever goin' to see that wet-behind-the-ears ninny Blake again. You're goin' to be my woman."

"You're crazy," she hissed through clenched teeth.

"I think maybe we'll settle in Savannah," he mused. "I can always find work at the docks there. We can get us a little house in the country, and you can grow a garden. We'll have us a good life, you'll see. And we'll have lots and lots of young'uns."

She squirmed against him, wishing she could loosen her wrists and get her hands on a knife. "I'd rather die than have you touch me," she swore.

"Well, touch you I will," he cackled, squeezing her breasts. "And if you don't shut up, I'll gag you again. I've got to find us a place to hole up for the night, and then I'll make you feel so good you'll beg me to take you over and over. You'll see."

Lightening split the sky, and he cried, "We're in luck. I see something over there. Looks like an old shack."

He rode the horse right through the door of the dilapidated structure. Water was pouring through holes in the roof, but one corner of the room was dry. He lowered Jacie to the dirt floor and dismounted. "I got a blanket in a canvas bag that shouldn't even be damp. We'll bed down here. Now get your clothes off. That fancy gown you got on is soakin' wet. I got some trousers and a shirt in my saddlebag you can put on later. Right now . . ." and he drank in the sight of her as the storm once more lit up the night, "you don't need no clothes."

Luke had also seen the deserted shack in the flash of light, for he had been leading Michael and his men for some time without them knowing how close they actually were to Zach Newton. He had used all his Comanche cunning to feel for broken branches along the way, feeling for raw edges that let him know they had been recently torn by a horse passing by. He had also dismounted to get down on his hands and knees to check the depth of tracks in the mud to determine there was not one rider on the horse but two.

And as the storm had intensified, Luke had been confident Newton would seek refuge and figured he was inside the shack.

But he was not about to tell Blake, well aware Blake intended to kill him the second he no longer had any use for him.

"I think we should take shelter there." Luke pointed as the storm again lit up the night. "I can't find any more tracks in all this rain."

Grudgingly, water running off the rim of his hat, Michael agreed. "All right. But only till it slacks up."

Luke swung down off his horse and began walking stealthily toward the shack. He knew Blake and the others would be right behind him and he had to hurry. Reaching the porch, which was not a porch any longer but a pile of rotted logs, he stepped through the debris and positioned himself at the window to await the next bolt of lightning.

It came.

And he saw them, a man and woman struggling on the floor.

This time there was no glass to shatter, but the Comanche war cry he gave as he somersaulted through the window and landed feet first inside the room split the air.

Taking Newton by surprise, he was able to easily tear Jacie from him. "Run!" he commanded her. "Get out of here—now!"

But Jacie was paralyzed with shock to hear Luke's voice. As another flash of lightning lit up the room, she fought to believe that it could actually be him.

At last she came alive. "Dear God. Oh, dear God, Luke . . ." She backed away as Luke and Zack began to grapple on the floor, cursing and grunting.

Michael and his men had heard the noise and rushed to the shack to charge inside with guns drawn. Seeing them, Jacie shrieked, "Don't shoot! You'll hit Luke."

"Jacie!" Michael leapt to her and shielded her as he yelled over his shoulder, "I've got her. Now kill them both."

But Jacie twisted away from him to throw herself in front of Luke and Zach as they continued to fight. "No. You can't kill him. I won't let you."

Michael came after her. "Get back here. Get down, damn it."

Bart roared, "Boss, she's in the way. We can't shoot without hittin' her."

Michael lunged for her again, not seeing the rotted log lying next to a washed-out hole in the floor. With a cry of pain, he pitched forward. His leg snapped, and his face hit the ground hard, momentarily dazing him.

At the same instant, there came another cracking sound, louder, more ominous, as Luke broke Zach Newton's neck with a quick flick of his wrists.

Jacie threw herself against Luke as a torch ignited to flood the shack with an eery, flickering light. "I don't believe it. Dear God, it's a miracle." She wrapped her arms about his neck and clung to him, sobbing with joy.

"Get away from him, Jacie." Michael lay on his side, his broken leg jutting out from his body at an awkward angle. He gritted his teeth against the white-hot stabs of pain. "Get away from him," he repeated in a deadly tone. "I can't let him take you away from me. I won't, damn it."

She stared at him in pity. "Oh, Michael, don't you understand? I was never really yours. I never said I loved you. I tried to love you, I swear I did. But I couldn't. And when I met Luke, it was like I'd been loving him my whole life, just waiting for fate to bring us together. The last thing I ever want to do is hurt you, but it's Luke I want. Please. Let me go." She faced him, trying to keep Luke behind her to shield him, believing as long as she did the men would not shoot him.

But Luke was taking no chances. Nor was he standing behind a woman. He saw the crazy look on the overseers' faces and knew one of them might be stupid enough to think he was a crack shot and could hit him and miss Jacie. He slung her to one side and fiercely reminded Michael, "We had a pact, damn you. You agreed to let her make up her own mind."

"I lied," Michael said with a triumphant smirk.

"Jacie has been through so much these past months she doesn't know what she wants. She certainly doesn't know what she's saying if she claims she prefers living with a savage to the kind of life I can give her. She can't be in her right mind.

"But maybe I shouldn't have you killed," he went on thoughtfully, motioning to Bart and his men to lower their guns for the moment. "I've just realized Jacie would hate me forever if I did. And I don't want that. But neither will I let her go away with you," he added staunchly. He looked at Jacie. "You only think you love him. Come here if you want him to live. Listen to what I have to say."

Jacie could only obey, but all the while her eyes were on Luke, drinking in the sight of his dear face. She wanted so desperately to feel his arms close around her, never to let her go.

Despite the throbbing of his injury, Michael drew her down beside him and took both her hands in his and spoke quietly, patiently. "You've been through an ordeal, and as I said, you can't be thinking clearly. Now, you know I love you more than my life, and you must understand that there is just no way I can let you go away with Luke, or any other man. It's out of the question. If you don't want to marry me right away, I'll understand. I'll give you time to forget all this. But you must promise to live in my house and let me take care of you. Give me your word you will do that, and I will let the Comanche go free. Otherwise, I'll kill him, Jacie."

She knew he meant it. "I'll never forgive you for this, Michael, but you leave me no choice. I give you my word."

"You will get over it, Jacie. I'll make you so happy

you'll forget you ever knew him." Then, to Luke he gloated, "Hear that, Indian? She's made me a promise. Now you get out of here as fast as you can and don't come back, or you're a dead man."

Woodenly, Luke could only concede. "I won't be back. She gave her word. I will not ask her to break it." He could not make himself look at Jacie again, could not bear to see his own anguish mirrored in the eyes he adored as he whispered, "Good-bye, my love."

Michael could not resist a final taunt. "I don't have to keep my word, you know. I can have you killed and still keep her."

Luke did not respond. He walked out, but Jacie pulled herself from Michael's grasp to run to the door and watch after him through her tears.

Then, her heart breaking into bits and pieces inside her, she turned back to Michael. "Yes, you could have killed him," she said coldly, remembering the time when she had begged Luke to slay the cougar. "But you don't have to kill everything you fear. Sometimes it goes away on its own, in peace. You should kill only to save yourself, Michael, and Luke was never a threat to you, only to what you think you feel for me."

"*Think?*" Michael echoed incredulously. "Oh, dear, beloved Jacie. I've never been more sure."

"Have you ever considered anything else?" she challenged to his further bewilderment. "I think not. You have wanted me since I was a child because I was a part of Red Oakes, and you had to own me like you own your slaves, your land, your precious mansion. It didn't matter whether I loved you, because you always got what you wanted. That's how it is with you and your rich family."

She turned from the door with a sigh wrenched

from her very soul. Luke had been swallowed by the night and had taken a part of her with him, but it was over. For him to live, it was the way it had to be, and her only solace was knowing her mother would be with him, would be cared for.

Long moments passed. There was no sound save for the wind of the storm, the rain pelting down on what was left of the tin roof.

The men shifted uneasily, not sure what was expected of them and afraid to ask.

"Go to him."

All eyes were on Michael, but Jacie was the only one to speak. "What did you say?"

"I said go to him—now. Before I change my mind." He nodded to Bart. "Give her my horse . . . *now*," he commanded. "Do what I say, damn it."

Jacie was not about to argue and ran toward the door but suddenly stopped. Looking back at him in wonder, she felt the need to say something in parting and began, "Michael, I will never forget you for this—"

"Just go!" he yelled again, waving a hand at her, then viciously rubbing at his eyes, because he would be damned if he would let his men see him cry.

And after she had gone to disappear into the dregs of the storm, Bart and the others hurried to gather scrap wood and make a litter to carry Michael.

When it was made and they were about to leave, Bart went to Michael and said, "I know it's your business, boss, but for the life of me, I can't understand why you let her go. She'd have got over him sooner or later."

"I don't expect you to understand," he responded thoughtfully. "It's only important that I do.

"Besides," he added with a sad little smile, "She's right. She never said the words . . . never said she loved me." *But I believe she's said it to him,* he thought miserably, *just as I believe she meant it when she did.*

With Bart leading the way as Michael's litter was dragged along behind his horse, they rode through the night, and it was nearly dawn when they arrived back at Red Oakes.

Elyse had kept a vigil by her window all night, and when she saw them approaching she hurried out to meet them. "You're hurt," she cried, running to kneel by the litter. Then, seeing it was only his leg, she breathed thankfully, "At least you're alive."

Michael saw her glancing about and knew she was wondering why Jacie was not with them. "She's gone," he said. "She went with him. It's what she wanted. I think . . ." He drew a ragged breath of resolve and let it out slowly before admitting, "It's probably for the best."

Elyse's heart skipped a beat. She did not know what it would ultimately mean for her future, and for the moment she dared not ask. There was still much for Michael to forgive her for—if he ever could.

She told the men to carry him inside.

As they lifted him up, Michael reached to take her hand and say, more to himself than to her, "Maybe Jacie was right. Maybe I haven't ever thought of anything else . . . or *anyone.*"

Luke and Jacie rode toward the sunrise, toward the future.

She rested against him; his arms wrapped about her tightly.